Getting Tricky

SCARLETT FINN

Also by Scarlett Finn

TO DIE FOR...
TO DIE FOR TRUTH
TO DIE FOR HONOR
TO DIE FOR VIRTUE
TO DIE FOR DUTY
TO DIE FOR LOVE

GO NOVELS
GO WITH IT
GO IT ALONE
GO ALL OUT
GO ALL IN
GO FULL CIRCLE

KINDRED SERIES
RAVEN
SWALLOW
CUCKOO
SWIFT
FALCON
FINCH

LOVE AGAINST THE ODDS STANDALONE COLLECTION
SWEET SEAS
HEIR'S AFFAIR
RESCUED
MAESTRO'S MUSE
GETTING TRICKY
THIRTEEN
REMEMBER WHEN...
RELUCTANT SUSPICION
XY FACTOR

EXILE
HIDE & SEEK
KISS CHASE

THE EXPLICIT SERIES
EXPLICIT INSTRUCTION
EXPLICIT DETAIL
EXPLICIT MEMORY

WRECK & RUIN
RUIN ME
RUIN HIM

MISTAKE DUET
MISTAKE ME NOT
SLEIGHT MISTAKE

NOTHING TO...
NOTHING TO HIDE
NOTHING TO LOSE
NOTHING TO DECLARE
NOTHING TO US
NOTHING TO SAY
NOTHING TO GAIN
NOTHING TO YOU
NOTHING TO THIS

THE BRANDED SERIES
BRANDED
SCARRED
MARKED

RISQUÉ & HARROW INTERTWINED
TAKE A RISK
FIGHTING FATE
RISK IT ALL
FIGHTING BACK
GAME OF RISK

FORBIDDEN PREQUEL DUET
ALL. ONLY.
ONLY YOURS

THE FORBIDDEN NOVELS
FORBIDDEN DESIRE
FORBIDDEN WANT
FORBIDDEN WISH
FORBIDDEN NEED

LOST & FOUND
LOST
FOUND

ONE

"LYLA MALLOY."

"Yes, Sir," Lyla said, sinking into the isolated steel-framed chair that stood in front of a panel of four people.

Only one of those people worked in her department, though all of them were executive-level employees with the entertainment channel she worked for. Channel Prem, one of the most successful commercial channels in the country.

"Do you know who Nairn Strickland is?" Alan Bunyan, the network director asked her.

Bunyan, who was sitting in a larger chair than the other three on the panel, was the only one who'd spoken thus far, but he was known for his need to be at the center of attention any time he was in a room.

His question was silly enough that Lyla stopped tugging on the cuffs of her oversized sweater and actually smiled; something she didn't think she'd be doing in this intimidating meeting. "Of course," she said, glancing at each face before continuing as it seemed they wanted her to do. "He's the station's biggest star. He hosts Boys Night three nights a week with Noah Tate and Nathaniel Green." Known as the 'Threens', the three of them were often seen around town together, drinking, partying with different women, and just generally being boys behaving badly. "He has a show on our radio station late Sunday night and he hosts Truth or Dare, one of our flagship quiz shows."

Truth was, Nairn was everywhere, and while his reputation appealed to adult audiences, he was huge on social media too with fans in most age ranges from teenagers to middle-aged men and women from many backgrounds. Men wanted to drink with him, women wanted to screw him, and the younger fans idolized him.

This was a first for Lyla, being addressed by the network director. When she'd been called into this meeting, she was sure that she was being fired because the only man she knew would be here was Ritchie, her direct superior. Though she had thought it was weird that he was pulling her into a meeting in one of the fancy boardrooms as opposed to into his office where she'd seen people lose their jobs before.

Ritchie was sitting at the end of the long table, saying nothing; he was more like a decorative paperweight than a bookend. He didn't seem to have any useful task other than to bulk out the numbers or fill space. Her boss was in his forties and always seemed stressed; she'd never once seen him crack a smile.

Bunyan was older than him, using the features of his appearance alone, the lines on his forehead and the thinning of his hair, she'd put him in his sixties, but she knew he was actually only in his mid-fifties. Maybe the trials of his job added years—she could understand that. But it would probably help if he kept himself in better shape. Although he was tall, he carried more weight than he needed to and seemed to sweat a lot too. Lyla wasn't sorry she hadn't spent more time around him, his bluster made her uneasy.

"Good," Bunyan said, looking to his colleagues before taking a breath and looking her square in the eye. Uh-oh. "We're going to need you to marry him."

The universe went onto pause. Lyla wasn't even sure what he'd said and she knew three languages; comprehension wasn't usually a problem for her. "I'm… I'm sorry, what?"

Bunyan clasped his hands together and took on a

learned air that was probably supposed to patronize her. "It started with this petition, about a month ago, remember, with the suicide kid?"

A teenager who'd been featured on one of Prem's reality shows had overdosed after taking part in the show. It didn't matter that the coroner found a verdict of accidental death; the public had launched a campaign against the channel. Someone had written a powerful letter blaming the media for his death, tearing into executives for using the desperate public as puppets who were taken advantage of by the money-hungry media simply because they were naive and believed fame and recognition would solve all life's problems.

"Yes, Sir, but I—"

"We were accused of liability in his death."

Everybody knew that, there were articles in all the papers and spread across online media about the case and the responsibility of entertainment providers. "Yes, Sir."

Bunyan's attitude wasn't one of remorse or even reflection; this whole thing seemed to be little more than an inconvenience. "It's ridiculous of course, but we decided we could not ignore the accusations in the letter attached to the petition." With the civil case being brought by the kid's parents, the channel needed to do some damage control. "So for our next project, we have to use our own people, to prove that we don't only take needless risks with the schmucks out there in the world, but that our shows are so safe and fair, that we would use our own people, even those we value most."

That explained why Nairn would be involved in this project, he was the face of the channel… after ten PM anyway. "I understand, Sir," Lyla said. "But why would you choose me to—"

"Interviews were conducted, covertly. We studied personnel records, spoke to staff, and the aim was to find a bride who was the most opposite to him. We still want to make great television. It'll be called Opposites Marry. You know, as opposed to Opposites Attract."

Yeah, she got it. Lyla's mouth opened in an 'oh' as the woman at the end of the table spoke up. "We couldn't allow the premise of the show to seem too obvious or easy.

The point is to put a real challenge to our people, make it as difficult and as fraught as possible. So," she said and smiled. "We chose you… There isn't a person on the premises who's more different to Trick than you."

Okay, so Lyla had to marry a man, not just any man, but a famous one, and it had just been confirmed that they had zero in common. "Forgive me, but… I'm not a celebrity… I've never been on TV, and I have no interest—"

"But you're still one of us," Bunyan spoke again. "You've worked for the company for five years."

Yes, she had, in her quiet, little anonymous corner where she was quite happy. "Yes, but I'm a researcher, I'm not—"

"Your role is perfect," Bunyan said. "We won't have to worry about conflicts with Trick's schedule, you can work around him. If you were another personality from the channel, it would seem gimmicky, no one would believe it. We want everyone to believe it."

"Believe it," Lyla said, still struggling to incorporate the reality of this conversation into her psyche. "Believe that Mr. Strickland and I are… getting married?"

"The public will know it's a setup, but over time, we'll decide how the relationship should progress. We will sell it as a real marriage; you guys have to appear to be in this to make it work. The premise of the show is simple," Bunyan said. "We'll keep both of you apart until the actual wedding. You'll be given discretion over your dress and that stuff, but the details of the day will be at Prem's discretion, you won't have to organize anything. We'll send a designer around to fit you for the dress you want. Hair, makeup, everything will be taken care of. You will meet Trick at the ceremony."

Lyla would meet the man she was supposed to marry on her wedding day. If she was inclined to swear, she'd probably try it now. "I… I can't marry a man I've never met."

Everyone on the panel laughed, she didn't get the joke. Bunyan threw up his hands. "That's the whole idea! Marrying a stranger, it's always a hit concept." Not a new one, but still, he was right, it was popular. "You're living a dream, marrying a popular celebrity who millions of women would love to be tied to."

Yes, millions, though she wasn't one of them and wasn't interested in fighting with the competition. "Wasn't he dating Kira Levine for a long time?"

Bunyan nodded. "Yes, but they broke up months ago. He's single."

Well that was always a point in the favor of any betrothed. But an underwear model, really? Why would he go from one of the world's sexiest women to… her? Lyla wasn't known for being sexy, she wasn't known for being anything. Her clothes were drab and oversized. She just didn't care about what she wore and would always choose comfort over style, not that she had any sense of style that she was trying to keep secret.

"Why would he agree to do this?" Lyla asked, thinking that maybe if he backed out, she wouldn't have to.

Again, everyone laughed. "Oh, Trick is up for anything," the woman at the end of the line said.

The blonde was familiar, she wasn't a board member and it only took a second for Lyla to identify her as remembering things was sort of her job. "You're Sadie Lawrence," Lyla said. "You're Mr. Strickland's producer."

"One of them," Sadie said. "And he prefers Trick… no one uses his full last name, and not even his mother calls him Nairn."

That prompted another thought. Lyla's attention went back to Bunyan. "Our families, what about our families?"

"They'll be invited to the wedding. Like I said, this will be a real marriage, the public want to see you fall in love… it doesn't matter that it's all a con," Bunyan said, becoming sedate as he explained. "The wedding will be your first meeting with Trick, you'll be given some time after the ceremony to talk with him. There will be pictures, a reception, the works. The wedding will take place on Wednesday, you'll go on honeymoon on the Thursday to return on the Sunday."

Thoughts of how her family would handle this and how comfortable she was conning the public fled when she heard the word *honeymoon*. "Four days," she said.

Away… alone… with Nairn Strickland… what the hell would they talk about? She knew nothing about sport or liquor or the latest entertainment hotspots.

"Yes," Bunyan said. "His radio show is live, everything else is, or can be, pre-recorded. The radio show is the only thing we can't alter, so he will have to be back in time for that."

His radio show. But no talk of her job. When Lyla turned to Ritchie, the head of her department and a man she'd only ever exchanged a few words with since her initial interview five years ago, she noted that he didn't seem to care much about that.

"Your workload will be adjusted as is required," Ritchie said. He was at the opposite end of the table from Sadie, and it seemed a bit unfair. If Sadie was here as a representative of Trick, and was his good friend, shouldn't Lyla have someone equally invested in her standing in her corner? Apparently not.

"Trick's apartment is right in the center of the city, just a ten-minute cab ride from the studios—"

"His apartment!" she exclaimed. God, that was a point, if she was supposed to marry him then she was supposed to live with him. "I couldn't move."

"You would have to," Bunyan said. "You have to live with your husband. These transitions will be what makes the show worth watching."

"Worth watching," she muttered. It didn't usually take her so long to catch on, but the shock of this had put her on her back foot. "You'd be recording everything."

"There would be cameras placed throughout the apartment, your office—"

"I don't have an office, I work in a bullpen," Lyla said.

"Wherever they're deemed necessary," Bunyan said like she was just being awkward and maybe she was. "And there will be a camera crew with you at all times too. There will be two shows a week. One with footage of what has happened, the reality aspect, the second will be interviews conducted with each of you and those around you, intercut with footage of incidents that have happened, and probably some unseen stuff. That will be worked out in editing."

Followed by a camera crew, her life bugged, taking part in weekly interviews where she'd be quizzed about the intimate details of her life with a man known for being highly sexed. Yeah, this was probably her worst nightmare.

In another testament to her shock, Lyla's next question burst out of her. "What about sex?" she asked. Intimacy was not a subject she frequently spoke about, but it was important for her to know what her husband would expect in that arena.

Sadie smirked and picked up her pen as if she needed a distraction. "You're not required to have sex with him."

But you will.

The final three words weren't said out loud, but they were in the eyes of everyone on the panel.

Why were they so sure of that? Because this Trick guy was so charming and irresistible that she'd never be able to put up any defense against his seduction? Shame that they didn't understand how non-sexed she was.

Lyla wouldn't want to make any assertions, because she hadn't met the guy and maybe he did have magical powers after all. To get into her panties, he'd need them. That or a miracle from above.

"No, I didn't think I would be," Lyla said, confident that she could keep her legs together. If the studio tried to write any kind of sexual obligation into the contract, they'd be opening themselves up to all kinds of law suits later; this show was meant to be solving problems, not creating them. "I meant him, will he be discreet with the women he's sleeping with? He's known for being on late night, how much coverage will there be—"

"We won't discount airing anything," Bunyan said. "One of the USPs of this show is that it will air after-dark, so it won't be censored. If you, or Trick, engage in any kind of intimate activity with each other or other people, we reserve the right to show everything."

Good, then she definitely wouldn't be sleeping with him. "Because it makes good TV." Would she be expected to perform? If she caught him in bed with another woman, was she supposed to flip out? She wouldn't, she couldn't care less who this stranger slept with.

"It does," Bunyan said. "This will be compelling television. Trick's name alone guarantees that the tabloids will be interested."

Inhaling, she pushed back her shoulders and returned Bunyan's stare. "Thank you for the opportunity," she said and rose. "But I have to decline, thank you."

Bunyan's confidence faltered for the first time, and he turned to the man at his side like maybe he needed a translation. "Decline? You can't decline," Bunyan said.

Lyla was confident that she could. It was an intriguing idea and if she wasn't so risk-averse she might think about giving this a go. But there wasn't any person less camera-ready than she was.

"You can't force me to marry a stranger and have my life scrutinized under a media microscope I never coveted."

Obviously, her refusal hadn't been factored into the schedule. "No, but… this is an incredible opportunity… and you will be compensated."

So she'd get a salary bump for entertaining the station's biggest star? "Thank you for considering me, really, I am flattered, but I'd move on to the next woman on your list."

At least she wasn't being wishy-washy, they had to give her that. Lyla was confident in her refusal. "No list," Bunyan said, thrusting to his feet. "There is no list. We all agreed. As soon as we saw you, we knew, there is no one better suited for this."

No one less like Trick. "Sir, I—"

"Take a day," Sadie said. "Twenty-four hours to think about it… I understand why your instinct is to say no, but it's fun, that's all. Don't think of it as a life commitment, it's only three months, and I can guarantee you one thing."

"What's that?"

Sadie smiled and her eyes flicked to the side for a second before returning, like she knew some big secret she wasn't sharing… yet. "You'll have fun with Trick. It's his life's mission to push people's boundaries and take them on an adventure. It'll be a wild ride."

Right. Except her name and the word "wild" were antonymous. "I'm sure he's a barrel of laughs," Lyla said. "But I don't want to be married to him."

"Sometimes it's the risks we take that define us," Sadie said. "That's one of Trick's mottos."

Maybe Sadie thought she was building on the mystique of the man who was a stranger to Lyla, the meek researcher. Instead, she was giving Lyla reasons to say no.

"You have until the end of business today," Bunyan said. "We'll expect your answer. We can't delay any longer."

No, because if the wedding was next Wednesday, that didn't give much time for planning as it was already Thursday. Lyla was pretty sure she wouldn't be the one walking down the aisle to marry Nairn Strickland and she sent out a silent prayer of luck for the poor woman who did.

TWO

LYLA WALKED OUT of that meeting feeling like she'd just taken a beating. She was at lunch alone in the canteen, nibbling on her rye crackers when three women from the research department closed in around her and sat down. This trio were always together. When they were supposed to be working, they were always gossiping about something. Lyla called them the Cronies, only in her head of course, but to her it seemed an apt description.

"Hey, what was that meeting with Ritchie?" Faith asked.

Faith was the head of the research clique and the most popular in the department. The beauty knew everything that was going on, and that might be why she and her two cronies had decided to descend on Lyla this lunchtime when usually she ate alone.

Lyla did everything alone, and that was just the way she liked it. Interacting took too much energy, and she never understood why people insisted it was healthy to be social all the time. Lyla was healthy; she ate well, ran every day, did yoga, and was always in bed by ten-thirty. She was a good girl. Happy. Content. Alone.

"You better not be getting promoted," Dinah, Faith's number two, said. "No way could you run the department."

Being in management didn't interest Lyla. For one thing if she was in a position of power, she'd have to talk to people, and she did that as little as possible. "No, I'm not getting promoted," Lyla said, picking up a carrot stick.

The meeting had sapped all of her reserves and dealing with these cackling women was exhausting. She didn't even care that they mocked her behind her back, although she knew they did, everyone in the department did.

Lyla was the odd-one-out in every room she walked in to and she always had been. Having plenty of practice at being the outcast, she didn't need to be taught how to shrug off the ridicule that came with it. It was habit now, second-nature, being impervious was a part of who she was.

"So, what then? Some top-secret project?" Chelsea, the third and probably most cutting of the group, said. Chelsea had the most to prove and was often battling with Faith for dominance in the passive aggressive way these women did.

Lyla had been told not to discuss the meeting and she wouldn't. If she was going to say no, it wasn't right that she go mouthing off about something the channel was trying to keep under wraps until the contracts were signed. And she wasn't supposed to have any contact with Trick, of course. They'd said that like there might be a chance of it happening.

The women snickered. "Who would ask her to do something that important?" Faith asked. "She sits in her little corner with the picture of her cat, she doesn't have the connections, or the finesse to pull off something big."

No, Lyla probably didn't, which was why after five years, she was still in the bullpen. "It's not—"

"Maybe they're taking a risk," Chelsea said.

"Or maybe she pitched her own project," Dinah said and all three women laughed before leaning closer. "Come on, Lyla, tell us what's going on."

They only wanted to know so they could spread the gossip around the whole building. "I can't," Lyla said, picking up her homemade smoothie to take a sip.

"Sure you can, we're your buddies," Faith said, taking

her hand. "What is it Ritchie wants? He ask you to suck his dick? That's usually what he wants from us."

The girls giggled, but it was Chelsea who threw her head back and laughed loudest. "Who the hell would ask her to blow them? No guy is that desperate! Have you ever sucked a cock, Lyla? Ever even touched a man?"

Sighing, Lyla would compare this to high school, but there was something so sad about it, pathetic. It was clear that this trio had hit the peak of their popularity in their cheerleading days and held onto the highs they got every day back then by trying to recapture their youth through mocking others.

Lyla had always thought that mean girls grew out of their bullying ways and matured. These three were examples of how that wasn't the reality.

"Probably never kissed one," Faith said and patted her hand. "Don't worry, I'm sure it'll happen. You'll find some creepy fifty-year-old virgin guy who lives in his mom's basement… maybe he'll let you play with him."

Chelsea scoffed. "Oh, come on, that would require her actually going out there into the world and doing something," she said. "She does nothing. Ever. Doesn't date. Doesn't take risks or have adventures. She's just gonna sit in her little crappy apartment, buying more cats, disappearing into that deep, dark hole of spinsterhood."

Sheesh, these women were something else. But they were the kind of women Lyla had been dealing with her whole life, women who thought they were better just because they were glamorous and got the attention of guys.

When she was treated like this, it didn't make her shrink anymore. High school had been a nightmare because she'd never fit in. College, for the most part, wasn't much better. But Lyla had gained a new perspective as she got older and more contented with who she was. So when bullies approached her, poked at her, now it just made her mad.

How dare these women act like they were superior to her when they weren't all that different. Yeah, Lyla didn't spend hours on her hair and makeup every morning. She didn't go through life flirting and teasing the opposite sex. But they all worked in the same department; all did a job and paid their bills. Did it matter if Lyla was happier at home with a book in the evening rather than out in a wine bar picking up guys? Why should that make her less than them?

"None of you are married," Lyla said, feeling an odd sort of fire building in her belly.

She was sick of it. Sick of people making assumptions. Sick of being the focus of other people's insecurities. It wasn't her fault that she was comfortable in her own skin and these women weren't, so they felt the need to lash out at her.

"Through choice," Faith said, accentuating her chest as she looked down her nose.

"And we'll have rings on our fingers when we're ready, and way before you," Chelsea said. "We have choices… you'll just have to take whatever you're forced to."

Biting into her carrot stick, Lyla chewed loudly. "Yeah, maybe I will."

Maybe she should. One thing she couldn't argue with was Chelsea's comments about her never taking risks. Lyla didn't like change and enjoyed her routine. Looking back on her life, she couldn't remember a single risk she'd ever taken.

Adventure. Sadie had said that marrying Trick would be an adventure and Lyla had never had one of those either.

Leaping into marriage with both feet was a huge risk. If it went wrong, she could be left heartbroken; except she knew how to protect her heart, knew how to shut down her emotions. So what could really go wrong? This Trick guy wasn't going to fall for her, so she didn't have to worry about breaking his heart.

The cameras would be intrusive, but they'd ensure her safety. Trick couldn't physically hurt her or force himself on her when there was a lens in his face. Anyway, he was a celebrity, if he was an asshole to her, he'd lose fans and Bunyan wouldn't want that.

As the trio from her department continued to ridicule and tease her, she reflected further. Wouldn't it be a shock for them to hear she was marrying the most popular guy on the network? It would be like the nerd marrying the star jock. It wasn't real, she knew that, but it might shut these women up to know that she wasn't quite the wallflower they considered her to be.

Lyla didn't take risks or have adventures, but she'd been presented with an opportunity to shock those around her into questioning their assumptions. Like Sadie had said, it was only three months. If Lyla said no, she'd stick to her routine, go about her life, and nothing would change.

But maybe if she took her first real risk in life, she'd have an adventure she could be proud of. At the very least, she'd shut the Cronies up for a while.

***

LYLA HADN'T BEEN due to come home this weekend. Her parents didn't ask any questions when she called to say she was coming, and her aunt, Ann, received her with a hug, while her thirteen-year-old twin cousins were as reticent as ever.

The family had eaten lunch and her father was sitting in the living room with the teenagers, Avril and Toby, while Lyla helped clean up with her mother and aunt.

All her family lived in this one two-story suburban home. Her aunt escaped her abusive relationship when the twins were just eight and since then the three had lived here in the home Lyla had grown up in.

Her mother, Cece, and her aunt were discussing something about the neighborhood and Lyla took a deep breath, she had to do this now. Ducking around the broad archway that separated the kitchen from the living room, she waved at her dad who was sitting in the armchair frowning at the twins who were on the couch having a debate about some video on the internet.

When he noticed her, she gestured him over and he drew his scowl from the youngsters to get up and come to her. "What's wrong, honey?" he asked.

Lyla took his hand and guided him to the breakfast table. "Can you guys sit down," she said to her aunt and mother as her father sat. "I have to tell you something."

"What is it? What's wrong?" Cece asked, grabbing for Ann's hand. "Did something happen? Are you sick?"

Her mother had hated it when she moved to the big city, she'd been so sure that some awful fate would befall her daughter. Cece often called Lyla up at the oddest times just to check she hadn't been attacked or robbed or something.

"No," Lyla said, giving them all a chance to settle. It was harder than she thought to explain what she'd signed up for and she was so worried that they'd be disappointed in her.

When she'd walked into Bunyan's office and said she would do it, he'd whipped out the contracts before she could take a breath. But she didn't care that he was so exuberant, Lyla was focused on her own triumph. This was a risk. A game. Fun. Something that proved she wasn't as closeted as everyone seemed to think she was. Bunyan was over the moon, and when she put pen to paper to sign, she felt invigorated.

Yesterday, Friday, was spent in and out of meetings with legal and with the executives and producers in charge of the show. She'd met Paul, who was the director and Cliff who would be his assistant and in charge of filming her.

They'd set a schedule for doing interviews at her apartment the following week, which was going to be a weird experience, but one she'd have to get used to. The men also explained how there would be a two-week lag between actual events and the show airing. Meaning after Lyla got married on Wednesday, and went on her honeymoon, she'd have been living in Nairn Strickland's apartment for ten nights before the first show aired.

The show would air on a Wednesday with the interviews and catch-up shows airing on Friday. So it worked out that Trick was on the schedule every night of the week. Boys Night was on Tuesdays, Thursdays, and Saturdays. The Truth or Dare Quiz was on a Monday and Opposites Marry would air on Wednesdays and Fridays. His radio show, Trick Talk, went out on Sunday nights.

Boys Night was a topical show. The guys would comment on sports events, and do reviews of movies and TV shows in their typical style. They had celebrity guests, did interviews, and there were games. Yes, the games. So many games. There were a whole variety of different games, which were basically just an excuse for the guys to push and tease each other.

Lyla had been given an extensive education on Nairn Strickland's history, on his current schedule, on what was coming up for him, even which celebrities would be guest starring on Truth and on Boys Night.

But she'd yet to meet Trick himself or anyone in his life, except Sadie.

Lyla couldn't quite figure out the beautiful blonde. Sadie obviously had great affection for Trick, they were close friends… maybe more. Lyla had seen Sadie talk on the phone with Trick and the woman was always laughing and tossing her hair, were they a thing? Maybe.

She should probably care more about her fiancé's fidelity. But this was fun. For a show. It wasn't real. Yes, they would be really married, but nothing was permanent in this day and age and it wasn't like she had a fortune to protect.

For the most part, this was still a secret around the studios, they were bound by confidentiality, but it would get out eventually and that was why she had to tell her family… today.

"I'm getting married," Lyla said. For a minute, there was nothing but stunned silence. "It's not real, I mean, it is real, it will be a real marriage, but… it's for Prem… I'm doing a reality show."

That sounded so ridiculous that she cringed. A show. Her? A reality show? This declaration was the equivalent of a Kardashian saying they were going to join a convent.

"You're… getting married?" Ann said and Lyla tensed when she saw tears in her aunt's eyes.

Her panic flew to her mother and, oh no, she was tearing up too. "Yes," Lyla said, opening her hands to try to calm the women. "But it's not… like I'm not in love or anything."

"Oh, but he'll fall in love with you!" Ann said and leaped up to rush over and hug her. "How could he not love you? Where is he?"

Her aunt looked around like the groom might pop out of the wall. "He's not here," Lyla said.

"Well, what's he like?" Ann asked.

"Uh…" Lyla didn't know how much late-night TV her family watched, but for the first time, she was really scared to say his name out loud. "I've never met him… I won't meet him until, you know, the day."

"That's part of the show?" Ann asked pulling her into her side. "We have to tell the kids!"

"I was thinking that maybe they shouldn't come to the wedding, you know," Lyla said. "You're all invited, of course, but it's this Wednesday so, if you can't make it—"

"We'll make it," Ann said, her grin making Lyla nervous to look at her parents who had been silent so far. Ann turned her around, but kept her close with an arm around her. "Isn't this good news?"

Was it good news? Lyla couldn't tell, Cece hadn't blinked, but the tears were still thick on her lashes. "You're getting married," Cece said.

Okay, at least her mother was snapping out of the waking coma. Lyla took her time to turn to her father who just looked… shocked. "Daddy?"

Something flickered on his expression, like he'd just been taken off pause and he shook his head. "Is he a good man?"

Oh God, that was such a father-like thing to ask and she had no idea what to say, she didn't have a clue about her groom's values. "I won't be in any danger," Lyla said. "There will be cameras following us around, so everything will be on film."

"Everything?" Ann asked.

Lyla didn't talk about sex with her family, didn't talk about men and relationships, and that had always been fine with her. If she could get away with saying nothing now, she would stay mute. Except she had to prepare them, it wouldn't be fair not to. A bit of discomfort now would be better than them tuning in to the show with the twins and maybe seeing something salacious.

Her husband had a reputation of being a ladies' man

and if he cheated on her, there would be questions, her father would be devastated, and if there were sexual scenes, it would be better if the twins didn't watch.

"Yes," Lyla said. "I'd prefer if you didn't watch. I don't know what they'll show or how it will be edited."

Her father was shaking his head as he pushed his hands onto the table and stood up. "I can't let you marry a man who'll make a fool of you."

Attempting a smile, she tried to be loose. "Daddy, it's fun," Lyla said, leaving Ann to go over and hold his hands. "I won't be made a fool of, the studio want viewers to have a positive experience."

"I don't understand why you would do this," he said. "You've never been interested in fame."

This wasn't her attempt to get famous. "I don't want fame," she said. "They picked me because Nairn Strickland is the star, I'm just supporting cast."

"Trick," Ann said. "You're marrying… Nairn Strickland?"

Lyla didn't expect any of her relatives to know who he was, but all three of them shared a look. "Yes," she said. "He's the station's biggest star."

"We know who he is," Cece said. "We watch that game show he does."

Of all the things he did, the game show was probably the tamest. Though Lyla had never really watched it before, she knew there was a lot of innuendo and some of the "dares" were risqué or immature, though as far as she knew there was no direct nudity.

"Your dad listens to his radio show sometimes," Ann said.

That surprised her because his show was renowned for having a lack of boundaries. "Are you sure you want to do this?" Cece asked. "It doesn't seem like you. You're not being coerced, are you?"

"Yes, you don't usually take risks like this," her father said. "We don't want you to do anything you'll regret."

It could be her imagination, but Lyla felt that her father's objections weren't as strong as they had been before he'd learned who her groom was to be.

"I'm not being coerced and I want to do this," Lyla said. "Yeah, it's a scary idea that is taking me way out of my comfort zone, but that's kind of the point. I want to push myself, to find my limit. I like my life, but I never have adventures."

She read about them in her books, and this was probably the closest she'd ever come to living that kind of exciting life.

"Strickland is… he's a gregarious guy," her father said. "He might force you out of your shell."

Is that what her father wanted? She'd never been made to feel like she wasn't enough for anyone in her family. Everyone here loved and encouraged each other and she'd do anything for her family, just as she assumed they would do for her.

"I want your support," she said to them all. "And, Daddy, I want you to walk me down the aisle."

Now it was his turn to tear up as he smiled. "Honey, if this is what you want we will support you and it would be my honor to walk you down the aisle, it's every father's dream."

Lyla was still nervous, but as her father hugged her, she felt a bit better. Telling her family was difficult, and it had given her a focus since she'd signed up to do this. With their support, the next thing to turn her attention to was the wedding itself and that brought its own set of anxieties for her to face. But she'd signed the contract so she was in it now.

THREE

SO THAT WAS HOW she ended up here, standing in what was little more than a glorified hotel coatroom, wearing a full-skirt wedding dress.

Lyla was so pleased she'd been allowed to pick her own dress because the suggestions of the designer were outrageous. Figure hugging, low-cut, all the things that Lyla wasn't.

Choosing the full skirt, without a train, she had long-sleeves and a high neck. None of that fussy sequins and lace stuff, just plain muslin. After a lot of persuading she'd agreed to let the designer put a plain white sash around her waist that fastened behind in a neat, straight bow. But that was it. She didn't want fuss.

The hair stylist went berserk with excitement when she took her hair down and her dark auburn waves cascaded to her waist. But when he started going on about flowers and lace and braids, Lyla had to interject. A chignon was just fine with her.

"Are you sure you want to do this?" Cece asked.

The hotel was lovely, a grand five-star affair. The wedding was taking place in a marble-floored room with tall columns and ribbon-wrapped chairs. The pictures would be taken in the external courtyard, then the meal would be served in a room upstairs.

Only her parents and her aunt were here representing her family. The teenagers had been sent to school. But from the noise outside her room, which was on the main thoroughfare to the ceremony room, Lyla would guess there were quite a few people here, probably extras brought in to fill out the seats because her guest list was so meager.

Lyla didn't know much about Trick's family. More time had been spent drumming his professional accomplishments into her than his personal ones. Lyla had done some research on her own and she knew that his parents weren't together anymore, though they were still civil from what she'd read. He'd grown up with a sister, Josie, but Lyla hadn't looked into aunts and cousins because she felt it wasn't her place to pry too deep into his personal life.

"Yes, Mom," Lyla said, pulling her skirt around as she turned toward the door. Instantly faced with the camera that had been on her tail all day, she blinked. "Hi."

Cliff, the assistant director who was assigned to her had a look of concern on his face. "How are you feeling, Lyla?" he asked.

"That depends," she said, allowing some of her rare sass to slip out. "Did the groom show up?"

She was comfortable enough with her parents that she didn't have to be aware of them in the room. The cameraman never said anything and the sound guy was always doing his best to stay out of the way, so the crew had begun to fade away into the background. It probably wasn't a good thing that they were becoming invisible because these people were capturing everything about her life and were prepared to share it with the world, so she should probably be more aware of what she was doing and saying.

When she imagined it was just her and Cliff, it was much easier to be relaxed and answer his questions. He'd always been nice to her and she explained to him that dealing with more than one person at a time often overwhelmed her. He'd done his best to accommodate her quirks, of which she had many.

Cliff laughed. "Yeah, Trick's out there. He's making jokes, seems pretty relaxed."

It was the oddest thing ever that this random guy had met her groom and she hadn't. "Okay, let's rock and roll," she said, feeling oddly calm about all of this, which wasn't like her at all.

Maybe it was adrenaline, but Lyla felt she had to do this now, while she was still feeling pumped from getting ready. If she got the chance to relax too much she might second-guess her decision.

"You don't want to make him wait a bit?" Cliff asked. "It's traditional for you to be late."

Lifting her eyes to the clock above the door, Lyla read one minute to three. "Three o'clock," she said. "I'm never late."

Cliff exchanged a look with the sound guy and shrugged. "Okay, Mom, you need to take your seat," he said. Turning her cheek toward her mother, Lyla accepted Cece's kiss and adjusted her veil to cover her face as her mother scurried out. "Remember, Lyla, just go straight ahead into the room. There's a white screen that will block you from view until you take a right down the aisle with your dad. Ignore the cameras. All of them."

She'd been told this before, but appreciated that he had a job to do and part of that job was to repeat the same instructions to her over and over. "Cliff, I'm going to be late," Lyla said, aware that she never missed a deadline.

"Right," he said.

The sound guy pulled open the door at his back to let the three men reverse out. Her father took her arm and she walked forward, trying to ignore the three men recording her.

They got to the hall and although they were still filming the crew picked up pace to give her some room to walk. This wasn't how her wedding day was supposed to be. But as she walked forward, she knew it didn't matter that this was no fairytale. Lyla had never really pictured her wedding day because she never really expected it to happen. Love wasn't something she'd spent any time looking for, she didn't need it, she was happy being just her.

"Everybody stand," someone declared as she and her father began to walk alongside the screen. There was no music, but she knew enough about productions to know that would be overlaid on the edit, now they wanted silence.

Rounding the end of the screen, she saw about ten rows of chairs with maybe six in the row, wow, no way did she know that many people. But before she could try to identify faces, she saw the monstrosity of red roses on the perimeter of the room, how much did they cost? And what were—

"Sorry, can you just stop, Lyla? Can we do that again?" Cliff's boss, Paul was at the corner of the room, walking forward, waving his hand. She did as told and stopped, waiting for him to come over. But he stopped in front of her mother. "Lyla, honey, can you look at him?"

"Oh," she said, and her exhale became a nervous laugh. "Right, sorry." Letting her eyes dart to the altar, she saw what almost seemed to be the illusion of a man standing next to the registrar. Yep, that was Nairn Strickland all right, and man, was he tall, and damn, yes, he was smiling, probably laughing at her for being an idiot. "I was looking at the flowers."

She hadn't really meant to say it to anyone in particular, but Trick seemed to think she was talking to him. "They're lovely."

"Yes, they are," she said, though he was still smiling and it was a bit unnerving to see how his eyes glittered with amusement. Yep, definitely laughing at her. "Bit over the top, but what do I know? I'm no set designer."

"Me either," he said. "Better than condom trees."

"Indeed," she said with an overly formal nod. Was this weird, them conducting a sort of conversation while twenty feet apart in a room of over a hundred onlookers? She wasn't pulling this back, so she rolled her eyes and bent to hike up her skirt with her flowers still in one hand and her arm still through her father's. "Come on, Daddy."

"Reset and go again."

Yep, they went again and this time she got all the way

to the altar before Paul called out for another take, this time he wanted a wide shot. "And you thought we were getting married today," Trick murmured, she was only five feet from him now, but this time he wasn't looking at her when he spoke. "Hope the honeymoon's refundable!"

The joke aimed at the director got a laugh. Glad someone thought it was funny, he wasn't the one in agony.

"Can I take my shoes off?" she asked Paul who looked horrified at the suggestion. "Six inches isn't an advantage in this context."

The room laughed and she turned around to look at them, why were they laughing? Why was that funny? God, had she made a fool of herself? Great, like it wasn't bad enough that she was screwing up this aisle thing. What kind of woman couldn't walk down an aisle?

"Lyla!" her mother chastised.

"Sorry, Mom," Lyla said, and switched her flowers into her other hand so she could hook her wrist over her father's shoulder to support herself as she could picked up her foot to try to adjust the sling-back of her shoe. Except when she tried to reach down, the damn skirt was in the way.

"Here." Lyla's head snapped to the side when she heard Trick's voice nearby. He was crouching at her side, picking up her skirt to reach underneath. He didn't go snooping, as she might have expected him to, he just pulled her shoe from her foot and squeezed her heel with his whole large hand. "Where does it hurt?"

Like a rabbit at the end of a hunter's gun, she said nothing, didn't breathe, didn't blink. Why the hell was Nairn Strickland kneeling beside her in a tux, holding her foot?

"No, you can't take them off," Paul said. "Continuity. Your height has to stay the same."

"Sorry, babe," Trick said, slipping her shoe back on and backing away.

'Babe'? She was a 'babe'? When did that happen? Next time it was the registrar that messed up, he coughed and knocked over a flower arrangement, which took ten minutes to be reset. Then there was a bee in the room that sent half the guests fleeing. A series of mishaps saw them resetting another six times.

As she and her father stood at the head of the aisle, waiting for another reset, her mom jumped to her feet and held her phone up. "Lyla, honey, your phone is ringing."

Course it was. At least it happened while they were waiting and not while she was walking down the aisle. She took one step and her feet screamed, so she gestured to her mom. "Can you bring it over? Who is it?"

Her mother read the screen then looked at her. "Curtis."

Panic widened her eyes and Lyla shook her hand at her mother, who stopped dead. "No, no, I can't answer that. Don't give it to me."

"Why not?"

Glancing around, Lyla bowed closer, though there was twenty feet between mother and daughter, and there was no way the dozens of guests around them wouldn't hear her. "I can't lie to him."

"You didn't tell him?" her mother asked.

"I really don't need your judgment, Mother," she said, scowling at her, but her mother was the queen of the sneer.

"You should've told him."

The phone stopped ringing, letting Lyla relax a fraction. "I wasn't allowed to, Mom. This is all a secret."

Probably because the producers were worried she or Trick would back out. So it wasn't until the ink was dry on the marriage certificate that the announcement would be made at work and the first commercials for the show were airing the next night.

Everyone on the production had signed confidentiality agreements that had to be adhered to until this was public knowledge. Though at this rate, it wouldn't be happening because of production issues not personnel ones.

"Okay," Paul announced to the room. "This is the live one. Mother of the bride, back to her seat." That was a bit rude, but Lyla was too exhausted to argue with him. "Lyla, smile." Smile, right. She made herself do her best. "And look at Trick." Smile. Look at Trick. Smile. Look at Trick. "And Trick—"

"Yeah, yeah, I'm ecstatic. Can we just do this, please?"

Her mother was in the room and wouldn't appreciate language like that; Lyla guessed his mother wasn't as particular. But Trick's mom was probably used to his mouth by now.

Smile. Look at Trick.

Did it matter if she smiled? She'd been wearing a veil all day, how could they tell? She got that they could tell if her head was facing in the wrong direction to be looking at Trick, but could they really tell if she was looking at him?

The answer to that was no, because she actually focused on a spot behind the man rather than on the man himself, and no one called for a reset. Her father said something to Trick as he put her hand over her groom's. She didn't hear what it was because her father leaned right in to whisper in her groom's ear, but he was talking for a minute before the men shared a long moment of eye contact and her father took his seat.

After that, the ceremony was a bit of an anti-climax. They got all the way through it like they were reciting lines. She was no actress, but maybe she should consider the profession… or maybe she could if she could deal with people.

As it stood, she was too exhausted to really think about what she was saying, so she just said the words as they were said to her without thinking about what they meant or the long-term picture. The good thing about this being like a production was that it had lost its authentic quality. It no longer felt like a real wedding or a real marriage, because they were just doing as they'd been directed to all day. Say this. Do this. Walk there. Hit your mark.

Even when it got to the, "You may kiss the bride" part of the ceremony, there was no big pulse-racing moment. Trick lifted her veil and she tipped her head to accept his lips just at the corner of her mouth.

The kiss was chaste and probably not what he was expecting if the way he'd lunged down at her was anything to go by. But she wasn't about to put on a show for the grumpy guests when she felt just as grumpy herself.

If Paul was unhappy with it, he'd have asked them to do it again. But as it was, the guy was getting more and more stressed because they'd lost so much time.

"Okay, we're doing this part in one take, just a wide shot," Paul said to them as they stood signing where they were directed. "Then it's outside for the pictures. We're losing the light, so we'll do a couple today and probably revisit another time."

"Another time?" she asked.

"Sure, pictures can be done any time," Paul said. "We dress you up, everyone takes their places…"

"Right," she said.

Of course. Nothing was real. It wasn't about capturing the day or the mood, it was about the show and they would only need a couple of pics to sell the story to the papers.

Trick finished signing and Paul grabbed his arm to pull him to her other side. There wasn't even any finesse in the way the director grabbed her hand and shoved it into Trick's elbow. The director could've just asked her to take his arm, or asked Trick to offer it, but no, he pulled and tugged on them like they were dolls being positioned.

"Feel better?" Trick asked.

When she glanced at him, she saw he was looking at the director. Her groom's face was as tight as she felt. It had been a long day for him too and probably a boring one for a guy who was used to being on the go all the time.

"Smiles," Paul said and backed away grinning, indicating that they should smile.

The director rushed over to his crew, whispered a few things, then asked the congregation to stand as he ran to the end of the aisle and indicated to her and Trick that they should start walking. They did, and she was so relieved that the ceremony was over that she didn't even think about what they'd just done.

"So you're Lyla," Trick said, from the corner of his mouth, behind his infamous smile.

"Yes, Mr. Strickland, I am," she said, restraining herself from asking what gave it away, the big dress and the vows maybe?

"Think it should be Trick, don't you?" he said.

Paul growled aloud and waved as he marched down the aisle toward them. "No talking! Can you just smile and walk please?"

"Damn," Trick muttered and began to walk backward, but he went too fast and she whooped as she tried to keep up.

Her groom's manners only went so far. Trick's patience might be stretched, but so was hers. Frustration was no excuse for him dragging her around by her arm that he had clamped under his.

Next time, they both did their best to smile and walked up the aisle without talking. Paul was grumbling and unhappy when they finished the shot, but Trick landed a glare on the director that made her shiver.

Oh yeah, he was pissed and he wasn't doing it again. That was just fine with her.

FOUR

PICTURES WEREN'T MUCH better. Everyone was in a bad mood. Smiles were forced and the group shot was probably the best one, and that was only because it was so wide. They only took half a dozen before Paul called his crew over.

Trick went to join his personal posse.

Lyla had seen the woman at the head of the group looking at her frequently throughout the day. She'd been in the front row on Trick's side, so Lyla guessed that the woman was Trick's mom. She was looking again and seemed to want to come over, but Trick put an arm around the front of her chest and drew her back.

"Okay," Paul said, rushing over to her, reaching Lyla even before her aunt and mother managed to. He put an arm around her and began to guide her away, but paused to look around. "Where's Trick?"

Turning, she pointed back. "With his family."

"Right. Trick!"

Trick turned, but took his time speaking to his family before he left them and came over to join her and Paul. "Now do we eat?" Trick asked when he got to them.

"In a minute," Paul said. "You're supposed to get an

hour to talk, we have to cut that, we just don't have time to get everything in. You can have fifteen minutes; the cameras will follow you up. There's a seating area at the top of the stairs, in the sunroom, it's lit."

"Wish I was," Trick said, digging his hands in his pockets.

Paul just grumbled at him and shooed them up the stairs. Trick didn't even wait for her, he took the stone steps two at a time and got to the building while she was just halfway up the staircase. Trying to negotiate her dress and ridiculous shoes without falling on her face delayed her, but Lyla would rather take her time than embarrass herself on film.

Lyla didn't know the layout of the hotel, so she was glad to get to the building at all. But when she entered the glass doors of the sunroom, she found herself alone. Huh. Trick had definitely been ahead of her, she couldn't see how he could get lost.

"Lose your groom?"

Turning around, she saw Cliff and the camera closing in on her. "Uh, looks that way," she said.

"How do you feel?" Cliff asked, gesturing at her to sit down from behind the camera.

Backing up toward the cushioned wicker couch, she looked down and then spread her hands on her dress without sitting. "The dress… can I crease the dress?"

"Are you going to stand all night?" Cliff asked. "You'll have to sit down for dinner."

"True," she said. "If there's a seamstress around, some of the layers are detachable."

"Continuity," Cliff said.

Damn that word. She exhaled and sank down, but lost most of herself in the skirt. Shoving it down, she stretched out her legs to point her toes, but it didn't matter to the camera because the operator crouched to film up at her.

"Are you trying to get a shot of my underwear?" she asked, pushing the air out of her skirt.

"Looks like you're sitting on a cloud," Cliff said, glancing at the image on the top of the camera. "So, forgetting the production stuff, how do you think the day went?"

"Oh God," she said. "Like a comedy of errors."

Cliff smiled. "Can you remember to repeat the question in your answer and… you know… try to stay positive, you just got married. Smile."

Sick of hearing that word, she was tempted to sink back, but still felt the bulk of the dress getting in her way. "I think the day went well," she said, wondering when she'd become such a convincing liar.

"And your groom, what do you think of him?"

Trailing her eyes toward the courtyard, and then the other way to the building that was attached to the room by a set of open double doors, she wondered where he'd got to and what she could say about him that was positive. "I think my groom is… funny."

Yeah, he was funny, great at cracking jokes, not so great at being where he was supposed to be.

"And what do you think he thinks of you?"

Of her? How was she supposed to answer that question when they'd exchanged so few words?

"He thinks her feet hurt."

The camera turned as they all did toward the double internal doors; Trick emerged from the dimly-lit bar beyond carrying two glasses of some kind of dark liquor. Sauntering over, Lyla expected him to offer her one of the glasses. But he didn't. He tossed one measure into his throat quickly followed by the other.

Crouching, he shoved the empty glasses onto an end table then dropped to his knees beside her and tucked a hand under the end of her dress to circle her ankle with his hand. Relief made her exhale when he pulled off her shoe. Her head fell back when he slid the other off.

"Way into a woman's panties, start by taking off the shoes," Trick said.

Horror made her head snap back up, but he was talking into the camera, not to her. His hand slid up the front of her leg as he rose to slide onto the couch beside her. Leaning over her, Trick let her skirt gather against his arm as his hand slid up over her knee.

"What are you doing?" she asked, her lungs getting

tighter.

"Getting to know you," he murmured and leaned in.

Planting her hands on his chest, Lyla gave him a hard shove and put space between them. Glancing at the camera before she looked back at her groom, she tried not to freak out. "I don't think that's what they meant."

"They meant whatever we want them to mean," he said and tried to kiss her again.

"I'm not ready to… I can't kiss you," she said, her eyes popping toward the camera and the other silent men in the room.

"Just ignore them, babe. You focus on me."

His hand went higher when he tried once again to kiss her, but she wasn't giving in. "Our families are right out there," she said.

In a glass room with other men was one thing, but outside the glass were their families and colleagues who would be making their way up to the hotel for dinner soon.

Trick snickered, his eyes heavy as he focused on her lips. "I wasn't gonna take you all the way right here… But if that's what you want, Mrs. Strickland, that dress will give us all the cover we'll need… you slide on over into your old man's lap."

Sitting back, he slouched and patted his thighs with both hands, which gave her the ability to sit up and try to regain some composure as she straightened out her dress. "I think, Mr. Strickland, you need to hold your horses and think about bringing a girl a drink before you put your hand up her dress."

"Liquor!" Trick announced, slapping his knees and sitting up straight. "My second favorite thing to do with a girl. We're not so opposite after all, are we, sweetheart?"

He leaned in and kissed her cheek so fast that she didn't even realize it was happening. Lyla was still gaping at Trick when Cliff spoke.

"Okay," the assistant director said on a laugh. "We'll cut it there. You guys have five minutes before we're coming to get you… enjoy it."

The assistant director took his cameraman and sound

guy out of the room and closed the doors, though did it matter when they were in a glass room? Lyla was pleased to have transparent walls because she didn't want to be alone with this Neanderthal of a man who was only interested in booze or sex.

She was about to chastise Trick for his behavior when he sagged and let his head fall against the back of the couch. "I had no idea that a wedding was so exhausting," he said, his eyes closed. "Don't put those shoes back on if they hurt your feet, screw continuity."

Who was this guy? This relaxed guy who was talking without that thread of innuendo in his tone? "Uh, Mr. Strickland…"

"Seriously, babe," he said and managed to catch her hand without opening his eyes. "Call me Trick. We're married."

"Right," she said, looking down at their joined hands that were resting on the cushion of her dress. "Married."

"Do you know what we're having for dinner?"

Why couldn't she stop looking at their joined hands and why did no one tell her that his hands were so big?

"No," she said.

"Doesn't matter, I guess, I'm starved, I'd eat just about anything right now… You know, they made the announcement at Prem about an hour ago, so I'd expect some of our colleagues to show up to this shindig tonight."

How did he know this? And who knew his fingers would be so thick between hers and feel so solid? But they were warm, and his fingertips were rough, why would his fingertips be so rough?

"Right," she mumbled.

"Hey, you okay? I mean… apart from the obvious whiplash of going from single to married in a day?"

Forcing herself to turn, she saw his head was tilted toward her, his eyes open to slits. "I'm… confused… you don't want in my underwear anymore?"

His smile almost turned into a laugh as he closed his eyes and let his head twist away again. "Yeah, that was full-on; I figured they warned you, you did good… Production did their job good though, finding a woman so opposite to me. I knew pretty much as soon as you walked around the corner of that screen that you weren't my type... So, we're good, I'll play it up; I know what I'm supposed to do. But it's damn clear you're not attracted to me, so just keep slapping me down and we'll be good... It's what the audience wants, right?"

"Great television?" she murmured.

"Exactly." The double doors opened and Paul appeared with a camera. "Time to turn it on, sweetheart," Trick whispered and grinned before leaping to his feet and pulling her up. "Gotta get my girl drunk enough to enjoy the wedding night."

It was obvious her groom was talking to the camera and it even got a wink as he dragged her past and into the bar that led to the dining room beyond.

***

"READY TO SPLIT?" Paul asked.

Lyla hadn't seen much of Trick all night.

The Prem crowd had been in and had cheered accordingly, but she had a lot of explaining to do. Specifically, to Curtis who had been her only friend in the building for a long time. He didn't get it, and she was sorry that he seemed so annoyed.

At least her parents liked the food and there was an open bar, that was something. The rest of the guests seemed to be having fun too. The night got progressively rowdier as the guests drank as much free alcohol as they could.

The first dance had been a war of the hands. Trick kept trying to grab her ass and pull her close as she fought to maintain a more traditional stance. He didn't seem to care much about them having an audience, both in terms of their friends and family members that were around the perimeter of the dancefloor, or the camera that kept coming in close to try to pick up their conversation.

The fifth time she had to duck his kiss was the last time.

After that, she pushed his hands from her body and excused herself for the ladies room. Lyla didn't make a big deal of it, just acted like she really needed to go. Except the truth was, she couldn't even use the bathroom because of the dress. She'd been holding it all night, so she hadn't drunk much, but that was fine with her. Trick was fast with his hands and his mouth. Lyla had to keep her wits about her when he was trying to steal from her what he wanted.

Her mother seemed to like him though. Cece thought he was mischievous. Lyla didn't get it. The man was constantly trying to grope her, always hugging other women and leaning in just a little too close, taking a good look down their dresses as he did. Yeah, he was mischievous, and a letch.

She still hadn't met any of Trick's family; they'd been at their own table all night and didn't venture far from it. Nathaniel and Noah, Trick's cohosts, spent a lot of the night at that table too, but the two of them she had met and danced with. They seemed to talk about sex as much as Trick did.

All in all, it had been an exhausting night and she was so relieved that Paul had come to offer a reprieve.

"Yes," she said, pushing away from the bar where she'd been loitering alone for almost an hour since her parents and aunt left.

It was a long journey home for them, so she didn't begrudge them leaving, especially since they still had to pick up the twins from their friends' houses. But Curtis hadn't stayed either, so she was left alone, in a dress she was still paranoid about creasing.

"Where's Trick?" Paul asked.

"You're asking me?" she asked, looking out across the room that was starting to thin a bit now.

The Strickland family table was empty and she couldn't even see Nathaniel or Noah anymore.

Cliff came running over to join them wearing a smile. "Good?" Cliff asked.

"Don't know where Trick is," Paul said.

Cliff blinked and poked a thumb over his shoulder. "He and the boys left with a posse a half-hour ago… they're going to that opening in town… he took his camera crew though, so we're good."

Paul nodded. "Okay, I guess, would've been nice to know."

Yeah, for her too, because she could've left when they did if she'd known they were going. "Can I go home then?"

The men exchanged a look and the camera suddenly came in to view behind them. That's right; she was being filmed all the time.

"There's a suite upstairs for your wedding night," Paul said. "Someone should use it."

"Let Trick take his party there," she said and grabbed her clutch from the bar.

Her mother had kept it for her all day and she was pleased she'd had the foresight to pack her phone and some cash.

Walking away from the men, she began to head for the exit and got as far as the lobby before she realized she was being followed.

Turning around, she stopped to address Cliff. "What are you doing?"

"Coming with you."

"Coming—what?"

"We have to," Cliff said.

"I'm going home to take a shower and go to bed," she said. "You have to film that?"

Cliff shrugged. "I guess the shower is optional if you're going to be in it alone."

Restraining her growl, she turned to continue onto the street. They weren't all going to fit in the back of a cab, but that didn't stop Cliff from joining her with a portable camera.

It was amazing that the directors and crews still seemed to be so motivated when she was struggling to keep her eyes open.

"Aren't you tired?" she asked after reciting her address to the driver. "Don't you have a family to go home to?"

"Nope," he said. "You want to grab a drink?"

The camera was on, so she had to guess he was

joking, but that wasn't exactly clear when she met his eye. As unimpressed as she felt, he was smiling. God, she was sick of men already. This was why she avoided them and did everything she could to not talk to them or draw attention to herself. As soon as she took her glasses off and let them know she had a waist, that was it, they all became complete idiots.

"Seriously?"

His smile only got wider. "It's your wedding night, right? No bride should sleep alone on her wedding night."

"I'll sleep with Risk," she said, without even being polite enough to smile.

"Risk?"

"My cat," she said. "He has better manners than every man I met today... minus my own family."

Cliff looked at his watch. "We could go to the club, get your groom."

Yeah, production would love that, if she stormed into a nightclub in her wedding dress and grabbed her groom to haul him home by his ear. No way, she'd done enough performing for today.

"No thanks."

"One last night of freedom before the whipping starts?" he asked.

Whatever he wanted her to say, she didn't care about trying to take his lead anymore. "No whipping," she muttered and closed her eyes. "I can't wait to get out of this damn dress."

"That we will be filming," he said and she didn't appreciate his teasing.

Though, in fairness, she was probably just too tired to really focus on his humor that seemed to just keep missing the mark.

"Do what you want," she murmured, unable to fight. "I just want to get to sleep."

"So you can wake up early and catch your flight. Excited about your honeymoon?"

"Sun, sea, sand, what's not to be excited about?" she asked. "Florida's like my dream destination."

"Really?" he asked and he was right to sound dubious.

She cracked an eye. "I'm more of an Alaska girl," she said. "Lots of layers and hot chocolate around an open fire."

"And a good book."

She smiled and closed her eyes again. "You're getting to know me so well, Cliff… Now will you let me take my clothes off in private?"

"Maybe," he said. "I'll have to text Paul."

So this was her life. One guy had to get another guy's permission to find out if she had to strip in private or on film. "You won't be missing anything. Trust me."

The contracts that she'd signed were extensive. She had signed her life over to the station for the foreseeable future. What was supposed to be an adventure was fast turning into a nightmare, but she was too tired to care tonight.

FIVE

LYLA DIDN'T HAVE time to care the next day either. The camera crew were at her door before she'd even brushed her teeth. She didn't let them slow her down though, and managed to get out of the apartment and made to the airport on time.

There was some sort of security alert, so it was taking longer to get through check in and security checkpoints. Since filming had started it seemed she was always waiting, waiting, waiting. Eventually, she did make it onto the flight and into her seat.

Cliff and the others were on the same plane too, but they were dotted around all over the place, meaning there wouldn't be any filming on the flight, which she was at peace with, even if it pissed Paul off.

The flight was late, but at least she was here. She hadn't seen Trick at all that morning, but that didn't mean he wasn't there. The seats all around her were taken, it seemed to be fully booked, so he could be anywhere on the plane.

Until someone came and told her that he wasn't here or she should get off the plane because there was no honeymoon, she was going to sit there, looking out of the window watching the airline employees scurrying around on the tarmac.

"Hey."

Turning to the sound of Trick's voice, Lyla wasn't surprised to find that he wasn't talking to her; he was never talking to her. He was talking to the guy in the seat paired with hers.

"Hey, I know you!" the passenger said. "You're… you're that late night guy with the buddies!"

"Yeah," Trick said.

When Trick's grin widened, she turned back to look at the men in their high-vis vests. Wondering about the point of the neon jackets, she blocked out of the conversation going on between the two men beside her and speculated on how long it might take a plane to stop after a pilot noticed the guys on the ground.

A minute later, the guy beside her got up and then someone else dropped in to the seat. Turning around, she saw Trick grinning at her. "Hey, baby." When he reached over in an attempt to touch her jaw, she dipped back and pulled her purse higher in her lap. "You're pissed?"

"Pissed?" she asked, pushing her oversized prescription shades higher on her nose. "No—well, yeah, I guess. I could've been in bed a half-hour earlier if I'd known you were taking off."

He curled a hand around her knee making her pleased that she'd chosen to wear the long sundress paired with the tie-dyed cotton poncho cover-up. But even though there was no skin contact, she still picked up his hand and put it on his own lap.

"Sorry, I'm tactile."

Apologetic was better than what he'd been last night, but was it the alcohol that made him handsy or the personality?

"There is no filming on the flight," she said. "You can give that gentleman his seat back."

Leaning out into the aisle, Trick seemed to be looking at something, the stewardess's ass probably. "You liked that *gentleman?* Doesn't seem like your type."

"What do you know about my type?" she asked,

narrowing her eyes when he lifted his sunglasses to prop them on the front of his forehead so he could pinch and rub the bridge of his nose. His eyes were bloodshot with dark circles beneath them and she recognized that he was hungover. Opening her purse, Lyla popped a couple of ibuprofen from their sheet and tipped a vitamin from its bottle, then picked up the water bottle she'd got from the stewardess. Holding both toward him, he opened his palm to accept the pills. "Stay hydrated."

"Ah, you're an angel," he said, tossing the pills back and gulping down the water. When the air stewardess walked by, he seized her wrist. "Hey, sweetheart, can we have a couple of bottles of water and half a dozen vodka miniatures. Leave them in plastic, you know?"

The air stewardess smiled like putty and giggled. "Of course, Mr. Strickland."

"I told you, it's Trick, and don't you go forgetting it, sweetheart."

He winked at the woman and Lyla rolled her eyes as she walked off. "Do you think more alcohol is a good idea? What time did you get home?"

"Haven't done that yet," he said, groaning and pushing back in his seat. "And I'm not gonna drink it, I'm just gonna let them think I am."

Lyla didn't know what that meant, but had learned already that there was plenty in his life that didn't make sense to her. She wasn't going to get herself lost in any labyrinth trying to figure it out. The air hostess came back with his things and she got another wink as Trick handed Lyla one of the full water bottles.

The stewardess left with a giggle and Trick dipped into the space between their knees to work covertly. Watching Trick tip the vodka into the almost empty water bottle, Lyla was surprised to see him stick it in the pouch in front of him and then refill the empty vodka bottles with water from one of the new full bottles. He turned his tray down and spread the vodka bottles across the tray, except now there was no vodka in them, it was just water.

Huh, he was a perplexing person. "Cliff says he's

going to give me a tour of the resort when we get there. You could sleep then."

"Who's Cliff?" Trick asked, stretching himself out so far that his hands flattened on the ceiling above them. "The hotel manager?"

"My assistant director," she said.

"Huh," he said, his eyes still closed. "Guess I never thought about Paul not being in two places at once."

If she'd been introduced to everyone, he must have been too. Obviously, he didn't pay attention in other areas too.

"Paul was pretty angry that you ditched him last night," she said, pulling her purse up to her torso again and hugging it close.

"Yeah, I got reamed for that," he said, smiling and turning onto his side in his chair to look at her. "He was more pissed than you are… You the perfect woman, or you just worried about coming off as a nag on the first day?"

"You made it clear yesterday what this was," she said, pulling the stack of papers out the pocket of the chairback in front of her.

"I did?" he asked. "I gotta be honest, sweetheart, I was pretty much drunk all day, so if I'm a little hazy on the facts…"

"We're not attracted to each other and we already know we have nothing in common, that's the whole idea of the show. You know, I was the only girl on the list because there wasn't one other person on payroll more different to you than I am. So…"

"So…?"

Turning to see him assessing her, she felt scrutinized, but was he trying to figure her out or just where this was going? "I think it's obvious we'll be getting a divorce."

He smiled, something he did easily, and it warmed his whole face. He was one of the most approachable guys she'd met. Always smiling, and everyone's best friend, nothing seemed to bother him.

"Why'd you come then?" he asked. "If it's over before it began?"

"It's a publicity stunt," she said. "Maybe I didn't

realize how deep that went, maybe I thought there would be…"

"Be what?" he asked and his hand slid over onto her knee again.

Lyla wasted no time in putting it back on his side of the chair arm. For some reason, that made his smile turn to a grin.

"Not that," she said. "You're physical, that's what you want… I'm not like that. Not even a little bit."

"You're not physical?" he asked. "You don't do anything physical?" His eyes dropped to her body, but they quickly became lost in the hood of a frown. "How come you always cover up every inch of yourself?"

Her thin cotton cover-up did have a high neck and it was long enough to drape to wrist and mid-thigh, not that it mattered, as her dress went to her ankles. Right now though, her stuffed purse was on her lap and hugged in to her body so tight it rested beneath her chest.

"What do you expect to see, Mr. Strickland?" she asked. "Would you like me to show more skin?"

He grinned. "Yes, that would be great."

"And what if the view's not as nice as you want it to be?" she asked. "Not Kira Levine nice."

His brows rose as his eyes drifted from her body to meet hers and his glasses fell over his eyes again. "Wow, straight into exes, okay. Kira was hot as hell, comparing you to her would be like comparing…"

"Apples to oranges?"

Nodding, he folded his arms, but stayed twisted toward her. "Yeah, but it doesn't matter. You wouldn't compare me to your exes, so it's not… you know… a big deal."

Sure, not a big deal, except her ex list had exactly one name on it and he wasn't an underwear model. "No, it's not a big deal," she said. "Because we know this is not going to be anything. And I came because who doesn't like a free trip to the beach? Yeah, I'll admit, I thought twice about it after dancing with you. But I figure, there are a bunch of clubs and a lot of beautiful women around, so I probably won't see you much… I actually didn't expect to see you on the flight at all."

Sorting through the information she'd taken from the chair-back pouch, she put back the security information just as the plane began to move. They taxied out and took off. Trick hadn't said anything else, so she figured he'd fallen asleep and was happy to leaf through the in-flight magazine reading about products available for purchase and the latest in tray-table innovations.

The novel in her purse was beginning to look more attractive by the second, but she didn't want to race to pick it up. She only had a limited number of books to get her through the full four days and she read fast.

"So, what are you?"

Trick's words were so unexpected that they startled her.

Lyla turned to find him fixated right on her, his glasses on his head. "Sorry?"

"If I'm physical and you're not, then what are you?"

"Cerebral," she said, turning the page of her magazine. "You need a woman with an immaculate figure to interest you and I need…"

"Brains," he said, pushing his shoulder in to the back of the chair to push up higher. "You think I'm an idiot."

Lyla didn't mean to smile, but she did, though she didn't take her attention away from the magazine article that she was no longer reading. "I think the things that I like to talk about and the things that you like to talk about couldn't be more different. I don't know anything about sports, or liquor, or breast implants."

"That's okay, I can teach you." She didn't laugh. "What do you like to talk about?"

"You don't care," she muttered, still smiling.

"I care," he said, taking the magazine away from her to stuff it into the chair-back before seizing her hand. "Humor me, babe, what do you like to talk about?"

Twisting around, she curled her body around her purse when she drew her knees up onto the seat and shifted her whole body in his direction. "Politics, history, philosophy," she said and his eyes kind of flared in a way that made her laugh. "See."

When she moved to return to her previous position, he reached over to grab her knees and pull her back. "No, wait, don't… just give me a minute, okay… history. I like history. You mean like the Wild West and stuff? Cowboys and all that crap?"

Grinning, she shook her head. "Actually, I like European history, the Roman emperors, the British monarchs… there are some amazing and fascinating stories. Their senates and courts were filled with intrigue, romance, drama, conflict… It's the greatest of adventures and the best part is, they're all true."

"Romans, huh," he said and she nodded. "You like powerful guys, emperors and kings. That what turns you on?" Typical that he should jump to some kind of sexual association. "Like Caesar and that stuff?"

"Caligula's actually one of my favorites, he's said to have been completely insane. He turned his palace into a brothel and was in love with his sister."

"Why shouldn't he love his sister?" he asked.

She laughed. "No, he was *in* love with her… had sex with her."

His whole face screwed up and she laughed again. "Really? He screwed his sister?" Clutching her hand, he gave it a squeeze. "I'm not sure my stomach is strong enough to listen to this right now."

If he was playing, he was doing a good job of it. "There are all kinds of stories like that. They're all dubious of course. Spread by the victor after the victim was killed. Most of the emperors and kings were assassinated… usually by those closest to them or their own family members who wanted to steal power."

"No kidding," he said. "Harsh."

"Yep," she said. "It's actually really interesting… if it's told right."

Giving him his hand back, Lyla reached for her magazine again, but he caught her hand and pulled it back to his, this time taking it onto his knee instead of hers. "So tell it," he said.

That wasn't funny. "What?" she asked.

"Tell me the stories."

Shaking her head, she tried to pull her hand away, but he kept hold of it. "I can't."

"Why not?"

"I'm not a good story-teller," she said. "I don't... I don't talk well."

She understood Trick's confusion—he relished talking to groups, commanding an audience, so he probably couldn't see how daunting a prospect performing was for her.

"You're talking great, babe. Tell me, I want to know."

The whole point of this marriage thing was for them to be different, but she hadn't read anywhere that they were supposed to suppress those differences. "What do you want to know?"

"Sex," he said, spreading his grin again. "Tell me more about that."

"The Romans were very sexual," she said. "And in contrast to widespread opinion they were much more liberal than we are in a lot of ways. They shared partners, wives; they slept with slaves and prostitutes openly, and often engaged in same-sex relations without shame. They decorated their walls with what we would classify as pornography."

"No way!"

That wasn't Trick's voice. In fact, her groom looked up at the same time she did to see the two guys from the seats in front were kneeling up looking over the back.

"S'up, guys?" Trick asked, snickering at them.

"Yeah, man, big fans," the guy said and reached down to shake Trick's hand in a weird slapping, twisty combination before his buddy did the same thing. "Tommy, look who this is!"

The other passenger called to his friends who were seated behind them and before she knew it there was a group of half a dozen college kids around, penning her in as they all tried to get Trick to notice them. They were starting to draw attention to themselves; Lyla felt herself shrink.

Extracting her fingers from Trick's, Lyla tried to push his knee aside, out of her way. "Excuse me," she murmured and clutched her purse tight as she stood up and wondered what the hell she was going to do to get by his tray table.

"Whoa, wait a second," Trick said, putting an arm out to urge her back down into her seat. "Where are you going, babe?"

"Restroom," she muttered, keeping her eyes down.

As his fingers stretched under her chin, he tried to lift her face, but she resisted. "Looking for a little mile high fun?"

The shock of this made her gaze leap to his and her mouth open. Could he really just have said that in front of all these guys? These… strangers. This… group.

"Trick," she hissed.

"Hey, you guys together?" one of the passengers asked. "She doesn't seem like your type."

"Yeah, I figured she was an assistant or something."

"Nah, guys," Trick announced and drove an arm around her. "This here's the little woman. She's my wife."

As the guys all expressed shock, Lyla gasped. Throwing her purse to the floor, she grabbed the hem of her poncho and Trick's collar. Yanking him toward her, she threw the end of her poncho up over both of their heads to hide them from the group.

"Trick," she whispered, frantic as she searched his eyes that were only a couple of inches from hers. "We're not supposed to tell."

"Relax, babe," he said, smiling as he let a curled finger touch her cheekbone. Although the contact startled Lyla and she tried to pull away, she couldn't go anywhere because there just wasn't room to withdraw while they were under this cloak. "The first ads will be on the network tonight and these guys will have a story to tell, it's all good publicity."

Good publicity, she was getting tired of hearing that. "Right. Whatever. Will you please let me pass so I can go to the restroom?"

"Do you really need to go or are you just trying to sneak away from me?"

Why would he think that? "No, I…" All she achieved by lowering her eyes was causing his finger to slide from her cheek to her chin to lever them up to his again. "I don't do well in groups," she whispered.

"Another thing we don't have in common," he said and smiled. Was he enjoying this? She admitted that she had a vulnerability and the first thing he did was smile like an idiot. "Just keep your eyes on me, babe, okay? Forget about everyone else, just look right at me."

A hand slithered onto her knee and began to ascend her leg. "Trick, take your hand off my thigh."

"What? I'm curious about what you're hiding." He grinned that impish grin. "We're married."

Thrusting the poncho down, she pulled his hand out from under it and deliberately locked her fingers between his. Yes, she could do hand-holding. While his hand was in hers, it wasn't misbehaving.

"No way you're married," the passenger said. Lyla hated how fascinated they'd all become with her. Before that announcement, she'd been ignored. "Were you making out under there?"

"Yep," Trick said to the grinning guys who had to all be in their early twenties. "We're going on our honeymoon. She's real hot for me, aren't you, babe?"

Without expression, Lyla stayed deadpan showing that she wasn't impressed by his grin. "Aflame."

"See, she knows all the sexiest words. I got myself a brainiac," he said, either he was making fun of her or he was meant to sound proud, she couldn't figure out which.

"You with brains? I thought every guy was supposed to go for boobs," the passenger said and all his buddies found this hilarious.

Rolling her eyes toward the window, she wondered how far up they were right now and if parachutes were an option. Lyla was trying to phase out when something touched her chest. Slapping it away, she was shocked to realize it was Trick's hand. With her mouth open, she blinked at him, thank God he hadn't done more than graze her through her clothes, but who the hell did he think he was?

"She's got those," Trick said, winking at her before turning back to his admirers.

"Can we see them?" the passenger asked.

She gasped. "Excuse me?"

The passenger shrugged. "Kira showed hers everywhere, still good jerk-off material. Up high!"

He held out his hand for a high five, which Trick actually gave him and a bunch of the others.

Wow, this was the man she'd married. The man who gave other guys high fives to celebrate his ex-girlfriend's breasts. Lyla would be interested to meet this Kira just to find out if she appreciated being objectified in that way. Lyla had no problem with the female form or men admiring it, but she'd like to think if there were real feelings between Kira and Trick there might have been more respect, but maybe not.

Turning back to the window, she exhaled. "I wonder if Kira high fives women who talk about your penis," she muttered and then smiled. "Probably not."

The guys whooped and hissed.

Lyla was shocked when Trick's hand curled around her jaw, holding her head static as he leaned across and touched his lips to her ear. "I love a woman with a smart mouth, Malloy."

She sucked her lower lip into her mouth and stopped breathing when he caught her earlobe with his tongue and drew it between her teeth to give her a light bite. No man had ever bitten her. Her shock must have been written across her face when she turned to him because his grin got bigger, but his eyes got narrower.

"Oh, hey, you guys have got some fire," the passenger said.

Fire was the last thing they had, except when Trick's gaze fell to her mouth, she had to acknowledge that he was a better actor than she'd thought he'd be. For a second, she almost believed that he wanted to kiss her.

Then she remembered the sunroom and how convincing he'd been when he put his hand up her skirt only minutes before admitting he had no interest in her. The man was good at his job; she had to give him credit for that.

Trick settled back in his seat, his attention intent on her. "Now, babe, what were you saying?"

"What was I saying?" she asked, thrown out of the

moment and into confusion. "About what?"

"The sister fucker," he said. "Finish the story."

She glanced around at the group of guys who were taking up space in front, behind, and in the aisle. "Yeah," the passenger said. "You said they had porn on the walls, that's cool."

Porn on the walls. Yes. Making eye contact with Trick, he nodded. "You… you want me to tell you about the emperors?"

"Sure," he said. "Talk to me, babe."

Well, it was better than sitting through a silent flight or fighting his hands. She'd prefer to be talking to one single person. As long as she just looked at Trick, Lyla could pretend it was just him, right? Okay, she took a deep breath. She could do this.

SIX

THE WOMAN WAS SMART.

He'd married a goddamn encyclopedia.

It had been a shock enough to Trick when he was told that she'd said yes, how the hell had that happened? He'd managed to bag the first woman he'd proposed to without actually ever meeting her.

Then she'd turned around the end of that screen and he'd been shocked. Her full skirt, long-sleeves and thick veil made it pretty obvious that she was hands-off. Before the actual wedding day, he hadn't given a lot of thought to who they'd lined up for him. The idea had been put to him and he'd thought, 'What the heck?' If it helped the station that had given him a home, then why shouldn't he toss a couple of months at this?

Trick had been surprised by how good a sport she was when the up and down the aisle debacle happened. The first part of his wife he'd ever touched was her foot. Her skin had been soft beneath his fingertips; he liked that, and the smell of coconut that came from her hair, he'd noticed that when she was next to him at the altar.

But that was it.

That was the extent of his awareness.

At least it had been until they were in the sunroom and her little mouth opened in outrage when he slid his hand up her leg. Her breathing had hitched in fits and starts as he got higher, and he'd really thought he was going to kiss her. Then she'd pushed him away.

Yep, Lyla Malloy couldn't be farther from his type.

There was his type on Neptune and then there was Lyla on Mercury. No doubt about it. She didn't have sass, just shock. Didn't flaunt her figure, she was buttoned up, right up to the tight knot that kept her hair in check. She didn't flirt with him, or with anyone. She answered questions, spoke politely, and if that flight was anything to go by, she knew everything.

Her face lit up when she spoke about these ancient pricks who she knew so much about. Telling the stories of these long-dead bastards and their busy cocks made her eyes widen and her mouth more expressive. It put color in her cheeks and made her body move as she told the tales from hundreds of years ago.

Her hands moved under that blanket thing that covered her body. Although she kept her purse near to her, she shifted in the chair, leaning in to give him a whiff of that coconut stuff, only to lean back and address the group.

She said she wasn't good in groups, but by the end of her little educational lecture, she had those guys drooling. He didn't know what it was that was so mesmerizing, the huge glasses that she peeked over the top of? The way her narrow shoulders moved beneath the thin purple tie-dyed material or the saucy curve of her lips as she murmured an illicit detail?

Didn't matter.

She wasn't his type.

Never would be.

***

THEY'D GOTTEN TO the hotel and he'd had a nap. Trick didn't know where she'd gone, didn't really care. If the directors were around then they would be looking after her.

So he didn't have to be worried about her safety and amusing her was someone else's problem. He'd have no chance of keeping a woman like that entertained. Somehow, he doubted his juggling bit would fly with a genius like her.

Paul had come in to the bedroom, woken him up, dragged him into the living room and told him to eat. "We want to get some shots at the pool," the director said as Trick ate a sandwich with one hand and scrubbed the other through his hair. "The light is good right now and we don't know what the weather will be like tomorrow."

"Lyla wants to go on the walking tour tomorrow," Cliff said.

Trick thought he recognized the scruffy-haired guy from the wedding, but had been introduced to him again when he came out of the bedroom anyway, so it didn't matter if they'd met before.

Facing the huge window on the far side of the living space, Trick winced as he realized that if the light was this bright inside, it was going to be worse outside.

One of the camera guys came over to stand next to Paul and that blocked out some of the glare from the sun, but not enough. There were other crew guys on the couches; Trick couldn't remember their names. He only remembered Cliff's name because when he heard Paul use it in reference to the scruffy-haired guy, Trick recalled hearing Malloy say it too. So that was the guy who'd taken her on a tour and been entertaining his wife while he slept.

Trick wondered how much Cliff knew about Roman emperors, maybe Lyla had been talking about the history stuff with him too.

"Yeah, she told me," Paul said. "But we do need some pool shots."

Glancing left and right, Trick sought out liquid. "Got any beer?"

One of the camera guys tossed him a bottle of water. "Lyla said you have to stay hydrated."

"We haven't been married twenty-four hours and she's turning the screws already," Trick said, but twisted off the cap of the bottle and gulped down all the liquid inside.

Yeah, water was good, he needed that… Hmm… maybe she knew what she was talking about.

"You have to change into your shorts," Paul said.

"I need a shower," he grumbled and belched before rubbing a hand on his chest.

He could do with going back to bed for a couple of hours because he was getting too old for staying out all night. Given his reputation, it was impossible to admit it, but Trick had been getting tired of it for the last few years.

Yawning, he heard a door open behind him and tried to remember if he'd even packed swimming shorts. This water was good. Reading the bottle, he tried to figure out if there was something special in it that was making him feel better.

"Cliff?"

"Yeah, Ly…"

The way Cliff's voice trailed off made Trick look up at the assistant director. Except before he got there, he saw his director, Paul and the camera guy gaping, wide-eyed, staring at something behind him.

Glancing past the guys in front of him, Trick saw that Cliff and the other camera guy, as well as the sound guys, had their tongues rolling from their mouths. What the hell was provoking boners all round? 'Cause he recognized the way they all shifted.

"My hair tie broke," Lyla said, her voice carrying from behind him. "And I need help with this lotion. I'm not going out without it; the sun is at its peak right now."

Turning around, Trick didn't know what to expect, but he felt his own heart flip over in his chest as his balls began to pant. That… that was Lyla…

The woman was standing there in a string bikini, with all that crazy wild hair that looked softer than cotton candy, cascading all around her. It fell all the way to her waist, and as she scooped it back over her shoulders, she revealed a body that actually made him squeak when he opened his mouth.

The tits, the ass… the abs… damn, who the hell was that?

When she was done scooping the waves of silken dark hair from her body, she looked up and blinked sultry eyes at all of them. Why had he never noticed how her eyes tapered until now? How they were so keen, yet alluring at the same time.

"What's wrong?" she asked, closing a hand over her breast as she took the bottle of lotion in to her cleavage. "I'm going to put my kaftan on, don't think I'm going to embarrass you all by going out like this."

She smiled like that was a joke.

Oh, holy hell, she smiled.

Where did that come from? Was that really the same smile he'd seen on the flight? He'd recognized that she had a pretty face, though he hadn't seen it without her glasses. And yesterday, she was either wearing her veil, or they were too far apart. Her little snit in the sunroom hadn't been conducive to smiling and he was grateful for that, because what the hell was that on her face now? Even the voice of his internal monologue squeaked, he was so taken aback.

His heart was pounding, his guts felt tight, and had she said embarrassed? No way was his wife going out into the world like that. She'd give men coronaries after they got the most intense hard-on of their lives.

"Sure, Lyla," Cliff said, obviously having recovered from his stupor enough that he could drag himself off the couch. "Sorry, sweetie." Sweetie? Trick snapped his scowl around to the guy who was literally sprinting across the room right now to grab the bottle of lotion from his wife. His wife! "Glad I didn't watch you taking your clothes off last night now."

Uh, what the hell? Trick had never felt rage like this. What was this prick doing thinking about watching her strip? Lyla laughed as she picked up her hair and began to gather it onto her head.

Cliff moved behind her and she tipped her chin to her shoulder. "Do you need me to untie the string?" she asked. "There are towels in the bathroom; if we go in there I can take it off."

"Whoa!" Trick said, startling the room as he began to march toward his wife and the prick who was flicking open the lotion bottle. When he got there, he snatched the bottle from the assistant director. "No one puts lotion on my wife except me."

Giving the assistant director's shoulder a shove, he muscled him out of the way.

"Trick!" Lyla said, turning to him wearing a frown. "What are you doing? I'm not going out without lotion."

Grabbing the bottle from him, he was left gaping when she seized Cliff's wrist and dragged him into the bathroom, slamming the door.

He exhaled annoyance when he heard the lock turn. Spinning around, he gaped at Paul. "What the hell was that?"

"She trusts him, they've been spending a lot of time together," Paul said.

"Trusts him?" he asked, marching across the room. "He's a dude! In there with my topless wife!"

Paul smirked. "She said she'd cover up with a towel. Besides, he took your wife home on her wedding night, if there was anything going on with them, it happened already."

Trick had never vibrated with anger like this before. He'd known the woman twenty-four hours, he wasn't supposed to care about who she got naked with, but this was a pride thing. Lyla was his wife; she shouldn't be screwing around on him. Did she think this was some kind of joke?

But as he was about to spin around and kick the damn door in, he remembered what had happened last night and why he hadn't been there to take her home.

Damn.

Trick had cared more about his reputation and playing to the crowd than he had about her, about his responsibilities. Well it wasn't what he cared about, so much as what he was told to care about, but Lyla didn't know that.

Running a hand through his hair, he couldn't figure out why he felt like he was coming apart at the seams. This was the weirdest sensation ever... It was jealousy, for someone he had no feelings for. Maybe just 'cause it turned out she was way hotter than he'd thought.

Except... he'd never really been as shallow as the persona he put on. Yeah, he loved a good figure, as much as the next guy, but it was never more important than that spark.

The spark.

Like the one he thought he'd felt when she made that comment on the flight right before he whispered in her ear, making her pulse speed against his hand.

God, he squeezed his eyes shut, his wife was hot.

Damn.

He'd thought he'd be fine. He could play the character and make her uncomfortable enough that she'd keep her barriers high and he'd never have to worry about feelings, or sex, getting involved in their relationship. It would make good TV and she'd dump him, getting him off the hook from being the one to do it. But how the hell was he going to sit next to her now like it was no big deal when he knew that was the figure she was packing.

Not physical, his ass. That was the kind of figure someone kept in check, and he'd make it his mission to catch her in the act if she was going to try to hide it.

When Paul put an arm around his back and patted it, he jumped. He hadn't even known the guy was standing that close.

"Go get changed," the director said. "Take her down to the pool and you can have your shower when you come back up."

It was on the tip of his tongue to ask if he was going to shower with his wife. What the hell? How had she become a different person just because he saw she had a decent pair of tits? He played at being that guy, but he'd never thought he really was that guy. God, he disgusted himself.

Turned out that on top of giving him a history education, Lyla Malloy was teaching him things about himself as well. Number one being, he was a prick.

***

LYLA DIDN'T KNOW what was wrong with Trick, but she'd guess that his hangover was catching up with him. She'd hoped that his nap would pull him back, but dinner had been a nightmare.

He hadn't just been a drag in the pool where he

wouldn't do anything except stand at the edge and glare with only his eyes and nose above the water level, but he'd been in a mood in the room as they got ready to eat.

Paul was ready to blow a gasket. The director had begged Trick to interact with her at the pool. He'd refused. So, she swam for an hour and talked, at length, to Cliff about the walking tour that she was really looking forward to.

The camera had been following them around, so she got showered and dressed in the bathroom with the door locked and was pleased with the shift dress she'd brought. It hung to her knees and although she'd prefer it to be longer, it was really baggy and the cut-out mosaic pattern at the top went all the way from her shoulder right around her neck.

It wasn't that she wanted to cover up, she just didn't like clothes that she had to worry about adjusting or displaying anything they shouldn't. When she was covered up, she was comfy and could relax.

But she did love to swim too and had a bunch of bikinis because she'd always go to the pool when she had an excuse. Lyla hadn't thought that much about bringing them, because they served a purpose and she enjoyed the feel of the water on her body.

"I think breakfast is served between eight and ten," she said, trying to find something to pick up the conversation that had stalled before the entrée. When two people had so little in common, it was difficult to keep conversation interesting. However, Paul kept gesturing at her, and the camera kept moving in close to their table in this quiet corner of the deck area of the restaurant. "Do you like to wake-up early? I figure we can take turns on the couch."

His eyes rose from his empty dessert plate to hers. "We're not sharing the bed?"

She shook her head. "And Paul said you have two bedrooms in your apartment, so I guess I'll take the guest room."

"If you want," Trick mumbled and dropped his eyes to his plate again.

It was weird, but she felt more than discomfort, she was actually... worried. Leaning over the table, she wished the camera would go away for a minute, except, when the camera was around, he was usually more "on" than he was at any other time.

"Nairn," she murmured.

His smile was slow, but he didn't look up, just fingered a prong on the fork next to his prone hand. "No one calls me that," he said.

Oh, she didn't care about being his buddy. Moving down a chair, she got closer to him. "I'm calling you that," she said, sliding a hand onto his face to draw it up so he'd look at her. Immediately, when their eyes met, she felt better. "Do you want out?"

The only thing she could figure was that he was having regrets about what they'd done. It made sense. He was a guy used to his freedom and he'd just tied himself down to the heaviest weight he'd ever met.

Slowly, his lips curled into a sinister kind of smile that didn't fill her with confidence. Sliding up in his chair, Trick didn't straighten, he leaned closer, guiding her hand from his face around his neck as he moved in. But instead of kissing her lips, he kissed her cheek, then moved around to her jaw and lower to the dip beneath her ear.

"Nairn," she whispered when he kissed her neck.

Her eyes got heavy until they closed and her head moved of its own free will, somehow knowing exactly how it had to shift and angle to let his lips find the spot they sought. His first name felt better on his lips than his nickname. It didn't make sense, but it made her feel more connected to him, made their connection more real.

Why was it okay to let the stoic, reticent Trick kiss her like this when she'd never dream of letting the handsy, arrogant chancer who'd held her on the dancefloor last night touch her this way?

His tongue trailed over her pulse point, bringing his lips to her ear at the same time she felt his fingertips on the inside of her knee beneath the table. "I'm gonna fuck your tight, desperate little pussy so hard tonight, baby, you're gonna forget your own damn name."

That was it.

Exactly what she needed to hear.

Standing up, she shoved away from that disgusting, entitled mouth and was infuriated to see it twist in a laugh. He opened his arms. "What? Baby, come on! You want it!"

Grabbing her water glass, Lyla tossed the liquid in his face and spun around to march away. If he thought she was happy to be spoken to in that way, he was mistaken. Whatever she'd done to make him think she was one of the hussies from his nightclubs, she'd have to figure it out and make sure she never did it again because she had a limit and he'd just found it.

SEVEN

LYLA HAD LOCKED the bedroom door, but he hadn't come knocking on it. She left him sleeping on the couch when she went to breakfast because she didn't even know what time he'd gotten back to the room.

For all she knew, he'd gone on another drinking binge. A guy like him could find friends, or rather drinking buddies, and a warm bed, in any state or country.

She'd gone for a wander around the resort and perused the gift shop before the walking tour group met in the lobby. Trick had shown up, just seconds before they were going out the door. His arrival delayed their departure another twenty minutes, as he signed autographs and told stories.

Yeah, the guy could turn it on for his fans, no doubt about that.

The tour included a picnic lunch, during which Trick was surrounded by people who wanted to be his new best friend meaning Lyla was spared having to talk to him all day.

Dinner that night was a buffet and they'd ended up at a table full of more adoring Trick fans, but she didn't care, in fact, she was grateful, because it saved her from a repeat of the previous night.

Trick told her to take the bedroom again that night and she was glad to because at least the door had a lock and she didn't have to worry about him accidently falling into bed with her. Lyla guessed he was happy to be out in the living room because it gave him freedom to come and go as he wanted, with whoever he wanted.

Saturday was spent by the pool. Trick missed breakfast again; she was learning that he didn't keep regular hours. While she swam and read, he stayed in the jacuzzi being adored by those who recognized him.

They did some interviews in the evening and ended up eating dinner in the room with the crew as Paul lectured them on interacting more.

But they had a flight to catch on the Sunday and by the time they packed and made it to the airport in their minibus, everyone seemed ready to leave Florida behind.

The next step for her was moving in to Trick's place.

The camera crew got every second of her packing up the last of her things in her apartment. Trick had to go to the studio and so he disappeared, leaving her and a couple of guys from the station who were dressed up like movers, to take her possessions out of her apartment.

She wasn't moving her furniture. In fact, Lyla was keeping her place because she wasn't ready to part with it yet and selling an apartment she loved was a big deal to her. If the honeymoon had taught them all anything it was that this relationship wasn't going to last beyond the contract.

It felt weird going into Trick's place without him there. Paul gave her a tour and then they did take after take of her snooping around the place, though she didn't say much about the things they set her up to find. So what if he drank a lot of beer and there were a ton of empty liquor bottles? Did it matter if he had a porn stash? And why was his internet search history her business? It wasn't.

It was nice that there was a note on the fridge from Trick saying she should make herself at home and that he wouldn't get back until she was asleep.

No, because his radio show was live from ten to midnight, and she had to get to work in the morning, so she wasn't going to wait up.

Sleeping in his guest room was no different to sleeping in a hotel or at a friend's house. Yes, it smelled like Trick and that was a little bit weird, but it didn't take her long to get to sleep.

Monday was one of the oddest days of her life.

No.

It was *the* oddest day of her life.

And that was including the day she'd married a complete stranger.

Some people at work went out of their way to come over to her. Most people just pointed and whispered.

Keeping her head down, Lyla tried her best to just do her work. That was all she wanted to do. Luckily, the camera crew had split before she got to her desk. So, this was just her, working.

"You know he only did it for the show."

Looking up from her desk, she saw the Cronies surrounding her. "I know," Lyla said to Faith.

The three women were holding cardboard coffee cups, and Lyla cast her eyes to the clock on her desk. Hmm. She'd missed lunch. Well that was fine, she didn't really relish the idea of sitting in the canteen with her packed lunch getting gawked at anyway.

"It's not like he knew who you were before he agreed to do it," Chelsea said.

"I know," Lyla said again. If these women thought they were going to get a rise out of her or upset her, they were sadly mistaken, she smiled. "Still got married before you did though."

The women faltered as someone squawked and hubbub started on the far side of the room. The trio around her desk turned to check it out; they did have to be the center of everything after all. Except as she glanced around to look over the shoulder-high screen that surrounded her desk, Lyla was surprised to see Trick there at the edge of the room scanning the space. People were crowding him, but he was looking right over their heads, something he didn't normally do. Usually he was attentive and patient with fans or anyone clamoring for his attention.

God, had something happened?

Pushing away from her desk, she rounded the Cronies, ignoring their questions and rushed from her secluded corner over to the man who was being mobbed by the research department; a group who weren't known for playing it cool.

Trick scanned right past her, then stopped and looked back, his head tilting in a smile as he recognized her and began to move through the people who were drafting around him. Trick reached toward her, she put her hand in his and he curled their fingers together like they were about to engage in a thumb war or something.

Trick pulled them together and with his other hand he picked her glasses off her nose to push them up into her hair as he dipped to kiss her cheek.

His lips rose to her ear. "Can I take you out for coffee?"

Looking left and right, Lyla felt it necessary to acknowledge that there were a dozen people around them still baying for his attention, not because they were there, she was getting used to his fans, but because it should make one point obvious.

"I'm working," she said.

"I know," he said, keeping the link of their hands tight together as he took her hand up to his lips. "But I managed to ditch Paul and I'll be filming all afternoon. I don't have long before the cameras catch up with us."

Then why did he seek her out? And why wasn't he trying to grab her boobs? This had to be important. "We shouldn't go out in public if you're worried about us having an audience," she said. It was weird how easily she managed to blank out the people crowding them as long as she kept her focus on his eyes just like he'd told her to on the plane. "Come here."

Keeping his hand, she led him away from the others to the far side of the room to one of the quiet study rooms they usually reserved for audio work. There was a glass panel in the wall that meant they'd still be visible from the bullpen.

But when Lyla closed the door and slid the lock, the engaged light came on. Like anyone who wanted in couldn't just look through the glass and see someone was working inside. Nope, they needed the light too apparently.

Except, well, she wasn't working, not as Trick guided her over to the desk and propped himself on the edge to draw her into the vee of his thighs, resting his hands on her hips.

"Is everything okay?" she asked, touching his face, then she remembered what had happened the last time she did that, so she dropped her hand.

"Have you seen the schedule this week?" She nodded. "It's insane." She nodded again. "We're not going to get any time alone."

"Have we ever had any time alone?" she asked.

It felt like every second they were under some kind of scrutiny. Even now, although he'd put her back to the part-glazed internal wall, she knew her colleagues would probably be watching. He straightened his back, then kind of sagged in a gesture suggesting he was about to say something, except he didn't speak.

When he swiped his tongue over his lip she got more impatient. "Trick, would you just—"

"I'm sorry."

Part of her wanted to look around for the camera, another part wanted to lift his tee-shirt to look for a wire. "You're what? For what?"

"This is messed up. I don't think either of us bargained on how messed up it would be."

Conceding a nod, Lyla had to admit she hadn't had a clue what a rollercoaster this would be. "Okay."

"I have to be a certain way for the cameras, you know, the… personality. It's—"

"An act," she said and nodded. "I know. I have figured that much out."

He smiled. "You're a smart one, Malloy."

In the sunroom, on the plane, even on their honeymoon when he offered her the bedroom every night, he showed a different side of himself. Trick didn't always say inappropriate things and act like a letch, he only did that when someone was watching them. Sure, sometimes his innuendos didn't hit the mark, and some of his jokes weren't funny, but he was much easier to get along with when they didn't have an audience.

"When we're alone you treat me with respect. When we're not, you don't."

"And that's why I'm sorry," he said. "I upset you when I said… what I said… at the dinner table."

Oh, so that was what he was talking about? Then why were his hands sliding up and down her hips now? Was he feeling more than he should? Was he about to take her by surprise with another insult?

Lyla slapped her hands onto his, stalling them against her hips. "You didn't have to say that. I know dinner was a bust and I shouldn't have touched your face, or… responded when you…"

"When I kissed you?" he asked, slipping one hand out from under hers to curl it around the side of her neck that he'd kissed. "I probably shouldn't have done that either."

"No," she said, taking both of his hands to bunch them in hers to move them between their bodies. "You do have a habit of touching me more than you need to… Trick, I'll admit to knowing that when you act in shocking ways you're doing it for a reaction from me, or for the cameras, I know that. But… I have to admit to not having a clue who you actually are behind the façade."

He let his hands fall from hers onto his thighs that she was still standing between and he shocked her again by letting his head fall against her shoulder. He just laid his head there for the longest time and she didn't have a clue what to do. It took her a good minute before she let her hand curl around the back of his neck.

"Malloy, you're not the only one," he mumbled.

Turning her lips toward his hair, she almost felt bad, but had to ask. "This isn't some sneaky way I haven't figured out for you to cop a feel, is it?"

He laughed and the heat of that exhale moved through her baggy sweater and managed to reach the sensitive peak of her breast that hadn't been awakened by a man in a long time. He blinked as he straightened, kind of, and looked at her. The exhaustion in him made her peer closer, what was he hiding? What was so awful that he had to keep up this front all the time?

But her contemplation was broken when his hands slid up under her sweater to cup her waist beneath it over her tank top. "Why do you wear this stuff?"

"What stuff?" she asked, trying to be subtle in her attempts to pull his hands out of her sweater because her coworkers would be watching every nuance.

She couldn't encourage this behavior, even if it wasn't an overtly sexual move.

"Your clothes. You pick all this baggy, shapeless stuff that covers every inch of you. Look at it. It goes right up to your neck, all the way to your wrists and your pants probably don't even have a decent ass in them, not that I can tell 'cause that sweater goes halfway down your legs."

Sneering at his exaggeration, Lyla only smiled when he mirrored her growl in a fake mocking. "I wear clothes that are comfortable," she said. "I don't have a figure that—"

His eyes widened with interest. "Oh, I can't wait for you to finish that sentence. Malloy, you have an amazing figure and if you say anything else, you're just flat-out lying to me… Why would you lie to your husband?"

Her smile got wider because this was the kind of teasing she could handle. "It's not that I don't have a figure, it's just… I don't see why everyone else has to see my body all the time and it… it changes things."

"What changes things?" he asked. Lyla was surprised that he appeared genuinely interested in what she was saying. "Your body?" She nodded. "Because when people see you have a killer body they…" He didn't finish the sentence, but his smile intrigued her. "You're goddamn smart, babe."

"I'm—"

"You didn't even see it. In the hotel, that first day when you came out of the bathroom in your bikini, all us guys were panting."

"You were…? Oh, Trick," she groaned, trying to push away, but he pulled her back so quickly that her body bounced into his.

He slid his hands from her waist around to splay them on her back, holding her to him.

Pressing her hands to his shoulders, Lyla didn't put up too much of a fight. This wasn't bad, he wasn't trying to be all over her, he was just holding her. Yes, she could encourage this kind of touching; it might discourage the other kind.

"We were," he said. "And you're right, our opinions of people do change based on their body type. It's not fair; it's just the way it is."

"I just like to be comfortable," she said.

"And not drooled on, I get that," he said. "But you're a married woman now, you can relax a bit."

She didn't understand. "Being married means I should take my clothes off?"

He nodded, selling his line as serious. "In the apartment, yes, as much as possible. In fact we introduced naked Tuesdays just last week."

Did he ever stop flirting or thinking about sex? The teasing… was this what Sadie had meant about her having fun with him or was this the kind of behavior that encouraged women to get naked with him?

"Have you had sex with Sadie?" she asked, making some connections in her mind.

"Yes," he said. Lyla was surprised that he didn't skirt the issue or try to avoid the question. "Years ago, we're just friends now." He peered at her. "Does that bother you? That I work with her?"

Lyla shook her head. "No, who you sleep with and who you work for are none of my business."

"It's a bit your business," he said. "We're married."

She didn't ask about Sadie as Trick's wife; it was curiosity that made her ask. The same thing that made her good at her job made her question probably more than she should.

"But we're not married for real," she said.

"Funny, I didn't print that marriage certificate from the internet, did you?"

Rolling her eyes, she pinched his shoulder. "No, I meant, it's not like we married for love. If we loved each other then yes, I would have a major problem with you seeing your ex every day. But we don't."

"She's not really an ex," he said, sort of considering it as he shrugged. "It was a casual thing, only lasted about a week."

"She's had you longer than I have."

Something about the way his eyes lit up made her wonder about the significance of what she'd said. Lyla wasn't great at reading between the lines.

"I never married her." True and she had to concede that. "You're the only woman I've ever married and that's why I had to come down here to apologize. You're right, we didn't marry for love. But we're married and we have to live together. I can't keep avoiding you or punishing you for my misconceptions."

"Your misconceptions?"

He tipped his head to the side and let one corner of his mouth curl. "Let's just say, my opinion of you changed when I saw you in that bikini too."

"Trick," she said and again tried to move out of his arms, but he didn't let her go. In fact, he tried the puppy-dog eyes on her as his hands slid further up her back to settle between her shoulder blades, beneath her sweater on top of the tank she wore under it. "I don't want you thinking about sex around me. It makes me uncomfortable."

"No kidding," he said and that earned him another pinch. "Paul tore me a new one this morning talking about how we have to have more conflict. The avoiding each other thing isn't working for them… So, I figured I could keep pushing you until you either have me arrested or you divorce me, or I could come down here and lay it out straight for you."

So the apology was a prologue. "Okay, lay it out straight."

"I'm gonna be a letch. I'm gonna piss you off trying to touch you and tease you. After Paul left, I called my sister and she seemed to think it was a good idea to let you know I'm not actually a pervert." Lyla let a laugh burst from her lips.

"I think I forget that people don't know that about me. That you don't know me. And I don't want you to ever be afraid of me, okay?"

Lyla sighed. "And my role in this is to put you in your place. To argue and object," she said and he nodded. It was just as possible that Paul had told Trick to talk to her, maybe this wasn't a genuine apology at all. Still, she appreciated being kept apprised of what was going on. Trick seemed to care more about her point of view than the studio did. "What if I want you to stop?"

"Tell me to stop."

She shook her head. "But if I'm pushing your hands away telling you not to do something, isn't that me telling you to stop? Would you act that way with a woman in a club?"

The amusement that sprang to his face was confusing. "I'll be honest, babe, most of the time when I tell a woman I want her, I get her," he said. When he saw that she wasn't smiling or even a tiny bit impressed, he cleared his throat. "But, uh, if a woman said no, I'd just move on to the next one… 'Cept I can't really do that with you."

It was sort of a sad existence in a way. Lyla wondered if he knew that. "You're worth more than someone will pay for you, Trick." The flash of his frown told her that he didn't get it. "You host these shows. You have your fame and your entourage when you go places… It's all one big machine that you're at the center of… It's sort of sad that there's no emotion involved, no real connections, it's all just… shallow."

"That's the point," he said. "That's the personality."

Which might have worked ten years ago, or more, when he started doing this, but he wasn't a stupid kid anymore.

"Is it ever difficult?" she asked, finding herself more curious about the man behind the mask now that he admitted to wearing it. "Don't you ever get tired of playing the playa?"

He shrugged. "It's easy money." Her brows rose and he exhaled a laugh. "Okay, I get it. How much someone will pay for me, okay." Taking a deep breath, he sank a bit lower in his slouch, widening his thighs around her. "I don't screw around as much as the press report. Most of the stories sold by women are bullshit."

"You never refute them."

"Why would I? It goes with the image and if the girls need a few bucks, why should I stop them from getting it?"

"Off your reputation," she said. "They're using you."

He nodded. "Yeah, but I used plenty of women when I was trying to build the rep, in the early days. It's karma, right? The screwing around is kinda tiring now, I mean not the screwing." He wiggled his brows. "I've got plenty of stamina, baby."

"That's good to know," she said almost like a parent being patient with a child.

"Just in case, you know," he said and winked at her. Yeah, there was a joker in him and a flirt. This level she could handle, it was the other guy who pushed her too far. "But yeah, the stranger in my apartment or waking up in a strange place, the small talk, the 'I'll call you' even though I wouldn't, yeah, that got old a while ago."

"And the drinking?"

"I like going out with my boys," he said. "But we probably only have one heavy night every month or two now. The others, we're out for an hour and home… Green's been with Samantha for two years now, she keeps his leash tight."

"I thought they broke up."

He nodded. "That's what the papers think. It works for his rep if the relationship looks rocky, you know? Together, apart, he screws up, she kicks him out… all that is orchestrated. They just put a down payment on a three-bed house, Sam wants kids."

That was shocking, one of the infamous Threens was settling down. It was a surprise. But it was more of a surprise that Trick was letting her in on the secret.

"Why are you trusting me now? Why did you come to me today? You could've pulled me aside on honeymoon and—"

"On honeymoon, my head was up my ass," he said. "I thought I had to play that guy all the time. With the cameras around so much, it's difficult to know when we have to be 'on'. I guess I got to my limit today when Paul came to the apartment to yell at me… I mean he was effectively telling me to sexually harass you. That's fine when we're in a public place, you know, in a glass room where a woman can scream for help if she really feels afraid. But they're talking about when we're home, when it's just us and a cameraman."

"They're setting up fixed cameras in the apartment too," she said. "There won't always be someone with us."

He groaned. "That's worse."

"You don't have to worry; I'm not going to sleep with you." With a half-smile, he laughed. "I mean, I know you don't really want to sleep with me. I wasn't suggesting that you did."

"All of that aside," he said, probably sensing that she was getting herself tied in knots. "If there are fixed cameras in there, we won't know when they're filming… some of them have lights to show when they're on, but it's not always possible to see depending on the angle. They could be watching us at any time."

So life in the apartment was going to be him constantly trying to touch her up. "I don't know how long we can do this for," she murmured.

"Is there something you don't eat or drink?"

"Something I… why?"

"If there's a specific food or drink that you don't like, we can use it as our code word. If it's mentioned we know the other wants to be alone and we can… I don't know, go out or go into the bathroom or something."

"The cameras will be in the bathroom," she said. "Cliff said there will be one in the shower anyway."

" 'Cause they think we're going to be doing it in the shower?" he grumbled and she shrugged. "Hell…"

It was sweet that he seemed really frustrated by this, though it was for his own benefit, not hers. "Blueberries," she said, catching his eye. "I don't like blueberries."

"Okay," he said with a flare of hope. "If we need to get blueberries, then we need to be alone, right? But if you just say the word on its own then I know you're through, okay? That we're done."

"And when one of us walks, we both do?" she asked and he nodded.

It was amazing how much better she felt after just one conversation.

"I'm so glad I called Josie," he said and some of her excitement wavered. "My sister. I called her after I spoke to Paul. She said the only thing to do was drop the act and be honest. I was worried you'd freak. But you're really... cool."

She laughed and looped her arms around his neck. "That is the first time in my life I have ever been called cool. Thank you, Mr. Strickland."

"No problem, Mrs. Strickland," he said grinning and lowering his face to let their foreheads touch. "We just have to be friends, okay?" She nodded against him, making their noses touch. "We be honest with each other and if one does something that the other doesn't like then we work it out. Compromise." Closing her eyes, Lyla felt herself relax. It was a start. A foundation of trust was imperative if this was going to work. "By the way." He leaned back enough that they could make eye contact, but his arms were tight around her ribs now, still under her sweater. "Did I see a cat in the apartment?"

"Risk," she said, wearing a grin. "He's my baby."

"His name is Risk? I love it."

"Do you like cats?"

"I guess I do now," he said. "Do I need to do anything with him?"

She shook her head. "I take care of him. It's been just him and me for five years now, he'll take some time, but he'll warm up to you."

"Five years," he said. "No boyfriend?"

"Nope," she said. "I actually like being on my own."

He laughed. "So, you went from being alone with Risk to twenty-four hour scrutiny? Good plan, babe." Something caught his eye behind her and his smile immediately dissolved. "Damn," he murmured and stood up. Keeping her in his arms, he rushed her back against the door, the only fully solid space on that glazed wall. "Let's not tell anyone about this conversation, okay, babe?"

Well yeah, obviously, but why had he changed so quickly? "What?" she asked, scared by the concern on his face.

"God, I hope you don't come out of this hating me,"

he murmured, but wasn't really talking to her as he reached up to drive his fingers into her hair.

"Ow, Trick…"

His digits caught on the pins in her hair, and as they got rougher, some fell out leaving her tumbled hair a mess. But she had just raised her hand to her temple when he began to grab handfuls of his own tee-shirt, webbing it with creases. Then he snatched her hand and squeezed her fingers out flat.

"Good, you have nails," he said and before she could even register what he was doing, he pulled her hand up. While squeezing her fingertips, he forced her nails in to the side of his neck, dragging them around and down to his throat, leaving long angry scratches on him.

"Trick," she hissed as someone started to bang on the door.

"I'll see you at home tonight," he said, unbuttoning his jeans with a yank. Bouncing up and down, he forced them to sag on his hips.

Grabbing the back of her neck, he pulled her forward and kissed her forehead, then he flashed her a smile before straightening his face and urging her aside to open the door. As soon as he did, he took one step then stopped, like he was surprised.

"Trick!"

Paul's voice echoed and Trip stepped aside to let her see the camera that was pointed in both of their faces. "Uh… just having some, uh… husband and wife time," Trick said, putting an arm around her and glancing down. "Oh, babe, you have…" He touched a rough fingertip to the corner of her mouth like he was rubbing something away. "We're good." Trick took a step forward then stopped and grabbed his belt. "Forgot about that." Making a big show of pulling up his jeans, he buttoned them and winked right at her in front of the lens that had to be reflecting her shock. "Good talk, babe."

Kissing her forehead again, he began to back away, nodding and waving at her stunned colleagues. Trick whistled. "Yo, camera! Star's over here!" He clicked his fingers and raised his arms to point down at himself as he walked backward through the department.

The cameraman turned to scurry after him and Trick winked again. Yeah, he was back to being a prick, at least Paul looked happier, even if her colleagues were all gawping at her. They had to know it was bullshit, she and Trick had been standing there in view for a long time. Except…

Moving in to the room, she looked through the glass to see that where they'd been standing wasn't fully in view. The room was only part glazed. There would be no way to see what was going on between the lower half of their bodies as she stood with her back to them with him wide-legged on the desk, had he done that on purpose? No, surely not.

But, yeah, she was a wife now, and apparently a slut too.

EIGHT

BEING MARRIED TO TRICK was a walk in the park… twenty percent of the time.

At night after the camera crew were gone, they'd started taking long walks in the park, which was somewhere they could be alone. Maybe the only place they could be alone. Occasionally, someone would stop them to ask for Trick's autograph, but for the most part, they were left alone.

It was nice because on their walks, he was honest with her. They talked about their families, their goals, and their day to day lives, who was annoying them and what their hopes were.

Trick was tactile with her, whether the cameras were on them or not. When they walked through the park, his arm was around her or their hands were linked. It was nice, sort of reassuring to be with him when he was being himself without the bullshit.

After they came home, they'd share a drink together on the couch in a way that would satisfy both their need to act for the camera and not push each other too far at the end of a long day. So they'd hold hands, or he'd pull her into his lap. Physical contact was becoming easier because she was getting used to trusting him to perform without threatening her safety.

He always pestered her to come into his bedroom and always tried to kiss her goodnight, but it was for show. They'd become friends. Fast friends through necessity, but close friends through choice and she did trust him. If he was truly like his persona he would be sneaking into her bedroom at night or finding excuses to walk in on her in the bathroom— he did neither. He didn't prank her or ping her bra or act like the immature idiot he portrayed. Most of the time, when they were in the apartment together, they just let each other be.

Trick had learned how to make it look like he was doing far more to her than he really was and her baggy clothes were a great cover. He could put his hands up her top and contort the fabric to make it look like he was groping her breasts or her ass, when in truth, he was not touching her at all or just grazing the tank top she wore beneath.

He still made shocking innuendos at every given moment and often embarrassed her in public with his outrageous comments and behavior, but she understood why he did that.

They'd been married for two weeks and the first episode was airing that night. A screening had been arranged at the Prem studios. She and Trick were in prime position on a couch in the center of the front row. But there were about twenty other people in the room behind them, mostly from production, but a couple of their colleagues too.

Lyla hadn't considered how she'd feel about watching herself on TV, but it was an odd experience. They were watching the show in time with everyone else in the nation who'd tuned in. There was a blurb at the start, explaining the premise and there was a brief title screen. A narrator spoke, and there was some footage of the interviews that had been done before the wedding, before they'd ever met.

Used to his persona now, she wasn't shocked to hear Trick's misogynistic comments, but Trick picked up her hand and gave it a squeeze so she looked at him and smiled when she saw that he was worried. He pulled her against him. Lyla didn't mind resting her head on his chest when he put his arm around her and laced their loose fingers together.

Given how tactile he was, Lyla was used to him doing things like that, so didn't think much of the friendly gesture. They had to get close every night when they curled on the couch together; she was accustomed to letting him take the lead.

The footage of the wedding itself made her smile, not because it was a particularly beautiful ceremony, although it did play lovely on screen with the added music and long shots of them apparently staring into each other's eyes. Yeah, that didn't happen; but it looked nice. It made her smile because it was so quick. It had taken them most of the day to get a shot of her walking down the aisle and it only took twenty seconds on screen.

When they got to the kiss-the-bride moment on screen, the turning of her head looked really abrupt. As she winced in real time, Trick pressed his lips into her knuckles. He was reassuring her; that was sweet of him.

They were two weeks beyond that wedding ceremony and still hadn't kissed properly, but why would they? He'd taken to kissing her forehead to say hello and goodbye. It was a nice, friendly gesture and she appreciated it.

Lyla had often wondered if he thought of her as a brother would a sister. He had a sister, so he had experience, and she often felt protected around him. Trick was always reassuring her, whenever he could, and he was respectful… when he was allowed to be.

The rest of the wedding reception was odd to watch. The pictures were little more than a glance on the screen. Their exchange in the sunroom was played, as was their first dance, where the highlight of the footage was her shoving Trick's hands away and storming off the dancefloor. They'd edited that well.

Then came the part of the night when Trick and his buddies were talking about cutting out. There was a big palaver about recruiting others and gathering up a group discreetly, then there seemed to be a lot of giggling and theatrics about not telling the bride they were stealing the groom, who was completely in on the subterfuge.

In the screening room, Trick's grip on her hand got tighter. No doubt he was worried about her freaking out, but, why would she? They didn't even know each other then and she'd come to learn how big his persona needed to be, how the character he played was just that, a character. It just so happened that the joke on the wedding night was her.

Lyla couldn't have begun to know how much.

Trick's posse went to one club, then another. The group got bigger, thinned out, grew, got smaller, then bigger again as the number of hangers-on fluctuated. They went to another club, and another. At the first establishment, there was a big deal made of it being his wedding night and that his bride wasn't giving it up for him.

Yeah, Lyla couldn't argue that, she wouldn't have given it up for him. But it would've been nice to be asked before she became the butt of a night-long joke. There was a montage of the night. Various pictures from a variety of the clubs they'd been in were flashed on the screen, and in every one Trick was kissing a different woman.

There was her husband on the screen with his tongue down the throat of one blonde, then another. Yeah, blondes were his thing. Inhaling, Lyla reminded herself how long ago this was. Well, okay, it was only two weeks ago, but she'd told him after that night that it was none of her business who he slept with and that hadn't changed.

They were friends. There was no love. It was just a friendship.

Rolling her eyes up to him, she wasn't surprised to see him pale and braced, but she grinned and pushed up to kiss the underside of his jaw, something she'd never done before.

Out there in the world, in front of the camera, she had to be outraged by his behavior because it was the persona that had been developed for her, and she'd kind of walked into it being the opposite of a promiscuous man.

So as the rest of the episode played out, Lyla wasn't surprised to see that her every rejection of Trick was stressed, just as his patience was emphasized when she knocked him back time and again.

But there were no other incidents of him kissing anyone else. So at least her speculation about the honeymoon was wrong. He hadn't been out partying or getting laid. Lyla watched to the end and when the show was over the viewing screen was turned off and the lights were turned up.

Stretching her arms and legs straight, Lyla blinked to adjust to the illumination. Paul came into view with Sadie and the others from the initial panel who'd propositioned her. Looking over the back of the couch, Lyla saw the door closing, everyone else was gone, leaving her, Trick, and the panel alone. The panel was taking seats on the couch under the large TV screen they'd just watched on or they were pulling swivel chairs from the side of the room.

Lyla didn't know that they'd been due to have a meeting. "Are we leaving for the team-building thing on Monday morning or in the afternoon?" she asked Paul. "I have work to finish before—"

"We'll pick it up," Ritchie said.

Bunyan sat in the center of the couch opposite theirs. "We like the show, but we're worried about how the series will progress, there's just not enough…"

"Conflict," Paul said.

"Tension," Bunyan corrected him.

"Damn," Trick said. "There's a line I can't cross, Bunny."

A smile quirked her lips, she'd never heard anyone call the executive that. The star of the channel obviously got away with more than others.

"Yes, we know that," Bunyan said. "And we can't force Lyla to relax her boundaries… we may have taken our need to find your opposite too far."

Great. So she was messing this up too. "You film me in the shower every morning," she said. "I'm guessing that's going to be on next week's show."

"Not unless Trick is in there with you."

Inhaling, she knew it would be easier for everyone if she'd just start sleeping with him. But the panel didn't understand how the couple had moved into a comfortable friendship zone. If she and Trick tried to force physical intimacy, it would just be weird.

At least he was saying they weren't going to show her body, that was a positive. Though she had taken to showering with her bikini on, so that might be why they weren't showing it.

"But we have an alternative," Bunyan said. "We've hired a new character."

A new character? Well at least they weren't all pretending to be who they actually were anymore. Of course, it could just be a figure of speech.

"A new character?" Trick asked, leaning forward, past her, his elbows coming to rest on his knees. "Who?"

"Kira."

Her mouth fell open. "Kira Levine?" Lyla heard herself asking. "You want him to sleep with his ex... on camera?"

Bunyan nodded and shrugged. "He has to sleep with someone."

Trick inhaled and his head lowered into his hands. Resting a hand on his back, Lyla stroked him in reassurance. This was just horrible.

"You can't ask them to do this," she said. "It's unfair. Trick and I is one thing, this whole thing was orchestrated, it's fake. But there was actual real emotion involved in his relationship with Kira. You're exploiting something real, something raw."

Trick sat back and picked up her hand to squeeze it in his as he kissed her fingers and focused on Bunyan.

"And what?" Trick asked. "I'm supposed to screw around with Kira behind Lyla's back? She's supposed to play ignorant?"

"You didn't mind on your wedding night," Bunyan said and Trick looked away from them all.

Trick couldn't feel guilty about that, shouldn't feel guilty. They were still strangers then and she'd given him permission to be intimate with anyone he wanted to be intimate with.

"It will only play like that until the show airs, after that, everyone will assume that Lyla has seen you together."

"So, she has to find out and flip," Trick said. "You want her to perform for you?"

"Isn't that what you've both been doing?" Bunyan said. "It's going to be great television, real drama. It gives the audience something to sink their teeth into. We need it to keep the show afloat. We can only play it with you as the horny husband and Lyla as the frigid wife for so long. You're just not gelling; I've seen some of the footage. People want sex or love by this point, and they're getting neither, so we have to introduce drama."

Bobbing her head in a nod, Lyla could see how that made sense.

"Lyla," Sadie said, drawing her attention. "Would you mind giving us a minute?"

"Oh, sure," she said, leaping to her feet.

Trick caught her hand. "Wait a sec, babe. Sadie, whatever you have to say, say it. You don't have to hide anything from Lyla, she's cool."

But Sadie just smiled at her, ignoring Trick. "Do you mind?"

Lyla shook her head. "Of course not."

It was sweet of Trick to think he should include her, but she wasn't the star. Lyla had come to learn how high up, or rather low down, she was in the order of things over the last couple of weeks.

Trick kissed her hand. "I'll come get you in a minute… We'll pick up that wine you like on the way home," he murmured and she nodded, letting her fingers run into his hair as she passed him to head for the door.

When Lyla glanced over her shoulder to see Trick was looking over the back of the couch at her, she smiled and got a wink, but a real one, that was joined by a genuine smile.

Stepping outside, she saw a group of colleagues nearby and Curtis was with them. She hadn't seen much of her old friend over the last couple of weeks, though they were still texting and talking on the phone. But as he came nearer, he didn't look particularly happy to see her.

"We need to talk," he said, taking hold of her shoulder.

"Okay," she said, worried that something might be wrong as he led her down the corridor and in to an empty office. "Is everything okay?"

***

"IS EVERYTHING OKAY?" Trick asked Sadie.

He didn't usually fall out with folks. He tried to get along with as many people as he could, especially his friends. But Sadie tossing Lyla out was a step over the line as far as he was concerned.

"Do you feel anything for her?" Sadie asked, crossing her legs and leaning toward him, blocking out the others. "You've been married for two weeks, is there any chemistry… at all?"

"Chemistry?" Trick asked, suspicious as he looked at everyone in the room. "Are you gonna tell me to ramp up the seduction? Come at her a different way? Sadie of all the people—"

"I think you should divorce her," Sadie said. Trick wasn't the only one in the room stunned by that suggestion, but his friend didn't back down. "Better yet, we'll look in to an annulment. You haven't slept together, right?"

"What the hell is the meaning of this?" Bunyan demanded. "We can't drop this yet. We've invested huge amounts of—"

"This is going to bite us on the ass," Sadie said, rising to her feet to point at the TV screen. "Either the public sees Trick as Mr. Stud Numero Uno, and Lyla becomes a laughing stock, or he's dubbed a sexual predator and we walk right in to a harassment suit… Did any of you watch the same show I did? You're making this woman out to be some sort of sexual simpleton!"

"That's the appeal! She doesn't have the experience of—"

"It's not about experience, Bunyan," Sadie argued. "You've shown that woman sitting at the bar alone on her wedding night while this bastard goes out screwing around town."

Trick flew to his feet. "Hey, I never had sex with—"

"How many women did you kiss that night? Because it sure looked like more than five, maybe more than ten, yet the bride goes home in a cab with the damn cameraman." Sadie lifted a finger at him. "Who, by the way, made a move on her... Yeah, no one showed that slice of footage. You're not the only man coming at her, which makes this so much worse!"

Balling his fists, Trick clenched his jaw. "That bastard, Cliff. I knew it! I knew he was a—"

"Would it have mattered what she'd done?" Sadie asked. "You were screwing around before the ink was dry on the marriage certificate. Yet, she sits in here watching it, smiling and kissing you, what the hell, Trick? You're using her. You're all using her."

"You knew what this was when you signed on," Bunyan said. "All of us did."

"Do you think she knew she'd be made a fool of like this? She looks like an idiot and now you're asking her to accept him screwing around with his ex after just two weeks! This isn't a marriage, this is just us exploiting her naivety. Haven't you heard the way she talks about herself?" Sadie snapped. Trick had never seen his friend this riled about any of their previous projects. "I've seen the interviews, you know, the ones that none of you have seen. She has like zero self-esteem. She's not down on herself, just accepts that she doesn't measure up, like somehow that's normal and okay. Those people she works with, they already ridicule and bully her, how the hell is this going to play? They're probably out there right now pointing and laughing." Sadie shook her head and fixated on him. "Either you feel something for her and you man up and make this real, or you divorce her, right now, Trick. Don't play these games with her. It's not fair. You're not only risking your rep, you're risking her sanity, which was exactly what we were trying to avoid." Sadie whirled around to pin her sights on Bunyan. "If you break this girl right in the middle of the damned lawsuit you're fighting, what happens then? Huh?" Sadie turned back to him. "How will you live with yourself, Trick? If she's ruined by this and turned into a joke?"

Pushing back in his seat, Trick slid his hands down his thighs and sealed his lips. Sadie was right. Lyla had low self-esteem; he'd seen the way she counted herself out all the time. It was often subtle, but it was definitely there.

Since they'd been living together, he'd grown to respect her in a way he'd never considered that he would. She was his friend. More than that, he worried about her, all the time. All the damn time. Especially when he was being an idiot.

But this… he let his eyes rise to the blank screen. The world needed someone to love and they loved a good joke. He couldn't let that joke become Lyla, even if she told him she understood the need for her role.

At the end of the day, he was her husband and there were responsibilities that came with that. He might not have understood it on their wedding night. Might have spent most of their honeymoon in a bad mood because he had a boner that wouldn't go away. But every minute he spent with her he admired her more, cared for her, and…

Twisting to look at the door she'd left by, he wondered about her, where was she, was she okay? Were there people out there giving her a hard time? It made him so mad to think that anyone could say anything negative about his Lyla. His Lyla.

That's exactly what she was…

His.

NINE

"I DON'T THINK you understand how it looks," Curtis said.

They were in the empty office, seated in swivel chairs, facing each other. Lyla was watching the way their hands laced together between Curtis' parted knees. His fingers weren't as long or strong as Trick's were.

"I know you're worried," she said and smiled at him when he slid one of his hands out of hers and on to the side of her neck. "You're my friend, Curt, you know how I feel about you. I would be worried about you too."

"He's using you. They're all using you."

She understood why it was difficult for him to understand the experience of living in a reality TV show, she hadn't understood it either.

"It's okay," Lyla said, smiling to reassure him. "It's just the way it is."

"I can't stand by and let you be hurt," Curtis said, his voice softening as his hand slid up to her cheek and his thumb grazed over her lips. "You're so vulnerable and you don't see it… You don't see what's happening. You trust too easily."

He leaned closer and she knew he was going to rest his forehead on her hairline, like he'd done before, but he never got that far because an angry male voice interrupted.

"What the hell is going on in here?"

Lyla couldn't have been more surprised to turn and see Trick just inside the office door. "Trick," she said. "This is Curtis and—"

"Yeah, I figured that out, babe," Trick said, his face set in a weird kind of angry frown that was glued on Curtis as her husband marched toward them. "Just trying to figure out what game he's playing."

When Trick got to them, he grabbed Curtis' shoulder, hauled him up out of his seat and rushed him to the nearby wall.

"Trick!" she screamed. "What are you doing?"

But he didn't listen to her, just thrust Curtis harder against the wall and pushed an arm to his chest as he got right into his face. "You wanna touch my wife, you ask for my permission… in writing, and don't hold your breath waiting for a response."

Pushing away, Trick winded Curtis with the power of his shove and backed off a step to throw an arm around her neck, but she shoved at him.

"How dare you," Lyla said, shrugging away from Trick's arm to go to Curtis. "I'm sorry."

"He's an idiot," Curtis said, his hand flat on his chest as he tried to catch his breath. "You deserve better than that, Ly."

"What the hell would you know?" Trick shouted and she felt his body heat rush against her back. Here she was sandwiched between the two of them. As she tried to soothe Curtis, she pushed herself back into Trick to keep him away from her friend.

"I know you're going to hurt her!" Curtis said. "You don't have a clue what you've done to her! Not a clue!"

Now Curtis was losing his temper and she was beginning to panic because if they both lost their cool she'd have no way to calm them down. "Curt," she said. "Don't!"

"What don't I know, nerd, huh?" Trick asked.

It was getting harder for her to keep any kind of pressure up on her husband because he was just too strong.

"You don't give her what she needs!" Curt argued.

Lyla didn't like how he spat the words over her; she didn't want these men fighting. Why would the only two men in the world she cared about fight like this? They were her friends, why weren't they acting like it?

Trick's laugh wasn't happy. "Oh, and I suppose you do? Is that it? You wanna screw my wife? Do you?"

"Trick!" she said. Shoving back hard, Lyla managed to give herself half a breath of space to spin on the spot to plant her hands on his chest. "Don't speak to him that way! What the hell has got into you, Nairn?"

His lips squeezed together and she felt the heat of his anger even though his eyes were pinned on the man at her back. The pure hatred in them gave her a chill, but she shoved him once more.

Trick bared his teeth and hissed. "You turn around and walk out that door with me right now or I put this prick through a wall. Your choice, Malloy."

"Lyla," Curtis said behind her, but she wasn't going to let her friend get hurt.

"Then let's go," she said, staring up at Trick, wishing that he'd look at her so she could tell if he really was angry or just playing the appropriate theatrical role. "Baby?"

Whispering the pet name she'd never used before made Trick drop his attention to her, and while the intensity lingered, his anger began to cool. This time when he put his arm around her neck and tugged her against him, Lyla didn't put up any kind of fight. She wanted to look back to see if Curtis was okay, but Trick was holding her too tight.

The camera crew was just by the door. Great, well they had their footage, and now she understood why Trick had been such a bastard. It was an act. But she was annoyed. For the first time, she actually was irritated by this stupid game. Curtis hadn't signed any contract, he didn't have a role to play, he was her friend, and he'd just been hurt because of her fake marriage.

***

THEY DIDN'T SPEAK in the car, not until Trick pulled off the road to park in front of the liquor store. "Just the wine or do we need—"

"I don't want wine," she said and folded her arms.

"You don't… well I'm here now, why the hell didn't you say that when you saw me turn down the block?"

It was just fine with her that he was angry because she was too. "Am I supposed to be in your brain?" she asked. "How am I supposed to know what you're going to do?"

He squeezed his fingers around the wheel and gritted his teeth. "You saw me driving this way, didn't you?"

"Yes, I saw you driving this way, but I figured, you know, being the insensitive jerk that you are, you'd probably be coming here for something you want. You haven't been drunk at all this week, so by my reckoning, it's overdue, right?"

His inhale was long and his grip tightened. "Is this about the kissing on our wedding night or 'cause I shouted at your pet?"

Offense made her twist to gape at him. "My…? Trick!"

When his gaze landed on hers, she saw that same intensity in him that he'd carried when he shouted at Curtis.

"We need goddamn blueberries," he growled.

Neither reacted to his comment, but they both knew what it meant. The car was rigged with cameras and audio recording devices. For a few seconds, they just stared at each other.

"No," she said and shook her head. "No, we don't… Go get your liquor, Trick."

"Get out of the car, Malloy."

Leaning closer, she hissed, "We are not going to have an argument in the middle of the street, Nairn."

"Rather have it in the apartment?"

The apartment that was as rigged as the car he was trying to contain his anger in. Growling aloud, she unclicked her seatbelt and tossed it away to shove out of the vehicle. Trick was already at her side of the car.

Grabbing her arm, he pulled her onto the sidewalk, but she yanked her limb away from him. "I don't need you to pull at me," she said, shoving him to put some distance between them as they both stalked down the block.

Having the argument where it might be picked up by the recording equipment in the car was dumb, so they had to get away from the vehicle. When they turned the corner, she went another five paces before she stopped.

"You had no right to do that," she said.

Trick spun on her. "You were messing around! What the hell, Ly! I'm sorry, okay? I know the wedding night was screwed up, but that was back then, before I was honest with you, before we were… us! You went out there after the show tonight and found him to—"

"To what? Did you think I would marry you and refuse to be intimate only to track down my friend and jump him just because you kissed a couple of strangers?"

"Did you?" he asked. "Was that the point? You wanted to make me mad, right? Well you succeeded, baby!"

"Don't get sarcastic," she sneered and put her hands out when he tried to approach her again. "And don't come near me!"

"Why? You didn't mind him getting up close," he said. "Is that why you married me? To make him jealous? Well it worked, guess you've got him now."

This side of Trick was the most infuriating. She knew how to deal with his "character" and she could deal with him when he was sulking about something. But when Trick was mad, he was just so difficult and there was nothing reasonable about his arguments.

"You don't know what you're talking about," she said, unable to believe that he'd picked this insignificant thing to get so mad about. "Curtis is my friend, he saw the show, he was worried. He doesn't… he doesn't understand."

Pacing away and back, Trick seemed to be having trouble staying still. "Doesn't understand what?" Trick asked. "What was he saying to you? Tell me!"

This anger was overwhelming, but there was plenty of space between them, so she didn't feel threatened despite the strength of his mood. For sure, she was safer with Trick than Curtis had been.

"He doesn't understand what it's like," she argued. "And he was looking out for me! We've been friends for a long time."

"Isn't that nice? Your best buddy. How come your bestie didn't even know we were getting married? Huh? Why were you so scared to answer your phone on our wedding day? It was him, right? He was the guy who called you while you were waiting to marry me?"

"Yes," she said. "And I didn't tell him because I wasn't allowed to. I wasn't as lucky as you, okay? I didn't have a friend on my side. You had Sadie looking out for you every step of the way. She was always there in your corner. I didn't have that. So yeah, maybe I have to build some bridges now, but that doesn't give you the right to put your hands on my friend in anger! I've been nothing but respectful to your friends, to Sadie, to your boys. I've been polite and understanding and—"

"Too polite!" he screamed and came back towards her. "You know what it was like to walk in on that? That prick was going to kiss you and you were just—"

"Curtis was never going to kiss me! He would never kiss me!"

He scoffed. "Yes, he would. That bastard wants you! He wants to screw you! But you are *my* wife!"

"And what does that mean, huh?" she asked. "It means nothing! In a few days you're going to be back in Kira's bed and all of this will be ridiculous!" Someone had to be rational and for some reason, Trick was having trouble seeing how stupid his anger was. "You hurt my friend. You hurt him and you hurt me... Curtis never signed up for this. He didn't sign up to be pinned to a wall and yelled at. He didn't sign up to make great television. So, yeah, well done, you'll be Bunyan's favorite again because you know they got all that on film. You blew your top because you knew it would look good on film, and now you're annoyed that I'm not shrugging it off like I shrug everything else off. You know what, Trick? You can be a jerk to me as much as you like. Shout at me. Pin me to walls. Grope me. Do your worst. But do not hurt the people I care about. Don't do it again."

"You're mad at me?" he asked. "You screw around and think you can—"

Lyla growled at him and threw up her hands. "Oh, Nairn Strickland, you are the most infuriating man! You get the bit in your teeth and you just won't let it go!"

Storming away down the block, she went past him and kept on walking.

"Where are you going? Malloy!" he shouted after her. "Where the hell are you going?"

Damn him and his mood. If he wanted to be a jerk then she would let him pace and grumble to himself as much as he liked. She was in control of herself and her own actions and she did not have to give him an audience.

"Away from you!" Lyla threw the words over her shoulder. "Go be a jerk somewhere else! Find another woman to act for; I'm not interested in being your audience or encouraging you. When you're ready to be the nice, calm, reasonable Nairn, you know, the real you who's decent to me, you give me a call!"

"Malloy!"

But she kept on going and didn't slow down. They spent so much time together that maybe they needed a night apart. Lyla sure wasn't going to stand there all night screaming in the street.

When she got to the corner, she glanced around to check for traffic and was surprised to see a figure in her periphery.

Turning around, she didn't expect to see Trick ten feet behind her. "What are you doing?"

"You can be as pissed at me as you like and walk a hundred miles, but I am not leaving you alone in the street at this time of night."

Where had his anger gone? Why was he staying away from her? "Who would attack me?" she asked looking down at the oversized coat she was wearing over her baggy clothes. She looked more like a bag lady than a primo target for a rapist. "Go away, Trick. I'm not in the mood to look at you. Just go back to your apartment."

Scanning, she saw no cars and crossed the street to

walk down the next block, her apartment was on the other side of town. But it was a nice night. Lyla decided that she'd walk for as long as she felt like walking and then she could get a cab.

Since she'd moved into Trick's place, she hadn't thought about going back to her apartment. But two weeks wasn't a bad run. She hadn't expected to settle into living with anyone after living on her own for so long.

On the next corner, she looked for traffic again, and yelped when she saw Trick was still behind her. "I'm not leaving you," he said without her asking for an explanation.

"And I'm not getting in a car with you," she said. "Stop following me. Go away. Don't be creepy, stalker guy. I'm telling you to go away. I'm giving you permission to leave. Go. Go away." But he was shaking his head. "Nairn—"

"If something happened to you—"

"I don't have anything worth stealing and a rapist would never get through all the layers I'm wearing," she said, realizing that they weren't shouting at each other anymore. Trick began to approach her. "I don't want you to come over here. I'm mad at you, Nairn."

But she didn't move away even when he came up so close that his body moved against hers. Trick ducked to brush his lips over the sensitive spot beneath her ear, just at the back of her jaw.

Oh… when his breath warmed her there, Lyla's whole body vibrated until her muscles loosened. Grateful that she had his form in front of hers, she exhaled and closed her eyes as she sank against him.

Scooping a hand around the other side of her head, Trick angled her and kissed her in that same place again. "I'm sorry," he whispered into her ear. "I'm sorry, baby."

"You hurt me," she said, tipping her head up to meet his eye and find he really did look repentant.

The man was a good actor, but he didn't usually lie to her when they were alone like this, so she believed the contrition in his eyes.

"I know, baby, I'm sorry," he said and dipped to kiss her forehead. "Let me take you home and get you liquored up… and when you're nice and loose, I'll give you a foot rub."

He made her smile and when she did, so did he. Turning them back the way they'd come, Trick tucked her under his arm and guided her back up the block. Yeah, Lyla was still pissed, but he was doing the brotherly protective thing again and she couldn't deny that it was sweet enough to sway her.

They'd both feel better after a good night's sleep. Maybe watching the show had affected both of them more than they'd realized.

Whatever the reason for their spat, they couldn't walk away from each other because they were both contractually bound. Oh yeah, and they were married.

TEN

BY MONDAY, everything was pretty much back to normal between her and Trick. Yeah, Lyla had given him the cold shoulder for a few days, but it played well to the camera and Paul was ecstatic about the drama.

Curtis had been emailing her, but Lyla kept that quiet because she didn't want to include him in the performance any more than was necessary.

Today they were going on a Prem corporate break. It was a few days away for team-building apparently, but it was really just a setup for the show. She hadn't been told that in explicit terms, but she was sure it was.

Some of her colleagues were here, as were some of Trick's, although she hadn't actually seen him yet this morning. He'd been run ragged these past few days filming the quiz, and pre-recording segments for Boys Night. Although he would be doing a live Boys Night episode via Skype while they were away, which she thought would be fun for him.

The Boys Night shows weren't always live, they only did a few live ones a year as a novelty. The audience loved them and were always demanding more because when things went wrong, they went really wrong. And there were often a few setups and surprises during the live shows.

There were also a series of Boys Nights specials due to begin filming in a few weeks where the boys would be required to do tasks and take part in missions in different locations. The audience loved the trio's interaction and the channel were taking advantage of Trick's boost in exposure and popularity. Though she'd miss it because filming would start after her three months with Trick were done.

The media had loved the first episode of Opposites Marry and were panting for more. She got her first paparazzi experience on Thursday and the cameras had been a pretty constant feature since the show aired. But Paul was so desperate to keep the footage of the couple secret that they now had security when they were out and about.

For the most part, the picture hounds had given up crowding them outside the apartment, though Trick was sure they were still being monitored via long lens, which made their walks feel much more exposed, so she'd been making them shorter.

Most everyone who was going was already on the bus that was going to drive them the hour or so to the hotel where they were having their getaway. Everyone except Trick and a few of his crew; no surprise there. Lyla was standing in the aisle of the bus having just pushed the handle of her suitcase down. She began to wonder how she'd reach the overhead compartment when the noise rose at the front of the bus.

She smiled, Lyla could always tell when Trick was approaching because he was followed by a rumble of conversation or laughter and there was usually some kind of greeting uproar. She didn't even bother to turn around. He'd seek her out, or he wouldn't, making eye contact wouldn't make a difference to his plans.

But within a few seconds, Trick's breath warmed her ear. "Save me a seat, Malloy?"

No one had ever wanted to sit with her, even now, but Lyla didn't grace him with an answer.

She just tapped the top of her case and pointed up. "I can't reach the overhead thingy."

"I got it," he said and picked up the case to shove it in to the overhead compartment.

They had a case. Yes, *they* had a case that was stowed in the trunk of the bus. There were just a few extras in this smaller case; it wasn't heavy, she was just short.

Lyla dropped into the seat and began to move toward the window because she'd prefer to be in a corner and if Trick wanted to sit with her, he'd prefer the aisle anyway because he'd be able to talk to interesting people that way.

Except she didn't get all the way over to the other side before Trick sank down next to her and scooped her up out of his way. He lay down on the seats and sat her right on top of him. Right on his stomach. Lyla grabbed the back of the seat in front and knew her cheeks flushed because everyone on the bus was looking right at them.

The woman opposite the aisle made a noise. Lyla turned to see that Trick had stretched his legs out, right across the aisle and propped his boot heel on the arm of the chair where he crossed his ankles.

"I'm sorry," Lyla said, smacking Trick's legs, he dropped his feet flat onto the floor of the aisle and Lyla smiled at the shocked woman who probably wouldn't have minded, except the move was so unexpected. Turning to Trick, Lyla saw his shoulders slouched against the wall under the window and his eyes closed. "You nearly kicked that woman."

"Sorry," he mumbled, then raised his voice to call out. "Sorry!"

"It's… it's okay," the woman said. "He can put his feet up, that's okay."

Trick lifted his feet, but Lyla planted her hands on his thighs to push them down. "No, he can't. But thank you."

Turning back to Trick, she couldn't be mad at him when he looked so tired, even with his eyes closed. "You haven't shaved," she said and brushed the back of her fingers on his stubble.

"Didn't have time," he said, but didn't bother to open his eyes.

Slipping off her shoes, she looked around for her magazine. "You're lying on my magazine," she said, remembering that she'd tossed it into her seat.

He kept his eyes closed, but lifted his shoulders, so she bowed over him to reach underneath to fish it out.

"Why aren't we driving yet?" he asked as she pushed her glasses up the bridge of her nose.

Glancing around, she saw that there were people still on their feet and there were still some empty seats. She'd been told there would be at most just one vacant seat, this was a popular trip.

"Not everyone is here yet," she said and smiled as she opened her magazine and picked up her feet to cross her legs. If Trick wanted to be her seat, she wasn't going to change her usual behavior. Lyla liked to cross her legs, and he didn't object, but he was probably used to it. She did this at home a lot, it helped the cameras have something to look at, so while she read and he watched TV, they would fashion themselves in all kind of overlapping seated positions. They'd be wrapped in each other or supporting the other's body making it look like they had a building intimacy. "Fancy you not being the last one to show up. That must be a first."

He snickered a fake laugh and yawned then rubbed the back of his neck. "It's warm in here."

"The air conditioning probably isn't on yet," she said and found the first article that she wanted to read.

Lyla read a couple of lines before he spoke again, a sure sign he was getting impatient.

"Read to me," he said, still in his semi-slumber.

"There are people here, babe," she said, glancing around at the others who were stealing looks at the couple, but she was getting used to it.

Being followed by a camera twenty-four seven gave her a new comfort level for being stared at.

She often read to him in the apartment when they were alone, but she didn't think the others there would appreciate it.

"I want to hear your voice," he said.

"Later," she said because she wasn't going to read to the whole bus. "You're going to get a crick in your neck if you stay like that." He tugged her sweater. "You need a pillow?"

"We could go to the back of the bus… lay down together."

Trust him to find a way to make innuendos even when he was sleeping. "There's a restroom at the back of the bus," she said, "not a full back seat."

"Then a pillow it is," he said and tugged her sweater again.

But she wasn't going to take it off even though she knew that's what he was getting at. Balancing herself on him and with a hand on the back of the chair in front, she picked up her purse from the floor and pulled out the inflatable pillow she'd brought. Yes, she knew him and knew that he'd be tired.

Laying her magazine on his chest, she shifted down his body a bit and began to blow in to the pillow. "I get so sick of reading about climate change," she said between puffs, her eye still moving over the article that was laid on him. "I mean, if half these journalists put their time and effort in to actually taking action rather than just writing about taking action, the problem would be solved, right?"

"That's true of a lot of things though, isn't it?" he asked, moving his hand from under the magazine on his chest to stroke her back probably to soothe her because he knew this was one of the things she got riled about. He'd heard her ranting about it often enough when she was reading articles from the internet aloud to him at home. "It's easier to comment than to act."

"Maybe," she said and kept blowing until the pillow was big enough for her to lean down and pick up his head.

Their close quarters didn't feel weird until he opened his eyes a fraction and she realized her chest was right there in his face.

"Hello, ladies," he said and blinked up at her with mischief in his eyes. "Motorboat?"

Pressing her hand over his eyes as she positioned the pillow behind his head, Lyla laughed because with her sweater over her body, there was nothing to see. As she sat back and picked up her magazine, she had to wriggle because she was uncomfortable. Trick's hands shot out to clasp her, one hand on her abdomen, the other on the small of her back.

"Did I hurt you?" she asked.

He hissed in a breath that showed his teeth and she worried she'd done damage. "I spend a lot of time thinking about my mother when you're sitting on me," he grumbled in a whisper.

His lips curled and he was certainly breathing funny.

She didn't really get it. "Your belt is jagging me."

"Then undo it," he said, still in that pained husky voice.

"Really?" she asked, having not considered doing that.

It would make more sense for her just to move seats, except she'd been told the bus was going to be full. When she looked over the seats, there seemed to be two free seats together about halfway down the bus.

"On second thoughts," he said and increased his grip to pick her up and lift her higher so she was sitting right on his chest.

Her whoop drew some attention, but as he smoothed the edge of her sweater from his face, he exhaled and smiled. "Can you breathe?" she asked.

"Easier," he said. "Figured having you sitting on my dick was about as close to the edge of my control as I could get. If your dainty little fingers start undressing me, I'll probably go off."

Inhaling, Lyla knew better than to take him seriously and went back to reading her magazine.

They must have sat like that for another ten minutes. Lyla was sure Trick was asleep, but noise started to rumble up the bus. Usually that kind of susurration only accompanied Trick, but he was already there, she knew that for sure.

Something buzzed and she glanced down to see a light against the seat. Trick lifted his pelvis, which tipped her hip closer to his face. But he didn't seem to notice as he settled back down, his broad shoulders squashed into this narrow space. It was a shame really that he had to shoehorn himself in here just for a few minutes of sleep. But as she ran her fingers into his hair, he turned his phone around to read something and his relaxed expression suddenly got tense.

"Damn," he whispered.

"What?" she asked as he took her hand from his hair and kissed the back of her fingers. "What's wrong?"

He brushed her fingers against his stubble and didn't even try to smile when he said, "Kira."

And at the same moment she realized what he was saying, the noise on the bus rose again and then there she was, Kira Levine, in the flesh.

"She's gorgeous," Lyla murmured as she watched the woman float up the aisle of the bus on her own personal invisible cloud chariot.

Picking her up, Trick put Lyla back in a seat as he sat up at the window. "More beautiful outside than in," he said and Kira spotted him.

The two of them held eye contact and Lyla looked between them, Kira seemed to be smirking, but why? Trick on the other hand, didn't look like a man in love, he looked tense and angry. Was he worried about what was going to happen?

Kira slid into a seat and stayed perfectly poised. Trick didn't flinch.

Lyla picked up his hand. "Go to her," she murmured. His attention snapped around to her, so she smiled. "It's where you're supposed to be, with her. You're supposed to be with her."

"But I—"

"No," she said and shook her head. "Go be him. Go do what you have to. Seduce her… you've earned it. We've been married nearly three weeks, have you had sex at all since?"

"No," he snapped, so offended by the suggestion that she laughed.

"Then there's your reward," Lyla said, turning to look at the back of Kira's perfect head. "Your prize is one of the most coveted women in the world."

She didn't expect to feel Trick's lips on the side of her neck, but after the long press of his kiss, she turned to look him in the eye. "I'm not gonna touch her."

"I understand," Lyla said, nodding. "I'm not

supposed to know. The affair is to be secret this week, remember? You'll be able to sleep with her for at least two weeks before the show catches up to what we're doing now."

His eyes closed slowly as his face fell against her shoulder. "I'm worth more than what someone will pay for me," he mumbled. "Isn't that what you said?"

"Yes," she said, turning her mouth into his hair as she stroked the back of his neck. "Sometimes it's the risks we take that define us, isn't that one of your mottos? Having an extramarital affair is a big risk, but the world will understand it. When you put Kira and me together, there's really no contest."

He lifted his head to look her in the eye again. But before he could say anything, the bus began to move and she slid out of her seat to pull him up. "Malloy—"

"Go say hello," she said, slipping in to the window seat and picking up her magazine. "I'm being boring anyway. Go on."

***

THERE WAS TRAFFIC that delayed them getting to the hotel, but she figured that kind of worked out because it gave Trick and Kira more time to reconnect. As soon as they stopped, there was a cheer and everyone seemed to stand in sync.

The nice guy from the row in front of her helped her pull her case down from the overhead and he introduced himself as Tony.

Tony was also the first person she saw at the welcome mixer that was taking place that night. Lyla didn't know where Trick was, she hadn't seen him at all since the melee of people getting off the bus kept them apart. But she didn't expect to see much of him on this excursion; she'd guess that was the whole point of setting this up, to give Trick and Kira time to get it on.

"I just don't see why anyone needs to get involved in anyone else's business," she said to Tony as they sat at the bar together.

There was a buffet against the far wall that was meant to serve as their dinner. Lyla and Tony had already made a trip over there, but were back on their stools at the bar, keeping to themselves rather than really mingling. But right now, most of the groups were keeping to those people they knew and given that she didn't know anyone except the Cronies, Lyla was happy to stick with Tony.

He laughed. "Says the woman who's the subject of her own show," he said.

Smiling, she conceded a half-shrug. "It's not my show, it's Trick's show," she said. "And if anything, that gives me a better understanding and appreciation of what it involves." Pushing her shoulders back, she showed the black stripe pinned to her neckline. "I live my entire life miked."

"It must have been a difficult adjustment," he said. "Going from anonymity to instant fame."

"It wasn't instant," she said. "The cameras were following us for a couple of weeks before the show aired, that kind of gave me a chance to get used to the intrusion."

"You don't seem like the type of woman to flaunt herself, but everyone in the room, probably the city, has seen you in a bikini. Doesn't that make you feel violated?"

Tipping her smile toward him, she was done with the food, and instead picked at the edge of her straw as they made eye contact. "You writing a story?"

Again, he laughed. "I work for Prem, honey, you don't have to worry about me keeping your secrets... I just... I think everyone was surprised by your decision to do it. Watching that first show was... painful."

"Great television," she muttered and picked up her glass to drink from her straw.

"Is that what they tell you?" he asked.

Why was his voice softening like that? Did he really expect her to open her heart to him? Even if she was willing to spill all her secrets, she didn't actually have any.

"Trick takes care of me."

Turning his body toward hers, Tony laid an arm across the back of her stool. "If that was true, he'd be here with you instead of over there with Kira Levine."

Oh. Straightening, she didn't even bother to look over her shoulder. If Tony said that Trick was there, then he was there. And just like she'd thought on the bus, it wouldn't make any difference if she looked at him or not. If he wanted to come to her, he would, if not, he wouldn't. With Kira around, he had no reason to come to her.

"They're friends," she said, drinking more. "They haven't seen each other for a while, they're just catching up."

"They've been catching up all day. Seems fair that a man would come and check in with his wife when they're at the same party."

Everyone loved to tell her everything that was wrong with Trick and she was sure that everyone did the same with him, telling him how wrong they were for each other. It didn't matter that it was true. Didn't people think that they knew that?

Trying not to get annoyed, she was so disappointed when Tony's hand slid onto her knee. Sheesh. Since the show had aired, male attention in her had sky rocketed. She didn't know why. She'd have to probe Trick for his thoughts on male motivations. Was it because she was married? Because she was married to Trick, a popular, virile guy and these guys wanted to test their appeal? Or was it because of what Tony had already admitted to seeing? The bikini.

If she was obvious about picking his hand off her leg, someone would see and the cameras were in the room. Lyla didn't know exactly where they were because she'd been trying to ignore them and not be obvious about seeking them out, but they were looming.

Her saving grace was Trick and Kira. With them at the party, it was unlikely that anyone was looking at her.

"Please don't," she murmured and tried to move her leg away.

"He's not watching… he's busy with her."

Maybe it was fame people wanted and guys thought that if she started messing with them they'd get screen time with Trick.

"Please take your hand off my leg," she said, so disappointed that a man who she'd thought was a genuine guy turned out to have an agenda.

"Someone should look after you," he said. "Trick's not going to do it."

Why would she want this guy to do anything for her? "We just met," she said, irritated by the movement of his fingers as they caressed her through her skirt. "Do you think I would cheat on my husband with a stranger because he says he'll look after me?" she hissed and grabbed her purse. "What do you think I need from you that Trick doesn't give me?"

"Attention for one thing."

"Whoa, you read that one wrong, buddy," she said, spinning away from him to leap off her stool. "My husband knows that the last thing I need is attention. I don't need him to pander and he doesn't expect me to simper."

"Lyla," he said and tried to reach for her, but she twisted away.

"Get over yourself, Tony. Stay away from me. And if you know what's good for you you'll stay away from my husband too. He doesn't like men who put their hands on me."

Where had that come from? Lyla asked herself the question as she turned to walk out of the bar and through the lobby to return to her room.

It was true, Trick had flipped out at Curtis for putting his hands on her, but that was for show because the cameras were there and it looked good for him to be possessive. Trick probably didn't give two hoots about who was feeling her up, not really. So why the hell had she said it?

ELEVEN

IT WAS CLOSE to an hour later, as she was rubbing moisturizing lotion into her arms, that she heard someone coming into their suite.

"Babe?"

Ah, it was Trick. "I'm in the bedroom," she called out, putting more lotion on her hands as she sat on the edge of the bed and picked up the hem of her nightdress that hung to her ankles.

Trick appeared in the doorway. He tossed his key card to the dresser and began to take off his jacket. "What happened? You ran out of there early…"

Turning on the bed, she began to knead lotion into her calves. "Can you tell me something about men?" she asked, rubbing the lotion in to her shins and knees.

"I can try," he said and pulled off his tee-shirt.

God, she hated it when he did that. The studio factored in gym time to his schedule and he went on his own time too, when he had it… not that he often did. The lines and angles of his torso had distracted her on their honeymoon. She'd thought their impact would lessen the longer they were together, so far, that hadn't been her experience.

Concentrating on her lotion, Lyla picked her nightdress higher so she could squirt lotion onto her thighs. "Do they see a wedding ring as a challenge?"

"Damn! I knew that guy was sleazing on you," he said, coming over to drop onto the bed facing her. "I was gonna come over, but Paul was buzzing around like a bad smell. I had to wait all this time to come upstairs because I wanted to be alone with you. I didn't want them following me up. I waited until he disappeared to do interviews with the other participants before I could slip out without him knowing I was gone. And Kira—"

"She's very beautiful," Lyla said, smiling as she wiped the residual lotion from her hand onto his bare shoulder. As soon as her hand landed on the solid mass of his muscle, she stopped. Her mouth opened and her smile faded. Why the hell had she thought it was okay for her to touch him like that? "Sorry, I—"

"It's okay," he said, widening his own smile and he curled his fingers around her wrist to do the wiping for her. "I touch you every day, 'bout time you returned the insult."

Typical that he should be sweet about reassuring her. "It's not an insult when you touch me," she said, drawing her hand away from his. Lying on the bed, she wondered what he was looking at, then remembered she hadn't pushed her nightdress back down. "The lotion needs a minute to soak in."

Self-conscious, she rubbed her legs together, but he rested a hand on her shin to grip her. "You've got gorgeous stems, Malloy," he said, bowing to kiss her knee.

Laughing, she pushed his head up, but was surprised to see that he wasn't smiling. In fact, he looked odd. His eyes were small, precision-focused, but she couldn't figure out what was going on in his head. So she scooted over to the other side of the bed, putting some space between them.

"Do you want the bed tonight?" she asked and carried on before he could make a joke. "The cameras aren't here, you don't need to proposition me."

His next inhale was long and tired. It had been a long few days for him, so she didn't say anything when he turned around to lie on the bed beside her. He deserved a chance to chill. A minute of silence stretched.

"Kira cheated on me."

Oh…

Sliding down the bed, she rested her head on her hand as she lay on her side next to Trick who was staring up at the ceiling. "I didn't know that," she said.

"Not a lot of people do," he said, taking another breath. "I know I'm a jerk most of the time, I know I do dumb shit, and I hurt a lot of women when I was a stupid kid playing to the cameras, but… When I'm in a relationship, I'm in. I've always been that way. I don't make promises I don't intend to keep. Don't make commitments to…" He trailed off and picked up his hand to look at his wedding ring. "I guess that's not true anymore."

Reaching over him, Lyla pushed his hand down. "You didn't make me any promises," she said, laying her hand over his on his chest. "You just recited your lines at the wedding; that was it. It didn't mean anything. It was a script."

Looking at her, Trick was doing that peering thing that always unnerved her. "Why do you always put yourself down?" he asked. "You act like you don't deserve respect… or love."

"We didn't get married for love or respect," she said. "So it doesn't count… And Kira cheating on you must have been devastating; it's obvious that you cared for her."

"Why do you think that?" he asked.

"Two reasons," she said. "First, you kept the secret. You found out about the indiscretion and ended your relationship, but you didn't go selling the story or slandering her, so you must have cared about her enough not to want to embarrass her or damage her career."

"And the second reason?"

Grinning, she got a fraction nearer to whisper. "You're a good person Nairn Strickland, and you feel things more deeply than you want the world to know. You were with her for a while and like you just said, you wouldn't have made promises to her if you didn't intend to keep them… It must be weird that Bunyan's asking you to sleep with her now…

Did you forgive her after the affair?"

He shook his head. "It wasn't like that. I found out she was screwing around, she said 'so what' and split... I didn't see her again... Maybe we weren't that into each other after all."

"Sometimes it's the people we care most about that we hurt the most," she said.

He scooped a hand up under her jaw to angle her head up so he could peer in to her again. "Who was your guy?" he asked. "You said it had been five years, you didn't tell me anything about him."

"Declan Gordon," she said, and didn't really want to look at Trick when she mentioned her ex's name. "It's been six years since we broke up, I don't talk about him much."

"Why not? Still hung up on him?"

She shook her head and let him thread their fingers together as was his habit. "Declan was the one who taught me the real value of being alone," she said. "I'd always been a loner at school. I met Declan in college and we were really inseparable. He'd been branded the odd-one-out in high school too. We kind of bonded over our mutual oddity."

"So, what happened?" he asked. "How come you're not still with him?"

Dropping to her back, she folded her hands on top of each other under her breasts. "Turned out, he wasn't who I thought he was."

"Ah," he said.

"He won this national competition thing for the college and got popular overnight. We hung on for a while after, but he changed... kept trying to change me too. He didn't want me to be me anymore, he wanted me to be what he thought he deserved. And he deserved a woman who'd worship him, especially in public. Didn't take me long to figure out I wasn't good enough for him. He kept telling me what a disappointment I was. How I should be grateful to him because he could do so much better. Eventually... he did."

Turning her head to watch Trick as he rolled onto his side, she didn't like the pity in his eyes, but it was probably mutual. "Sounds like a dickwad, want me to look him up? We can pay him a visit."

"And what? Make out on his couch?" she asked.

He grinned and bowed forward to touch his lips to her forehead. "Or we could just go at it… I'll rough him up a bit first, hurt him for hurting my girl, then when he's lying there bleeding, I'll eat your pussy right there in front of him, make him watch me worship you."

Giving him a shove, Lyla was touched that he would make the suggestion, even if it would never happen. But she put him back on his side of the bed, and then flopped to her back and gestured downward over her hips. "The only…

"Pussy?" he asked.

"Yes, that… the only one of those you should be thinking about right now is Kira's." It was funny, if perplexing, to see his expression turn to disgust as he rolled flat again. "Did you leave her in the bar? I know that this is difficult for you, but Bunyan seems to think it's guaranteed to pull in the ratings. And you did agree—"

"It's sex," he said, "sex always sells."

"So why are you lying here with your buddy instead of seducing a babe?"

"My buddy," he muttered.

She'd meant it to be a joke, now she feared she'd missed the mark. Lyla wasn't renowned for her sense of humor or delivery or reading people, especially men.

"Was that presumptuous? We're not friends, we're—"

He laughed and turned to his side, resting his face near enough to hers that his chin prodded her shoulder when he spoke. "We're married, Malloy, we're more than friends… Getting close to you, spending time with you like this … it's been the best part of this stupid show… Haven't you had any fun? Even a smidge?"

Turning her face to his, he was too close for her to focus properly, but she smiled anyway. "Maybe a tiny smidge," she said. "I like listening to you play your guitar on Saturday mornings."

"Yeah?" he asked, his voice laced with comedic male pride. "I'm real good at that, huh? You like my music?"

She nodded. "Because when I hear that, wherever I am in the apartment, I know both your hands are occupied and they won't be coming at me."

He laughed and tilted to kiss her shoulder. In an unusual move, he left his lips there for a second, then began to graze them back and forth. "You know, Bunyan just needs me to have sex with someone," he said and his fingertips began to gather her nightdress at her hip, pulling it high over her thigh, though they were both still flat on the bed. "He didn't say it couldn't be you."

"No," she said, slapping a hand down on top of his. "I said that… And we're alone, what are you thinking of, bringing *him* out?"

As far as Lyla was concerned, the other Trick, his over the top persona, had no place when there was no one around to watch him perform.

"If he was here, he'd be on top of you already. You'd never be this relaxed with him this close to you," he said and rose to look down at her. "Do you trust me, Malloy? At all?"

Touching his face, she felt the need to connect with the man who was going through torture of his own. It must be horrific for him to be spending time with the ex who'd broken his heart. Not only that, he had to sleep with the woman when his own feelings about her infidelity were probably still raw.

"Completely," she said. "And I can relax around him these days, because I know you control him, and you'd never hurt me. You're the protective big brother I never had."

"Brother, huh," he said and was looking at her mouth again for some odd reason. Lyla began to worry that she might have smudged toothpaste on her cheek or something. "Never thought I'd get where your Caligula guy was coming from…"

Excitement made her turn toward him. "You remembered his name!"

"I do listen when you talk, sweetheart," he said, draping an arm over her hip as she touched her palms to his chest.

They'd never laid like this before, in bed, together, facing each other, her body almost nestled to his, just a couple of inches between their forms as her fingers spread on the warm flesh of his hard chest.

It felt peculiar to be so close to him, so close that the heat of him was permeating the thin cotton of her nightdress and warming her nude body beneath.

Maybe that was it. All she was wearing was this thin nightdress. Yes, the garment had wide straps and hung down to her ankles, though it was gathered high around her thighs now, but she'd never been so accessible to him. Even the bikini would've taken more effort to get off as it had knots. This nightdress would take only seconds to shed.

Why was she thinking about taking off her clothes? Lyla knew she'd never get naked with Trick. Just. Never.

"Malloy?"

The sound of his voice startled her and she tipped her head back to see him looking down at her, his arm curled beneath his head for support.

"Why does your voice sound all low like that?" she asked, but her heart was doing something weird.

It could be a palpitation. Maybe it was a coronary. It wasn't painful, but her pulse was definitely irregular. Her stomach was agitated too, like it was roiling and jumping; but it was happy, not unpleasant.

Picking up her chin in his thumb and forefinger, Trick tipped her head back farther and rubbed his thumb back and forth just a fraction. Lyla couldn't work out why he wasn't answering her or why he seemed to be falling asleep as his eyelids got heavy. Maybe there was a gas leak and he was feeling the same effects she was.

But before she could ask if he felt ill, sound carried from the suite. "Where are you? You bastard!" Paul shouted.

"Damn," Trick said, flopping on to his back to rub his hands on his face.

"Wait… are you both in the bedroom? Together?" Paul called. "Where is the camera? Get over here!"

Trick unbuttoned his pants and grumbled as he tugged them down a bit. "You take the room tonight, baby," he whispered. "Kick me out and lock the door, okay?"

"Kick you out? Why—"

Rolling over on top of her, Trick thrust an arm around her back just as the camera appeared in the bedroom doorway. "Come on, baby, just a little nookie," he said, rubbing his face in her hair.

"Trick," she screeched and pushed at him. "Get off me!"

"Oh, baby, you get me hard then turn it off. Don't go cold, hot stuff. Play with me."

He pressed a hand to her waist, not her breast or between her legs, but her waist, then he growled against her neck.

"Stop it," she said and this time when she gave him a shove, he rolled all the way off her and exhaled. "Get out of here! All of you!"

Moving off the bed, Trick muttered something to himself and then began to stomp off toward the camera, holding his jeans up with one hand as he did.

When he got to the camera, he gave it a push. "If I'm not getting any, you're not getting an eyeful, shift it."

Climbing off the bed, Lyla rushed over to the door to close it behind all of them when they were over the threshold. Turning around, she fell against it and closed her eyes. Pressing her hand to her forehead, she felt bad for Trick, out there taking the heat from Paul who would be pissed that he'd been ditched and because Trick was not with Kira as he was supposed to be.

This felt like it was getting complicated, but she couldn't figure out why. Nothing had changed. Had it?

Except now that she knew Kira had hurt Trick so badly, she really didn't want him to sleep with her. Didn't want him to lie in bed with her and open himself up to her, he could get hurt again and…

Her hand slid down to her mouth to stifle her gasp.

She was jealous!

Lyla didn't want Trick lying in bed with Kira, sharing his secrets with his ex, not now that he did that with her, his wife. Lyla wanted to be his outlet for emotion. If he was stressed or needed to vent, she wanted to be the one he came to, just like tonight. He'd needed to tell someone about Kira, and indirectly to tell someone how difficult this was for him, and he'd chosen to tell her.

Rushing to the bed, Lyla climbed on and hid under the cover. She was his friend. That's all it was. She wanted to be his friend, his close friend. Being allowed to see the truth of the man behind the character was a privilege and as dumb as it was, she wanted to be something special to him.

His life was filled with people, male and female, and she still didn't know all of them, she may never know all of them. Trick had friends at every level of every definition of the word, who the hell was she to think that she might ever qualify in the upper echelons of that?

He made her laugh. Made her feel safe. Played with her. Helped her to relax, even about the sex stuff that she was clueless about. Trick just made everything easy and he didn't judge her. Lyla had to be careful. If she started to think he was important to her and started to think that she might want to be important to him, she could lose more than her dignity. She could lose her heart.

TWELVE

LYLA HAD BEEN weird all day.

Trick couldn't figure out what was wrong with her, but she wouldn't look at him. They'd had to do a bunch of bullshit team-building stuff in the hotel today and he hated every second of it. Mostly because the cameras were there, getting in everyone's faces, asking questions, and urging him to get as close to Kira as possible.

Exactly what Paul was lecturing him about now.

Sitting on the couch in the lounge area of the suite he was sharing with Lyla, Trick couldn't stop thinking about his wife in the bedroom, alone. He was surrounded by the crew, focused on the director pacing back and forth on the other side of the coffee table in front of the opposite couch.

"So as soon as you can sneak off, do it," Paul said. "Kira knows this is why she's here, so she's not going to put up any fight. Be polite, buy her a drink, flirt, we'll catch as much of it as we can, but don't be too obvious. This is extramarital, remember? We want it to be clandestine; that makes it hotter."

Trick felt sick.

He couldn't relax.

Curling one hand around a fist, he squeezed and gave himself a silent pep talk. Goddamnit, this was Kira, he'd had sex with her a thousand times. They weren't asking him to do anything he hadn't done before. And she was hot, if he just thought about her features, and not her personality, he'd get it up, he could do this.

Her boobs… was that what had done it for him before? No, they weren't responsive, weren't as high and full as Lyla's, hadn't featured in any of his recent fantasies, not the way his wife's had.

Her ass, that was it, he could just grab hold and… Skinny and flat, that was how he remembered Kira's ass now. Her ass didn't register at all, even in the tightest dress. She was all bone, no tone, not like the way Lyla's looked in her bikini when he—

"Hey, are you listening to me?" Paul asked, snapping his fingers and pulling Trick from his reflection.

"No," Trick said, getting more agitated as his anger level rose. "I wasn't. You want me to fuck her, so I'll fuck her. I don't need a step-by-step guide."

"Good," Paul said and reached into the equipment case that was on the couch behind him to pull something out. Tossing it over to him, Trick had to think fast to catch it… and he took a second to register what it was: a box of condoms. "Be safe. Give us ten minutes to get setup, then come down."

Paul herded the guys out of the suite. Trick listened to the automatic lock click in to place. Inhaling, he blew out his breath and shoved up from the couch. He had to see Lyla before he went out. Trick already knew this was going to be the most awkward conversation of their relationship.

Last night, in bed with her, he'd felt accepted, needed… just like a regular guy lying with his woman. If Paul hadn't interrupted them, he'd have kissed her for sure. She seemed to have put this line between the real him and the character he played. She believed that the character would letch over her, but believed it was impossible for the real him to have any kind of intimate feelings for her. And her comment about him being a brother? He didn't know whether to laugh at that or spit.

Going around the couch, past the armchair at the head of the table, he stuffed the box of rubbers into his jacket pocket and gave the bedroom door a push to let it swing open on its hinges. There she was, his wife, on the floor at the end of the bed, standing on her head in her yoga gear. Man, she had a body, and she didn't even know it. He loved watching her do her yoga; she evened her breathing and closed her eyes, and just seemed to lose herself in it.

He knew she did something to stay in shape and yoga was just a part of her regime; she was way more physical than she realized.

When her eyes popped open and she noticed him, she smiled and let her body descend into an elegant crab shape before slowly rising to her feet. "Oh, good, I wanted to ask you something before I forgot."

At least she wasn't being as distant as she had been all day. Today, he hadn't felt that she was pleased to have him within three feet of her or even to hear his voice. She'd just closed down. But now she was smiling, was she pleased that he was going to Kira? That he was going to be intimate with another woman?

"Ask away," he said as she went to her laptop case in the corner of the room.

If she asked him to stay, he would, he'd already made that promise to himself and to Sadie who had been glaring at him for most of the last two days, since Kira showed up. He'd thought having one of his closest friends on this trip with him would give him support. As it was, he felt a bit like his network was falling apart. Sadie was pissed at him, Lyla was being distant, and Kira… well she would just love that he needed her help.

"Will you sign a picture for me?"

"Will I…?" Lyla actually pulled a picture out the front of her laptop case and brought it over with a Sharpie, wearing a grin. Did she know what was going on here? "You want me to sign a picture for you?"

"Not for me," she said, putting the pen in his hand as she spread the picture on the dresser. "It's for my cousin,

Avril. She asked before the wedding and I forgot, I didn't think it would be appropriate to ask you then."

"But you thought it was appropriate now?" he asked, watching her pop the cap off the pen for him.

"We're friends now," she said. "You said we were buddies last night."

"Friends?"

Lyla pushed his hand down toward the picture, what was she doing? And why would she still not look at him? Well if this was what she wanted, he would do it for her. As Trick moved the pen to the paper to sign it, he began to think about what he wouldn't do for her… was there anything on that list?

"Thank you!" she exclaimed when he was done and picked up the shiny sheet to blow on the ink to dry it.

All he could see was his woman standing there with her back to him, paying such careful attention to the picture while ignoring the real him. Putting the pen on the dresser, Trick took a step forward and slid his hand around her waist. He was going to kiss her neck, in that sweet little spot beneath her ear that made her whimper.

Except she took his hand away from her belly and moved it aside so she could walk across the room and slip the picture back into a folder in her laptop case. "Lyla—"

"Paul already told everyone I was sick, so just tell them you left me up here in bed and you won't have to worry about saying anything else," she said, chipper as she turned to lean against the wall between the chair and the nightstand. "I feel sort of guilty that I get a night off and you have to do all the work."

Only Lyla could say she felt guilty on the night her husband was going off to sleep with another woman. Pinning his eyes on hers, Trick wished he could make her understand how important she was and how she deserved so much better than this.

"Ask me to stay," he muttered.

He hadn't meant to say it. But he had to let her know, if there was a choice, he was choosing her.

But she just smiled that Lyla smile that told him she was about to say something self-sacrificing like it was no big deal. Something no other woman would ever say.

"Don't be silly," she said. "I wouldn't do that to you. This is what you want… I'm happy for you, honey."

Happy for him because she thought Kira was such a catch? Except he'd caught that fish long ago and let her swim free without chasing her because he knew she wasn't worth it. Kira wasn't half the woman Lyla was.

"If you change your mind, call down, okay?" he said and she nodded.

"I won't, but thank you for considering me," Lyla said and her smile got even wider. "Now go have fun… Go on!"

She encouraged him out the door with a wave of her hands and there was nothing else he could say, so he went. Leaving the bedroom, he marched across the suite and out into the hallway to head for the elevator.

Lyla was going to spend the night alone in their suite and he was going to spend the night with Kira. His wife didn't give him grief or make him feel guilty about what the studio were asking him to do. But happy for him? Could she really be happy for him? Maybe she was happy for him because she knew the start of the affair was the beginning of the end of their marriage. How many weeks would the studio ask him to string both women along? After sleeping with Kira, his chances of ever getting intimate with Lyla dropped into a minus percentage.

His stride slowed.

He knew already that his chances of ever getting with her for real were slim, but she'd never allow herself to be two-timed. Their friendship had gone from strength to strength since their conversation in her department, but he'd lose that after being with Kira.

And Kira, would she expect a relationship? Did she want the show to focus on them? If she did, he'd never get rid of her.

This wouldn't be a temporary fling, not if Kira caught a whiff of the limelight.

Lyla would be pushed out.

She'd leave his apartment.

They'd get a divorce.

It would be over.

Stopping in the middle of the hallway, he was suddenly hit with all kinds of emotions and ideas.

What he wanted… What did he want? Lyla had said that this was what he wanted. But he didn't. He'd never craved Kira. He'd been relieved to get out of that relationship and had no desire to go back to it and…

Returning to his thoughts on the couch, he realized how every time he compared the women, it wasn't Kira who got him hot, it was Lyla.

Lyla's body.

Lyla's laugh.

Her mind.

Her smile.

Her.

He couldn't even bring himself to fondle his wife's ass or her boobs. Yeah, because he knew she didn't want it and it would be disrespectful, but also because his body couldn't take the teasing torment.

On that bus, when she'd been sitting on him, wriggling her ass on his cock, he couldn't stop himself from getting hard, and he didn't want to scare or upset her, so he had to move her onto his chest.

All through their honeymoon he'd stayed in the water and in the jacuzzi because of his hard-on. But it wasn't just her body that got to him. No. He loved how she took care of him, making sure he stayed hydrated, made smoothies for him for energy and took note of his sleeping and grooming habits.

She could read him. They'd been married for a day shy of three weeks now, and spent every waking minute together that they weren't working. And he'd never once been bored with her.

Sometimes it was intense and full-on and he felt awful for the way he had to act around her for the show. Lyla made him want to be better. Made him value himself more and his character less. She brought out every protective instinct he'd ever had because she was so vulnerable. Even if she didn't see it, her naivety about men and sex made her a target for others.

Lyla carried herself with composure and never griped

or complained. She wanted everyone else to be happy, went out of her way to be accommodating, and no one stepped up for her.

Turning on the spot, Trick began to walk down the corridor, slow at first and then faster as he got closer. Lyla deserved better than this.

Screw the show.

Someone had to step up for her. She deserved better than what she'd been put through. She needed someone to prioritize her, no one ever had… until now.

Lyla was the full package, she was real, and he would be a fool to lose the best thing that had ever happened to him.

Trick wanted her.

In his life.

In his bed.

In his heart.

Lyla was his and he was going to make it his mission to make her see just how much he cared about her.

No. That wasn't enough. He cared about Sadie. About Josie. About the guys.

No, Lyla was different. She was more special. The most special person he'd ever known.

She was his wife.

His best friend.

The person he trusted most in the world.

He didn't just care about her.

He loved her.

THIRTEEN

LYLA WASN'T PARTICULARLY hungry, but if she didn't eat something now, she'd get hungry later and she didn't like to eat late. It was already approaching nine PM, way later than she'd usually have dinner. But the day had run late and then they'd done interviews after their briefing about the next few days. So time had just gotten away from her.

She'd gone into the living room to try to find the room service menu, but stopped to consider whether she could order anything or if maybe that would look suspicious. If she was really sick, she wouldn't be ordering dinner, would she? She wouldn't be in the mood to eat.

Maybe if she just picked something light or—

The suite door opened, which was weird. No one should be coming in. Everyone should be busy downstairs.

Spinning around, she saw Trick barreling toward her, a man on a mission. "Forget something?" she asked, but barely got the words out before he grabbed her face and pulled her up to him.

Lyla was so stunned by the pressure of his mouth that she didn't react for a good ten seconds. But when his tongue touched her lip, she thrust a fist to his chest and struggled to get away.

"What the hell?" she asked, leaping back and wiping her mouth with the back of her hand that was still clutching the room service menus.

His chest was moving up and down fast, his eyes were determined and unblinking, and he didn't hesitate to start moving toward her again. "I love you."

"What the hell, Trick!" she said again. "There's no one here! It's not funny to—"

"I'm not laughing," he said, moving another step in her direction.

But she squawked and held up the menus, thrusting her fist into the air once and twice to stop him from moving forward and keeping a good six feet between them. He smiled, but it wasn't an expression she recognized, he looked... relieved.

Trying her best to breathe and find some sense in this whacked out moment, Lyla was still recovering from that kiss... He'd kissed her.

Trick had kissed her!

Touching her lips, she lost herself for a second, had he really kissed her? He'd never done that before.

"I don't understand," she whispered.

"I know, baby," he said and this time when he walked forward, she let him pass her menu-clasping hand and put his arms around her waist.

But she still felt disconnected from reality and herself.

Lowering his face to her hair, Trick nuzzled his mouth down to above her ear, which meant he had to open his legs around her in a crouch and when she felt the rub of something decidedly erection shaped, she squawked again and tried to push away. To her surprise, he let her go, but there wasn't much space. With the window at her back, a cabinet on the wall at her side and the bedroom door just beyond that, behind where Trick was, she was cornered.

Without even thinking about letting herself look downward, Lyla found his smiling eyes. "You have to go. Kira is waiting for you. You have to have sex with her and—"

"No," he said, shaking his head and opening his arms

as he exhaled a sound of relief. "The only woman I want to have sex with is you. You are the only woman I want… God, Malloy, you don't know what a relief it is to finally figure out why I've been feeling this way. I want to be near you all the time. I don't want to lose you. I want us to do this. To be this. All the way. For real. I want this to be real. I want us to be together."

Wow, he was good. He really made that speech seem cathartic.

Glancing left and right, Lyla wondered where the hidden camera was as she twisted and leaned toward him to whisper, "I didn't get a script for this, Trick."

They didn't exactly get scripts, but if something big was supposed to happen, they did usually get direction.

"Not Trick, Nairn," he said, coming to her to take her hand. Pulling the menus away, he tossed them to the floor and pressed her hand against his chest. "And there's no script, baby. This is it. Me. Just me. Asking you to be mine. Everything real. All the way."

Narrowing her eyes, she couldn't help but be suspicious. "All the way like sex?"

"Yes," he said, nodding his head. For some reason, he couldn't take his eyes from hers and the scrutiny was beginning to make her prickle. "Sex, yes, we'll have sex. But not now. Whenever you want it. Whenever you're ready. I don't care if it takes ten years. I want you, Malloy. No, I want you to be Strickland. Mrs. Strickland, my Mrs. Strickland. Completely. No expiration date. No backing out. No walking away. No setups and scripts. Just us. A man and a woman making it work. Compromise. Figuring it out. Communicating. Together… Hell, I've known you three weeks and I'm so in love with you… Damn, how did I miss it? I knew I was attracted to you, but geez, Malloy, you're… you're my everything. You're so smart." Keeping one hand over hers on his chest, he used the other to stroke her face. "So beautiful. Funny. Kind. Considerate. You're warm and talented and—damn, baby, I could go on all day."

What the hell was this? Why was he looking at her like that? Why did he look so happy just to be standing there?

"Trick," she murmured. "You have to sleep with Kira."

"No," he said and seemed so sure as he stepped in closer to her. "I'm your guy. I promise you, baby. I won't ever be with another woman. Never again. I belong to you and I want you to belong to me. We're going to be together in every way two people can be. I want to be your best friend. Your lover. Your husband. I want us to do it all. For real."

"You just… You just said 'promise', but you… you never make promises."

"Unless I mean them," he said, squeezing her hand in his. He was working it in his fist as he took it up to his mouth. When he kissed her knuckles, he closed his eyes like she was the most delectable thing he'd ever had near his mouth. "I mean it, baby. I'm going to be there for you. For everything. I'll spend the rest of my life proving to you that I'm worth it. I know… I know you're so much better than I am, worthy of so much more than a dumb schmuck like me, but I—"

"Trick," she said, stepping in to touch his lips.

She didn't want to hear him saying anything negative about himself. It actually hurt her to think that he might believe he was in any way better than her.

"I love you," he whispered, looking straight into her, straight through her. "This isn't a game. This isn't a show. Right now. We're alone. All alone. A husband with his wife… I love you, Lyla Malloy, for real. All the way."

It was liberating for her to see this man she cared so much for freed. He really did seem to be lighter, though she couldn't begin to understand why he was saying these things. How could he love her? How could he be making promises to her and turning away from Kira to come back to her?

"I want to be special to you," she admitted in a whisper.

After tossing and turning all night, she did eventually fall asleep, but woke up feeling guilty. She couldn't ask anything of Trick, he'd never made her any promises. It made her feel awkward to be near him when she knew how she'd been stupid enough to care for him so deeply. It felt ridiculous to ask him to return those feelings when he was Nairn

Strickland, *the* Nairn Strickland.

Except here he was, making her promises. Was this for real?

"You are," he said on a wide smile that turned into a laugh. "Geez, baby, don't you hear me? I love you! You are the single most special person in my life. You. No one else. You are my priority. This is it for me now. We're going to do this and I don't care if I have to jack in the show, the career, everything. Whatever it takes to make you happy, I'm going to do it. You just say the word and I'll do it. Anything."

"Anything," she breathed. "Is this real? Trick, if you're playing me—"

"No playing," he said, dropping the smile and gathering her in to his arms again. "I promise you, sweetheart. I wouldn't do that to you. I wouldn't hurt you or use you like that."

He'd corrected her to call him Nairn and that was something she only did when she thought they were having an intense or genuine moment.

"This is crazy," she said and wriggled out of his arms. "You can't love me… you just… you can't! You're Nairn Strickland!"

"And you're Lyla Strickland," he said, watching as she bowed her head and walked past him.

"All that means is you'll do anything on a dare… is that what this is?"

"A dare?" he asked, shocked by the implication. "No! You think I'd go that low?" No, she didn't, not really. She'd told him last night that she trusted him and she'd meant it. "Are you telling me you don't feel anything for me? That these three weeks? It's all meant… it's meant nothing to you? Eating together, our walks, hanging out… the phone calls, the conversation… All the touching, sitting wrapped in reach other all the time… it's meant nothing to you?"

"No," she said, spinning around to see the angry disappointment written all over his face. "I care about you… I care about you a lot. But I—"

"No but," he said with a flare of hope in his step as he lunged toward her. "Care is good, care I can build on. I know it's hard for you to respect me when I've acted like such an idiot, but I'll stop all that, I promise. It's all real from now on, just me being… me."

"But the show—"

"I don't give a damn about the show," he said, scowling at her. "The show can go to hell. Let them drop me from the network, I don't give a damn. I have savings. I can look after us for a while and I'll always find work somewhere."

Look after us.

He was thinking of the future and taking her with him wherever he went. Could it be true? Could he love her? Taking the chance that he meant it was a massive risk, and there was a high likelihood that she'd get her heart broken, especially if this all turned out to be some big con.

Lyla had already figured out that morning that she was losing him anyway. Once he slept with Kira, Lyla knew she'd be phased out and Kira phased in, which made sense because both Kira and Trick were stars.

But it did mean her life would change. She'd lose her roommate. Her friend. The man she cared so much about that she'd felt physical pain when she thought of being without him.

Could she…?

Could she be in love with him too?

Lyla knew herself well enough to know she could convince herself of anything. She could also block out and dampen her emotions. It was how she managed to let all the negative comments roll off. She said they didn't hurt, but they probably would, if she let them.

So, what would happen if she let herself love Trick… for real… all the way?

FOURTEEN

INHALING, she rolled her lips into her mouth to moisten them and began to walk. Ignoring the hammering of her heart, Lyla kept on going. She could do this. Yes, she could do this. Taking a handful of his tee-shirt between the edges of his jacket, she moved him a quarter turn and urged him to the back of the couch. He was too tall for her to access on her own, so it was only when he was propped on the back of the couch that she could move between his bent thighs and slide her hands to his face.

Feeling like she'd missed the first one, Lyla pulled him to her to enjoy this kiss now that she was prepared for it.

For three weeks, she'd avoided this mouth. Avoided the dedication of this kiss. If she'd given in to his insistent lips too quickly, it would never have felt like this. Lyla didn't want the same generic kiss that he gave to every other woman he came across.

Trick's arms curled around her body and he exhaled a groan of pleasure when she urged his lips apart with her own. He wasn't hurrying her, maybe he was afraid of scaring her away, and she appreciated that because she could be easily spooked. Lyla wanted to be sure that she was kissing Nairn and not the idiot who'd thrown himself on her so many times.

But the real him cared about her, that was why he prepared her before he did shocking things and always did his best to keep her torment to a minimum.

His mouth tasted amazing, it was so warm and his tongue so sure as it met hers. When he pushed a little harder, she moaned. But Lyla didn't know if it was excitement or anticipation that made her hormones pulse. This was more thrilling than anything she'd ever done before, and this was just a kiss in the living room.

What would sex with him be like?

Opening her hands, she pushed them up to the front of his shoulders under his jacket and eased away. "They're going to come looking for you," she whispered.

His eyes were so drowsy that he looked drugged. Lyla could feel how her lips were swollen. It had been a long time since she'd made out, or done anything sexual, with anyone. She was so out of practice and with one of the most practiced men on the planet, she should probably be self-conscious about that.

For some reason, Lyla couldn't bring herself to feel insecure with him. Maybe it was the strength of his arms around her waist or the haze that seemed to be making it difficult for him to focus. Was he really enjoying this that much?

"We have some time," he murmured and leaned forward to kiss her again.

But she took a step back, out of his arms. Lyla didn't let his look of disappointment settle, she took his hand and pulled him away from the couch. His reputation for being late would buy them some time, how much was a mystery, but she was going to make sure they took advantage of it because they might never have another minute alone. As soon as Paul came in here to find Trick that would be it, their chance to be intimate would be gone. They couldn't do it for the first time on film. Lyla couldn't… have sex on tape.

Trick was heavy and dragging his feet.

"Come on," she said, trying to pull him harder.

"Where are we going?" he asked. "Let's go back to

the couch… kissing you is a high."

"Then what will sex with me be like?"

His eyes grew and he'd never moved so fast in his life. Lyla laughed as he rushed forward, scooping her off her feet and carrying her through to the bedroom as she wrapped her legs around his waist.

She was winded when his weight landed on top of hers on the bed. Lyla opened her mouth to gasp and laugh simultaneously at his eagerness to get his mouth back onto hers. The insistence of his lips to open hers was quicker this time and his tongue delved deep into her mouth. He was consuming her, building the need of their bodies to a place they'd never let it reach.

"Wait," he said and lifted up to look at her with that same daze in his eyes that she'd seen in the living room. "This isn't a test, is it? Am I supposed to suggest we wait?"

Smiling, Lyla rubbed her hands over his body beneath his jacket. "Do you want to wait?" He shook his head, his lips already moving towards her again. "And if I do?"

Clamping his lips shut, Trick stopped his advance, but took a second to clench before he spoke, "Then we wait."

Releasing her legs from their place at his back, she was pinned down by his body, but was too high up to know the answer to her next question, "Nairn… are you hard?" Lifting his hips, he rose a fraction and tilted to push the bulk of his erection against her core. Grinding down, he left no mystery about the need of his mass. "Is that for me?"

He grinned and she enjoyed knowing she'd put that sparkle in his eyes. "Only for you from here on out."

"Do you have protection?" she asked. "I'm not on any kind of birth control."

For a second, he looked worried and she thought their interlude might be over before it started. Then he laughed and pulled one of his arms from under her to reach into his jacket pocket and a second later, he pulled out a box of condoms to hold it aloft in triumph.

"Courtesy of Prem." There was something ironic about Paul providing the condoms and then missing the event. Her racing pulse and tickling skin were burning in anticipation; this was utterly terrifying and overwhelmingly exhilarating all at the same time. "Ironic thing is, Kira's on an IUD so we—"

Lyla's smile fell and some of her need dispersed. "You wouldn't have used protection with her?"

Kira cheated on him. God only knew who she'd been with since they'd broken up. Panic seized Trick and he sank down to kiss her. "Oh no," he said, "mood come back, come back. Forget that, forget it, baby, relax. There's the mood, see how good that feels? See how good your man can make you feel, baby?"

His lips moved across her cheek to her jaw and down to her neck. This man knew how to kiss, knew how to contort a woman's pleasure until she was aching for him. Lyla knew it because as the gentle caress of his lips slid down her neck to her throat, she couldn't help but relax.

Pushing his jacket off his shoulders, she welcomed the chance to run her hands down his arms, he had incredible arms. Strong and muscular, they were perfect for making a woman feel safe. He could pick her up, carry her around, pin her down, and take control.

Except now, he wasn't doing any of that. He was taking his time, kissing her neck, her mouth, her face, and it was as she enjoyed this kissing that Lyla remembered she'd changed into her sweats after he left and she was covered up, everywhere. He was probably worried about getting too handsy in case she was reminded of his alter ego.

But she wanted to know what it would be like to be touched by her husband, the man who'd said he loved her.

"Trick," she breathed against him when he kissed her again and she ran her hands through his hair. "Can we get naked?"

He whispered a laugh. "There's a question I never say no to." As soon as he said the words, he rose a fraction higher and seemed to be scowling at himself. "I'm sorry, babe. I don't know what's wrong with me."

It was funny to see him off-kilter and as she eased him away, she laughed and sat up. "It's okay, honey. I know you're not a virgin."

Pulling her sweater off over her head, she cast off her vest next and it was only as she slid her fingers under the waistband of her pants that she noticed he was just sitting there watching her. Stopping, she twisted to face him and crossed her legs, waiting for him to catch up.

Lifting his tee-shirt off over his head, he tossed it away and smiled. "Your turn."

The box of condoms was in the middle of the bed between them and as she fixated on it, her anxiety began to rise… she should never have stopped kissing him.

"Trick," she murmured. "This is going to be awful."

"No, no," he said, bounding up the bed toward her, shoving the condoms aside. "Look at me, baby." Grabbing her chin, he forced her to look at him. "I love you, okay? This is not just a casual whatever. I'm sorry I keep saying stupid things. I'm nervous, would you believe it? Me nervous about sex? I've had dozens of women, hundreds maybe. I haven't been nervous about sex since… Okay." He frowned and shook his head. "I'm doing it again. Damn… Listen, it's okay, I'm going to dedicate myself to showing you I'm a decent guy. We're going to be together and—"

"Not the relationship," she said. "The sex. The sex is going to be awful!"

His smile was slow and he leaned forward to bump his forehead on hers. "Don't worry about that, sweetheart. You just lie back and let me—"

"That's what I'm worried about! I have no skills. I'm useless with men. Always have been. What the hell do I know about sex? And sex with a guy like you who's been with hundreds of women…? I'll bore you."

When she moved to rise, he grabbed her wrist and pulled her back onto the bed. But instead of saying anything, he just pinned those narrow intense eyes of his on her for the longest time. There was something immobilizing about the way he looked at her like that.

When she finally stopped breathing, he toed off his shoes without breaking the stare. He leaned down and pulled off his socks, still without breaking eye contact.

Next went his jeans and he really proved his skills by

removing those while still fixating on her. But Lyla was grateful that he had because it became imperative for her to return that eye contact. He was naked. Oh, sheesh, Nairn Strickland was in bed with her, naked.

Panic closed her throat, but she was still frozen, not breathing, not moving. Trick took her trembling hand and moved closer to her. As he curled her fingers around his solid dick, she squeezed her eyes shut and turned her lower lip into her mouth.

Lyla was so tense that she didn't feel him lean in, all she felt was how his hand began to move hers, up and down, stroking him.

"All you need to do to satisfy me is be you," he murmured into her hair at her ear.

Blinking her eyes open, she didn't have a chance to focus on anything before his mouth met hers again. It was easier to relax when he was kissing her. All she had to do was think about those lips, the slick motion of his tongue sliding over hers, curling around to tempt her into his mouth as he pushed back to salve the tip of her tongue with his own.

Lyla didn't notice him removing her bra. But when his hands closed over her bare breasts she exhaled the weight of her pleasure into his mouth. And she realized something else; she was still squeezing and sliding her hand up and down his dick. All on her own, she was pleasuring him. Her hand moved as he did. She didn't want to let go of him, it felt empowering to have a hold of him like this, especially when she knew he was enjoying it. And being honest with herself, she knew if she let go, she might never touch him again.

Trick moved onto his knees between her legs. "One sec, babe," he said, taking his mouth from hers and easing her hand off his penis.

Lyla was disappointed enough that her next exhale sounded petulant, even to her ears. Trick grinned at her and kissed her quickly. "Just a second then it's all yours all night," he said and slipped his fingers into the waistband of her pants. "Can I take these off?"

She wanted to say no, it was instinct to keep that last barrier in place. But a refusal was such a contradiction to what her body wanted. Her mind was conscious of her body image and ability, but her body was screaming at her to welcome him inside of her.

"I—"

"It's okay to say no," he said and all her doubts about his sincerity vanished there and then.

There was no way this man could be looking at her with that patient tenderness, while his dick clearly had an agenda, and not love her.

Lyla was going to let herself love him back, no more hiding. No more protecting her heart. She was going to open herself to him; it was the only way to embrace the adventure. Either this would be forever or he would be the greatest love affair of her life. He already was and they hadn't even done anything yet.

Trick obviously guessed that she wasn't ready because he let his hands ascend as he leaned forward to kiss her again, but she slanted away. "Nairn," she said, grabbing his wrist to stall it. "Make love to me… please."

"You sure? We can wait until you're sure you're ready. I don't want you to feel rushed or—"

She laughed. "Stop trying to talk me out of it! Would you take my pants off and have sex with me, please?"

He grinned like a kid at Christmas as he bounced down the bed, pulling her pants and underwear with him as he went. "She keeps saying please like she's not a goddamn wet dream," he muttered and as soon as her pants were out of the way, he grabbed her thighs, yanked them apart and bowed to kiss her center.

"Trick!" Lyla screeched.

Her torso rose from the bed as she grabbed his head and pulled it up.

He pouted. "Let me eat your pussy, baby, please," he grumbled like she was taking away his favorite toy.

Laughing, she ran her fingers into his hair. "We might not have time to—"

"If I can make you come, it will be worth it."

His fingers slid down through her folds, opening her wide, teasing and learning her. He kept his eyes pinned to hers when he bobbed his head downward once, then twice, like he was asking her permission to let his mouth descend to eat her.

But when his fingertip touched her opening, Lyla froze again and as he let the digit slide inside, her mouth opened in increments with every millimeter of his progression.

Usually when she was alone, she played with her clit to make herself come, but had never really bothered with penetration since she'd never come that way, so it had been a long time since anyone had been in that space.

Trick's teasing turned into concern, and when she tensed at the sight of his concern, he got even more worried. "What?" she asked, grabbing for his wrist as she pulled her hips up the bed. That was all she needed, to be told her anatomy was somehow wrong. "What's wrong?"

"Wrong?" he asked, and his worry disappeared when he looked at her next and the curl of his lips got downright obscene. "You have the tightest pussy I've ever been in." Taking his finger to his lips, he put the whole thing inside, sucking it clean, and making her squeak. " 'Fraid you're gonna have to get used to me eating you out, baby. You're going to need serious prep and we'll have to schedule huge amounts of foreplay time."

"Trick," she whined and tried to close her legs, but he was still lying on his chest between them.

"Relax, sweetheart," he said, pushing up to find her lips with his, pressing his naked form down on hers. "I'm just teasing. You're incredible… this is going to be incredible."

The sensation of his body on hers, skin to skin, gave her something to focus on in addition to the talent of his mouth. So when he began to fondle her breasts, she let his tongue take the lead while she moved her torso in response to his hands.

"That feels so good," she murmured as he kissed her chin and down the line of her throat.

"Let's try this one out," he said, sinking lower, he replaced one of his hands with his mouth.

Kissing, sucking, and nibbling on her breast, he gave every inch of her the attention of his tantalizing tongue.

"Oh, Trick," she gasped, but he wasn't done. His free hand slid between their bodies and he began to circle her clit with the tip of his finger. "Uh…"

Panting, her mouth stayed wide as she gasped and moaned at his teasing.

"That's my girl," he whispered, blowing circles on her damp nipple.

It was literally thirty seconds later when her hips pushed up into his hand and her orgasm exploded, sending the natural drug of endorphins shimmering through her blood to her every crevice. "Nairn!"

His finger slid into her and he joined it with another and he lifted his head to smile down at her. "You're wet, real wet, baby, perfect. Your man's thirsty… you're a good girl."

But when he began to slide down her body, she grabbed for his shoulder, a mixture of anticipation and panic made Lyla swallow a fresh dose of adrenaline. "I want you to…" It was insane that she could be naked with him, she could orgasm for him, but she still couldn't say the words.

"Want what, baby?" he asked, kissing her hard. "I'll do anything that will make you feel good."

But although his expression was open behind his obvious arousal she couldn't bring herself to say it. So instead of speaking, she lifted her knees higher on his ribs and reached down to take hold of him. One side of his mouth curled high.

"That," she said. "I want that."

He kissed her again. "And that you'll get… but I don't want to hurt you."

"Try," she said. "Please, Nairn."

Was it the please or the use of his first name that made him groan? Whatever it was, when he sagged forward and found her mouth, she did her best to angle for him and tried to guide him forward into her.

"Patience, baby," he grumbled against her. "Patience."

Her smile rose and then she laughed. He couldn't have been expecting the sound because he rose, showing a question in his gaze. "Are you giving me a taste of my own medicine?"

Returning her laugh, he kissed her quick. "Yeah, that's what it is, now you know how it feels."

Lyla knew he was teasing, she could see that mischievous light in his eye. "What if I beg?" she asked, biting her lower lip. "What if I say pretty please?"

He reached over the bed and with one hand he fumbled a condom from the box, he pulled the pack open with his teeth and managed to put the protection on without even looking at what he was doing.

Pressure against her opening made her mouth open in a silent gasp and with his eyes locked to hers, he pushed harder.

But he stopped and shook his head. "I've never been so scared to hurt a girl in my life."

Lyla didn't know if that was extraordinarily sweet or if she should feel inadequate. Splaying her fingers on his cheeks, she kissed him, knowing that his mouth had the ability to calm all her fears and anxieties. "Then let me do it," she said and began to ease him aside so she could squeeze out from under him.

"Hey, no, where'd you think you're going?" he asked.

But Lyla wasn't leaving him, she turned over, forcing him to go with her as she let her mouth dance in front of his. When Trick was on his back, she climbed on top of him and taking his lead, she copied what he'd done by curling her fingers around him and holding him tight while their eyes stayed locked.

Lowering herself slowly, she understood what he meant about pain as his girth pushed her limits. Trick tensed when she winced and he grabbed her hips, but as he tried to pick her up, she shook her head and laid her hands over his.

"If I don't make friends with him you're going to be celibate for a very long time," she said, trying her best to smile as she rocked her hips side to side. "You said love, right?"

He laughed and that helped to relax her. She slid further down him as he moved his hands to the back of his head.

"You're a walking fantasy, Malloy," he said, lifting his hips and easing them back, helping her by moving in opposition to her. "I did good."

Shoving down, she yelped and he curled up in a hiss. "Oh God," she said, cupping her breasts.

This was it.

This felt good.

Oh, the rhythm of him with her encouraged her juices and as they coated him, she moved faster and he went deeper. "That's my girl," he said, his voice gruff. "Oh, yeah. You got it, girl."

Lyla thought she was doing okay, but Trick can't have thought so, because he threw his arms around her and tossed her on to her back. But she couldn't be offended because his rhythm was better, faster, longer, harder.

Working hard to match him, she panted and squealed as he hit her deep and massaged her clit every time their bodies met. "Trick," she squeaked. "Oh, Trick, I'm… I'm gonna…"

"Go, baby," he called out, and that was it, she screamed and her whole body clenched as it rose toward his.

"Nairn! Oh, fuck!" she hollered, driving her nails into his upper arms.

"Lyla," he growled in response, shoving into her once and again, as he released himself in climax.

FIFTEEN

THE BACK OF HER hand fell to her sticky forehead and while she blinked to clear her spotty vision, she saw Trick there, still above her, grinning.

"I'm feeling pretty good right now," she panted. "Please don't make fun of me."

But his grin only got bigger. "You said you were gonna be no good... that was the best damn lay I ever had."

Letting herself smile and feel satisfaction collide with relief, Lyla was consumed by the positive endorphins that made her feel like she could do anything, like she was the most powerful woman in the world.

Bowing lower, Trick was about to kiss her, so she moistened her lips. Except the suite door opened and they both turned to see that the bedroom door was still ajar.

"Damn," Trick said and leapt off her to run to the door. He slammed it just as Paul turned the partition wall that separated the entry hallway from the living room.

"I saw you, you bastard!" Paul called from the other side of the door as Trick locked the door and turned to fall against it.

He pulled off the condom and tossed it in the trash,

but stayed by the door.

"Why do you look like you're having a heart attack?" Lyla asked, pushing on to her elbows. "We don't have to tell anyone if you're embarrassed about—"

"Embarrassed?" he said, returning to that scowl he always got when she offended him. "No, I just…" He smiled, a kind of dopey, easy smile she hadn't seen him use before. "I don't want to share you."

Okay, that was a nice line and she flopped down onto her back as Paul began to hammer on the door.

"We can't leave him out there all night."

"Why not?" he asked, sauntering back to the bed.

It was a real shame that Paul was out there having a fit. It wasn't nice that the director had been ditched, and Kira was probably pissed off too. They'd waited well beyond what would be normal Trick lateness.

Trick dropped to his knees on the floor at the side of the bed. "For one thing," Lyla said, rolling away, so she could grab the condom box to hand it over to him. "We only have two condoms left."

"Hmm," he said, frowning at the pack. "I see the dilemma."

"So, the longest we can stay in here with him locked out there is two more nights."

His avid attention rose from the condom box to her. "You think we're going to have sex once a night?"

Oops, was that wrong? Lyla took a turn at frowning. "We're not? Every other night? Once a week?"

"What kind of an idiot were you with?" he asked and laughed as he rose up over her and climbed back on top of her on the bed. "Gimme ten minutes and we'll be going again."

"Again?" she asked, her eyes bulging like they were on stalks. "You can't really—"

"Oh, I can," he said, nodding at her shock and brushing his nose on hers. "We're gonna have a lot of fun, Mrs. Strickland… I've wanted you for a while, so I've got a lot of tension to work out."

"And then we go to once a week?" she asked and he

laughed again as he kissed her.

"Baby, we can have sex any time you want to have sex."

"Any time? Like in the morning?"

"In the morning, the afternoon, inside, outside, in the shower, in the office—"

"In the office? You mean at Prem? We can have sex at Prem?" She gasped. "You have a dressing room, don't you?"

Trick didn't have an office, he had a whole living space in the Prem building. Lyla had never been in it, but because all his filming was done in the main studio building, he had a permanent dressing room. With a lock and everything she'd bet.

Her exuberance encouraged him and he seemed so enamored right now. "How have we been married three weeks and you've never seen my dressing room?"

"I've never seen you work," she said and shrugged. "Well, I guess you could say I've seen you work." Because whenever he adopted his character, even if it was just for fans, he was working. "But I've never been near you when you've been filming any show other than this one."

"This isn't a show," he said, kissing her. "Not anymore. Not in here. This is just a husband and wife, enjoying each other."

Paul began pounding on the door again. "I'll have security up here in a minute! I'll tell them you're ODing in there."

They couldn't have that kind of scene or drama on the show. "Trick," she said, squeezing his shoulders. "You have to talk to him."

"What do you want me to tell him?" he asked, kissing her and then licking her lip.

"Nothing," she said, curling her arms up under his to hook them around his shoulders from beneath. "I mean, you don't have to admit that we... you know."

"Had sex?" he said and grinned before kissing her again. "You don't say any of the words."

Scratching her fingernail on him, Lyla turned her

head away from his next attempt at a kiss. "You knew what I meant."

"You'll get comfortable with this stuff, you're just out of practice… it'll take time. But you can push any boundary you like with me. You know when it comes to you I don't really have any. So anything you want to do or try, I'm up for it. Just do what feels right for you… for us."

"I…" She was nervous about what she wanted to say next because Lyla wasn't quite sure where the emotional boundaries lay. He'd said he loved her, but that was before sex, maybe he'd changed his mind. "Trick, I…"

"What?" he asked, his tone laced with concern. "Is something wrong? If you think about dumping me now that—"

"No!" she said, wouldn't it be funny if the rookie had used him for sex only to cast him aside after. "I'm not having second thoughts, I… I want to be with you. Now more than ever."

He bobbed his head in cocky acceptance. "Yeah, I'm killer between the sheets."

It was nice that she could laugh when he was being an idiot, but Lyla understood it was just his sense of humor. "You were incredible, baby."

"Hmm," he hummed. "I sense round two getting closer by the second."

He tipped his head to kiss her, but before he touched his lips to hers, she blurted out. "I don't want you to sleep with Kira."

Lifting his head, Trick was frowning at her. "What?"

"I don't know if it's my place to say that to you or not, but… as soon as we open that door, Paul will want to drag you downstairs to do… well, what you were supposed to do and… it would make me really uncomfortable if—"

"God, you're adorable," he said and kissed her hard, letting his tongue slide deep against the roof of her mouth to taste as much of her as he could reach before withdrawing. "I love you. I'll be faithful, a hundred percent. But you have to be as well."

Laughing was an instinct, though it may not have

been appropriate. "Trick, who am I going to sleep with?"

He wasn't laughing, in fact he looked pissed. "I know plenty of guys who want to screw you," he said. "But it's not just about sex… I don't want you sneaking into empty offices with Curtis and letting him touch your face. I don't want you sitting at bars with random guys who proposition you… I don't want you getting into cabs with lecherous assistant directors who think it's okay to ask if they can film you getting undressed."

He was so passionate about each point that she was left dumbstruck for a minute when he was done. "Okay, well… I guess that helps me figure out what the rules are between us."

"The rules are we're together," he said. "Not for the show. Not for the studio. We're together. For real."

Outside the room, Paul was screaming at the crew who had to be out in the living room too.

"What are we going to do about the show?" she asked.

"The world knows we're married and I'm proud of us. I'm proud of you. Don't ever say I'd be embarrassed to be with you again, it hurts me."

That was honest, clear, and shocking, but in a good way. "Okay, I'm sorry," she said. "So, we don't mind if they know we had sex?" she asked and he shook his head. "We'll have to figure out how much we let them… see…"

"That's completely down to you," he said. "Just like before, okay?"

"You'll still be hitting on me?"

His glee made her laugh. "Probably more."

"But you won't… you won't say derogatory things about me when I'm not around, will you?"

"I wouldn't say derogatory things when you were around either," he said. "But you have to guide me on this. You know sometimes I'm a prick. I wouldn't say anything mean, but… are there words you don't want me to say or… what am I talking about? Let's just tell them we're out. Tell them we're through with the show and you don't ever have to worry about me being like that ever again."

But she shook her head. "We made a commitment and just because we actually developed real feelings doesn't mean we should back out of that. We'll figure it out as we go. Just… I don't mind you talking about us… sleeping together, just don't… talk about doing me anywhere that's not…"

"Up the ass," he said. "Stuff like that."

Her mouth fell open and she hissed, "Trick!"

"I'll be respectful, I promise, baby," he said and kissed her before he jumped off the bed and swiped his jeans from the floor. "You stay in here, I'll go talk to Paul and tell him it isn't happening."

Pulling up his jeans as he hopped toward the door, she sank back on the bed and exhaled when he turned and winked at her before going out and closing the door behind him.

SIXTEEN

"OKAY, WHAT SEEMS to be the trouble?" Trick asked as he sauntered away from the closed bedroom door.

Man, this was going to be tough. How did he play this cool when really all he wanted to do was open his mouth and yell? On a scale of one to ten, one being utter humiliation and disaster, and ten being every guy's ultimate fantasy, telling Lyla he loved her had come in at about a fifteen.

Sex.

They'd had sex!

Never in his wildest dreams would he have guessed that she'd trust him enough to let him take her like that. Now that she had, he wasn't going to do anything to mess this up. No way. But that shouldn't be hard. His dick wasn't going to go sniffing anywhere else and they spent every minute they weren't working together anyway.

No. He was going to be the perfect husband, when he wasn't being… a prick.

Paul was pacing again and the camera guy was in the armchair at the head of the table with the sound guy on the couch behind Paul. So Trick rounded the couch opposite him and dropped himself down in the middle of it to stretch his arms along the back. He'd never felt so good. Never in his life had he felt this light and this… happy.

Paul gaped at him for the longest time, so he raised his brows in expectation. "You're kidding, right?" Paul asked. "You prick, we were sitting down there waiting for you. Where the hell have you been?"

Turning his hands, Trick didn't move his arms. "What?" he asked. "I'm where you left me. Exactly where you left me."

His balls were lighter and his heart stronger, but yeah, Trick was in exactly the same physical spot he'd been when Paul last saw him. Damn. It was amazing how quickly life could flip around.

"I'm gonna have to hold your hand and lead you everywhere," Paul said, driving his fingers into his hair.

Glancing from one of his hands to the other, Trick smiled. "Don't think you want to hold my hand right now." But Paul didn't seem to be listening, he'd gone back to his pacing. "Listen, man, chill, okay? Nobody died. If someone had a heart attack every time I didn't show some place I'd been invited, there'd be a lot of dead people on my conscience."

Paul stopped to glare. "You're crazy! You weren't invited someplace, this is your job! Get it together, we're going downstairs. Now! Kira won't wait all night, she's spitting nails."

Trick snickered. "I'll bet."

"You think this is funny? She's a difficult woman when she wants to be, beautiful, but damn difficult."

Presenting a hand to the director, Trick smiled. "Hey, that's it! You need to get yourself laid! You'll chill if you get some pussy! Kira is single and I've got it on good authority she showed up here to be screwed."

"By you! Get your ass downstairs and—"

Returning his hand to the back of the couch, Trick shook his head. "Not gonna happen, my friend. Sorry…" He laughed again. "That's funny, I'm apologizing to you for refusing to screw my ex!" Trick sighed out what was left of his laugh. "Ah, that's funny."

"I'm glad someone's laughing," Paul said, his face

getting redder. "You are gonna do this, you don't have a choice!"

Trick wasn't worried about Paul's insistence, but his nonchalance only riled the director more. "I'm not sure what the rules are on rape via third party," he said. "No means no, right? Even for guys. So, yeah, I'm saying no."

"You can't say no!"

Although he knew it would upset his director more, Trick had to smile. "What are you gonna do? Force my dick into Kira's pussy? Yeah, that's romantic and not great TV. That's a lawsuit right there. You think you can trick me into it? Get me drunk enough that I don't know what I'm screwing? Believe me, bud, I'll know. And you try putting your hands on me, I'll take you apart. Done deal, man… I won't screw Kira. Won't be happening."

The bedroom door opened. Trick hadn't expected Lyla to come out of the bedroom, but when he turned to look over the back of the couch and saw his rumple-haired, rosy-skinned beauty looking at him with those sultry eyes, he couldn't say he was sorry to see her, and neither was his dick.

"Babe?"

"I don't know if I want to eat or shower," she said and yawned as she came toward the couch wrapped in a fluffy white hotel robe.

"I can offer a third option," he said as she sank down onto the couch beside him.

He couldn't share her. He couldn't do it. Which meant he'd have to give up spending the night in her bed.

Damnit.

He'd been thinking of how he could have her stuff moved from the guest bedroom at the apartment into his bedroom while he was still here, so it was done by the time they got back. Now he was looking at her thinking how he didn't want to give up any of their intimacies to the baying masses.

He'd have to piss her off, do something out of line to make her mad so she'd relegate him to the couch. If he didn't, Paul would find a way to wheedle a camera in to the bedroom.

Even if they were just sleeping, it felt wrong to be

watched. All he wanted to do was hold her. Falling asleep with her in his arms would be a Technicolor dream. But his selfish want would have to wait until he got used to sharing her… if he ever did.

But Trick was still going to move her into the master in their apartment.

If he got kicked out for being a dick, he'd sleep on the couch or he'd be the one in the guest room just as it worked in any real marriage.

He'd be a real husband to her; he'd make sure that single purpose drove him on every day.

***

TRICK WAS LOOKING at her funny. He was sort of doing the peering thing, but there was something knowing behind his eyes, something deeper.

Lyla smiled, hoping that interpreting his expression as a positive was right. "Are you okay, honey?" she asked and put a hand to his thigh to push nearer and touch her lips to the corner of his.

It was a short kiss, closed-mouth, but a kiss nonetheless and one that a wife would give to her husband. God, she hoped she was doing this right. She had so little relationship experience and there she was married to a man who could write "sexual aficionado" and "relationship master" as special skills on his résumé. How the hell did that happen?

But when she drew back, he was smiling. Yes, good sign. Moving his arm from the back of the couch, Trick curled it around her and pulled her against his side, tucking her in close.

Curling her legs under her, Lyla relaxed into him as she folded her robe over her thighs. It was going to take some time to get used to Trick being affectionate. Rather, it would take time for her to get used to not spurring those advances.

While she'd gotten used to his over-the-top behavior being nothing more than a performance, she had adapted to her role of chastising him. It would be interesting to see how she'd react if he did anything overtly sexual when they were alone.

Usually when Trick tried to kiss her, they were in front of a camera and she knew how to respond to that. Now… now she'd be able to accept his kiss. Except he'd given her carte blanche to draw their boundaries and he'd accept her limit.

So, if she wanted to refuse his mouth or push him away, she still could, still would, because it was weird to think of them doing anything genuine, or intimate, in front of the lens.

Right now, Trick slouched lower and let his mouth disappear into her hair. "I love that smell," he mumbled. "God, baby, I could bathe in your scent."

Wow, she'd always thought when he used lines on her it was for show, but now she wondered… could he mean it? Sliding her hand deeper into the vee of his parted thighs, Lyla wasn't surprised when he lifted his hips a fraction, urging her hand closer to his groin.

That was the kind of thing over-the-top Trick would do, yet this move was much subtler than she was used to from him. Was it a genuine invitation or was he toning down the character now that they were… together?

Twisting to look up at him, Lyla didn't expect his face to be so close to hers. But she couldn't kiss him, because there were dormant cameras in the room, crew in the room, witnesses.

"Hold the phone," Paul said and when she turned to look at him, she read a variety of emotions on his face, shock, confusion, disbelief. "What were you two doing in the bedroom? Alone… for more than an hour?"

"More than an hour?" Trick said and turned his face into her hair again. "See, baby, I told you I had stamina."

Responding with a quiet laugh, Lyla dug her nails into his thigh and he squeezed her tighter. She had a feeling that a lot of their affection was going to be subtle like this, they didn't make a big show of changing position or moving, just used their present connection to have an intimate conversation.

Paul's hands went into the air. "You were screwing! You have sex for the first time and we weren't even there!"

"Wasn't really a group session," Trick said. "We were confident enough to give it a go ourselves... Turns out, we did okay."

That raised an interesting question. "Have you had group sex?" she asked, tipping her chin up.

"Yes," he said. Geez, was there anything he hadn't done or anything he wouldn't admit to? "But it was years ago, baby. I swear I've been a good boy for a long time."

Well he broke up with Kira months ago and she didn't remember reading about him being with anyone else since then. That being said, he had been open to casual liaisons if their wedding night was any kind of indicator.

Paul snapped his fingers and she became aware of the camera crew mobilizing, they hadn't been on film until now. It only took seconds for the camera guy to get the equipment onto his shoulder. He stayed seated on the couch opposite them, on the other side of the coffee table, with Paul just out of shot as his leg stayed to the side of the lens.

The sound guy didn't have to go far either. He picked up his boom, played with his dials and leaned forward in his armchair.

"Really, guys?" Trick asked. "Way to be subtle."

"So, what was it like?" Paul asked, jumping in to interview mode.

"What was it like?" Trick asked. "What was what like?"

Smiling, she turned her amusement against his chest because it was just like Trick to find a new way to infuriate their director.

"You know what I'm talking about," Paul said.

"The game last night?" Trick asked and leaned forward to pick up the room service menus that had somehow ended up on the coffee table. She guessed that one of the crew must have picked them up during Paul's tirade. Trick handed them over to her and touched a kiss to her hair. "Missed it. Had to watch it on my damn phone. Nightmare. You try following a conversation with the highest maintenance woman on the planet while keeping it quiet that you'd rather be watching the Patriots under the table."

"Lyla, how do you feel about being described as high maintenance?" Paul asked.

Reading over the menu, nothing was grabbing her. "He wasn't talking about me," she muttered and took a breath. "Is soup a good thing to get when you're hungry?" Considering it, she hummed. "Never mind, I don't want bread in my system this late."

So as she went back to her reading, Lyla let the conversation between the men fade out. Trick was being obtuse, though he was clear that he'd been talking about Kira being the high maintenance one.

Paul was getting more and more pissed off by the second. "You enjoy this," Paul screamed.

Lyla kept reading. "Trick, will you eat my bacon?"

He laughed. "Damn right, baby. You don't gotta ask, just lay it out for me," he said. "Race you to the bedroom."

She clucked her tongue as she looked over her shoulder. "They put bacon in the salad. I don't want the bacon. But I don't want it going to waste."

He scrunched his fingers in her hair, his eyes shining as they fixated on her. "We'll ask them to leave it out."

"Hmm," she said, going back to the menu. "I don't want to be any trouble… one of these guys will eat it… or I could just get the chicken."

"Who gives a crap about chicken?" Paul said, his frustration making his ire rise.

"Are you shouting at my wife?" Trick asked and he didn't sound like he was having fun anymore. "Just so I have something to tell the judge, I want to be clear about what's going on before I put my fist through your face… Are you shouting at my wife?"

"Trick," she soothed, rubbing his thigh as she turned the menu over. "The steak is good here, least that's what I heard, do you want steak?" Turning around, she blinked at her husband when she saw the severity of the gaze that he was still pinning on Paul. "Baby, I'm not offended, you've riled him up… I know how infuriating you can be. I sympathize with him."

Glancing at her, Trick slid his hand up her back when she leaned forward. "Want me to stop playing with him?"

Smiling, she shook her head. "No, it's fun to watch."

Curling his finger under her chin, he bowed forward as if to kiss her. The whole room seemed to lean in and a collective breath was held.

Trick froze and his eyes brightened when they landed on hers. "Did you feel that?" he asked and she nodded before he laughed and sat back. "Damn, you guys are all pervs."

That was a good test run, she'd still had time to pull away, but he'd done it first. They'd have to kiss in front of the camera eventually. Lyla hoped they'd get to a point where they kissed without really thinking about it. Right now, every joining of their lips still seemed profound because it was so new.

Something on Trick's arm caught her eye and she gasped when she saw the angry red streaks on his shoulders that ran down his upper arm. "Oh my God," she said, grabbing for him and touching the edge of a scratch. "How did you do that?"

"Seriously?" he asked, cupping her face with one hand. "I didn't."

"Then how did…" Sorrow made her eyes fly to his. "Oh God, it was me, when we… Baby, I'm sorry!"

But conceit bled from his wide smile. "Battle scars… I wear them with pride, sweetheart."

Leaning forward, he rested his forehead on hers. It wasn't a kiss, but it was an intimate gesture from him, her man, not his character.

A knock on the door broke the moment. "It's open," Paul said. Trick must have been frowning because the director shrugged. "We unlocked it for security when we thought there was going to be a scene."

Glancing up, she saw Cliff coming around the partition and offered him a smile, but went back to her menus, feeling the pressure of deciding. The others would need to make their selections too, it wasn't right that she was monopolizing the list.

"What's going on? Shouldn't you guys all be down the stairs? I thought you were going to be at the party?" she heard Cliff ask.

"Yeah, bro, you're not the only one who expected to be at the function," Paul snapped.

The director was getting angry again. The poor guy really did put up with a lot, but if he wanted his life to be easy, he should've chosen a different career and not chosen to hang out with larger than life celebrities.

"What happened?" Cliff asked.

Maybe she should get fish. But fish from room service… would it be good fish? It would have to travel all the way from the kitchen up to the room, would it get cold or maybe it would be soggy?

Crossing her legs off the couch, she propped her fist under her chin while thinking, 'Come on, Lyla, make a decision.'

"This damn idiot happened," Paul said. "We're down there waiting with our thumbs up our asses like pricks and Trick didn't come!"

"He did," she said and when the room became silent, she lifted her eyes to Paul and then to the others. "Trick did… come…"

Oh… yeah, she'd totally read that wrong.

Turning her eyes to Trick, Lyla was sure she was blushing.

"Ha!" Trick let out a single burst of laughter and then pointed at her as he tried to straighten his grin. "Yes, I did. She's actually right about that. I did come… hard."

Letting her hand slide over her eyes, Lyla caught the weight of her head that wasn't close to the mass of her mortification. They hadn't meant that… It had been something of an achievement for her that Trick had enjoyed her so much he'd reached climax. Maybe that was what was playing in her subconscious when she'd heard Paul's statement and her response just came out of her, it just… came out.

"Oh God," she exhaled.

Trick's hand curled around the back of her neck and

he leaned in to kiss the back of her head as he gave her a single-handed massage. "Thank you, baby. You're a good wife, defending her man. Don't let them talk smack about me." He sat back, but his hand stayed on her neck. "Yep, guys, it's official. I did come… right there inside my wife."

"Trick!" she squawked and bounced away from him to twist and gape at him as she hit his thigh.

"What?" he shrugged.

Glancing at the camera, she didn't know where she should look. "We used protection."

Trick leaned in at her side, his face right against hers. "Yes, kids, this is a public service announcement: wrap it."

"Oh, Trick," she said, hitting his thigh again and using her whole upper body to push him back.

He did go to the back of the couch, but threw an arm around her to take her with him, so she was nestled into his side again.

"You had sex?" Cliff asked and sat on the arm of the couch behind Paul. "Ly, you actually had sex with him?"

"Wait a minute," Trick said like he was trying to figure something out. "You thought we were all at the party, you didn't know I didn't show."

"Yeah," Cliff said. "So?"

"Why did you come here?"

"Thought I'd check in on Lyla."

Everyone knew she wasn't really sick, even the camera would know that now. She wouldn't be sitting here talking about having sex and eating food if she was unwell. But they'd probably edit the sickness part out for the show now that it wasn't necessary.

"You thought you'd come to my private hotel room to see my wife who was here… alone? You wanted to be alone with my wife?"

"We're alone all the time," Cliff said like it was no big deal.

Trick was building to something and it made her nervous that she didn't know what it was. "Trick," she said, warning him as she put the menus aside.

"No, babe, give me a minute," he said, lifting his arm

away from her to shift to the edge of the couch and pin his focus right on Cliff. "Do you want to fuck my wife?"

"What?" Cliff snapped. "No!"

"Trick," she said and tried to reach for him, but he shifted down the couch a few inches, in Cliff's direction.

"No? So how come you wanted to film her stripping on our wedding night? Huh?" he asked and Cliff started to look worried. "Yeah, I've seen the footage… You're gonna watch your step, you bastard, 'cause I've got my eye on you and if I think you're out of line I'll knock you back into it, do you understand me?"

"Trick," she said, but he wasn't listening. No one was.

"I don't want to be with Lyla," Cliff said.

"I don't believe you," Trick said. "You're telling me if she loosened that robe…" Sitting back, he pushed her to the back of the couch and dug his hand around the knot of her belt. "What you got on under that, baby?"

"Nothing," she whispered, letting her eyes flick up to the camera before they fell again.

Trick kept his fist around the belt as he turned back to Cliff. "If she loosens that robe, lies down, and opens those hot legs for you, you're telling me you'd walk away instead of sliding yourself into her hungry pussy?"

Cliff swallowed hard, and she didn't even know what to say or how to respond, outrage seemed too mild.

"You're being a dick," Paul said. "Lyla's stacked, okay? We all admit that. There's plenty of guys who'd do her, Cliff's no different."

Trick threw his head back in a sinister laugh. "Oh, that's goddamn great, so every guy in here wants to fuck my wife?" Taking his glare from Cliff, to Paul, and then to the other two, his tension was making her nervous. "Do you? Huh? You want to do her? Do you?"

Trick actually seemed to be waiting for the sound guy to answer.

"Trick," she said, trying to keep her voice soft.

He grabbed her arm and pulled her forward to the edge of the couch beside him and yanked her spine to his chest. "What is it you like best?" he projected the question to the room.

Sweeping her hair away from her neck, he was rough about yanking her head to the side and when his mouth closed around her carotid, she gasped. "Trick."

"It's okay, baby. I got ya," he whispered, the others would've heard it and they would see the way her pulse point was racing in her throat as her husband ran his lips down the side of her neck. "You like this, boys? This what you want to see? You want more?" His hands ran up her arms to the lapels of her robe and he gripped it tight before tugging it open, not all the way, just enough to expose a triangle of her upper chest. Pushing the heels of his hands into her breasts through the robe, he pushed them up and together, giving the room an eyeful of cleavage. "Open your legs, baby, they want a show."

"Trick!" she called out and thrust her elbow back into his ribs. He let go and she shot to her feet, spinning around and gathering her robe back together. "You just don't have any limits at all, do you?"

Marching away from the group, Lyla went into the bedroom, making a big show of slamming the door and locking it.

He wasn't going to spend the night with her.

Things had just been so good and then he'd turned. Which meant one thing… He wasn't ready to share her.

Being the prick, going over the top, he was making sure the world knew he'd been stuck on the couch… again.

SEVENTEEN

IT TOOK TOO LONG to get rid of the crew.

Trick wanted to kick them out the minute Lyla slammed the bedroom door, but they lingered. They kept on filming for quite a while, probably trying to catch Lyla coming back out of the bedroom.

She didn't.

Good.

He didn't want her to.

He wanted her to stay in there. Safe away from the lens that scrutinized them. But he'd never felt like this, so hollow and sick and disgusted. It was difficult to push her at the best of times, now he'd just pledged to be a decent guy and he'd gone and done… that.

Lying in the dark on his back on the couch, he covered his eyes with the back of his wrist. He probably wouldn't be getting much sleep, he just wished he knew that she was sleeping. If she was sleeping, she was relaxed, and there was a chance she didn't hate him.

A small chance.

A tiny one.

Paul had spoken about setting up a static camera in

the room, luckily, they hadn't brought any because no one had assumed that the couple would be getting it on. The couple being first on that list.

Lyla hadn't eaten. She hadn't gotten her shower either. She'd been locked up in that bedroom for two hours.

Paul and the others eventually left after he assured them he'd call with any developments or if there was a chance of sex. He wouldn't. But it didn't take much to persuade them that Lyla was pissed.

She usually pushed away from him and often squealed his name with outrage, but she never threw any comments at him, not like she had tonight.

Trick couldn't help but replay the words in his mind. Had she meant them for the show, or had they been for him? If he'd hurt her, really hurt her, he'd never forgive himself. He just wouldn't. He wouldn't even argue if she wanted to dump his ass and split, he'd deserve it.

When the bedroom door opened, he didn't move. If she needed the bathroom or wanted to go for a shower, he wasn't going to start up with her. The woman deserved some breathing space and that meant he'd live with his own torment and give her peace.

"Trick," she murmured.

His arm slid away from his head, but with him on his back on the couch, they couldn't actually see each other. "Yeah?"

"Come to bed."

What?

Sitting upright, he looked over the back of the couch, but she was already gone. The bedroom door was open but vacant. Had he just dreamed that? Leaping up from the couch, Trick wasn't about to take the risk that it hadn't been real.

Rushing to the bedroom, he saw her there, sitting up in the middle of the bed, scooting over to the opposite side as she pulled the covers back on the empty side. "Babe?" he asked, staying near the door in case she decided to throw something at him.

"Come to bed," she said, sliding down beneath the comforter to rest her head on her folded hands on the pillow.

She was wearing the baggy white dress thing she'd been wearing when she slathered that lotion stuff all over her body, driving him crazy with the same scent of coconut he recognized from the shampoo that infused her hair.

"You… you want me to come to bed with you?"

"It's got to be more comfortable than the couch," she said. "You don't have to touch me if you don't want to."

She sounded serious enough. Damn, his woman just kept surprising him over and over. Dashing to the bed, he leapt onto it and shifted over, right to the middle and dropped his head onto her pillow with hers. She laughed. Oh, that sound… He loved making her laugh.

"And if I do want to?" he asked, his hand hovering over her hip.

"Did they leave cameras or audio—"

"No," he soothed, lifting his hand to her face to brush the back of his fingers over her cheek. "I'm sorry I was a prick, babe. I—"

"I know why you did it," she said, taking his hand and directing it around to her back so she could move against him. "You did that so we could do this… alone."

Squeezing his eyes shut, Trick didn't lose his guilt, but was washed by relief. "How did I get with such a smart cookie?"

"I felt… nervous… but I knew you'd never really expose my body to anyone… would you?"

"What? No! Of course not, baby. I can't share you. I can't do it… As soon as I heard Paul coming I knew I'd do whatever I could to protect this… I'm sorry if I scared you. Babe, I know I go too far, but I get into that—"

"I think a part of me liked it." Wow, okay, so this was what stunned silence felt like. "Is that… bad?"

"Nothing that turns you on is bad," he said and was stoked that she was sharing her sexual feelings with him so openly. "What was it you liked about it?" Because if he knew, he'd be sure to do it again.

"I always assumed that any time you were being possessive it was because of the camera, you know, it made great television. But tonight I… I thought maybe you might…"

"Mean it?" he asked, pulling her closer to him in hope that she might feel the boner pulsing between them and react in a way that would give him the green light… or not. "I do mean it. I don't want any guy trying to move in on you. That bastard snuck up here when he knew I wouldn't be here, 'cause he knew you were alone and vulnerable."

"I wasn't actually sick," she said and when she opened her mouth on his throat, he had to close his eyes and remind himself to be patient.

"You're always vulnerable, sweetheart. Least you were until you had me. From now on, any guy asks for your number, you give him mine instead."

She wriggled even closer. "Give him your number?" she asked and laughed. "How would that work?"

"Easy, I'll tell him I'm your pimp and organize somewhere to meet."

"Why would I want to meet him?" she asked.

This was exactly why she was vulnerable, she just didn't get it. "You wouldn't," he said, rubbing his mouth in her hair. "I would. Me and my boys."

"I can't condone violence," she said. "You shouldn't be hitting people."

"Sometimes a scare is enough," he said. "But I reserve the right to do whatever I want if any bastard pushes me too far."

As he felt himself getting angry about any guy who might try to touch his precious Lyla, he felt something damp against his chest.

Damn, was that her tongue?

Green light.

Skimming one hand down her back, he let it settle over the rise of her gorgeous ass and began to gather up her nightdress. "How do you feel about sleeping naked?"

"I might get cold."

"In my bed?" he asked and snickered. "Not gonna happen."

"You're not naked," she said, and when her hand skimmed his hip to curve around his ass, he swore under his breath.

Lyla didn't usually touch him. Her confidence was growing and that meant he was in trouble. The more they did this. The closer they got. The more she'd touch him. His control was frayed enough already without her exploring him.

Flipping onto his back, Trick wanted to whip off his underwear as fast as possible so she didn't have to be out of his arms for a second longer than was necessary. "Am now," he said, flipping to his front, he scooped her beneath him.

It felt so good that her legs opened automatically for him and settling between them was like coming home. But he wasn't going to bury himself inside her yet, they had unfinished business. He'd figured out that kissing her made her relax. So he occupied her mouth with his and went to work lifting her nightdress up over her hips. He'd keep on going and pull the damn thing off, if it didn't mean he'd have to stop kissing her.

"Nairn," she whispered, when he slid his fingers through the seam of her body.

Because she was pushing and stroking his chest, he deduced that she liked his torso. Good. The more things she liked, the more likely she'd be to stay with him. He wasn't beyond manipulation or blackmail. If he needed to use either to keep the woman he loved, he'd do it.

"Love?" he asked and her eyes slipped up to his, why did she look so grateful? "I do love you, Lyla."

"I know," she said. When she smiled, he began to massage her clit again and tried to kiss her, but she inhaled and gave him another push. "I'm a bit… sore…" Hell, he'd hurt her, exactly what he didn't want to do. "It's okay." Smoothing her hands up his body, she stroked his face. She was just so delicate, so gentle with him. Everything she did felt so tender, like he was precious to her. No one touched him like that. "I like it. It reminds me of what we did, but… can we go slow?"

Slow? If she was in pain, his dick wasn't going anywhere near her pussy, not until she was completely ready for him again. He wouldn't cause her pain, wasn't capable of it.

"How about you trust me to make you feel good?" he

asked and stole a kiss before crawling down her body, kissing his route south.

Her whole body tensed when he kissed her clit, but he slid his hands up over her torso, beneath her nightdress to her breasts. Massaging and reassuring her, he carried on with his feast. She'd get used to having him down here, and she'd learn that even when sex wasn't an option, he could make her feel good because he was dedicated to her in every way a man should be dedicated to his wife.

EIGHTEEN

THEY HADN'T MADE LOVE again last night, but that didn't stop Trick from taking her to climax after climax. Lyla hadn't admitted to him that no man had ever used his mouth on her before he did. Now she felt like a veteran. But he didn't just use his mouth. He used his hands, his fingers and his penis, letting her wriggle and writhe all over him to lose herself in the bliss of orgasm.

When she woke up to him kissing her, she'd asked him to make love to her again, and he did after a little pleading on her part. He was so preoccupied with the idea that he might hurt her that he was reluctant. What he didn't get was that she liked the feeling of him stretching her. It was overwhelming, just like him and the emotions he was invoking in her.

Taking his sweet time, he wouldn't push too hard or be too rough, and it was the most incredible way to welcome the day. They'd literally just come when Paul came storming in to the suite again. Trick had leapt out of bed, grabbed his own robe and ran out without telling her the plan.

She overheard Trick greeting Paul and deliberately glazing over all their director's questions about any intimacies they might have shared since he left.

Breakfast was brought to the room because they had a long day ahead.

The hotel was on the outskirts of a national park, so this morning, they'd all been piled onto the bus for a quick journey up through the park to the two-story outdoor center, which was built to resemble an old stone fort.

Their directors were talking to the guides while everyone rambled around. They'd all been given proper hiking boots, told to wear jeans, layers, and provided with a waterproof jacket which had a hood and a whole bunch of pockets.

"I don't know how to read a compass," Sadie said coming over to where Lyla was sitting on one of the concrete picnic tables erected outside the fort.

The producer, who wasn't here as a producer but as one of Trick's colleagues, was looking at the plastic device that she was holding up in the air like a cell phone.

Standing on the bench, Lyla turned Sadie and put her arm around her to reposition the compass flat. "Just keep turning until the needle points north," Lyla said, looking at the compass over Sadie's shoulder.

"How do I know which way to turn?" Sadie asked, going clockwise, then counter-clockwise.

Lyla laughed. "It doesn't matter, you'll get there eventually."

While still wrapped around Sadie, Lyla could only go so far before she came to the edge of the bench and when they got to that limit, both women laughed. "What's all the hilarity?" Trick asked, coming over. "There's to be no jokes I'm not in on."

Sadie took her eyes from the compass to glance at him. "Lyla's making my needle point north," she said.

Trick got to them and leaned in to whisper to his friend. "Don't beat yourself up, she does the same thing to mine."

Sadie tutted and exhaled, but took the bottle of water Trick handed her, and turned around to face Lyla. Lyla sat back down on the table, keeping her feet on the bench, and took the bottle Trick gave her as he went to the head of the table to prop his ass against it.

"This place is beautiful," Sadie said, looking up at the building behind Lyla. "I wonder if they do weddings."

Trick finished gulping his water and twisted the cap back on. "Who are you marrying? I thought Adam went to Poland… and he was never going to marry you… just saying."

"Ukraine," Sadie said. "He left three months ago. I'm just, you know, for… whenever."

"Well I recommend it," Trick said, leaning back to bump Lyla's arm with his back. "Marriage is great."

Sadie smiled. "You've got that big, 'I just got laid' smile on your face, it's been there all day."

Trick shrugged. "Won't see me hiding it. I'm happy. Who'd have thought it, huh? That I'd be married before you… Watch out for spinsterhood, Say, that shit sneaks up on a girl."

"Uh," Lyla said, her head coming up from reading the back of the water bottle. "I'm offended."

"You?" Sadie asked. "I'm the singleton."

"Trick didn't marry me because he loved me, he did it because he thought it was a lark," Lyla said. "I would say 'ouch' except I only did it because…"

Trick twisted toward them so he could look at her. "That's a point, I never asked, why did you do this?"

Hmm, well, she picked at the edge of her label. "Because the Cronies said I never took risks, never had adventures, and because… they said the only man who'd sleep with me was a fifty-year-old virgin who lived in his mom's basement."

"Look good for your age," Sadie said to Trick, then turned to her. "The Cronies, that's what you call them?"

"Faith, Dinah, and Chelsea from my department," she said. "I call them that in my head—but I don't mean it as a way to disparage them, no. The word 'crony' comes from the Greek language, it's a beautiful language, it's like art when you see it written on the page… I need to take the time to really study it. I've always wanted to visit Greece. It's a gorgeous country, beautiful beaches and the history… The period of Classical Ancient Greece has been of particular interest to me for a long time, that's around 800 to 500 B.C, give or take… There were major advances in art and technology during that time period. It's surprising to know how much of their culture reverberates through to ours. Oh, and one for you, Trick, honey, they held the first Olympic Games in 776… B.C., of course… though there is evidence to suggest they actually started before then. The games were held in honor of Zeus and carried on for hundreds of years. All contestants were male… and nudity was common." Smiling at Sadie, Lyla shrugged. "If I can relate something to sex or sport, it's more likely to stick in his mind.

"Anyway, the word 'crony' means long-term, and those three have been friends forever, far as I can tell they're friends anyway." Frowning at the trio who were loitering at the edge of the pack, Lyla wondered at their internal politics. "They're always together, but sometimes it feels like they don't like each other that much, I don't know, I don't understand it."

"You're too nice to understand women like that," Trick said, folding his arms.

Sadie was staring at her, but Lyla didn't notice until she spoke. "You know that in your head?"

Lyla hadn't thought about it and didn't have time to say anything because Trick spoke with a grin in his voice. "Hot as hell, isn't she? Keep your hands off, she's mine."

"Really? You know all that," Sadie said and looked at each of their faces. "What the hell do you two talk about?"

"I don't need to say anything," Trick said and uncapped his water bottle. "I could listen to her talk all night."

As he lifted the bottle to his lips, Lyla put her hand on his. "Don't drink it all. We'll have to get physical. Save some for after."

The instant joy and innuendo on his face made her sag, she'd done it again, said a stupid thing. "You got it, baby. Stand back, everyone, husband emergency! I got this one," he said, prodding his water bottle at Sadie who grabbed it just before Trick hooked Lyla's closest leg and thrust it straight up in the air to put her on her back and twist her around so her ass was at the head of the table where he'd been propped. "Damn jeans, no problem, I can work around 'em." As his hands went to work unfastening his own jeans, he bowed his forehead to hers, "How do you feel about doggy style?"

"Trick!" Sadie was the one who called out his name this time and the exclamation made him straighten.

"Okay, everyone, if I can have your attention?"

The guide from the outdoor center was moving to the middle of the scattered group with his hands in the air and a clipboard held aloft. Sadie turned and took a few strides toward the guide.

Trick opened his mouth and inhaled, Lyla sat up so fast that her body hit his. "Don't," she said, pressing a finger to his lips to silence him.

She just knew that her husband was going to make a joke and draw attention to them. Their eyes met and suddenly she couldn't hear, or focus properly. What was wrong with her? They'd had sex. Sitting on a concrete table with him between her thighs shouldn't be making her awareness grow in time with the speed of her heart.

Her leg curled around his and she saw her hand coiling around the side of his neck before she even knew it had moved.

Turning her nails into the back of his neck, she felt the pressure of them digging in and winced. "Sorry," she whispered and relaxed her hand. "I don't know why I keep doing that."

Bowing toward her, Trick brushed his nose over hers. "Because it feels good, baby. It's passion, it makes you want to put your mark on me and I love it… I told you, there are no rules for you, no limits, no boundaries to what you're allowed to do to me."

"But I don't want to hurt you," she whispered.

Tipping his head, he made hers move with his until their lips were just a fraction apart. "Then don't ever leave me," he murmured.

The words hit her hard. He meant them. This relationship was everything to him. Some of his own vulnerability showed as his eyes closed and she realized she hadn't returned his enthusiasm. In bed, sure, he had her, but she hadn't told him how she really felt about him.

"What do you think about Greece?" she asked.

"The movie?" he asked, scooping his hands around her ass to pull her closer to him.

It didn't take him long to switch back into playful mode. "The country," she said. "Maybe we could go one day. Maybe in spring, after the show's done."

Bending his knees, he kept her ass in his hands as he got lower. "For real?"

"They have nightclubs," she said and had to half-shrug. "I've never been in a nightclub, but yeah… I'm sure they have them."

He was grinning. "You'd come to a club for me?"

"If you'd come to the Acropolis with me," she said.

Trick laughed. "I don't even know what that is, but if you're there, I'll be with you… It could be our honeymoon."

"We had a honeymoon."

He sneered. "Nah, it doesn't count if there's no sex."

Laughing, she leaned back. "So you expect to go clubbing and…"

"Get laid?" he asked. "Yep, if there are no cameras, you have no excuses."

That was true. If there were no cameras, she didn't have any reason to say no… and wouldn't want to. "Uh, excuse me! Mr. Strickland!"

Trick didn't pay attention to the guide who was shouting at him because he was too busy trying to kiss her. Lyla had to lean back and give him a push. "Honey, that man is talking to you," she said because she didn't know the guide's name.

"Not possible," Trick said, trying to kiss her again. "We're the only two people on Earth."

Laughing, Lyla pressed both hands to his shoulders and straightened her arms to put space between them. Trick growled and turned toward the guy who was closer than he had been, and had drawn the attention of the whole group to their private conversation.

Though "private" was a relative term. The cameras were on and had been for most of the morning though the crew were keeping their distance.

"I'm sorry, sir, we need everyone to be safe," the guide said.

One of Trick's hands slid off her ass, but he kept the other arm hooked over her shoulders. "It's okay. We're married. We're both clean and open to the idea of children, so, thanks man, but we're good with the protection thing."

She shouldn't laugh and didn't know what the camera was picking up, so she turned her head away to hide her face. It probably appeared that she was embarrassed, which was good because it fit with her role in the performance. But she was too used to Trick and his ways now, so she actually found his behavior funny not offensive.

"Oh, no, I…" The guide sounded mortified, Trick really knew how to embarrass people, he'd done it to her enough, but she was accustomed to it now, others weren't as lucky. "I mean, we need a demonstration."

Trick exhaled impatience and sagged before straightening, like the suggestion was a major inconvenience. "Okay, fine, man, but you owe me. I'm not packing rubbers, so you'll have to provide, and she's wearing jeans, so are we all okay if I come at her from behind?"

"Trick," Lyla said, and frowned at him as she gave his shoulder a slap.

"What?" Trick asked, exuding innocence. "The guy asked for a safety demonstration."

"Not a safe sex demonstration," she hissed at him then smiled past him at the guide. "I'm sorry for him. Really." Scanning the group, she saw some smiling faces who were amused and others who were shocked, like the Cronies. "He can't help but… be him."

Nuzzling his face against her temple, Trick let his lips slide around to her ear. "There's something hot about you apologizing for me."

His breath tickled her neck, making her shiver. "You think everything's hot," she murmured.

"Everything about you, sure."

Sadie cleared her throat. "Maybe you two should, uh…"

"Get a room?" Trick asked. "What is it with me

having to finish women's sentences these days?"

Lyla nudged him. "I think she meant we should cool it and stop being rude. Sit down there."

"What?" he gaped. "You're benching me?"

But he didn't argue, just stomped the step to drop onto the bench her feet had been on when she was sitting here initially. Folding his arms, Trick slouched back against the table, grumbling to himself. But Lyla wasn't punishing him and to prove it, she brought her legs onto the table and twisted to hook her knees over his shoulders.

He didn't expect her to do something so physical, or intimate, but he welcomed it by curving his hands around her shins. When he tried to tip his head back to look at her, Lyla put her hands on his face and directed it toward the guide, then when Trick was looking at the guy, she ran her fingers through her husband's hair then let her hands slide down his body until her chest was on his head. Holding him firm like this meant he'd keep his eyes front, which was what everyone wanted.

"We're listening," Lyla said to the guide and smiled. "Please carry on."

Everyone was given a whistle to go with their compass and the guide gave instructions on what they should do if they got lost or hurt because cell phone coverage was non-existent out here.

The guide was coming to the end of his speech. "I'll call out a name and that person will pick their partner for the day. You are responsible for your partner's safety. If anything happens to them it's your responsibility to stay with them, keep them calm and provide any medical care that's required. You must not leave your partner alone, not for any reason. Pairs will each be given a map, and on the map are three checkpoints. You must find the checkpoints, retrieve the ribbon, and move to the next checkpoint before you return here to this rendezvous. Right here. Some checkpoints are individual, others will overlap. Some people will hit all the same checkpoints, some will have one or two checkpoints that overlap. Every pair will set out with another pair, but may split ways for the second or third checkpoints. The four of you may help each other, but you must maintain your link to your original partner at all times."

Trick turned his face toward her knee. "We have to maintain our link, did you hear that? How does he know about our link? Do you think they need pictures? I guess he's not an advocate for the pull-out method."

"Trick," Lyla murmured, burying her face in the top of his head. "You're not listening to the man. He's trying to keep all of us alive."

"Uh, hello? Husband," he said, clutching her legs tighter, squeezing them around his head. "I'll keep you alive… We should do some mouth-to-mouth practice though, just in case."

"So when I call out your name, simply state who you want to be paired with," the guide said, consulting his clipboard. "Kira Levine!"

Why shouldn't one of the most beautiful women in the world be first? She'd been on the bus this morning, but Trick had stayed with Lyla. Even when Lyla tried to get him to talk to his ex, to at least apologize for standing her up, he wouldn't. As much as Lyla appreciated his loyalty, it wasn't really fair to Kira that she'd been brought here and then messed around.

"Trick," Kira said and strode into view on the other side of the seating area behind the guide.

"Could've seen that one coming," Sadie said, returning to them and seating herself next to Trick.

"Okay," the guide said, taking notes and calling out another name.

Lyla started to open her legs to free Trick, but he snatched them and pulled them closed around him. "Don't you dare," Trick said, maintaining eye contact with the model who was fixated on him, waiting. "I'm not going nowhere."

Combing her fingers through his hair, Lyla kissed his head. "Don't make a scene. You're the only person here who she really knows," Lyla said. "I'm not getting into a cat fight. It's one day, you can be polite, go on, go to her."

He hissed. "I hate how you say that," he said, but exhaled and let her move her legs away from his body.

Turning around to show her his displeasure, Trick's eyes sank to her mouth. Lyla stood on the bench and bent over to put her arms around him before smacking a kiss to his cheek and whispering in his ear. "Don't have sex with her."

Trick knew she was joking because he smirked out a fake and unimpressed, laugh. "If that Tony guy says your name I'll put him in traction before I'll let him walk an inch out of my eyeline with you," he said, backing away.

"Sadie Lawrence!" the guide called out as Trick turned to march over to Kira.

"I'll go with Lyla," Sadie said, picking up Lyla's hand.

"Thank you," Lyla said as the guide noted down the pairing. "I thought it was going to be like gym when whoever was left was just stuck with me."

Sadie nodded to the Cronies. "Looks like there are some issues over there. Guess it doesn't pay to have an odd number in your group," she said, then turned to Trick and Kira. "He's really pissed off."

"I don't see why," Lyla said. "Kira hasn't done anything wrong."

"Oh, come on," Sadie said. "You two have been all over each other all morning, then the first chance she gets, she throws a spanner in the works."

"Please don't forget that I'm miked," Lyla said, pushing her chest toward Sadie who glanced down at the device attached to her jacket.

"Hey, the point of reality TV is to be real," Sadie said and leaned down to the microphone. "Kira Levine is a brat who deserves to be taken down a peg or two."

The guide finished pairing everyone. They were given a new bottle of water and a chance to use the restroom. Paul was talking to the guide when Lyla came back from the bathroom and Sadie came over with their map.

"Do you know how to read maps?" Sadie asked.

Sheesh, this was going to be a day. In a world of modern technology, the participants today were going to struggle. Some were already trying to open the maps in their phones, but it didn't matter, they didn't have GPS coordinates and there was no signal to patch into the satellites.

The map was in a plastic pouch that was around Sadie's neck. They'd have their work cut out today, the map print was small and it gave her an idea. "Trick has a Swiss Army thing on his keys."

Weaving through the other groups who were all poring over their maps, Lyla approached Trick from behind. "I don't care, Kira, I really don't," Trick was saying.

"I think you do, or I think you should," Kira drawled.

"Uh, excuse me," Lyla said, hesitant to interrupt, but she also didn't want to be accused of eavesdropping.

Trick turned around and his fed-up expression became happy. "Babe. Did you miss me?"

"Desperately," she said, her eyes flicked to Kira, but she didn't want to stare, so returned her focus to Trick. "Do you have your house keys on you?"

"My house keys?" he asked. "No. They're at the hotel. Why? Are we making a break for it? 'Cause we can swing by—"

"No. No problem," Lyla said and turned away to see Sadie approaching with Paul and the camera crews, both of them.

"Turns out we're on the same path for the first two checkpoints," Sadie said as she got closer.

Of course they were. It made sense now why Paul had spent time with the guide, they were matching up the group, Lyla probably should've seen that coming. Everyone began to head off in different directions, and the four of them had no choice but to go together.

With one camera crew far in front and another behind, everyone was miked before they started the trek, but it took a good five minutes of walking before anyone spoke. They were on a worn grassy path with a ditch on either side and trees flanking them.

"So, Trick," Kira said, her voice was slow and sultry, perfect for seduction, but her accent was too manufactured to be real. "Your dick's been in every pussy here... does that make this awkward for you?"

"Nope," Trick said.

Lyla and Kira hadn't been formally introduced. But

Lyla didn't mind foregoing that mortifying pleasure. Introductions would be a bit of an insult to the successful model, shouldn't everyone in the country know who Kira Levine was? And who was Lyla? A nobody as far as Kira was concerned.

"What about you Lyla, is it awkward for you?" Kira asked.

"Kira," Trick warned.

But Lyla wasn't intimidated, she switched on her ability to let rude comments roll off. Kira wanted a reaction, so the last thing Lyla was going to do was give her one. "No," Lyla said, but didn't stop there. "And to be fair to Trick, I don't imagine this situation is unique… Every time he goes into a nightclub there are probably several women he's had trysts with… And we're all adults here."

Kira wasn't deterred. "But it must be difficult to know that your husband has such a… colorful past."

"I can't judge him for where he's been," Lyla said. "I wasn't around for any of that. We didn't know each other… The only thing I care about is the future and what he does from here on out."

"But on the show, on your wedding night, he was—"

"We were strangers," Lyla said and smiled.

The path narrowed, so Lyla and Sadie fell back to walk behind Kira and Trick. "Other women would not be so understanding," Kira said, casting a glance over her shoulder.

"If I were the same as every other woman on the planet, Trick might not feel for me the way he does."

Trick laughed. "Oh, snap, baby," he said. "She's got a point, Key, so just drop it, okay?"

Kira and Trick exchanged a few more comments between themselves before Sadie took Lyla's arm and drew her to a stop. When she glanced at those in front, Lyla guessed they were waiting for some distance to grow before they spoke.

"Are you okay?" Lyla asked her partner. The rear camera crew was a good twenty feet away and had stopped when they had. The front crew would focus on Trick and Kira who were still walking and probably hadn't noticed that the women had stopped.

"Are you really okay with it?" Sadie asked, seeming confused and shocked at the same time. Lyla smiled and nodded. "I didn't even know that you knew about Trick and me."

"He told me," Lyla said and then shrugged. "Well, I asked him… it was pretty obvious."

"Pretty… how was it obvious?"

"It's in the way you talk about him, you just… you know."

Sadie was taken aback and opened her mouth then huffed and closed it as she tried to figure Lyla out. "I know what?"

"The effect he has on women," Lyla said. "You get this look in your eyes."

Sadie's mouth opened and she paled. "I don't… I don't feel anything toward him now, I mean we're friends, I care about him, but… there's nothing between us."

"I know that," Lyla said with a nod. She really wasn't stressed, no matter how much everyone else wished she would be.

"How are you so cool with this?" Sadie asked like she just couldn't get a grasp on how calm Lyla was.

"Look, this is the way it is," Lyla said. "I can't ask him to apologize for a past that I wasn't a part of. Sure, there are times I worry that I won't live up to the thrills he's had before. But when it comes to specific women and will he, won't he?" Biting her lip, Lyla tried to figure out how she could make it clear, but didn't really have the language, so she just exhaled and turned her eyes back to Sadie. "If he's going to screw around, then he's going to. If he's going to dump me, then he's going to. Would I be heartbroken? Sure. But… I have to enjoy him while I have him. I can't stress about what might or might not happen, and if I start driving him crazy with my paranoia, I'll kill the relationship. If I have worries, I tell him what they are. But I try to be sensible about it."

Sadie folded her arms, assessing her friend's wife. "I have noticed, you know."

"Noticed what?"

"That he's different, he's different with you."

She hoped in a good way. "I can't speak to that. I didn't know him before me, did I?"

"You knew the stories, the media portrayal," Sadie said and when Lyla dropped her eyes and smiled, Sadie got closer, making Lyla look up at her.

The women shared a moment of silence, just examining each other and slowly Sadie smiled too. They both knew it. The Trick that played up to the camera wasn't the same one that made them smile like this. They both loved him, in different ways, and tolerating, or playing with, the character was part of embracing him.

"Yo, what's the problem?" Trick's voice carried from further up the path and they both turned to catch up. It took them a minute, but as they got closer, Lyla read the concern in his eyes and it didn't lessen even after she smiled. "You okay?" he asked her when she got within ten feet. "If you need something, sweetheart, we can go back to the—"

Reaching up, Lyla closed her hands around his face and pulled him down. He came without any fight and she closed her eyes as she opened her mouth under his. The camera could have their field day and the public wanted love. But all she wanted to do was show her man how proud she was of him.

He wrapped his arms around her and pulled her off her feet when she touched his tongue with hers. Squeezing her tighter and tighter as their fervor grew, Trick held her close, making it hard for her to breathe, but all these layers between them would be frustrating him.

When her head fell back, she moaned and threw her arms around his neck, as he kissed her throat once. "Okay, I wasn't expecting that," Sadie said.

Trick rubbed his cheek against her neck before Lyla brought her head forward and pushed on his shoulders to ask for her feet back. "Thanks, Say," Trick said, keeping his arms around his wife. "Whatever you said to her down there, it worked."

This time when he tried to kiss her, Lyla let their lips

touch, but she kept it short. "I didn't say anything that would warrant… that," Sadie said.

"I kind of like that no one gets it," Lyla said, smiling at her husband. "And shocking people is kind of fun."

"You sure shocked me… and feel free to do that any time," he said and lowered to kiss her, but she bowed back.

When he groaned, she laughed, he'd just never know what he'd get with her in any given minute. "Can I have a ride?" she asked and his brow crooked as he lifted his gaze to the woods behind her. "A piggy-back ride."

"Not as fun as what I was thinking, but sure," he said and turned around to let her leap up onto his back.

"Uh, he's my partner and I have to look out for his wellbeing," Kira said as they started to walk again. "And I really think that if he's carrying anyone, it should be me."

"And she's the only one allowed to suck his dick, so yeah, she gets priority, deal with it, Kira," Sadie said.

Locking her arms around Trick's neck, Lyla rubbed her face in his hair and opened her hands on his jacket. But she didn't want to feel the fabric, so she fumbled for the zip and pulled it down to the middle of his chest then unbuttoned the shirt he had on underneath. She knew he was wearing a vest and a tee-shirt, but still moved her lips to the back of his ear.

"Tell me if you get cold," she said, sliding her flat hands inside his shirt to spread them on the planes of his warm, hard chest.

Lyla hadn't meant for this to be intimate, but she kissed behind his ear, then kissed him again, and again. She'd been on the receiving end of his neck kisses and knew how good they felt. She hadn't realized it would feel good to give them.

Boosting higher, she used his grip on her thighs as her anchor point to slide her hands deeper into his shirt and reach more of his neck with her mouth.

"Is this a team-building exercise or a dirty vacation?" Kira sneered.

"When my wife's around, my thoughts are never far from dirty," he said.

"She's all over you," Kira said. "Does she know there are other people here? I thought this show of yours was in trouble because she didn't want you."

Lyla stopped kissing her husband.

Paul wouldn't mind that being stated because anything could be cut in editing, but she didn't like the way Kira said it. The show portrayed her as a prude, Lyla knew that, and she'd learned to adopt that role in front of the cameras. Now that she'd been intimate with Trick, she didn't feel so inhibited, she felt… free, and it was enlivening to think she might get to explore the sexuality she'd always kept closed off inside herself.

But, the cameras were rolling. Oops. "Put me down," Lyla said, pushing at Trick's shoulders.

"No," Trick said, squeezing her thighs tighter. "She's just being a bitch, baby. Ignore her. You kiss me any damn place you like."

"She's jealous," Sadie said.

"I'm not," Kira said. "Why the hell would I be jealous? I could've had him if I wanted him."

"Oh, really?" Trick asked on a disbelieving laugh. "When are we talking about? 'Cause I don't remember ever thinking about proposing to you."

"You didn't propose to her," Kira said and laughed. "Your manager probably did, or Sadie."

"You want to see me propose to her? You want to see—"

Lyla planted her hand over his mouth. "Okay, everyone needs to calm down. This is silly. Kira, I apologize if I made you uncomfortable. You're absolutely right that my behavior is inappropriate. Trick, put me down, please." He stopped, but didn't let her down. "Please, Trick. Just behave for a minute." Grumbling, he bent his knees and put her on her feet, but he immediately pulled her to his side. "Let's just all work together to find these checkpoints and avoid talking about personal issues."

No one agreed with her, but no one argued either. It was going to take a lot to get this group working together, but for the sake of the camera, Lyla had to keep her cool and forget about her intimacy with Trick for the day. She had to remember her role and it wasn't to be a woman in the throes of early passion.

Her role in this show was to be smart and sensible. Smart and sensible women didn't grab men and kiss them. No, they read the map, helped with directions, and gave everyone a chance to participate... and they kept their mouths to themselves.

NINETEEN

TRICK HAD BEEN LIKE a petulant child when it came time for them to separate. They'd managed to find two checkpoints together as a group, but the third was different for the two pairs. She and Sadie had to go one way, while Trick and Kira went the other.

But he'd loitered on the path and when Lyla went to check if he was okay, he kissed her and held her close, refusing to let her go. Eventually, he had to, because the day was getting on.

She and Sadie found their marker and were back somewhere in the middle of the pack. Trick and Kira were dead last, not by a short amount of time either, they were back almost an hour after everyone else. While Lyla joked about Trick having to make an entrance, he didn't laugh, and he wasn't in a good mood.

Her husband wasn't in a good mood for the journey back or throughout the group dinner. She didn't understand, but didn't have time to question him.

When they returned to the suite, she got together the items she needed for her shower and went into the bathroom to wash her hair while the crew set up the equipment Trick needed to host Boys Night from right there in their suite.

Tonight, Boys Night was a live one-off Wednesday night special, except, Trick wasn't there in the studio. So, the crew for Opposites were setting up a camera, lights, and two laptops to let him Skype into the studio with the guys. Everything was being setup on the coffee table to face the armchair at the end of the table, with the window behind it.

The position was good. Lyla wondered if Trick had picked it because no one would be able to see into the room, no chance of anything "extra" being picked up if the camera wasn't turned off in time.

Lyla hadn't meant to be so long in the bathroom, and by the time she came out, Trick was alone in the armchair. But with his elbow on the arm of the chair and his scowl aimed at the coffee table, she didn't think he was on air yet.

Glancing at the clock, she saw that there was still some time. She'd intended just to sneak into the bedroom where she was going to read while he worked. But that face wasn't of the fun-loving Trick needed for Boys Night.

She got worried. "I'm wearing your tee-shirt," she said, tiptoeing toward him. "Is that okay?"

"Hmm?" he asked and lifted his head to look at her. "Oh, yeah, babe, whatever you want."

When he sank forward and planted his hands on his forehead as he propped his elbows on his knees, she knew something was wrong. "Trick," she said, but he didn't move.

Creeping toward him, she checked that the light on the camera was off. It was. The light would come on when the camera was recording and transmitting. The first laptop on the table beneath would show Trick what the studio were seeing of him here in the room, right now it was on a test screen. The other laptop would show the studio, the guys, what was being broadcast to the public and that was on a test screen too.

Putting a hand to his shoulder, Lyla startled him by pushing him back in the seat and sinking onto his lap. "Babe, I only have a few minutes."

With her hands on his cheeks, she used her thumbs to turn his lips up at the corners. "Where's this guy?" she asked. Her slight concern became full-blown panic when she tried to kiss him and he turned his mouth down. "Nairn?"

"How come you ran away from me today, huh?" he asked. "You leaped off my back, and said your behavior was inappropriate, how come you did that? You asked if I was embarrassed to be with you. I never asked if you were embarrassed to be with me."

"What?" she exhaled. "Are you playing with me?"

"Playing?" he snapped. "No, I'm not playing. Tell me, are you embarrassed about us?"

How could he even think that? "No! God, baby, no," she said, cupping his face to stop him from looking away. "No, I... I didn't ask you to put me down because I didn't want to be up there. I didn't even do it because of Kira. I did it because..."

"Why?" he barked, his eyes dark with anger. "Why did you do it? I get you pushing me away if I'm a prick, but I did nothing, nothing that—"

"Hey," she said, smiling and pressing her mouth onto his even though his didn't respond. "I'm not embarrassed to be with you, Trick. I love you."

His anger vanished and shock took its place. "You... you love me?"

Nodding, she couldn't stop her grin from spreading. "And I'm so proud of us."

"Then why did you—"

"Because it suddenly occurred to me that I had my own character to play and kissing you, jumping on you, that's not what my character does... not all of a sudden."

Relaxing, he seemed to be considering this. "You weren't embarrassed?"

"No," she said. "I kissed you because I'm proud of you, because I was tired of hiding how I felt. I wanted us to be able to kiss without worrying about the cameras. But I took it too far. The piggy-back, kissing your neck, it was too much for my character. We'll have to ease into that, or you'll have to take the lead. It was only because of the show."

"So when we're not filming the show..."

Kissing the end of his nose then his cheek, she grinned. "Expect me to be all over you."

"Oh, thank God for that," he said and his whole body loosened when he smiled and put his arms around her.

This time when she kissed him, he responded. "But I don't understand," she said, "you weren't in a bad mood after that. I mean you were, but… you weren't pissed at me when we were saying goodbye before you went with Kira, I don't—"

"She made a move on me," he said, sliding his hand up the front of her thigh. "When we were looking for the third thingy, she hit on me and we had this big blow out right there in the woods."

"And that upset you?" she asked, stroking his face. "Sometimes old wounds aren't as healed as we thought. When we care about people—"

"That's not why I've been in a mood," he said, watching his hand smooth up and down her thigh.

"Then why have—"

"I'm worried about how it will look on the show," he said. "How it will look to you."

That was why he was in a bad mood? He was worried that Kira hitting on him and the argument they'd had would play out as feelings being aired or maybe it would look like they got more than a little bit physical.

"Oh, honey," she sighed.

"If they cut it to look like I did something with her… I thought you were pulling away, that what Kira said got to you and if you were having second thoughts about us and then you saw that…"

Sometimes he was so sweet. "Baby, don't worry about that, I know how editing works," she said. "You're man enough that if you'd…"

"Fucked her."

"Yes, if you'd done that, you would tell me. What would be the point of lying about it when it's out there on film? You said you loved me… I'm taking you at your word. And if you love me, you won't want to hurt me. If you slept with another woman, it would hurt me… If you kissed another woman, it would hurt me."

Taking hold of her upper arms, Trick put some space

between them so he could meet her eye to show her how serious he was. "I didn't kiss her. I didn't touch her. I promise you, baby."

"I know," she whispered, stroking his face. "Will you do me a favor tomorrow?"

"Anything," he asked as she scratched her nails through his stubble.

"Don't shave," she said and smiled. "I like this."

"It'll dry your skin," he said, but let his hand carry on up to her hip, over the elastic of her underwear.

Kissing him once, she licked his lower lip. "I have good moisturizer."

"Yes," he grinned. "You do."

"If you don't want to, I—"

"Baby, if that's all it takes to make you happy, I'm the luckiest man alive… and it'll free up time in the shower." He wiggled his brows and she laughed.

"There is one more thing that makes me happy," she said, slouching in his lap a little more as she lifted her crossed legs over the opposite arm of the chair.

"What's that, baby?" he murmured.

"When you kiss me."

Lowering his mouth onto hers, he took his time tasting her lips, teasing her left and right. Licking her lips, he dipped the tip of his tongue between her lips only to withdraw it and his teasing made her whimper.

"Trick," she whispered against him, curling her fingers around his neck to pull him closer to her. She sank down to rest her head against the wide arm of the chair. "Touch me."

The breath of the words warmed his lips; she lifted her head to seek out his mouth again. Skimming her hand from the back of his neck down the length of his strong arm, Lyla found his hand on her thigh and urged it higher to let his fingers graze over the crotch of her panties and she drew her knee up to set her foot on the arm of the chair she was draped over.

"Uh, you guys need a minute?"

The third voice in the room made her tense and when

she turned her face to see the light on the camera and the view of her and Trick on the laptop next to the second screen that showed the Boys Night studio, she squealed and leaped up out of her husband's lap to dart toward the bedroom.

"Oh, cheers, buddy," Trick said to the camera as he rubbed a hand over his mouth. He leaned away from the chair to grab a cushion off the couch, which he positioned over his lap. "I'll remember this next time you're getting a little honey from your old lady. You guys couldn't have waited five minutes?"

Standing at the bedroom door, Lyla's embarrassment morphed into pride. She leaned on the frame, watching her husband in that chair, his smile wide. That smile. She'd put that there. Five minutes ago, he'd been upset, in a bad mood, now he was him again.

"I don't have an old lady. I'm free and clear, buddy, no ball and chain," Noah Tate said, getting a laugh from the audience. "And five minutes? What would you do with the other four minutes thirty seconds?"

Another laugh. "We had an appointment, you prick. Nookie happens on your time," Nathaniel Green said, his voice carrying through the speaker beneath the camera.

"Actually, it happens on hers. You think I'm pissed, you should see her face right now," Trick said and glanced over at her to wink.

"Guess all that bullshit about you not getting any from the wife has just been blown out the water," Green said.

"Guess it has," Trick said, lifting his feet onto the table and stretching out like Mr. Cock of the Walk.

Turning to go into the bedroom, Lyla wasn't going to stand and watch him all night although she could. Seeing him there, holding court, handsome, powerful, the center of attention, it was alluring. But she wasn't allowed to be aroused right now, she had to wait an hour for that.

***

IT WAS ABOUT FORTY-FIVE minutes later that Lyla reached for her laptop. When she pulled it out of the case, the case toppled. Everything fell out and crashed into the lamp, sending it falling to the floor where the bulb flickered and then went out.

Cringing, she tensed and closed her eyes. Trick was still out in the living room hosting Boys Night. She was supposed to be quiet, but the bedroom door was open.

"I have no idea," Trick said. "It's the missus trashing the hotel room. What can I say? She's rock 'n' roll. You okay, baby?" When he called out to her, she tucked her chin in toward her neck. Oops. He'd heard her. The clattering had carried through to the living room. Lyla had wrecked his show. "No, I hope not…"

If she didn't show him that she was okay, he'd leave his seat, which he wasn't supposed to do until the show was over. Putting everything down, she went to the door and smiled at him, probably coming across as sheepish as she felt. "I'm okay," she mouthed.

"You can talk out loud, baby," he said. "The audience wants to know you're safe."

No they didn't. They would probably love it if she killed herself live on TV… at least the studio execs would. "I'm okay," she said aloud, but quietly.

Trick gestured to her. "Come over here." Her eyes widened and she shook her head, which made him smile. "Don't look so scared, it's the guys, you know the guys."

She'd met them at the wedding, but she didn't know them. Maybe for the purposes of Boys Night, she was supposed to pretend that she did. Did she have to play a different character for this show? Maybe they should've talked about it before he went on air. But she'd already made a mess of things by appearing way more wanton on Boys Night than she had on Opposites. It did air at midnight, so basically anything was allowed on Boys Night.

Dipping down, she pulled a beer from the fridge and opened it. If she had a reason to go to him, she could go and then come straight back. His grin widened. "Wow, what a babe," he said when she held up the beer. "Look at this, guys, she takes care of everything I need."

Carrying it to him, Lyla stretched her arm toward him

and he rose enough to take the beer, but he grabbed her wrist to pull her over too. "Trick," she said and glanced to the laptop to see that her legs were in the shot.

"Geez," Green said. "Your wife's got stems."

"Mm," Trick said, taking the beer bottle from his lips to put it on the side table. Yanking her between his open legs, he pulled the tee-shirt that was draped over her tight across the top of her thighs. "Doesn't she?"

The laptop showed that only her thighs and knees were really on show. Letting her knees buckle, she sank down onto the floor between Trick's feet. It meant her face was in the shot, but wearing Trick's tee shirt meant nothing else was on show. Not that she minded showing skin, as such, but it felt weird to hear anyone say anything nice about her body.

"Hey, Lyla," Green and Tate chorused.

"Hi," she said, touching the edge of the coffee table.

"Are you keeping our boy in check?"

"Trying my best," she said. "But does anyone keep Trick in check?"

"Many have tried," Green said.

Rolling her eyes, she lifted an elbow to Trick's knee. "Many, many… many."

"Hey," Trick said, taking another drink from his beer. She could tell what he was doing, because she could see the laptop that showed what was being beamed to the massive screen behind the couch that the 'Threens' hung out on to do the show. "Are you all calling me a slut?"

"Little bit," Green said and she actually held a hand over her head with her thumb and forefinger an inch apart.

Trick laughed and caught her hand to close his own around it. "Okay, they're safe 'cause they're in the studio. You think you're safe sitting here, Mrs. Strickland?"

Twisting around, she put her back to the camera and smiled at him. "I'm safe," she said, pressing her hands onto his knees.

His eyes got heavy and he slid the beer onto the end table again. "Oh, yeah? You think you're safe?"

Nodding her head, Lyla slowly straightened her arms to rise and angle herself over his slouched body. The whole world could probably see her ass as she leaned in to kiss her husband, but they'd all seen her in a bikini from every angle. And once a person had been filmed in the shower every day for three weeks, they got over modesty fast. Whether the footage was used or not, someone had seen it.

"Mm," Trick said and scooped his hand around her jaw to tip her head higher as he bowed to part her lips with his. "You taste good… sweet… you've been eating those candies I left on the nightstand. You always taste good."

He was aroused by her, she could feel the length of his erection against her torso as she pressed herself against him. Leaving the floor, she pushed his legs closer together so she could climb onto his chair to straddle him.

Pressing her lips onto his, Lyla forced her tongue into his mouth. It was clear he meant to keep the kiss intimate, but restrained. She didn't feel restrained.

Her man had worried she was embarrassed about being with him. Replaying that accusation while in the bedroom had angered her, it upset her, it hurt her, and she understood what he'd said about being hurt when she said the same thing about him.

When she drew back from the kiss, she began to rock her hips over his, something the whole world would see. There was a whoop behind her, but she just smiled at the man under her who was clearly stunned. "I bet I feel better than I taste, do I?" she murmured and swayed forward to kiss him again. "Do I?"

He nodded, but the camera wouldn't pick up his slow, clumsy move that was driven by his shock because she was in the way. Lyla had told Trick earlier that she was beginning to like shocking people and she was learning that the number one person she liked to shock was Trick.

Taking off her glasses, she dumped them next to the beer bottle and reached for the hem of her tee shirt. Pulling it off over her head, she dropped it over the arm of the chair, and winked at him before relaxing her chest to his and kissing him hard.

"Screw the show. Everyone shut the hell up, this is quality television," Tate said behind her and she heard noise from the studio audience cheering. All they'd be able to see was her bare back and maybe her panties as she rocked herself over the erection in Trick's jeans.

Next time she broke the kiss, she started to unbutton his shirt, but he was slouched, lying on it, so she couldn't actually take it off. "I'm not waiting another ten minutes for you, Trick," she whispered, brushing her lips left and right on his. "I want you… now."

Something about her husky request made him get with it. Bringing up his legs as he lifted his torso, his arms came around her. They held her so tight that her torso was pressed to his. He was protecting her, covering her up as he stood up and took half a step to put her on her back on the couch, perpendicular to the chair he'd just been on and parallel to the coffee table, which meant they were just out of shot.

The guys in the studio called out to protest. Trick stuck an arm out across the table and waved as if he was trying to shoo them away. Lyla laughed and opened her hands on his neck to receive the full force of his next kiss.

God, he felt good, so good, too good. "Trick," she gasped when he pulled her leg higher around his torso and started to kiss her neck. "Oh, God, Trick."

Pulling at his belt, he whipped it free of its loops and tossed it out the way. It flew in the direction of the camera, either the studio saw it or Trick just broke something because there was a cheer from the speaker.

"Babe, just—" Instinct made her grab for his dick that he'd just freed from his pants and he groaned when she squeezed him tight. "Damn, baby… that's it, yeah."

"Like this?" she asked, her innocent question made him growl through his clenched teeth.

"Oh yeah," he said, forcing each word from his throat.

Rising, she kissed his Adam's apple. Something spikey, that wasn't a shirt button, grazed her breast. Glancing down to see what it was, she laughed and curled her fist around it. "Trick, you're still miked," she said, turning her lips into her mouth.

"Yeah, man, uh, we're still here."

"Crap," Trick said and rose onto his knees.

The microphone was clipped onto the edge of his open shirt. Since doing Opposites, Lyla had learned how these things worked. She put both arms around him to pull the battery pack from his belt, then tossed it to the coffee table.

The pack went first, but Trick kept hold of the actual microphone as he put an elbow on the coffee table and moved back into view of the camera. His face would be in shot anyway though it was probably way too close to the lens, but with his lower body still pinning her leg to the couch, he panted into the mike he held an inch from his mouth.

"Guys, you've got this right? It's like five minutes," Trick said, driving his other hand up over his hair.

"Seven minutes," Green said. "And I dunno, hmm… what do you think? Should we give him a break?"

Trick's face sank toward the table. "Come on!"

Lyla laughed because her husband really did sound frayed. "You'll make a horny wife very happy," she called out.

Trick kept his elbow on the table but whipped around to look at her and his surprise became a quick smile. "You're gorgeous, baby," he said then dropped the mike. "Let them fire me… You're on your own, guys."

Trick scooped her up from the couch and forced her legs around his hips as he started toward the bedroom. "Bros before hoes, man!"

Someone called out and he stopped but she caught Trick's lower lip in her teeth. "He wasn't calling me a ho," she whispered and stroked his face. "Keep walking, husband… please… I need you inside me."

That was enough to make him keep on going.

This side of her was new, but she liked it. Who knew that finding a man she could trust to guide her between the sheets would be so invigorating? She'd had no idea, none, that it could be like this. She felt so alive and desired.

Trick had said there were no boundaries and she loved learning to push her own. Lyla was far more sexual than she'd ever realized and she'd only figured it out because of him. Trick made it okay to try things, to make mistakes, to learn, and to love wholly, freely, and completely.

She loved her man and he loved her. She'd been promised an adventure, and that was exactly what she'd found.

TWENTY

TRICK WAS WALKING through the lobby of the Prem building when he saw the gang of guys hanging outside the canteen, but he didn't really think anything about it. Yeah, there were like thirty of them, but he knew how these things worked, one guy saw something, called a few friends over, who called the next group and it didn't take long to get a posse going.

He recognized it for what it was, a celebrity sighting. Most people around here were cool with the regular names, but once in a while someone came in for an interview or to cameo in something and it caused a stir.

His plan was to keep going right on by, but then someone at the back of the group spotted him. "Oh, hey, hey, Trick, you'll appreciate this, come check it out."

Okay, yeah, he could turn it on and admire whatever the guys were ogling. It was pretty safe to assume that it was a woman because everyone in the panting group were guys.

Diverting his path, he went toward them and found himself patted and cajoled to the front of the pack. They were gawking through the glass pane in the canteen door. "Check out the babe in the red dress."

Babe in the red dress, babe in the red dress… he wasn't really bothered about their slobbering until one of the guys pointed over his shoulder in the direction of the food line. "There, right at the end of the line, you see her? She spent ages at the fridge looking at the bottles. Man… you see her?"

Did he see her? Uh, yeah, he saw her. He saw the shapely legs, the short skirt and the pert ass. He saw the tiny waist just peeking from behind the mass of her shining auburn waves that he knew from experience smelled like coconut.

Looking over his shoulder, he examined each face. "You're not serious," Trick said. But the men were nodding and panting like dogs. "You are serious."

"She's hot, she hasn't turned around, no one can figure out who she is."

Ah, Trick had to smile. Yeah, he was pissed at all these guys checking out his woman, but man she had them all owned. "Check out that ass," one of the guys said and they all seemed to exhale in unison. "I'd give a hundred bucks to the guy who had the balls to go over there and grab that ass."

Oh, an opportunity.

Maneuvering his back to the door, Trick hoped to block the view and that she didn't turn around. "Hundred bucks a piece from every guy here says I go in there and do it."

"What?" the first guy said as the second one stuttered. "But, hey, you'd probably get away with it, 'cause of who you are."

"Are you allowed to do that? Aren't you married or something?" guy two said.

"Okay, then I won't," Trick said and took a step away, but they all chorused their objections. Ha, suckers. "Let's see the green."

Everyone fumbled around until the money was in guy one's hand. Trick held out his hand. "You gotta do it first," guy one said.

Trick plucked the bills from him. "You know my face, I don't do it, come after me. I'm not chasing down thirty guys I don't know."

"Okay, but you gotta squeeze it real hard," guy two

said, "not just like touch her by accident and apologize."

Trick had to laugh, these guys were real dweebs. Taking a backward step, he felt the canteen door at his spine. "Word to the wise," Trick said. "Before you make a bet with a guy about a woman, make sure the guy isn't sleeping with her. Oh, and if I catch any of you pervs drooling over my wife again, it'll cost you a thousand times as much… in medical bills. Now, because you paid, I'll let you watch, but after that, get lost."

Backing through the door as their objections followed, he turned to stride across the room and folded the money to tuck it into his back pocket.

Tossing one leg then the other over the metal barrier that separated the line from the rest of the room, Trick walked up behind her, and slid a hand down her hip over her ass where he squeezed her real hard and glanced back at the door.

There, he'd done what he'd promised.

Lyla gasped and twisted toward him, but when she saw it was him, she just swatted his chest without any force. "Sheesh, Trick, don't do that to a girl. You scared me."

"Who else would be grabbing your ass?" he asked and pushed her hair aside to kiss her temple as he put his arms around her from behind. "Hold on, let me rephrase that, anyone else grabs your ass and you call me, immediately." Kissing her temple again, he noticed something was missing. "Where are your glasses?"

"I put my contacts in," she said, looking at the illuminated menu above the kitchen. "I went back to the apartment to change. Ritchie said he didn't need me for the rest of the day." They'd got back from their team-building weekend that day and been brought back to the Prem building for everyone to get straight back to work. "I didn't have time to make lunch."

"You're hungry? I can take you out somewhere," he said.

He liked it when she bumped her head back against his shoulder, holding her weight like this showed a trust that he never realized he cared about having with a woman. "We're not supposed to be together right now. Paul only lets us off without cameras if we're at work and not interacting… this feels like interacting."

"I told him I'd check in with him when I got back from the gym. But since when do we care what Paul thinks?" he asked, enjoying her hair though he didn't know why she'd let it loose.

"We got in so much trouble for last night," she said. "You don't think we should cut him some slack?"

Paul had gone postal at them for getting busy on Boys Night when they hadn't even given Opposites any decent intimate footage. Trick didn't care. Apparently, Lyla was nice enough to feel bad.

Splaying his hands on her stomach, he wasn't sure he liked that he could feel the contours of her abs through the material. He was used to there being layers over her beautiful form. Everything she usually wore had no shape, which gave him the honor of being the only one able to check out her body.

Even he hadn't had the luxury of seeing it every day, not until they were sleeping together. Yeah, the world had seen her in her bikini, but he liked to think about that as little as possible now that she was officially his woman.

"It's too late for lunch anyway," she said, holding up the smoothie bottle in her hand. "I just wanted to put something in my stomach… I'm not sure if I like this one, it's been so long since I drank the pre-packaged stuff; you know I prefer to make my own… All this drama has made me realize that I'm a homebody. When we go away places, my routine gets all screwed up." Turning her face toward him, he felt her smile. "Risk was so pleased to see me though, he was purring and bunting me for the longest time. He was following me all over the apartment too. I almost didn't want to leave him."

She really loved that cat. Trick had never thought of himself as a pet person, but the black fur-ball wasn't bad… for a feline. When she moved forward a step, he went with her. "He's a smart cat," Trick said. "I rub myself all over you as much as I can too."

"He wants affection or food," she said, curving an arm around to loop her thumb into one of his belt loops between their bodies. "Your motives aren't as pure."

Yeah, he wasn't going to deny that. "Hey, I like getting me some affection," he said, turning his mouth against her. "And you know I'm always happy to eat you."

"Trick," she whispered and although he couldn't see it, he could hear the blush in her voice, which led him back into the thoughts he'd been having for most of the day.

After the bus dropped them off at work, he'd done his rounds at the studio and gone to the gym because he wouldn't have to work until later.

All day he'd been wondering what would happen tonight, would they be sharing his bedroom? Would he be able to make love to her knowing that there were cameras focused on the bed? Would he be able to sleep knowing that they were being watched?

But before he asked her about that, he had to solve another mystery. "What's with the get-up?" he asked. "You're creating a drool tsunami in the hallway."

"I'm... what?"

"I grabbed your ass to win a bet with the guys in the lobby perving on you, so expect flowers at your desk every day next week." When she twisted around to look towards the door, he got a look at how low cut the dress was. Despite looking almost corporate from behind, except the length, he was learning fast the garment was anything but demure. "You're letting the ladies out to play?" he asked, trying his best to hold onto his temper though his mood was taking a nosedive.

Her gaze fell from the door to her boobs that were spilling over the top of a neckline he considered too low. "I don't really have many social outfits," she said. "This is actually a size too small. I bought it on the internet like a year ago for a date I thought about going on for half a second. The dress was too small and the date never happened, but I never bothered to return it. This was the best I could do at short notice."

"Best you could do for what?" he asked, trying not to think too much about who she'd been thinking about dating.

"Sadie's taking me out for drinks," she said and

smiled.

He didn't mind Lyla getting close to his friends, but he did mind the two of them out alone while his wife was dressed like that and the star of a TV show.

"Tonight?" he asked and she nodded. "Babe, do you think that's a good idea?"

Her smile dropped away. "Sadie said it would be fine. She won't leave me standing anywhere on my own... We worked well together at the team-building thing. I like Sadie."

Mm hmm, his wife was so trusting and naïve. "Yeah, I like Sadie too," he said.

When they got to the front of the line, she opened her purse, but he'd already pulled a bill from his back pocket and paid for the drink before she got near her wallet. Urging her out of the line, Trick guided her over to the nearest table and tossed a leg over the fixed bench so he could straddle it while she sat with her back to the table, wearing a flummoxed look.

He rested his hands on her thigh. "Did I do something wrong?" she asked.

"No," he said and smiled to calm her. "But I just want you to know what you're getting into. Sadie knows how to party and you said you'd never been to a nightclub before, so I—"

"Oh, don't worry about that. We're just going to the wine bar a couple of blocks over, we're not going dancing or anything."

She didn't get how agreeing to go to a bar for a drink after work could lead to an all-nighter. "Right, but the cameras will be with you, that draws attention... the wrong kind of attention." Holding up his hands, Trick wanted to be clear. "Don't get me wrong, baby, I have no problem with you going out and enjoying yourself. No problem at all." Her blank expression made his heart grow; she didn't even understand how innocent she was. "But there's a lot of attention on you right now, people will want to talk to you, to get near you, and when there's alcohol involved, sometimes people don't realize they're pushing too far." Sometimes they did and it was those people he was really worried about. "I just want you to be safe.

You and Sadie alone—"

"Oh, we won't be alone," she said, grinning as she slid a comforting hand onto his shoulder.

If she even thought about citing the camera guy or the director who wanted into her panties, Trick would snap. "You won't?"

When she shook her head, her hair moved over her breasts and for a second he was distracted by memories of last night when she'd been sitting on him... in bed... her pussy wrapped around his—

"Sadie asked Noah and Nathaniel to come with us."

That deluge of ice-water over his head was more intense than the ice-bucket challenge had been. His mouth opened and his chin moved forward, but there were no words. "You..." How did he even process this? "You're going out with Tate and Green?" he asked and she nodded. Damn. She was smiling. Smiling! Oh hell, this was a disaster. "You, Lyla Malloy, are going on a night out with Noah Tate and Nathaniel Green?"

Again, she nodded. "And Sadie too... I'm looking forward to it."

Grabbing her hand, he clutched it to his chest like he was struggling to find his last breath. "Baby... you can't. You have no idea what the hell you're getting into."

Her frown didn't slow his heart rate. "But you didn't want me to go out alone. Noah and Nathaniel will be there to look after me and Sadie. You don't have to worry about other guys—"

"Other guys?" he asked, his eyes growing. "I'm not worried about other guys! I'm worried about those guys."

Her eyes moved left to right and she leaned in. "You said Nathaniel was with Samantha. And Noah wouldn't hit on me, would he? I'm married."

Trick laughed. "Tate doesn't care if a woman's married or not. But I'm not worried about them trying to sleep with you. You're right, both of them would defend you with their lives. You'll be safe from other guys, but you won't be safe from them. They don't know how to say no!"

Lyla gasped. "You think that I would proposition

them? That I would invite your closest friends into my body?"

"This is not about sex," he said, straightening his back. "If you tell them you want to strip naked and go skinny dipping in the river, they'll jump in right beside you…"

Laughing, she touched her lips to his. "The river is far too cold at this time of year for swimming."

Oh, hell.

Damn.

His head was shaking, but he couldn't shake the panic clenching around him. "That's not the right answer, baby. It doesn't matter what it is, they'll encourage it. This is about your safety! This is about your life!"

"But you go out with them all the time. You've been hanging around with them for like a decade and you're still alive."

Yeah, barely. She didn't have a clue about half the crazy stuff they'd done. Most of it never even made the papers, especially the stuff that happened overseas. Some of it he'd just got out of by the skin of his teeth.

He was stronger than her, more street smart, less trusting. If she got drunk—and she would because his friends knew how to drink—and someone suggested something crazy, either she'd do it and get hurt, or she'd be left alone while the others went off to be nuts.

"Sweetheart, will you please just trust me and wait until we can go out with them together?" At least if he was there, he could keep an eye on her. "I promise, we'll do it soon."

Sliding closer, she angled a little and lifted her legs to let them hook over one of his thighs. Man, she was so hot, and the way she was gaining in confidence with touching him was incredible. She was more relaxed without their Opposites camera crews around, but didn't even seem to care that the people in the vast canteen were openly gawping at them.

"What if I promise to be home by midnight, can I go out then?" she asked, tucking her head against his shoulder.

The warmth of her breath and that innocent tone laced through her voice undid him. Letting his eyes close, his hand slid up the curve of her waist. "Ten," he said. "If you're home by ten PM… and you call me every half hour."

"You'll be filming," she said, tipping her head back.

"I don't care," he said, understanding her want to get to know the men he spent so much time with and appreciating it, even if it was giving him palpitations. "I'll work around it. You're the most important thing."

"I'll text," she said. "That way you can put your phone on silent and it won't interrupt you."

Trick had no idea he was so good at compromise. What he wanted to do was tie her up and lock her in the apartment, but part of her newfound confidence was his fault. He'd encouraged her to try new things, and introduced these people into her life. It wouldn't be right of him to try to dampen her curiosity when it suited his inability to be rational.

"Okay," he said and linked his fingers into hers. "You said Ritchie didn't need you for the rest of the day?"

"Uh huh," she said, stroking his chest.

Damn.

She was just so… her, and his dick was having trouble remembering that they were in public. "What time are you meeting Say?"

"Six," she said.

Six to ten, that was four hours. The guys could do a lot of damage in four hours. But he'd take the flak from them about his protectiveness and call every ten minutes if he had to. It wasn't like he'd never been the butt of their teasing before; they'd all taken their turns being that. Trick was proud of his wife and his desire to keep her safe. "What time is it now?"

"Almost three," she said. "I thought I'd get a head start on a couple of things since we don't know exactly what our schedule will be over the next two months."

Yeah, and he was supposed to be meeting his agent, but that wouldn't be happening. "Yeah," he said, pulling her up to her feet. "That will wait."

He towed her toward the back of the canteen. "Wait for what?" she asked.

There was a staff door here that the majority of employees didn't use. He didn't use it because he didn't usually use the canteen, but he knew the stairwell it led to because it led somewhere else. "Where are we going, Trick?" she asked when he pulled her through the door and started up the stairs.

"You said you wanted to see my dressing room, right?"

Exhaling a laugh, she tried to pull her hand away, but he kept hold of it and kept ascending. "Trick, we can't, what if we get caught?"

"Who cares?" he asked. "You think the world doesn't know we're together?" Keying in a code at the door to the right level, he pushed into the corridor and wound through the route he knew well. "It's easier to find when you come at it from the other side."

"I won't ever be coming here by myself," she said.

They pushed through a double door and he saw one of the Boys Night crew standing there reading from a clipboard. "Trick?" Cohen said.

But Trick didn't slow down. "You didn't see me, man."

He winked and pulled Lyla through the door behind him. Cohen got a goofy smile on his face, either he liked the look of Lyla or he knew exactly where the couple was going.

Tugging his key from his pocket, Trick rounded the corner to the door that had his last name on it.

"Trick, this is a bad idea," Lyla said, but she was smiling when he yanked her between him and the door.

"Lookit," he said, pointing to the label on the door. "What does that say?"

Tipping her head back, she read the word. "Strickland."

"Right," he said, ducking to kiss her jaw because he just couldn't resist. "And I'm pretty sure that's your name too. So, this here is our property and… there are no cameras in here, sweetheart. Alone. We'll be alone… How sweet is that?"

Kicking the door open, he shoved her inside and rushed forward to close it behind him. Turning the key in the lock again, he trapped them both inside before spinning around to pin his desire on his wife.

Yeah, they were alone and without the cameras. They

were going to take full advantage of the seclusion; he'd make sure of it.

TWENTY-ONE

THE DRESSING ROOM was large.

There was a big desk with a mirror over it against the wall. Although there was a laptop on the desk, it was also covered with a bunch of other stuff, gifts and letters mostly, and food, all kinds of food.

The door to the full-bathroom was located on that same wall and the bulk of the room was setup like a big living room. But there was a step up to a separate space in the corner that had a curtain open over it. The curtain was tied back against the wall when they arrived in the room, but Trick told her it could be closed.

She didn't get why she would want to close the curtain over a couch until he went over and opened it into a bed. Ah, it was a pull out couch! Above was a cabinet and he'd pulled out pillows and a blanket to spread on the bed. When it was made, Trick had sat down and patted the space beside him and she knew exactly what he had on his mind.

He had a bed in the building!

It felt so good to take advantage of the space when, for once, no one knew where they were or what they were doing. There was no pressure to be "on" they could just be them. Themselves, together, alone, no expectations.

Sex without any chance of being interrupted made for an intense experience. Both of them could relax and explore each other, and they had, for she had no idea how long.

After, they'd laid together for a while, but he'd got up to use the bathroom and left her alone to reflect on how her life had changed, and how his had now that he was a married man.

"How many other women have you had sex with in this bed?" Lyla asked, spreading her legs to let one curl around the blanket that was strewn over her body.

Trick had just come out of the bathroom and was over at the desk, picking through a fruit basket, in full naked glory. "Uh…" He turned around, his mouth full of grapes, and elevated his eyes to the ceiling to begin counting off on his fingers, seeming to go through a mental list.

One finger, two, three, four. He moved onto the second hand and then back to the first. Still counting. Swallowing, she slowly sat up wishing she hadn't asked and was about to say that when he set her in his sights.

"Yeah… none."

He returned to his fruit. "Really?" she asked, pulling her knee higher.

"I know the man whore thing is a great joke," he said, pulling a bunch of grapes off the main stalk. Bringing them back to the bed, he sat down beside her and pulled one off to pop it into her mouth. "But Kira's the only woman I've been with in like three years." Her chewing slowed until her jaw stopped altogether. "Well, Kira and you."

Uh huh, her… Sitting straighter, Lyla leaned over to put a hand on his chest. "Two women? In three years?"

He nodded and tossed a grape into the air to catch it in his mouth. "Everyone forgets, I got my first show when I was eighteen. They painted me as the bad boy and back then, I was happy to play to it. No problem. I bounced around networks for a while, each played on the same kind of theme. I was… twenty-three when I first appeared with Green and Tate. Twenty-three, Ly, yeah, I was an idiot, I won't deny it. We went to the opening of an envelope if there was an open bar and I fucked anything with a pulse. We had cash and we were adored. Anytime we walked in anywhere there was this cheer like the party had arrived, and we played to that. We all did… Everything was free, we ate for free, drank for free, got season tickets to every stadium, people threw stuff at us and the networks went wild trying to get us signed up for shows, so we cashed in, and that meant partying hard."

At twenty-three she was working her first job out of college, still getting over Declan, and thinking about getting a cat. Trick was living it large, sleeping around, drinking heavily, and living a life most people would envy at that age.

"But that changed when you met Kira?" she asked.

He held up the bunch of grapes to pick off a good one for her. "I was about… twenty-eight when things started to change. Josie was mugged about a block from where I was partying… I was too drunk to take the call."

"Josie? Your sister, Josie?" she asked.

That must have been an awful thing to wake up to hear. His need to follow her after their argument made more sense now. Trick wouldn't leave her vulnerable in the street because he probably still lived with the guilt over his sister's mugging, he wouldn't want more if anything happened to his wife.

"She was okay, just shaken up, the guy didn't hurt her. Thank God she just handed over her purse. But my dad called me the next day and ripped into me, I didn't even remember what had happened. I was in bed with… someone. I didn't even know where I was or what had happened. I felt like crap, but I thought if I partied harder I'd forget how much of a dick I was…. Then a few months later, I met Tanya…" He circled his lips in an oh; like just the memory of her got him hot.

"You fell in love with her?"

He shook his head. "Not love, lust. I was infatuated with her, chased her all over the world. She went to Australia, so did I. She went to Japan, I was right there too. Almost lost everything for her. The guys tried to cover for me, but I was missing deadlines, skipping filming, really falling apart. Looking back, it was all an excuse; I just needed to get away from everything. I was done with the bullshit, shallow stuff and she made me think for a minute that maybe my life had some kind of meaning."

Learning about Trick was fascinating and his trust was humbling. "So where is she now? What happened?"

"Kira happened," he said. "Tanya was a model too, they moved in kinda the same circles. I only met Kira because of Tan. We all partied together… spent the night… together."

"Together? But… oh…" He spent the night with both of them. "A threesome?"

He nodded. "We were a threesome for a while, everybody knew it. I thought I was it, you know? I mean, come on, I didn't just have one model, I had two!"

Sure, that was every guy's ultimate fantasy. "So, what happened?"

"Tanya left," he said. "I was devastated. I'd only got with Kira because Tanya said she wanted it, least that's what I said… but what guy would say no? Not a dumb idiot like me anyway. I followed Tan to Milan, told her she was it, told her we'd ditch Kira… I almost asked her to marry me… Almost, but I didn't."

"Why not?"

Inhaling, Trick tossed the grapes to the nightstand and turned around to lie on his back and lock his fingers behind his head as he focused on the ceiling. "She laughed at me. Told me I was a joke. I'd been dropped from every show, I was writing a column back then and that was my only source of income, my travels with my models across the world; that was all I had… The sad part? I didn't even write most of it, I got one of the girls to do it for me. Tanya told it to me straight, I'd lost everything, ruined everything. I was sad, pathetic, washed up… And damnit… she was right."

"I'm sorry, honey," Lyla said, spreading her hand on his stomach.

He picked it up and when he pulled it to his mouth, she was forced to lie against him. But she didn't mind giving him comfort if he needed it. With her breasts crushed against him, she kissed his chest and stroked her free hand up and down his torso.

"No, she did me a favor. I came back home and

buckled down. Made it up to the guys, begged the networks to take me back, and picked up the radio show. It was gradual, but I got it all back. It could've been worse, I'd been off the reservation for about a year, but I had to really prove my dedication to everyone, I had to work harder, and I did. I knew I couldn't mess it up."

"And Kira?"

"Showed up on my doorstep a while after I was home," he said. "We talked, agreed to give it a shot." And that lasted a couple of years before he found out she was cheating on him. "Since Milan, I've… I've just been going through the motions, I guess. I know what people expect, and I do it… But think about it, how many women have you seen me hit on…? Other than you?"

None. Now that she thought about it. No, he didn't make moves on women. Yes, he could make a correlation between any subject and sex. He said outrageous things and had no shame when it came to using sexual language and innuendo, but he didn't sleaze on strangers.

"Other than the kissing on our wedding night, I—" He exhaled a short, disgusted laugh and she brought her eyes to him to see he was glaring straight up at the ceiling. "Trick?"

His eyes dropped to hers. "You didn't think it was weird that they showed a montage? They didn't show me moving in on any of those girls."

"They set the girls up?" she asked, but he shook his head as he smiled.

"It was all old footage," he said, "stuff from through the years or tabloid shots. If I'd been making out with women, I wouldn't have waited for the camera to line up the perfectly angled shot, would I? Most clubs aren't lit for picking up shots like that in the corners or in booths. It wasn't tough for them to set it up. All they needed to do was make sure I was wearing the right kind of shirt in the footage, or no shirt, that my hair style wasn't obviously different. They've got whole libraries of me and the guys doing stupid things."

"Oh my God," she said, sitting up to gape down at him. "Why didn't you tell me?"

"We did go to the club, for about an hour; some of

the partying footage was real."

"But most of it…?"

Shaking his head, he reached for her hand, but she took it away and moved off the end of the bed to crouch and pick up her panties. "Babe?" he asked, sitting up. "What's wrong? I knew if I stayed at the reception, if I stayed with you, that they'd expect us to, you know… be together on our wedding night. We were strangers, I didn't want to put you in that kind of position. I sure didn't want to force myself on you. I didn't know anything about you or if you'd have the confidence to say no even if you were against the idea of us sleeping together. Going to the club was a way of getting us both out of that situation. Baby? I didn't kiss those women. I didn't kiss anyone that night. The only person I've kissed since our wedding day, since we met, is you… Shouldn't you be pleased?"

"I am," she said, but the burn of tears was making her sinuses sting. Her bra was down the stair, so she crawled forward and picked it up to pull it on. But her hands were shaking and tears were blurring her vision. Oh, she had to get out of here, fast. Where was her dress? And her stupid hair, why did it keep getting in her face? Why the hell had she worn it down? Sniffing, Lyla managed to hook her bra, but as soon as she let go of the strap, she knew that it was twisted. "Damnit."

Trick crouched beside her and when he tried to hook her hair away from her face, she curved away from him. "Baby?"

"I'm fine," she said, and unhooked her bra. Her fingers wouldn't work and she couldn't get the stupid thing untwisted. His fingers covered hers and she let her hands drop when he took over the task. Trick untwisted it and hooked the clasp again. "Thank you." Her quiet words were almost a whisper.

"Look at me, Malloy," he murmured, his fingers combing through her hair, he tried to be subtler about turning her head.

His touch was so soothing that she let her legs curl out from under her so she could sit on the stair. Lifting her head, her wet eyes rose to his. "Nairn," she whispered.

His expression became so pained that she lost her fight to contain the tears. "Oh, baby," he said and put his arms around her to pull her to his chest.

Her tears fell for more than a minute before she pushed back. Being in his arms felt so good that she could've stayed there all day, but the last thing he wanted was a crazy emotional person sitting on the floor of his dressing room.

"I'm sorry," she said and tried to brush the dampness from her face.

"It's okay," he said, cupping her jaw to rub his thumbs back and forth on her cheeks. "I'm sorry I made you cry, baby. God, I'm a fucking idiot."

Gritting his teeth, he swore at himself with such hatred that she was infused with a need to console him. "No," she said, moving up onto her knees. "It's not..." Her chin wobbled and he exhaled another pant of pain. "I don't know how you do it... How you let them do it to you... You're just so... You're this amazing guy, but you let the world think you're this selfish, cocky, player, and you're just not like that..."

It took a minute, but his brows came slowly down over his eyes. "You're... you're crying for me? *For* me?"

Pulling away, she began to stand up. "I'm stupid, I—"

He yanked her so hard that she fell against his body, but he caught her in his arms. "I love you, Lyla Strickland," he murmured and drove his hand into her hair behind her ear to pull her mouth to his.

Every kiss they'd ever shared was intense, but this was something else. This was like an exchange of souls. He kissed her so deeply as he lay down on the floor, taking her down on top of him before turning her onto her back where he continued his worship of her mouth.

When her body was pulsing with the strength of her need and her tears were long forgotten, she let her head relax on the floor and spoke before he could kiss her again. "We're out of condoms."

Grinning, he kissed her fast and hard before he leapt

into a crouch and darted over to the desk to pick up a large tin. He brought it over and tossed it onto the bed before bending to scoop her up. He laid her on the bed so gently and kissed her again before reaching over her for the tin and popping open the lid.

Inside there had to be five hundred condoms, and she gasped.

Trick stayed on his side, his arm crooked over her shoulder to support his head, while she was on her back beneath him. "They're something people like to send me," he said, raking through the hoard. "We have just about every brand known to man in here, ribbed for your pleasure." Picking up one, he put it on her stomach and then went back to the box to pull out another. "Glow in the dark." He put that one beside the other and she laughed. "Blueberry flavor." He picked that one out, scowled at it, and tossed it away over his shoulder. "Won't ever need that one."

"Why would they need flavors?" she asked, putting her hand in the tin to rummage around.

"Well," he said and cleared his throat. "Sometimes a girl might like to—"

"Oral," she said and turned her head to smile at him. Lyla was surprised to see how heavy and happy his eyes were. Taking her hand from the tin, she touched his chest. "Would you like me to…"

"Blow me?" he asked and she was sure her cheeks reddened as she rolled toward him to bury her face against him for a brief second.

But she inhaled and relaxed to her back again. This was her man, and he didn't have an ounce of shame… and she loved it. "I was never any good at… that."

"Who says?" he asked, dropping his fist from his temple to rub his thumb on her forehead. "I think if you so much as breathed on my dick I'd go off."

If she didn't laugh, she'd probably scream. "Trick!"

"What?" he asked, shrugging and returning his fist to the side of his head. "I've had crazy fantasies about that mouth."

He exhaled and his eyes sank to her mouth as if he

was languishing in memories of those fantasies.

Tilting her head, she wondered, "Have you ever thought about me? Like that… if you…"

"Jerk off?" he asked and seemed to enjoy her smile so much that he had to kiss her. "To be honest, since we got married, I haven't really."

"Of course not," she said, scowling at herself and shaking her head.

He curled a finger under her chin. "Not because of why you're thinking," he said. "Because of the cameras. There are cameras in the shower, in my bedroom, everywhere I might think of having some quality time with myself… I did on honeymoon after I saw you in that bikini. But I don't guess there were a lot of guys who didn't after they saw that."

Skimming his hand down over her belly, he bowed over her to kiss the swell of her breast. "It was just a bathing suit," she said. "I like swimming and it's functional. It wasn't sexual."

"Oh, it was," he murmured, opening his hand to squeeze it between her back and the bed. When she realized what he was doing, she lifted to let his hand in. Unclasping her bra with one hand, Trick proved his skills, and she helped him pull the straps down her arms to cast it aside. "These are beautiful."

Watching his hand as it ran across her breasts, he squeezed each one, then bowed to kiss her nipple before he breathed it into his mouth. His mouth was incredible, he sucked hard and gentle, teasing her into a whimper, and a moan. One of his hands slithered down her body and down the front of her panties.

Opening her legs for him, she lifted her hips when he slid a finger into her. "Oh, God, Trick," she exhaled. Her heart was going so hard that she lost her breath. "Stop… please, stop."

Taking his mouth off her breast, he took a minute to focus on her eyes because there seemed to be a glaze over his. His hand stopped moving, but he didn't take his finger out of her. "How can I make you feel good, love?"

It was almost laughable that he was asking her for

suggestions when he was the professional and she was the novice. "It does feel good," she said, curling her body toward his. "I just… I need a minute."

Putting his arm around her, he pulled her to him and sank onto his back to hold her. After she let her eyes open, the first thing she saw was the proud protrusion of his penis sticking up toward her. His need was obvious, but he'd wanted to take care of hers first and even now, he was happy to just hold her when she said she wasn't ready to be overwhelmed by him again.

Reaching for him, curiosity made Lyla curl her fingers around him. This had been inside her. She'd gotten intimate with a part of his body that she'd never spent any time getting to know. Drawing a fingertip from the tip of him to his base, she let it move back and forth. He was long, but what did she know about how long penises should be? Thinking about doing research on the subject, Lyla decided it didn't matter if he was bigger or smaller than what was average because what he had was perfect for her.

His hand skimmed down her arm toward her hip and he began to lever her weight back, but she didn't want him taking over, so she moved his hand back to her upper arm and then returned hers to his dick.

Opening her hand, she spread the span of it flat on him then pushed down to gently rub his testicles beneath.

"Damn," he hissed.

Instantly, her hand leapt away and she coiled her fingers into her palm. "Sorry," she said.

But he grabbed her wrist and pushed her hand back down. "No, baby, that feels good. That was good cursing."

Good cursing, okay.

Encouraged, she slid away from his curled arm and moved her face onto his abdomen so she was literally face to face with the head of his penis. She didn't even realize her hand had moved to his upper thigh until he rested a hand on her head and began to comb his finger through her hair to spread it across his upper torso.

"What do you think it's going to do?" he asked with a smile in his voice.

"Am I making you uncomfortable?" she asked, aware of the weight of her head on his abdomen.

But when she started to rise, he dropped his palm to her temple and pushed her back down. "Actually, can't think of anywhere else on earth I'd rather be right now," he said.

Smiling, she was so flattered by how genuine he sounded that she turned her face and kissed his abs. Her cheek grazed the tip of his penis and she felt a shiver go through him. Wrapping her fingers around his shaft again, she edged forward, extending her tongue.

At the first flicker of contact, he tensed and his fingers twined in her hair. "Don't let me hurt you," she said as she lifted a little to move lower.

"Mm hmm," he growled, the strained sound coming from the back of his throat. "Malloy, you don't have to—"

"I want to try," she said, keeping her focus on his dick as she slid her fist up and down his shaft.

She was never going to be a pro, and he'd probably had enough oral sex to last him a lifetime… or two. But she was curious and the best research was hands on.

Kissing his head, she opened her lips and dipped to take him into her mouth. The mass of him was difficult to accommodate. Sucking him as far in as she could, she forgot to breathe and pulled back fast.

Hmm, this wasn't like she remembered it.

Declan was the only man she'd tried oral with and he hadn't been impressed by her efforts, so she had just assumed it wasn't one of her strengths.

But, for some reason, Lyla felt a real urge to do this. It had been Declan's suggestion when they were together, but this was her choice. She wanted to do this for Trick; she had to at least give it a good try.

"Come on, Lyla," she muttered to herself and rose to her knees as she gathered her hair in her hands and held it in one hand at the back of her head.

This was a challenge and she wasn't giving up without a fight.

Holding him tight, she bent over and kissed him again. Instead of going straight for the hard suck, she circled his head a few times. Sliding her tongue around the smooth crown, she dipped it lower over the ridge to his shaft. He'd said it felt good when she stroked his balls, so she slipped her hand from his shaft down over them, but that took him from her lips.

Twisting to seek him out, Lyla was surprised to find that Trick was watching her. His head was propped on a pillow, his eyes were little more than slits, but he was definitely looking at her.

"Will you hold my hair, please?" she asked because she didn't have any ties on her. Scooping his hand up the back of her neck, he curled his fingers around hers to take over management of her hair. She smiled. "Thank you."

He kept his fingers tight around her hair, but managed not to restrict her movement as she went back to licking and tasting him. It helped her to have both hands freed up because she could explore and support him as much as she wanted to and while her mouth opened around him again, she sucked hard and squeezed her fingers around his base. Trick groaned and his hips rose, which pushed him deeper into her mouth.

Drawing in a breath through her nose, Lyla tried her best to go with it. "Damn," Trick moaned. "I'm sorry, baby."

But she'd got this far, and she was doing it. So she smiled and twisted to blink at him as she pulled back and went down to suck him deeper again. He bared his teeth and hissed. Yes, this was it, breathe, suck, it was all about the rhythm. Taking her time, she didn't push too far and let him move in her one increment at a time.

Her confidence grew and she kept going, letting her hand spread on his belly as the other fondled him, she twisted her head on the next descent and he swore.

"Baby, I'm gonna come. You need to move."

Tugging her hair, he began to pull her up. But she whimpered and grabbed for his hand, frowning as she shook her head and sucked him again. Pulling his hand from her hair, she tossed it backward and saw his smile just a fraction of a second before her hair cascaded down over her face.

Lyla gasped when he smacked her ass and gave her a

squeeze, but her concentration was absolute. Making him come was her ultimate goal and if she could do it on her first try—

"Damn," he said and clenched as the warm, thick milk from his body burst into her mouth.

Rising some, she kept her mouth around him, but didn't want to choke, so she swallowed over and over, keeping the seal of her mouth around him until she was sure he was done.

When Lyla rolled to her side, her head flopped back to the spot it had started on and she exhaled. "How was that?" she asked, pressing her hand to her hammering heart.

"How was…?" Trick didn't finish his sentence, he just took a breath and then laughed out loud.

Hmm, maybe not the response she wanted. When she flipped her head over, he probably didn't have time to read her frown before he grabbed her arms and hauled her up the bed to put her on her back.

Pushing her hair up out of her face, she took a second to catch her breath. "Some women aren't as naturally talented at this stuff," she said. "I'm trying, Trick. I don't think it's right for you to laugh at me when—"

"Laugh at you? Baby, I'm in love. How was that? It was incredible! And you swallowed, you didn't have to do that, love."

"I wanted to," she said, "was that wrong?"

Shaking his head, he dipped to kiss her jaw then her neck. "No, baby, it was incredible. You're incredible. You get top marks, extra credit, and a gold star… If I had the world, I'd give it to you right now. Geez, Malloy, what are you doing with a schmuck like me?" Tracing a fingertip up and down his chest, she was pleased that he was so happy, but suddenly felt a web of anxiety closing around her, which Trick must have sensed. "Baby, talk to me. You never have to do that again if you didn't enjoy it. Never, Ly. I don't need that—"

"No," she said, her eyes bouncing to his. "It's not that, I was just thinking… I've… I've never felt like this before, Nairn."

"Good," he said, curving a hand around the side of

her neck when her eyes dropped to her finger again. "It's selfish of me, and arrogant, but I want to be the only guy you ever feel this way for."

"We're married."

"Yeah."

"We're part of this show."

"Yeah."

"What if it's all fake?"

He drew back an inch. "You think I'm messing with you? That I'm lying about how I feel?"

"No," she said, grabbing his shoulder before he could pull away. "I mean, what if the show and them forcing us together, what if it's making us feel this way? Intensifying things, you know? Like with Tanya, you said you were infatuated, what if that's what it is? What if we're just infatuated because we've been forced to be together?"

"I know the difference between infatuation and love," he said. "I've experienced both… have you?"

Had she? Maybe… But didn't they say if you weren't sure, then you hadn't? "I guess I just wonder… how will this work when the show is done? When the cameras are switched off and the lights go down? What happens next?"

He exhaled. "Malloy, I love you, I know that for sure. This is real for me. All the way… But if you don't feel that way…"

Lyla had switched off her emotions plenty of times over the years. It was the best way to avoid getting hurt. She'd said that she was going to let herself love Trick, but every second she spent with him was intensifying the emotion that she wasn't sure she was equipped to handle.

His phone rang. When he rolled away, straight off the other side of the bed, she couldn't stop him from going. Staying on her back, Lyla focused on the ceiling, something she'd seen Trick do plenty of times.

"Yeah," he said. "Yeah, gimme five." Something landed on the end of the bed. "Ly, I've got to get in the shower."

He was working tonight, or maybe he was meant to be working now, she didn't even know what time it was.

"Right," she said and forced herself to get up, wrapping the blanket around her body as she scooted to the edge of the bed.

"You don't have to get up if you don't want to," he said.

"Don't you have to put the bed away?"

He shook his head. "Not if you're using it."

"Won't you get in trouble if you leave me here? If I'm in here without you?"

"You're my wife, Ly," he muttered.

Oh no, he wouldn't look at her. She'd seen this guy before. Pissed off, dejected, grumpy, she'd broken him… again. "Can I use your shower when you're done?"

His attention rose to hers. "When I'm done?"

"You're pissed at me," she said. "You don't want me in there with you when you're pissed off… do you?"

"Malloy," he exhaled and smiled as he shook his head and ran a hand into his hair. "Baby, I'm not pissed at you."

Going over, she squeezed herself in close to him, still clutching the blanket at her chest in both hands. "But you're doing your grumpy face thing and I said a stupid thing. I upset you and I—"

"You didn't say a stupid thing," he said, holding her face. "You were honest and I want you to tell me what you're thinking. Always. Okay?" She nodded. "Promise me, baby?"

"I promise," she said and then squirmed. "So why are you doing your grumpy face?"

"Because I'm thinking that karma is a bitch," he said, peeling each of her fingers away from the blanket, forcing it to fall to the floor. Resting his hands around her narrow waist, he stepped back to admire her body. "I think that with all the crap I've done in my life, it would be the perfect punishment if the woman I love more than I've loved any other couldn't love me back." Her mouth fell open, but he used a single finger beneath her chin to close it before she could speak. Smiling, he bowed to rub his face in her hair. "I don't want you to ever lie to me, okay? And never feel guilty if this isn't enough for you… I'm going to do what I can to be everything you ever need. But if there comes a point I'm not satisfying you, cut me off. If you get a better offer from a better guy, take it. Don't hesitate. Don't think about it. You just do it, because you deserve the world, Lyla Malloy. Understand?" Again, she nodded and after a second, he kissed her forehead then smiled at her. "Now, who said something about sharing the shower?"

TWENTY-TWO

NOAH WAS HILARIOUS. Nathaniel, who she'd learned preferred just Nath, was more serious, and he was smart, *really* smart. They hadn't ventured out of the wine bar, and Lyla enjoyed having some time to bond with the other two members of the Threens. Sadie stuck to her side, and Lyla was just beginning to relax when Cliff came over to tap her on the shoulder.

"We need to get back to the studio," Cliff said into her ear.

"What?" she asked, looking at her watch to see that it was just after eight PM, she still had time. But Cliff looked so serious that she panicked. "Is it Trick? Is something wrong?"

But he didn't answer her, just nodded sideways and backed off. Saying her goodbyes in record time, she paid no attention to the guys' pleas that she should stay put. Sadie said she was coming with her and Lyla was so desperate to find out what was wrong that she didn't even argue.

Racing back to the studio, she followed Cliff through the dark lobby and up in the elevator to the executive floor. Oh, God, if something had happened to Trick, she didn't even know what she'd do. They'd had sex in his dressing room shower, but she'd been kicking herself for voicing doubts about their relationship. She didn't have doubts, not really. She just opened her mouth and said things; it was idle speculation, conjecture. She didn't think that her words could really upset him.

Her, Lyla Malloy, how on earth could she have the ability to hurt the megalith that was Nairn Strickland?

Sadie was at her back as she went into the office after Cliff, but she slowed in her pace when she saw Bunyan and Paul seated on either side of what she guessed was Bunyan's desk because she'd never actually been in his office, until now.

"Where's Trick?" Lyla asked.

Sadie closed the door behind them. "Was there an accident?"

"We need you to sign something," Bunyan said.

"Sign…" Lyla glanced back at Sadie who looked just as confused as she did. "You called me here with an emergency… And the emergency is… you need me to sign something?"

"Yes," Bunyan said.

Her new friend stayed at her side. "Wow," Sadie said. "I think we need to get you a dictionary for Christmas."

"You've caused a problem with legal," Bunyan said. "On Boys Night… you should never have appeared on the show and especially not in the way you did."

"It's a sexual release," Paul said.

Lyla was pleased to hear Cliff laugh. "Damn," she breathed. "Trick would've had a great comeback for that. Where is my husband when we really need him?"

Sadie smiled, but Bunyan scoffed. "You seem to have forgotten what this is, Miss Malloy," Bunyan said. "You are the property of this network and while you are, you act in the best interest of this studio. This isn't a game. This is business and you are an asset. That's all you are. And when assets stop working out for us, we sell them."

"Sell them?" Sadie said. "Now I know why Trick isn't here. If you spoke to her that way while he was in the room—"

"Yes, yes, he'd fly off the handle. He'd get defensive

and threaten us all. Well, he's not here, he's working, for the studio. As we speak, he's filming his quiz for us."

"Yeah," Sadie said and pulled her phone from her pocket. "He's in the building and he's expecting to hear from Lyla in five minutes. If he doesn't, I guarantee you he'll walk off set."

Lyla couldn't refute that. He'd been worried about her going out with his friends and what trouble she might end up in. If she didn't text, he might assume that she was in trouble and feel it necessary to come chasing after her.

"No, he won't," Bunyan said and picked up a sheet of paper. "Because this will only take a minute… All we need you to do is sign this."

"Oh," Lyla said and began to move, but Sadie put a hand on her shoulder to stop her.

"She's going to have her lawyer look at that first."

"Lawyer?" Lyla said in time with Bunyan and Paul. Lyla didn't even have a lawyer, though she could get a lawyer if it was necessary.

"Why would she need a lawyer?" Bunyan asked. "She signed the initial contracts without a lawyer."

"Yeah," Sadie said. "And that was just three weeks ago. Follow up contracts this quickly usually mean something was missed in the first contract or someone wants to change the rules of the game… Which is it? 'Cause if this was about Boys Night, Damon would be here."

"Damon?" Lyla asked Sadie.

"Their executive producer and director," Sadie said.

Bunyan glanced at Paul. "We need to ensure there won't be a lawsuit brought by Miss Malloy about the footage aired on Boys Night last night."

"Why would Lyla bring a lawsuit?" Sadie asked. "She knew Trick was live. Knew what was happening. She addressed the studio and spoke to the guys even after she was on her back." Sadie put her hand on Lyla's shoulder again. "Sorry, honey." Lyla shook her head because Sadie was right. "And that's exactly what a lawyer would say if this ended up in court… What is it you want, Bunyan? You won't find a person more accommodating than Lyla, so if you spell it out, she's the most likely person to agree."

Paul stood up. "We need you and Trick to go back to the hotel."

"The hotel? Which hotel?" Lyla asked.

"Where you had sex," Bunyan said.

"We can build a set," Paul said. "But it will be easier just to reserve the suite for an hour."

Bunyan projected his voice. "We need footage."

"Footage," Sadie said. "Of them having sex?"

"Just the usual," Bunyan shrugged like it was no big deal. "We're not filming porn. We have no problem with them staying under a blanket or trying to conceal what they're doing."

Sadie laughed. "You can't be serious."

Bunyan's expression got sterner. "This is not your business, Miss Lawrence. This is between the studio and our cast. We need the footage. It is necessary and they have to comply. It's in the initial contract. They both gave up rights to any and all intimate acts. We are allowed to have footage of it. We could sue them for subverting our access to the act."

"Sue them?" Sadie spat out, then nodded at the desk. "Is that what that contract is?"

"No, actually," Paul said. "This is an out."

"His idea, not mine," Bunyan muttered.

"It's a waiver that allows us to use stand-ins," Paul said. "If she signs this, we can get actors to recreate the moment."

Recreate the moment she and Trick had first been intimate? The idea made Lyla feel sick. "How can you do that? You get look-a-likes? Won't people notice it's not us?"

"More of the action will happen under the covers."

"But we didn't do it under the covers," Lyla said.

Sadie looped her arm through hers. "Don't give them any details. That was your special moment with Trick. Don't sell it to them."

Bunyan laughed. "Both of them sold themselves to us when they agreed to do the show. This isn't deviant curiosity. We need to enhance the appeal of the show. If viewers think they'll get better footage on Boys Night, they'll switch."

Oops, yes, that was true. Lyla worried her lip as she tried to decide what they should do. "I don't feel right about faking it," Lyla said.

Cliff laughed. "I think Trick would have a follow-up line for that too."

Yes, he would. Geez, all she ever did was say stupid things. "You won't have to fake anything," Paul said. "Sign the paper and we'll use stand-ins."

Other people, pretending to be them? How would she watch that? What if they did something that embarrassed her or Trick? If Bunyan was pissed enough he could make it seem like she was unsatisfied or that Trick was no good in bed.

And they'd never catch the emotional intensity of their joining. They could make it dirty and cheap. An actress could make her sound loud and ridiculous, or an actor could make Trick seem like a sleaze, something the studio was good at.

"No," she said. "I won't... I don't want you to use stand-ins."

"Then you have to go back to the hotel with him and do it yourselves," Bunyan said. "It's that or..."

"Or what?"

"We need something bigger," Bunyan said. "Something that will make our viewers forget they missed the first time."

"Something not under the covers," Sadie said like she was translating and it turned out she was right because Bunyan nodded.

"Ideally it wouldn't be in the bedroom either, it should seem spontaneous and..."

"Dirty," Cliff said and it was sort of sweet that he sounded annoyed.

But Lyla couldn't focus on that. Spontaneous and dirty... Turning to Sadie, Lyla set her determination. "You usually work on the quiz, right?"

Sadie glanced at everyone. "Uh, yeah, I took tonight off because of the team-building thing, I thought I'd have a backlog."

"Can you get me into the studio?"

TWENTY-THREE

LYLA WAS NERVOUS.

Thinking about it now, her question to Sadie had been stupid because they'd been in one of the top execs offices, anyone could've gotten her into the studio. But it was access she needed. Access to Trick.

Sadie was with her as she walked into the studio through a hidden door. "Are you sure you want to do this?" Sadie whispered to her.

"Don't have a lot of choice," Lyla said, trying her best to ignore her trembling hands.

Sadie grabbed a runner. "Spread word in the audience that the stunner about to walk on set is Lyla Strickland," Sadie said, presuming that people wouldn't recognize her without her baggy clothes, glasses, and tight chignon. "Keep it quiet from Trick."

The runner nodded and ran off; Sadie put an arm around her. "It's no big deal," Lyla said. "I've slept with Trick before."

"But not on film," Sadie said. "Not like this."

Her new friend's expression was full of contrition. But Lyla couldn't think too much about it, she had to be confident. Yes, confidence and determination, that's what would get her through… and if she just focused on Trick…

"We'll cut there and setup for the next game…" Someone called from the front of the fixed bleachers that she was standing in the shadow of now.

"Okay," Lyla said and smiled at Sadie. "Sex with my husband. Piece of cake."

Whirling around, she kept her spine straight and her shoulders back as she strode around to the front of the audience. As she moved through the space between the bleachers and the edge of the set, a cheer went up, a big one, one she wasn't expecting.

Widening her smile, Lyla waved to the audience and then turned to the set. There were two desks of contestants on either side of the quiz host's desk. Trick's chair had been turned away, but when he heard the cheer, he turned and followed the audience's focus.

To say he was surprised to see her was an understatement, but he smiled and left his seat, digging his phone into his back pocket as he rose. He must have been checking for her overdue message, but it didn't matter, she was here now.

He jumped down from the raised platform his desk was on and ran across the floor to meet her halfway. "Babe," he said, brushing his fingers across her cheek. "What's wrong?"

Taking his hand, she smiled at the panel members who tried to say hello and offered them a wave. She pulled Trick around to the back of the set, away from everyone. Going to a door at the rear of the huge studio, she dragged him through it. This was a backstage area, one that would be deliberately deserted. Except for those who were planted there.

Taking him down the half-dozen metal stairs, Lyla said nothing just moved a dark curtain aside to go into another part of the space. She'd been directed to go to the square area with its door on the far wall, a door which had a glass panel in it…

Dropping the curtain, she pushed him to the wall and swallowed her nerves while trying to keep her smile in place. If he thought she was nervous, he wouldn't want to do this. Locking her eyes onto his, Lyla read his confusion, but pushed on. Confidence. Determination. Yes, that was it, just keep looking at Trick.

"Kiss me, Trick," she whispered, pulling his shirt from the front of his jeans.

"What?" he asked, but sank his hand into her hair to take hold of her neck. "Here?"

Biting her lip, she tried to keep on smiling and nodded as she slid his belt from its buckle. Dipping down, he kissed her.

Yes, sinking into the pleasure of his mouth, Lyla let herself ride the wave. If she could get aroused, like she usually did when he kissed her, then she could forget that they were being spied on. Surely, she could.

"Dressing room," he murmured against her and took her hand.

But she put her hands to his chest and pushed him back against the wall when he tried to move away. "No," she said, unbuttoning his jeans to slide her hand into his underwear. "Here."

"Here?" he asked and something crossed his gaze.

Oh no.

He was suspicious.

But he couldn't guess, surely, he couldn't guess what was going on. Lyla would never ask him to expose himself or to do anything intimate without telling him they were on film. But he'd said there were no boundaries, that she could do anything with him that she wanted to… did that include this?

Reaching around to unzip her dress, she pulled it only part way down, so that when she guided her arms out of the wide straps and drew the top part of the dress down, her skirt stayed on her hips.

Trick grinned and tossed his head back in a laugh as he wound his arms around her. "Okay, I get it," he said and kissed her forehead before he grabbed her upper arms and spun her around to thrust her against the wall. Pushing himself closer, he laid a forearm on the wall above her head as he drew her face up with a finger. Instead of kissing her, he kept his lips a whisper away from hers. "The guys put you up to this… It's a bet, right? A dare?" He kissed her quickly. "You don't have to do it, baby. Of all the things I thought they'd ask you to do… Okay… this is up there as one of their better ideas…" His next kiss was longer, harder, more relaxed, but his assumption made her feel worse. He thought this was a game for his friends when this couldn't be further from a fun game. His voice dropped to a growl. "That said, if you want me to do you hard and fast right here, baby, you just hop on up and my cock will do the job."

Some of the heat in his gaze chilled when their eyes next met, could he tell from the way her heart was racing that something was wrong? Bunyan had told her not to tell him, Bunyan had said it would be smart not to, but she couldn't lie to him, she'd promised not to.

Picking up his loose hand, she pressed it to her throat. His hands were so big, so talented, so amazing that she didn't ever want to take them away from her. But letting her eyes wander up to his, she slid his hand down her front to her breast and he was happy to take a handful of her.

Lyla covered his hand and moved his thumb under hers, guiding it to graze the tiny portable microphone that Paul had positioned on the edge of the lace cup while telling her that its range would still pick up their voices even if she took the bra off.

As soon as she saw the moment of clarity in Trick's eyes, she squashed herself back and slid down the wall. She wouldn't ask him to perform for her, or for them, but she could perform herself. Keeping her bent knees together between his legs, Lyla put her hand into his jeans and opened her mouth.

But before she could take him out, Trick stepped back and grabbed her arms again to haul her up. With fierce anger in his eyes, he grabbed the neck of her dress and stuffed her arms back in the sleeves.

"Where?" he grumbled and she turned her attention to the door.

He spun around and began to stalk toward it. "Trick!" she called out and hurried to follow him, but he was already throwing the door open. Paul, Bunyan, and Sadie were all there with the camera crew, who were falling back on themselves to get out of the path of this raging bull.

"You?" Trick shouted at Sadie. "What the hell, Say!"

"I didn't know," Sadie said.

"You let her go through with this? You let her do it?"

Darting around her man, Lyla put herself between him and everyone else because she didn't know where this mood would end up. The last thing Lyla wanted was for Trick to get himself into trouble.

"They didn't give her a choice," Sadie said. "Trust me, this was the best of a bad bunch of options."

When Trick's attention flew to Bunyan, Lyla felt the heat of his fury. "Trick!" she said and reached for his face, but he threw her hand away. "Please, baby, it's fine!"

"You have a contractual obligation," Bunyan said and although Lyla heard a lot of bluster, she heard fear as well. "You have to fulfill your duties to this station!"

"My duty is to my wife and hers is to me. Did you tell her to lie to me? Did you?" Trick shouted so loud, that Lyla's ears started to ring. When Bunyan didn't answer, Trick tried to take a step forward, but she pressed into him with everything she had. Lyla didn't stop him from moving, but she hoped to slow him down enough to give the others a head start. "Don't you ever speak to my wife without me, ever! Any of you bastards go anywhere near her without me and I'll take every one of you apart, understand?"

"Trick," Sadie said. "Don't threaten them."

Lyla liked to think Sadie was worried about Bunyan being litigious, but it didn't seem that her husband thought that. "Don't talk to me, Say. Screw you. Seriously? She trusted you! I trusted you! A drink? Did you plan to take her out or was it all a setup?"

"No!" Sadie called. "We were out, with the guys, we got called in. We thought something was wrong with you! We came here and... They wanted her to sign a follow-up contract!"

Like he knew what that meant without further explanation, Trick's attention fell to her, but he didn't look any less angry. Lyla nodded. "They wanted to use stand-ins to recreate our first night together. I couldn't let them do that, Trick. What if they… What if they made it dirty or sordid? What if they made you out to be something… depraved or inferior?"

The studio could get him into a lot of trouble. They already had footage of him touching her and her arguing with him, telling him to keep his hands to himself. If they chose to make it look like he'd forced her into sex then he could find himself in hot water. It might be great television and create extensive publicity, but it would ruin him.

"They threatened you," he murmured and his anger flared with renewed energy when he raised his attention and his voice at the men behind her. "You threatened my wife?"

"Oh, give us a break," Bunyan spat out, not seeming to get that it wasn't smart for him to adopt an attitude right now. "Your wife? This is all bullshit! It's a setup! A goddamn show! And you do this right, you'll be a star! Don't be a moron! Everything we're doing will benefit you and your career! You, Strickland!"

Someone touched her back, and Lyla glanced back to see Sadie was zipping up her dress. Trick kept his focus on the men who were somewhere in the background. It seemed only right if someone was worried about her modesty that she should be worried about Trick's. So, with an exhale, Lyla began to button his jeans and when he draped an arm around the back of her neck, she hoped it was a sign he might forgive her.

"You ever wonder why we're protective of this?" Trick said to Bunyan.

The anger was still in her husband's eyes, but his voice was calmer.

"You're protective of her because you're an idiot," Bunyan said. Lyla planted her hands on Trick's abs before he could lunge, but he did growl. "You've got some hard-on for the vulnerable nerd thing she's got going on, but look at her! She's got this! She's a babe who won't remember your name in six months. I promise you! You think you know what this show will do for you? Think about what it will do for her! She's going to be famous! Probably more than you! She trapped the playboy Nairn Strickland! Got him panting like a puppy! Him and half the nation! You dumb bastard. Fine! You want to run this? Run it. But don't think for a second she's not playing you! You think she's not a thousand times smarter than you? You think she hasn't played it through to the end?" Bunyan scoffed in disgust. "You're an idiot, Strickland."

Lyla didn't want to look up, but she heard the retreating footsteps and assumed the others had left when Sadie moved into her peripheral vision. "You okay, honey?" Sadie asked and took her hand. But as she tried to take Trick's, he snatched it away and backed away from both of them. "Trick?"

"Take Lyla home," he said, his sneer fixed over their heads. "I've got a show to shoot."

Turning away, he stormed through the door that would take him into the studio. Sadie sighed and put an arm around her. "He'll be fine when he calms down." Sadie turned Lyla around and began to lead her away.

"Sadie," Lyla said, feeling the shudders that came after the adrenaline wore off. "I don't want to be famous."

"I know, honey," Sadie said, stroking her back.

They got another ten paces before Lyla stopped and turned around to look back the way she'd come. "You need to go back there and make sure Trick doesn't hurt himself."

"He wouldn't—"

"He's angry," Lyla said, her attention darting to the producer. "If he shouts at someone, or… hits them… Please, he won't keep it together if he doesn't vent, let him vent at you."

"What about you?" Sadie asked. "He'll never forgive me for leaving you alone."

Lyla smiled. "I'll get in a cab. I'm only going home. I won't talk to anyone, I promise."

Sadie nodded and gave her a hug. "Don't let Bunyan get you down. You and Trick have something special. Something real."

Lyla nodded, hoping that Sadie was right. "Please, hurry."

Sadie gave her hand another squeeze before turning to hurry back toward the studio where Trick would be.

When Lyla was alone, she fell back against the wall and covered her face with her hands.

What she'd said to Trick in his dressing room today had already affected him, probably enough that Bunyan's words would be worming their way into his mind. Lyla knew her husband. She knew that Trick played the character because he'd been taught over and over that his true self wasn't good enough.

He didn't believe he deserved her and if he got it into his head that she needed to be free of him, he'd do something stupid.

If that something stupid involved another woman…

Lyla squeezed her hands around her throat. She wouldn't be able to stop herself, she'd hate him, she'd never be able to forgive any infidelity. If Trick was hers, he had to be hers, only hers.

But she didn't believe he'd ever cheat on her, not ever. He hadn't been able to cheat on her on their wedding night and he could have. He wasn't what the media made him out to be. He was decent, kind, and oh so caring. Trick *was* hers. Only hers.

They weren't strangers anymore. They were lovers… and that was where all the problems had started.

Shoving off the wall, she knew what she had to do.

Bunyan wouldn't like it.

Paul wouldn't either.

But she was only interested in doing what was best for her man… while he still was her man.

***

WHEN LYLA HEARD the hammering on her apartment door, she knew there could only be one person on the other side of it.

Sliding the chain from its runner, she pushed her hair from her eyes and opened the door. Still half-asleep, she didn't expect the door to fly toward her or for Trick to come barreling inside.

"A note on the fridge, Malloy, really?" he yelled, storming into her living room.

Lyla had come back to her own apartment as much to get her own head straight as to put physical distance between her and her husband. She had no clue what time it was now, but it had to be seriously late. Filming would've run into the wee hours and Trick would've had to get home before he would've known she wasn't there.

"I didn't want you to worry," she said, clearing her throat and finger-combing her hair from her temples.

"Then you should've been in my bed when I got home," he said, whirling around to glare at her. "You think that stunt tonight was bad? This is a thousand times worse. Did they put you up to this? Huh? They tell you to leave me to piss me off and create drama? Is this all part of the plan to make me look like a maniac?"

She knew it! She'd known that Bunyan's words would've wormed their way into his psyche. Considering her husband for a second, Lyla didn't want to think about the cameras on the wall that would be capturing this fraught moment.

Going to the front door, she opened it and pointed outside. "I don't think so, Malloy," he said. "You are not kicking me out, no way!"

"We need blueberries," she said, focusing her own scowl on him.

There was no way their code was going to fly under the radar now, but what choice did she have? The hallway was the only place that wasn't monitored by the studio, as a public space it was too difficult to get permission to film out there twenty-four-seven.

Trick lunged over to grab the throw from the back of her couch and although she didn't get why he wanted it, she didn't argue, because he did march over the room to pass her to enter the hallway.

Lyla made sure the door wouldn't lock behind her and then went out, closing the door behind them to limit what the audio recording may pick up. Trick threw the blanket around her shoulders and tightened it around her chest. Was he worried about her modesty? She was wearing her nightdress that covered her all the way to her ankles.

But folding her arms around the throw, she kept it on and leaned away when he bowed toward her and she caught the smell of alcohol on his breath. "Have you been drinking?" she asked, pushing on his chest as he crowded her closer to the wall. "Geez, Trick—"

"I came home to find out my wife left me," he said, punching the door frame above her head, he gritted his teeth. "Ly! You left me!"

"Trick, calm down," she said, keeping the throw hooked around her hands, she rested them on the inside of his elbows. Sober Trick was hard enough to reason with when he was mad; intoxicated Trick would be even less reasonable. "Please, we don't want to make a scene, if we wake up the neighbors and they get this on their camera phones, we'll end up on the internet and—"

"Isn't that what you want?" he asked. "You want to be famous, baby?" Crouching, he buried his face in her hair and kissed her neck. "If we do some real nasty things on film, you'll get your payday."

Smacking his chest, Lyla shoved him with all her strength. "Don't you speak to me that way, Nairn. I don't want to be famous and you know that! Don't let that… that…"

"Bastard?" he asked, clutching the side of her neck. "I know how to loosen that tongue, baby. We've never done it in your bed; let's christen it tonight."

"No," she said, torn between being upset and annoyed that this more vicious version of himself had shown up. "There are cameras in there, did you forget?"

"That's what you wanted," he said, holding her hips to angle their bodies together. "You wanted to get filthy on film and I'm here. I'm saying, let's do it."

"No! Stop this. Stop being like this. What is wrong with you?"

He hissed a breath through his teeth as he swung down to get in her face. "I love you and I'm not enough for you. You know what that does to a guy? You know what it was like walking into that apartment and finding you gone?"

Lyla reached for his face with a slow hand, but he ducked away and stormed a few paces down the corridor. "I don't want to be famous and you know better than to believe Bunyan or anything he says. If you believed I was like that, you wouldn't be in love with me… My problem isn't with you, it's with… everything else. I was so confused in Bunyan's office without you. I didn't know what to do and he told me… he said I should seduce you, that I should let them film it without telling you. Do you know what that felt like?"

"You did tell me," he muttered. "You did what you were supposed to."

Lyla was glad that she'd been honest with him. Despite the way things turned out, she would rather deal with this than exploit Trick in the way so many other people had. "I don't like seeing you upset. I don't like causing that upset."

Spinning around, he held open an arm. "Then come back to me," he said. "I told you the only way to hurt me was to leave me… Come back to me, Malloy, and we'll be just fine."

"Come back to what?" she asked. "Do you want to share a bed with me when there's a lens recording everything we do? Every time you touch me in front of that camera, it cheapens this, it makes me wonder if…"

"If it's all fake," he said and his arm fell.

Just like she'd said in his dressing room. Lyla was new to this celebrity thing and new to being monitored and deconstructed. She didn't know how to deal with intimidating executives or contracts and sexual setups.

Her love for Trick felt so real and solid when they were just them. But when the camera turned on and they had to become their characters, she felt like they lost a bit of what made their bond so strong. Maybe she just needed time to get used to it. If she had her confidence, and knew how to tell Bunyan to leave her alone, then maybe she could be what Trick needed.

But Lyla didn't want to ever be in Bunyan's office in that same position again. She didn't want to be standing in Trick's arms wondering if he was suspicious of her motives, and she didn't want to ever be suspicious of his.

And that fight. She didn't want to be the reason Trick was mad or the cause of him being sued or hurting someone. Sending Sadie after him was supposed to offer him a relief valve, but he was here tonight, just as keyed up as he had been earlier.

"I didn't ever think in a million years that I would actually fall in love with you," she said, recalling what she'd thought during the panel when Sadie had seemed so sure that Lyla would sleep with Trick.

Lyla hadn't believed it was possible, yet here she was, standing in her hallway with tears streaking her cheeks, looking at the man she loved who didn't appear to be angry anymore.

A kind of resigned dejection settled over him. He exhaled and dug his hands into his pockets. "Go back inside, it's cold out here."

"Nairn," she whispered, but when she tried to reach for him, he took a step backwards.

"I told you if I didn't satisfy you that you had to cut me off. I told you not to hesitate… You promised never to lie to me, Malloy, and all you're doing is being honest, right? I can't tell you to do that then flip at you for it." His tight smile wasn't convincing. "You're a good girl and you know yourself. I'm sorry I wasn't enough, baby… I'll leave you alone."

Trick walked away down the corridor and she opened her mouth to call him back, but no sound came out. She couldn't call him back. What would she say? She wasn't going to invite him in to her apartment, and she wasn't going back to his place with him either.

Conversations in the hallway weren't secure and fighting would be guaranteed to bring the neighbors out of their apartments. Even after he was gone, she stayed put. Numbness had taken her over and she felt that cold he'd referred to.

She'd left him. Had she really left him?

Lyla loved him; she hadn't meant him to think anything else. He knew that, didn't he? But until she could be comfortable with their relationship being in front of the lens, she couldn't be what he needed her to be and couldn't share the marital bed with him.

Why was it she could be so confident in front of the Boys Night lens and so uncomfortable filming Opposites?

Because one was spontaneous and fun. The other was contrived and contorted.

Being on Boys Night was her choice and they'd captured a genuine moment between new lovers. Opposites was artificial. It was cut and reset over and over until the producers got exactly the shot they wanted.

Lyla didn't want to recreate her first night with Trick. Didn't want to be told when or how to seduce him. All she wanted was to be a woman in love with her man and as long as Alan Bunyan was in charge of that show, he was in charge of their relationship too and that was one element of control she just wasn't willing to relinquish.

TWENTY-FOUR

LYLA HAD THOUGHT that Bunyan and Paul would go postal about her moving back to her apartment.

They didn't.

They said it was believable for there to be bumps in the relationship since the couple were so different from each other. The drama was exactly what they wanted.

She and Trick got through a whole week without seeing each other. Until Trick, Lyla had never missed a person so much that her body hurt whenever she thought about them. And she thought about her husband a lot.

It would be easy to go and knock on his door. Easy to call him up and ask him to come and visit her. But with the cameras set up in both of their apartments the studio were determined not to miss a thing and she didn't want to share him, just like he'd said he didn't want to share her.

So, the cameras followed her and they followed Trick. Separately. Her interviews revolved around being told stories about what Trick was up to and being asked to comment. Apparently, he'd been out clubbing a few nights this week and the interviewers were very interested to find out how she felt about that. Lyla tried to keep her responses short, knowing that they really wanted Trick. They didn't want her. So, she tried her best to be polite, but vague.

The pressure was on Trick right now to carry the show. Lyla wasn't clubbing or hanging out with famous people. Her life was as boring as it had ever been.

The show that aired last night had revolved around their second week of marriage. Seeing them back then, still new to each other, learning how to live together, was nostalgic. If it was possible to feel that way about something that happened two weeks ago.

Lyla was at work, in her old routine, sitting in the canteen, eating her packed lunch and sipping her smoothie when a shadow made her look up.

Ah, the Cronies, it had been a while.

"I guess it was only a matter of time before you did it," Faith said.

"What?" Lyla asked, turning the page of her open magazine and picking up another carrot stick.

The three women sat down with her, two opposite, and one at the end of the table. "Do you feel ridiculous for doing it?" Chelsea asked.

"I still don't know what 'it' is," Lyla said.

"We saw what you were like with him at the team-building thing," Faith said. "How did you get him to look at you like that? Is he that good an actor?"

"He?" Lyla asked, realizing she'd learned something from her husband about being a smart ass.

"Trick," Dinah said. "We heard… you messed it up. It's over… right?"

Ah, yes, the good old rumor mill. It was difficult to always be on top of the current titbit. Lyla knew she'd been a subject on the gossip list regularly since marrying Trick. But with the show airing two weeks after events, sometimes the masses were behind the curve.

The Cronies must be getting fresh information from somewhere. Good for them. It was reassuring to find that some things never changed.

"Yep," Lyla said, biting into her stick. "I messed it up."

"Aww," Faith said, but Lyla didn't believe she meant the sorrow in the exclamation. "Well, you did your best."

"Sure, and I'm sure he's only sleeping with five or six other women by now," Dinah said.

"Least we can all be sure that's a list none of you will ever be on."

Looking up from her magazine, the last person Lyla expected to see standing behind the Cronies was Trick. But there he was.

Tilting her head in question, she watched him come around the table to slide onto the bench beside her, with one leg on each side of the seat.

Picking up her hand from the table, he held it in both of his and fixed his eyes on hers as he took it up to his lips. "You ladies want the skinny, watch the show, in the meantime… get lost. You don't deserve to be in the presence of my beautiful, perfect wife. She's worth a thousand of you black-hearted bitches."

The Cronies squawked and objected, but when Trick turned a glare on them, it didn't take long for them to scarper.

Only when the trio was gone, did he look at her. "Trick?" Lyla asked.

He'd been doing such a good job of avoiding her that she had wondered if they'd ever talk again. "I broke," he murmured, kissing her knuckles again.

Sucking in a breath, Lyla tossed her carrot stick back in the box and drew her knee up on the bench to turn toward him. "Broke?"

His brows came down as his hand fell to the bench, taking hers with it. "I didn't screw around. I broke by coming to see you… I was trying not to do that."

"Oh," she said. Lyla didn't know if it was offensive that he was trying not to see her. "I knew you were avoiding me. I figured you had your reasons."

"I did, but it's not like you think," he said, putting her hand back on her own leg. "I told you, I'm not what they say I am… I'm not a whore."

"I didn't say that you were," she said, having not considered that he might be here to confess an affair.

But Trick was building up steam and didn't seem to hear her. "Baby, you're the one who came to me and threw me against a wall because you wanted to have sex on camera. If I'd done that to you, you'd have cursed me up and down every alley in the city."

Lyla couldn't deny how she would've reacted if the shoe was on the other foot. "I know," she said, nodding. "That's why I thought I could let you know—"

"Not before you gave them something," he said. "You know we're going to have to watch that? They have you unzipping your dress, flashing your tits at me… you putting your hand in my pants… They have that, and they will use it."

Yes, they would because it was the juiciest thing they had on show. "I didn't know what to do, Trick. They cornered me. Told me we had to do something spontaneous and—"

"And you didn't think you should've said no? If you'd said you wouldn't do a damn thing without bringing me into the meeting, do you think that blow out would've happened?"

So he blamed her for everything. "I… I didn't mean for everyone to fight like that… I had no idea that Bunyan felt that way about me."

"And the first thing you did after was leave me." He sighed. "You did the right thing. I told you as soon as I wasn't good enough for you that you should split and you did," he said and stood up to pull something out of his back pocket. Throwing it on the table, he took his leg out from under the table. "It's an invite to my birthday thing next Friday. I want you there. Show up or don't, it's your call."

Looking at the white envelope on the table, Lyla was stunned. But when he turned to go, she grabbed his hand, halting him. "Nairn," she whispered, and the heat behind her eyes quickly became tears. "I… I feel lost without you."

Lyla was terrified as she lifted her gaze, and her fears weren't allayed when she found that he wasn't looking at her. But he didn't try to pull away. After a second of nothing, he turned his hand into hers and just held her for a minute.

Twisting toward her, Trick bent over and touched his mouth to hers. "Come home," he murmured and eased back a couple of inches to scrutinize her response to his request.

"I want to," she whispered.

"Come back to my bed," he said. "Whenever you're ready."

His next kiss was softer, longer, and made a tear slip from her eye. But she kept them closed as his hand slipped out of hers. She didn't want to watch him go. Couldn't watch him leave her.

This was just a glimpse of how he must have felt when he got back to his apartment and found the note on his fridge from her saying she was going back to her place. It must have seemed to him that she'd given up on them. She hadn't. She just needed him to be hers… she didn't want them to belong to the world.

TWENTY-FIVE

TRICK ORDERED ANOTHER DRINK.

Well, he had his answer.

Lyla wasn't coming.

With both arms folded on the bar, he leaned over it waiting for the bartender to come back with the bottle he'd ordered. If there was ever a reason to get blitzed, being dumped by his wife was it.

But he couldn't blame her, not after the way the show had been cut on Wednesday. Turned out his fears were justified. The studio had cut the team-building break to look like Lyla was the jealous one, and Kira was the seductive goddess. So when they made it look like he and his ex had got it on in the forest, he couldn't really blame Lyla for wanting rid of him.

He actually hated himself for loving her so much. If he could just get her out of his system, she'd be so much better off without him. All along he'd known that she deserved more. But in that canteen when he'd given her the invitation to the party, he'd really expected her to come back to him.

Seeing that tear on her cheek had made him want to hit something.

Hard.

The only reason he hadn't harassed her every day after she moved back to her place was because he thought it was her choice to leave him. Because she'd figured out what he knew all along, she was a goddess who deserved more than he could give her.

She'd said she was lost without him.

Yet, here he was, eight days later, standing at the bar, at his own birthday party…

Alone.

Folks came over to pat his back and shake his hand, but he didn't want to engage with anyone. Doing only what he had to, he dismissed them and turned his back as soon as he could. He'd told Green and Tate that he was going for a slash, that was ten minutes ago. He intended to go back to the top table and he would… soon. He'd turn it on… after a few more shots.

"I'm not giving you your present until Sunday."

Turning to look over his shoulder, he was pissed off to see Sadie sliding onto a stool beside him. For some reason, his friend reminded him of Lyla. He didn't blame them for what had happened, didn't blame anyone, except Bunyan.

"There's a whole table of presents somewhere," he said. "I don't care about presents."

The blonde at the end of the bar made eye contact with him and he smiled. Maybe that was how he would get over his wife, and he'd give her a reason to hate him at the same time and then they'd all be happy.

"Don't even think about it," Sadie said, snatching his chin to haul his gaze away from the blonde. "No. You hear me? No."

"What?" he asked, fixating on the blonde again. "Can't do any harm."

"It can do a lot of harm and you know it. You're not that guy anymore. Geez, Trick, it's been, what? Four years? Five? Since you screwed anything with a pretty smile and nice tits."

"She has great tits," he said, turning around to lean on one elbow as he winked at the blonde who looked away on a giggle. "Yep, I'm in."

"You're always in," Sadie said and put a hand on his chest to slide it up to his face in what was far too intimate a gesture for a friend to use.

"What the hell?" he asked, grabbing her hand and tossing it away.

Sadie grinned. "If you can't handle me doing that, how are you going to handle that sucking your dick?" she asked, nodding backwards at the woman she hadn't even looked at. Elevating her chin, Sadie leaned closer. "Are her tits nicer than Lyla's?"

Scowling, he twisted to drop both forearms back to the bar as he sought out the bartender. "Why did you do that? You ruined it."

But that was exactly what his friend wanted to do. "Why? Because thinking about Lyla activates your conscience?"

"I'm always thinking about Lyla," he muttered.

"And that should tell you something."

Looking up and down the bar, he was searching for the bartender he'd ordered with. "Where is my drink?"

Sadie took a big breath. "It's not coming."

Flipping around, he got more pissed at the woman who couldn't pull off innocent. "What the hell?"

"I don't want you getting drunk tonight," Sadie said.

"It's my birthday, I'm allowed to get drunk…" He glanced up to see the blonde still watching him. "And laid."

"It's not your birthday until Sunday," Sadie said. "Hence what I said about my gift to you. However…"

She made a show of opening her purse and pulling out a small gift-wrapped box to place it on the bar. With a finger on the top of it, she pushed it toward him.

Why would she say she wasn't giving him a gift and then put a gift on the bar? "What is that?" he asked.

"It's a keychain," Sadie said.

He hadn't actually expected her to tell him what it was. "Why do I need a keychain from you?"

"It's not from me."

"Then how do you know what's in it?"

"Because Lyla wanted to know if it was too cheesy… I think she was worried that you might make fun of her. I told her it was sweet and if you didn't think so then you didn't deserve her."

Letting his eyes fall to the small black box with its gold bow, he was curious, but sort of afraid too. "She gave you a gift to give to me, but she didn't show up?"

Sadie shifted in her seat, twisting her crossed legs toward the bar as she took her eyes away from him. "Well, she was supposed to give it to you herself. But… she couldn't be here. I said I would pass it on. Open it."

He didn't want to. But if he made a big deal of it then he would draw attention to his crappy mood. Pulling off the lid, Trick tried to huff like this was just inconvenient. It was a keychain, he saw it as he unwrapped the black tissue folded over the top, it was a heavy one, in the shape of a key, the top was a heart with words inscribed. *'Nairn, the key to my heart belongs to you"* it read on the front and when he turned it over the words were larger. *"Always, your love, Malloy."*

Curling his fingers around the token, he clenched his teeth. "Damn," he hissed.

When he noticed the blonde at the end of the bar still checking him out, he dropped his gaze and bowed his head. Had he really thought about touching any other woman? Being honest with himself, Trick had to admit that acting like he was thinking about it didn't mean he'd ever have let his feet move.

Sadie put a hand on his arm and got closer. "Her faith in you hasn't wavered," she murmured. "Every interview, they push her, they ask if she thinks you're cheating. Every time she smiles. She smiles, Trick, like they're making a joke. Last time they asked she said there wasn't an atom in her body that could believe for a nanosecond that you'd even think about being with another woman. She loves you. Don't forget that when peppy little blondes are making eyes at you thinking about their five minutes in the limelight."

Sadie spun her stool away, and was about to leave when he lunged around to grab her arm. "Then, where is she?" he asked. "We could be together, right now. I told her to come back to me and she hasn't even called me." When her eyes dropped again, he got worried. "Say?"

"I'm not allowed to tell you," Sadie said.

"She told you not to tell me?" he asked, his mind racing with ideas.

Where could she be that he couldn't know? Could she be with another guy? If she was, why would she give him this key?

"Not her," Sadie said. "The studio."

Tightening his fist around the key, Trick felt the need to break something, preferably Bunyan's face. "I don't give a crap about the studio!"

"Shh," she said, closing the last of the space between them. "Her dad died."

Panic and worry slapped him hard. "What?"

"She got a call on Sunday night. Her dad was rushed to hospital with chest pain. They kept him overnight, said it was fine and let him out. Lyla stayed with her parents, and thank God she did… on Wednesday he dropped dead, right there in the kitchen, right in front of her… She did CPR for twenty minutes until the paramedics showed up… but he was gone."

Trick didn't even think; he had to get to her now. Except Sadie grabbed him. "You can't go to her," she said. "The only reason the studio are keeping this quiet and giving her a break is because of this, your birthday. Haven't you noticed that they've been all over you with events this week?"

He had, and he hadn't liked it, but he didn't mind if it took pressure from Lyla who struggled with being the center of attention. "Sadie," he said, "I told her this was for real… I love her. I don't give a damn about the show or the studio. My wife is in pain. Where should I be?"

The whole thing felt shallow. It always had felt frivolous, but now he felt like a prize prick. He was standing here at a party while the woman he loved was going through one of the most traumatic things she'd ever endure. That didn't scream "real" relationship.

Sadie's hand fell from his arm and she stepped back. "I'll text you her parents address… I'll cover as long as I can."

"Thank you," he mouthed, backing away from her and taking his fist to his chest.

Everything in his world made sense as he paced out of that hotel ballroom.

Everything.

He ignored every person who tried to come near him and kept his focus on one thing.

His wife.

She needed him and they'd been apart for too long.

TWENTY-SIX

LYLA DRIED HER HANDS and hung the towel over the long handle of the oven. The kitchen was at the back of her parents' house. She walked past the breakfast table, under the large arch, and into the living room where her aunt was sitting on the couch.

"Go on up to bed, Auntie Ann," she said, watching how the woman struggled to keep her eyes open.

"No, it's fine. I have to read these," Ann said.

It was almost impossible to believe that there was so much paperwork involved after someone passed away. But it wasn't right that her aunt was trying to be so strong when this had to be difficult for her.

A knock on the front door made Lyla exhale.

Damn.

It was late.

She didn't want the kids to be woken up. Ann turned to look over the back of the couch, probably thinking the same thing, but Lyla smiled. "It's okay, I've got it."

People had been coming all day, yesterday too. Her father had been a popular guy in the neighborhood because he was always helping someone out. Now the family had so much food that there was nowhere left to store it. The freezer was full. They'd never have to make another dinner again. If there was just one more casserole—

Lyla opened the front door and her thoughts halted when she saw Trick there, on her parents' porch. Her hand shot to the left to immediately turned off the porch light that was above him.

Going outside, she pulled the door closed behind herself. "Trick," she whispered. "What are you doing here?"

"Sadie told me."

Her heart sank. "Oh," she sighed. "You weren't supposed to find out." Trying to see around him, she wondered how he'd got here. "Thank you for coming, but the cameras—my mom—"

"It's just me, baby," he said, taking her hand. "Just me. For real."

How she'd needed him. How she'd missed him. But she'd deliberately done her best to hold her tears inside, and couldn't let them come now. "Like I said, thank you for coming." His tender smile fell. As soon as she said it, she'd wanted to take it back. "That was cold," she whispered and sagged. Her eyes dropped. "Oh, God, Nairn, I don't know what I'm doing... what am I doing?"

"You're doing what you always do. You're putting everyone else first and trying to keep it together," he said.

When his hand moved onto her face, she closed her eyes and turned her cheek against it. "God, I've needed you so much."

"You'll never be without me again," he said.

When her eyes opened a tear fell, but he smiled, a small but real expression of his devotion to her. "Promise me something. Promise me anything," she said, in need of an anchor, or at least a glimmer of hope. "You said you never make promises that you won't keep. Make me a promise, Nairn. Right now, make me a promise that you'll never ever break."

"I promise that I love you," he said and opened her hand to press it against his chest. "And I promise that this will always belong to you."

She wanted to believe him, wanted to fall into his arms and let him hold her because in his arms, her world would make sense again. But Lyla shook her head and took a backward step. "No, you have to be at your party. Your birthday. Your friends… the studio and Bunyan—"

"I belong to you, Lyla. And I don't care if I have to camp on this damn porch to prove it to you. I'm not going anywhere. I'm your husband." Holding up his hand, he showed her his wedding ring. "If this family faces tragedy, I face it too. I'm not interested in being around part-time. I don't want all the good times and none of the bad. I want all of you, Lyla. I want you at your highest and at your lowest. Your father gave you to me, Lyla." Her eyes blurred. "He put your hand in mine and he told me to look after you… and I fell in love with you, baby. All the way, over the top, forever love that I'll give everything up for if I have to. I love you and you either understand that and want it or you question me and doubt me every day. Either way, I'm here. I'll always be right here… with you. All I want you to do is use me. Take advantage. Lean on me, baby. You need someone. I want that someone to be me. I want to be special to you. Remember, just like you said? I'm just asking for the same thing. Let me be special to you. Lean on me, baby, and know it will always be okay. Just lean."

"Trick," she whispered, her voice cracking at the end of the word. "Nairn."

"I'm here, baby," he murmured and moved in to take her hand again.

"He… he died… right there and I… I couldn't do anything," she sobbed and sucked in a long breath. "I couldn't do anything."

"Shh," he said and pulled her forward into his arms.

Letting out her emotion, Lyla sobbed and wailed, burying the sound in his solid chest that gave her comfort and security. He made it okay to be broken. Made it okay to hurt and to show how she felt. Trick held her so tight that she could believe he was capable of fending off every hurt.

Even as her knees buckled and she screamed into him, he held her up. Squeezing her body to his, he picked her up and carried her inside. Lyla didn't know how he found the basement or how he got her into bed. All she remembered was lying in his arms, crying and listening to his words of comfort for the rest of the night.

***

LYLA WOKE UP with a killer headache.

She was in her white nightdress and she was alone.

It took her a minute to remember that she was in her bedroom in her parents' basement.

After her good for nothing Uncle Earl cut out on Ann and the kids, the trio had moved in here. The three bedrooms upstairs in the house were taken up by Ann, and her thirteen-year-old twins, Avril and Todd.

Lyla's mom and dad had converted the basement so it had two bedrooms and a bathroom. Even after she'd moved out they wanted Lyla to know that she had somewhere to come home to, so one of the bedrooms was dubbed hers.

Stretching, she blinked up to the blinds that covered the narrow windows that ran along the wall up at the ceiling above the head of the bed.

Trick.

Sitting up, she looked around the room and was so disappointed to find that he wasn't there. But she shouldn't be surprised. He had to carry the show single-handedly while she was hiding here. He must have gone back to the city to appease the studio.

Lyla hadn't slept this late all week and so kept her shower fast and dressed even faster. Her mom would need her to make breakfast and keep answering the door to the well-meaning neighbors; she shouldn't be loitering in bed.

But as she ascended the stairs a sound stalled her. What was that? Was that…? Laughing?

Hurrying upward, Lyla rushed through the kitchen and stopped dead in the archway that led to the living room. There was Trick, in front of the fireplace juggling what looked to be four balls while balancing a skittle on his head. All around him were kids. Pre-teen through teen. They were all transfixed, cheering and clapping for the man who was showing off like an endearing idiot.

Lyla grinned. She had no idea that he could do that. Turning her back to the frame of the archway, she folded her hands and leaned against them to watch him move with such impressive skill.

"Someone ask me a question," he said, confident in his rhythm and from what she could see, he had every reason to be.

"Why?" one of the kids laughed as everyone kept cheering him on.

"The point is to put me off," Trick said. "Come on, ask me something, anything…"

Lyla would put good money on him learning to do this while drunk, so doing it sober would be a breeze. "What's two plus two?" someone called out.

"Oh, come on, challenge me," Trick said, but quickly followed up. "But not with math… don't challenge my math, I'll only make you feel inferior."

"Have you ever broken a bone?" one of the younger ones called out.

"Most of 'em," he said.

"Have you met Gisele?"

"Yep," he said. "She's overrated. No sense of humor."

"How many women have you kissed?" a girl asked.

"Until I've kissed a girl as beautiful as you, not enough," he said.

It was a skill that he could juggle, another that he could balance that thing on his head, now he was listening and being witty. "What year did they hold the first Olympics in Ancient Greece?" she called out and everyone turned around.

Trick ducked to thrust the skittle in the air and caught it under his arm after each of the balls fell back into his hands. He smiled right at her. "776," he said. "B.C. of course… though there's evidence they may have started before then." Taking the skittle from under his arm, he dropped it and the balls to the coffee table and began to saunter toward her.

"They were held in honor of Zeus... contestants were male..."

"And?" she asked as he came up close and rested his forearm on the frame above her.

"Nudity was common," he said. While the youngsters giggled and whooped, he ducked to kiss her. "How did you sleep?"

"Better than I have since we were last together," she said, resting her hands on his chest. "Where is everyone? How did you end up with—"

"Your mom is upstairs in a special Strickland bubble bath."

Grinning, she almost laughed. "You drew my mom a bath?"

Pride made him boast. "Not just any bubble bath, the king bubble bath of all bubble baths," he said.

"Hmm," she said, overwhelmed and in love, she linked her fingers at the back of his neck. "I might be jealous."

Bumping his head down to hers, Trick murmured, "All your bubble baths come with me in them from now on."

An addition her mother wouldn't have appreciated. Straightening her arms, Lyla arched up. "And my Auntie Ann?"

"At the store with a neighborhood posse, they're buying up the place so we can have a cookout this afternoon. Getting everyone over all at once is the best way to stop the door a-knocking every minute."

How did he know this stuff? It made such good sense. "The funeral is on Monday," she said, returning to reality. "We couldn't do it at the weekend."

"I know, Ann told me... and you need pallbearers."

Reality sucked. She exhaled and found the worry that she'd been without for the last few minutes. "I know, I don't even know who to—"

"Hey," he said, smoothing his hand down her cheek. "I've got it. Don't even worry about it for another second."

Pulling her body closer to his, she wanted to climb inside him where it was safe. "When are you leaving?"

Lyla didn't want to face the idea of being without him, but she didn't want to be blind-sided by his departure.

"I'm not," he said. "Josie is on her way over with stuff from my place, and from yours. We'll have clothes, whatever we need, and Sadie is taking care of Risk."

This was like some kind of parallel universe; Trick was taking care of her. Calm, rational, organized, this was the real Trick. No joking, no being unreliable, he was a rock. "But the show—"

"I told Bunyan where he could stick the show," Trick said. "I told him he's got two weeks of footage, if he wants to run it, he can and we'll see where we are after. If—and that's a big if—we decide to carry on we should talk about last Wednesday's show, I don't know if you saw it, but—"

Smiling, Lyla shook her head and pulled him down for a kiss. "Please don't insult me by suggesting I might think you did anything to hurt me," she whispered. "I don't care what the world thinks. I care what we think. I care that I love you. I care that you're here. I care that…"

Her voice wobbled and she had to suck in a breath to catch her tears.

"Baby," he murmured. "You go back downstairs and I'll—"

"No, they're not sad tears, I… I'm just overwhelmed. You're being so incredible and I… I was really struggling, I couldn't admit it, but… I lost you and then losing my dad so soon after… I thought I was being punished."

"What the hell could you be punished for?" he asked. "You're the most amazing woman in the world, and you didn't lose me… You'll never lose me."

"All the way?" she asked. "This is us, all the way?"

He nodded, but someone behind them laughed. "Lyla asked Trick to go all the way."

Trick turned his back on her and she let her face fall against his spine as he addressed the kid who was probably the same age as the twins. "We're married, dork-weed, all the way is in the contract," Trick said and she smacked his hip.

"You can't call kids that," she whispered.

"You're lucky I didn't swear," Trick tossed over his shoulder.

"You better not," she said, wrapping her hands around him to hook her thumbs into his front belt loops. It felt so good to be able to press her body into his like this, to take his strength and lean, just like he'd said.

Another kid guffawed. "Her hands are right there at your junk."

Trick laughed too. Geez, teenage boys were really something, and her husband was apparently at their level. "Maybe, hubby, you should remember how vulnerable your junk is when my fingernails are this sharp," she said and when he stopped laughing, she smiled.

She was playing, and he knew that, but this was what she needed, to just be herself with the man she loved. "If my wife is threatening our fun times, we're all in trouble," Trick said. "You kids, out back, all of you, we've got setting up to do." Trick moved back a step, pressing her to the wall of the archway again, though she kept her place nuzzled against his back. "No one crosses the property line! Everyone stay in the yard and if you see a stranger scream fire."

Laughing, Lyla waited until the herd was gone before she asked, "Fire?"

He shrugged. "No one comes when you shout rape… I tried it."

"You tried shouting rape?" she asked. He unhooked her thumbs and turned around. "I can actually believe that you did."

"I've gotta go setup for this cookout. I've got tables that need set and catering on the way," he said. "If I get you a blanket and a good book, can I trust you alone for an hour?"

"Alone?" she asked. "I don't get to help out back?"

Stretching an arm above her head, he leaned over her and scowled an apology. "I'm sorry, sweetheart, I'm just worried that you might be a bad influence on these kids. They're at a very impressionable age and with your questionable reputation—"

"I'm not wearing panties right now."

He immediately grinned and exhaled a laugh. "See, stuff like that," he said, but his glittering interest betrayed he wasn't going to take the risk she was only playing. "Really? Are you really not?"

Scooping a hand under her skirt, he fondled her ass and she laughed when he felt the cotton and grumbled in disappointment. "I had you."

"You always have me," he said and bowed to kiss her.

Taking her hand, Trick led her through the kitchen and down the stairs to the back porch. "What would you have done if I wasn't?" she asked.

"Walked around with a boner for the rest of the day," he said. "The kids would've been traumatized."

"Traumatized?" she asked. "Your penis isn't that scary."

"Well, thank you, but I would've kept it in my pants," he said, stopping at the edge of the yard to pull her against him. Wrapping her in his arms from behind, Trick propped his chin on her head, and settled against the rail at the outer edge of their deck. "Most of these boys are getting to the age where they're terrified of the dreaded spontaneous boner. How bad would it be for them if they saw me, a grown guy, unable to contain his? They'd think it happens forever, that they never get over it."

That was kind of a contradiction. "But if you can't control it? Doesn't that mean they never will get over it?"

"I got over it for a decade and a half… and then you came into my life."

"Are you trying to flatter me?" she asked, wriggling deeper into the vee of his thighs.

"Why would I do that? Because if you like me, there's the prospect of me getting laid? No, why would I do that…?" Lowering his mouth to her hair, he breathed in. "Why? Is it working?"

"Wait until I take my panties off later and we'll find out," she said, pulling his arms further around her body. "Shouldn't we help them?"

The kids were running around trying to open folding tables and crates of utensils. "Nah," he said. "What's the point of having minions if we don't take advantage of them?" She tutted at her husband and moved forward, but he tensed his arms and she bounced back. "I'm thinking about my mom."

She didn't get it, until she remembered what he'd said on the bus once upon a time and she arched her back to push her ass into his groin. "I thought you didn't have a boner."

"I lied," he said, "we'll just wait here a minute until it goes away."

It had been a couple of weeks since they'd had sex, he probably had some pent up frustration lingering in his system. "Okay," she said and exhaled to lean on him again. "I used to think you thought of me as a sister."

"Yeah," he said, with a scowl in his tone. "Where did that come from by the way? What the hell did I ever do to make you think Caligula and me were bros?"

It was funny, but so attractive, when he referenced anything she'd told him about history. "You didn't want to sleep with me, not back at the start."

"Who said that?"

Sheesh, he had a short memory. "You did," she said. "You said at the wedding that you weren't attracted to me."

"Ha," he said in a single laugh. "No, I didn't. I said you weren't my type and you're not. The women I went for before you were easy, blonde, bimbos… You're none of those things, love."

Maybe not all of them. "I'm pretty easy," she said.

They both thought about it for a second. "Yeah, okay, you are pretty easy."

"And I could go blonde."

"Nope," he said. "I love your hair. Don't touch it."

"I could pretend to—"

"I love your mind more than I love your hair," he said, anticipating what she was going to say. "And what was it you said to Kira? If you were the same as every girl who came before, this wouldn't be what it is, would it? I never loved any of the other girls. I love you. And I don't want you to change a damn thing about yourself."

"Mr. Strickland!" one of the girls called out.

"Shit," he said with a smile in his voice. "She makes me sound like a damn hockey coach."

Trick kissed the back of her head and eased her forward so he could go over to help the girl who was struggling with the table.

That was him, her husband. He was nowhere close to resembling any hockey coach, but he was hers, and he was here, taking care of business. Lyla had never been more in love or certain of her future than she was right now.

TWENTY-SEVEN

"THANK YOU FOR COMING," Lyla said and the neighbor whose hand she was shaking began to guide her toward the house like they wanted to be walked out through the building.

Trick had been impressed by his wife's fortitude loads of times, but just when he thought she couldn't do any more, she surpassed herself.

Far as he could tell, the cookout had been a good idea. It seemed to be a success and it had turned into an impromptu celebration of the life of the man he wished he'd had time to get to know better.

Standing at the edge of the yard, Trick scanned those who were still seated around the tables and made sure no one looked to need anything. The kid at the end of the table closest to him noticed him looking and averted his eyes.

Hmm, interesting.

The kid was Lyla's cousin, Todd. She'd said he was thirteen, not a great age. The kid was just starting his journey to adulthood. Trick decided he'd have to stay away from the teenager, make sure not to have any negative impact on the boy who was probably a good kid.

Todd glanced at him again, and Trick slipped his hands into his pockets.

The neighbors had fallen into two categories that he was familiar with. The ones who did everything they could to be as near him for as long as possible, and those who were terrified to get within twenty feet of him. He'd thought he'd done okay with the family. It was important that he did given that he'd be seeing a lot more of them, but the kid seemed nervous.

As he considered what he might have done to scare the kid, Trick saw Todd rise from the table and start toward him. Good, okay, so he wasn't scared, that was good. But why the hell did he look so shifty?

"S'up?" Todd asked when he got to him.

Okay, so they were just two cool dudes hanging out, Trick could do that without corrupting the kid. "Nothing," Trick said. "How you doing, kid?"

"Good… I'm cool."

Trick didn't want to smile, but the kid was really trying his best to be gangsta.

Grabbing his shoulder, Trick gave him a shake. "Don't try so hard, man," he said, laughing and punching his arm. "I'm the one trying to impress you, okay? And we're family now, right?"

Todd did seem to relax; he smiled at least, so Trick took that as a good sign. "So you're… you're sticking around?"

"Sticking around?" he asked. "Yeah. Why wouldn't I?"

"Joy says you're only here 'cause of the show, that you and Ly aren't really married."

Great, everyone had an opinion. Taking a mental breath, Trick reminded himself that these were just kids. "I'm sticking around. I love Lyla, I'm in this for the long haul."

He had respect for the kid trying his best to step up for his cousin, even if there was fifteen years between them. If it ever came to it, Trick would let Todd kick his ass for hurting Lyla, not that he ever planned to. But if he did, he'd let the kid do his worst and wouldn't fight back, just 'cause it was the right thing to do.

"But Lyla's so… plain… that's what everyone says."

Backtracking, Trick folded his arms and frowned. "Really? Who says?"

Todd blinked and took a half-step backward as he blanched. "I… I love Lyla, but she's… she never had guys around. Mom says she's got high standards."

Trick smiled. "Then she married me and you realized they were bullshitting you?" Damn, it was hard not to swear. He put an arm around the kid's shoulders. "Listen, man, most women fall into a category, some of them you'll know already, some of them you'll learn. But once in a while, like once in a blue moon, a woman comes along who doesn't fall into a category… Your cousin Lyla is one of those women. She's smart. Headstrong. Modest. Kind… And the sexiest woman I ever met. You want to find yourself a woman just like her and don't settle for anything less than a woman who grabs your heart so tight you feel it in your balls, you know?"

The kid's eyes were wide for a second, then he blinked and looked away like he had at the table. "And how do you… get her to like you back?"

"Kid, you've got time, plenty of time to…" Todd looked to the table, and then away again. When Trick followed his gaze, he saw a freckle-faced redhead steal a look at them and he couldn't stop his grin as he cajoled the kid with a shake. "Hey, man, you've got one on the hook."

Todd's face went bright red and Trick turned them away from the table to huddle. "What's her name?"

It better not be Joy who thought his girl was plain.

"Stacy," Todd mumbled, looking at the grass beneath their feet. "She's Joy's twin, like me and Avril."

Nodding, he gave the kid's chest a pat. "Good, something in common, good springboard… You talk to her? You hang out?"

Todd shook his head. "Joy asked me to the Halloween boy-girl dance."

Sisters. Interesting. Complicated. "But you want Stacy?"

Todd's head shot up. "I want to go with Stacy. I don't want… I don't *want* Stacy."

"Right," Trick said, "my mistake." Apparently, there was a difference, he was out of practice with teenage lingo. "Did you ask her?" Again, Todd shook his head. "There's your problem." Slapping the kid between the shoulder blades, he grinned. "Go ask her."

He might as well have suggested the kid run for President, Todd managed to look terrified and bereft all at the same time. "I can't do that! I can't… I can't just… ask her."

"Sure you can," Trick said. "Joy asked you. Just do it like she did." He frowned. "You did say no to the sister, right?"

"I… I said I'd think about it."

Okay, that was better than agreeing, but worse than a flat no. "That's okay," Trick said, giving him a pat. "That's okay, we can pull this back."

"We?" Todd asked, searching his eyes.

Trick had never seen anyone look so grateful and hopeful in all his life. "You need help with homework, call Lyla… You want advice on women…" Trick winked. "You call me."

"I can… I can call you? Like… on the phone?"

"Sure," Trick said. "Like I said, we're family."

Glancing over the kid's head, he saw Stacy looking at them again. The kid was fine. He had this. That girl was already his; he just didn't have the confidence to claim her. But as Trick was about to reassure the kid, he saw Cece in the shadow on the back porch waving at him, but trying not to draw the attention of the rest of the guests.

"I don't know how to get her to like me," Todd said.

"Lesson one," Trick muttered, worried by how frantic Cece looked. "Make her laugh."

"What? How do I do that? Is that how you got Lyla?"

Trick took a step away and smiled, trying to be as relaxed as he could, so as not to draw Todd's attention to whatever issue that must have risen. "Lyla fell in love with me when I took her shoes off," he said. "Have a think about it. Stay here. I'll be back in a minute."

Walking backwards, Trick eyed the girl then winked at Todd. Yep, great way to get into the family, keep the teenagers away from the drama. Todd turned away and seemed to be wracking his mind.

Good, if Todd was thinking about pussy… or girls, whatever teenagers thought about, he wasn't paying attention to his aunt.

Vaulting up the stairs, Trick found Cece just inside the sliding back door. "What's wrong?" he asked her as he put an arm around her shoulders.

"Earl is at the door."

"Earl?" he asked.

"The twins' father. We haven't seen him for five years. We can't let the kids see him. Lyla is trying to—"

Trick put his hands on her shoulders. "I've got this. Go out back, keep everyone away from the front of the house."

Cece exhaled and managed a smile. "I'm sorry this has been so difficult. I hope we aren't scaring you off. You haven't had much time to adjust to your role, have you?"

"My role?" he asked, thinking about his wife alone with this Earl guy.

"Head of the family," she said. "You are the most senior male we have now." Trick was still absorbing the idea when she touched his cheek. "You're good for our Lyla. You've been a godsend today. Thank you."

She turned and left him still thinking about how he'd ended up as head of a family.

"No!"

Lyla's call from the front of the house took him out of his daze and he turned in a snap to march toward the front door. Trick had taken on all kinds of roles for his career, but he'd never had one more important than this.

***

"I SAID NO, EARL," Lyla said and stepped into his path again.

She was so pissed off that he'd made it over the threshold. But she'd do this dance with him all day if she had to. All she had to do was out-wait him. As Earl took a step left, she took one right, getting in his way, keeping him trapped between the front door and the bottom of the stairs.

"I have a right to—"

"I don't think so."

Lyla heard Trick before she knew he was there. As threatening as his words were, he said them with a smile, so maybe he was going to try diplomacy, meaning there really was a first time for everything.

"Trick!" Earl said. His hostile manner quickly faded in lieu of a smile. "Hey, man! I'm a big fan!"

"Shame," Trick said. "I usually pride myself on being nice to fans… Excuse me, sweetheart." Trick took her shoulders to move her aside gently. He took one stride past her to grab Earl by his shirt. Throwing him against the wall by the door, Trick pulled the shorter man to the tips of his toes and got down into his face to snarl at him. "You're not welcome in this house. You're not welcome at the funeral. You're not welcome in this family. Come back again, talk to, or try to contact anyone even remotely related to this family and we're gonna talk again. In private. Understand?"

Earl might have been thinking about objecting, but when he glanced past Trick's shoulder at her, Trick pulled him forward and slammed him against the wall again. "You look at my wife again and I'll rip your eyeballs out of your skull with my bare hands," Trick growled. "Now I'm gonna open this door and toss you out on your ass. If you don't run away back to whatever hole you came from and stay there, me and my boys will have a lot of fun chasing you down and stringing you up like a piñata." Trick's sinister smile sloped his lips. "And if you're a real fan, I don't have to tell you how good I am at party games. Do we understand each other?"

Nodding, Earl swallowed. Trick reached past him and opened the door. Dragging him forward, he did exactly what he'd said and threw Earl out the door. He went after him and Lyla kept an eye out the glass panel in the door to see her husband standing on the porch, watching Earl run away down the path and across the street until he was out of sight.

Trick stayed out there another minute before coming back inside. Closing the door, he brushed his hands together and grinned. "I love taking out the trash."

Considering him for a minute, Lyla tried to imagine how she'd have handled Earl if Trick hadn't come into her life. "Why did you do that?" she asked.

His grin fell. "He upset you and your mom… you didn't want me to do that?" He pointed a thumb back over his shoulder. "I can go get him back."

Trick was the only person in the world who probably could threaten a guy with physical bodily harm and then chase him down thirty seconds later to charm him into being his best buddy.

Inhaling, Lyla went to him and lifted her hands to his shoulders. "I love you, Nairn Strickland," she sighed and pulled him down for a kiss. "He upset me and my mom, that's really why you did that? You don't even know the full story."

"Don't need to," he said, touching her hair. "Anyone who upsets you deserves a beating. He got off lightly."

"Trick," she whispered and pulled him down for another kiss.

The man surprised her every minute. Opening her mouth wide, she edged backward and kept her arms tight around him as she lowered to sit on the stairs. He made a noise of surprise, but it didn't make her release him. Tightening her arms, she tilted her head. Kissing him deeper, she slanted back and opened her legs wider to curl them around his thighs.

When the confidence of his mouth took over the angle of the kiss, and his hands slid up to start pulling pins from her hair, she guided his hips back to start unbuckling his belt.

"Am I getting lucky on the stairs?" he panted against her mouth.

She ripped open the buttons of his jeans and slid her hand inside to tighten her fist around him. When he groaned, she grinned, Lyla loved pleasuring him, teasing him, being with him.

Kissing him again, she shook her head, rubbing their lips together as she did. "I am."

"Perfect," he grumbled.

A and a breath later he yanked his pelvis from hers and rose to push her legs together.

"Trick—"

"Shh," he said and put his hands up her skirt to pull her panties down her legs.

When he had them off and hooked around his thumb, he kissed her once and winked. Oh, that wink, he had mischief in mind.

Bumping his feet down to the bottom of the stairs, he lifted her skirt and stuck his head up underneath, tossing the fabric down his back. Oh God, that wasn't what she'd meant! She'd meant that she was the lucky one to be with him, not that she wanted him to…

"Trick!" she called and grabbed for his shoulders, which were under her skirt.

He forced her legs apart and licked the length of her pussy before driving his tongue into her.

Laughter left her lips as the sensation of pleasure warmed her from within. "Mm, Malloy, I've missed your taste."

"Trick," she whimpered when he sucked her clit hard. Her body arched and as she exhaled another moan of pleasure, she lifted her head. There was a knock at the door. Oh! Whoever was on the other side of the door hadn't looked through the glass, until now. "Oh, Trick."

"Yeah, baby," he hummed.

"No," she said, trying to close her legs and push him away as the two women beyond the front door made eye contact with her and waved. "Trick, there's someone at the door… watching us."

Lyla lifted her hand in a pathetic wave as Trick pulled her skirt from his head and turned to lean on an elbow to look out the glass, his body still between her thighs.

"Oh, well that's crappy timing," he said and vaulted onto his feet to march over to the door. "That's sick, weird, and twisted. Don't sneak up on a guy like that. I was busy!"

Oh no! How could he be so annoyed and shouting at these poor women?

"Trick!" Lyla called and leaped up to run down the stairs. It wasn't until the women stepped forward that she realized who they were.

"Discretion is a thing you know," the younger woman said as the older one stepped forward.

"Yeah, Jose, whatever," Trick sneered at the speaker before ducking toward the other woman. "Hey, mom."

Lyla bounced between him and his mother, giving him a shove back with her body. He really couldn't kiss his mother right now, not when his mouth had just been…

"Oh, Lyla, sweetie," his mother said and pulled her into her arms.

The emotional shift that this required kept Lyla frozen for a few seconds. "We brought everything you asked for, Trick," Josie said.

"Thanks, sis," he said.

Just like that, they were friends again. Maybe that's what it was like to have a sibling. When his mom let her go, Lyla stepped back, but his mom kept hold of her arms and was smiling at her.

"How are you holding up, sweetie?"

"Uh…" Lyla said and tipped her head back. She wasn't sure if she was supposed to be talking to his mother, he'd wanted them apart at the wedding. "Trick?"

"Right, uh, Ly, this is my mom, Andrea, everyone just calls her Drea, and this is Josie," he said and held up a hand to indicate his sister who was still behind his mother.

To her horror, Lyla saw her panties there, still hanging on his thumb, now swinging between her and Drea.

Reaching up, Lyla grabbed them down and balled them in her hands. "Uh, it's very nice to meet you," Lyla said and pushed Trick back to turn and welcome their guests inside. "Everyone is uh, outside in the back yard. There's, uh… There's still food, I think… and, uh… you should feel free to, uh… you know… uh—"

"Head out back, we'll be there in a minute," Trick said.

Yes, she was freaking out, but did he have to sound so damn amused? Josie was grinning, even Drea was smiling. Great, so she was the butt of the family joke already.

The women headed through the house and Lyla did her best to stay upright until they were gone.

"Oh, God," she said, crumpling into a crouch as soon as the women were gone.

Covering her face with both hands, she let her palms slide up over her head so she could squeeze her skull.

"Babe, I can't get to your pussy from this angle... I guess unless I just..."

His voice was right behind her and when she pivoted in her crouch, she ended up cross-legged in front of him. "Trick!"

"Usually you're calling my name after I've done the job."

Smacking his shoulder, Lyla couldn't even figure out how he was so casual about this. "How are you still thinking about sex! Your mom just saw you... she saw... and my underwear!"

Holding up the offending item, she was too embarrassed to look at it, but Trick took it from her and shoved them into his back pocket.

"Baby, it's no big deal," he said. "She doesn't care... she's probably happy."

"Happy?" she screeched, wondering if they were having the same conversation. "On what planet—"

"I'm a considerate lover, I take care of my woman... not every guy does that. You're very lucky, sweetheart," he said and combed his fingers through her disheveled hair that had to be in disarray, half-up, half-not.

"Trick!" she called, grabbing his hand to pull it down, but before she could object anymore, he leaned forward and kissed her.

Some of her mortification dwindled as the beat of his heart increased against her palm. Oh, his chest was so solid, her pillow, her comfort. As long as she had this heart near her, everything else went away.

Pushing him, she put him on his ass on the floor, against the wall, and climbed into his lap. His hands slid under her skirt and cupped her naked butt as she rubbed her clit against the bulk of his erection.

The urgency of her want built and she dragged his shirt up to stroke his chest. "Babe, I've got a rubber in my wallet," he murmured just beneath her ear.

But she mumbled without making words and shook her head as she tucked her hair behind her ears. "Why?"

"I brought it to the party, in case you showed up," he said, caressing her back, spending extra time around the area of her bra clasp without actually popping it open.

"No, I…"

She couldn't remember her name, or what was going on as she looked at his lips. All she knew was that she needed to kiss this man under her.

Grabbing his face, she forced her mouth over his and silently begged him to stay with her always.

Trick took her into his arms and stood up, carrying her through the house and kissing her every step of the way. He even managed to maintain the tangle of their tongues as he descended the stairs and took her into her basement bedroom.

When she was on her back, he left her and she cried out, grabbing for him before he could get off the bed.

"I need to get protection," he said, curving his hand around her cheek.

Trying to breathe in and out in the right order, she shook her head. "Don't need it."

He frowned. "Baby, I love you, but kids, right now—"

"I'm on the pill," she said and he blinked away his frown. "I… went and got it, the day we got back from the team-building course… Before you found me in the canteen, that's where I was… why I never had time to make lunch at home."

Coming back down on top of her, Trick was grinning as he stroked his fingers from her cheeks into her hair. "You didn't say anything."

"I... was going to, but I... it takes seven days to work, so I... I wanted it to be a surprise."

"Oh, baby," he groaned and pressed his nose and forehead to hers.

"I kept taking it because I... I wanted to be ready for you." Ready for him because she'd always belonged to him. "I was always too scared to... Declan never wanted to risk it... What I'm saying is, I... I've never had sex without a condom..."

He kissed her and slid his hands down her body. "Until today."

"Should we wait?" she asked and was amused by his petulant scowl. "Until tomorrow... on your birthday."

"It's my birthday today."

Smiling, she hugged him. "It is not."

"I've got the best present in the whole world here under me right now. Alone in a bedroom with my wife... no cameras. No audience. Just us alone... I'd say this is better than every birthday I've ever had." Being with Trick made her so happy, but as she stroked his body, her focus fell to his throat. "Babe?"

"I... I'm so happy with you... but I'm devastated about my dad, I... it's a difficult juxtaposition," she whispered, still stroking him. "I feel like I need you, now, more than I've ever needed you... maybe more than I'll ever need you until..."

"Until?" he asked. "We lose someone else?"

"Or gain someone," she said and stole a look at him. "We've never really talked about what we want from the future..."

"Kids," he said. "Are you asking about kids?" She nodded. "Do you want kids?"

"I was always content that I wouldn't have them because I didn't want to mess up my life. I was happy alone. But now... you've changed so much about my outlook, Trick. I don't really know that I can see myself as a mom, but... I think you'd make an incredible father and I know it would be an honor for me to..."

"Get knocked up?"

Always making jokes, but it was nice of him to lighten a heavy moment. "Nicer than that, but… yeah."

"It's funny, 'cause I'd have said it the other way around," he said. "You'll make an amazing mom, but I don't know what I could teach a kid. Given my past, how could I say no or discipline a kid when every mistake I've ever made is recorded… with pictures."

But none of that changed her opinion. "Doesn't that make you smarter? Think of the wealth of experience you have to pass on to kids, you could guide them away from those mistakes."

"Yeah, but my kids will be smart-ass little pricks who'll call me a hypocrite."

"Mine won't," she said, scratching her nails on his throat.

He kissed her. "You know, we should have kids, a bunch of them. I guarantee they'll worship you and hate me."

"We'll adore you," she murmured. "All of us. The girls will never be allowed to have boyfriends and their brothers will beat on any guy who looks at them sideways."

He laughed. "That's exactly how I'd raise them." After another kiss, he got that far off look in his eyes as he searched hers. "You'd really have kids with me?"

"Maybe not tomorrow, but… yeah. There isn't a man alive I'd rather procreate with."

He failed to fight against the curl of his lips. "I'm actually jealous of whatever dead guy you're thinking about right now."

Squeezing her eyes closed, she tipped her head back and squealed. Because as soon as she'd said that she recognized the distinction it implied too. "God, I hate that you can see inside my brain like that."

"So, who is he? Huh?" he asked, licking her throat, then kissing her chin. "A king? An emperor? Some fancy scientist, brainy guy?"

Shaking her head, she ran her fingers into his hair, and pretended to really ponder the possibilities. "If every man who ever lived was lined up right now, alongside every man who will ever live…?"

"Yeah, who's on the list?" he asked. "Who's your number one for the baby daddy spot?"

"One name," she said.

"One?"

"Only you, my love… When we're ready, if we decide it's right… I want to have your babies, Nairn Strickland."

Sinking down, he found her mouth with his. "Well, wife, there's something kinda hot about that request… but let me make one of my own."

TWENTY-EIGHT

LYLA COULDN'T HAVE begun to know how those words would haunt her.

The funeral went as well as a funeral could. Everyone had left the house, everyone except for her family, Drea and Josie, who had become fast friends with her mother, aunt, and cousins.

Lyla and Trick had done most of the hosting, the greetings and farewells. While Drea and Josie took care of the practical details like food and jackets.

The last neighbor had just walked off the porch when Trick put his arm around her shoulders. "You okay, babe?" he asked, kissing her head.

He'd been there every step of the way today and when his boys turned up to carry her father's coffin, she hadn't been able to stop the tears. None of them had ego, none tried to steal the show, they were all demure and respectful. They greeted her mother and Trick's with kisses and comfort.

Todd was too short to carry with the others, but Trick made sure to put him front and center as the others did the heavy lifting. Watching her husband walk slowly, wearing that somber look on his face, she almost didn't recognize him as the same man who'd first tried to kiss her.

"We have to go back to the city tomorrow," she said, turning toward Trick to accept his arms around her.

"It can wait," he said. "Until you're ready."

"My dad was big on taking care of our commitments," she said. "And the kids have to go back to school and get back to normality… We can't hide here forever."

"I can take you away," he said, holding her close and kissing her hair. "Anywhere in the world, we can take some time together, as much as you need."

"You know what I want?" she asked. "I want to just get this damn show over with so we can live our lives. For real. So, I say let's go back, do what they want us to do, keep our heads down, and get through it."

"Sounds like fun."

Letting her head fall back, she smiled at him. "I want to move back into your apartment. I want to sell my place and sleep in your bed every night." Maybe it was surprise, but he said nothing. "Does that sound like fun?"

"Sounds damn close to perfect, but are you sure? You moved out fast. You were just gone."

"I know and I'm sorry," she said, feeling awful for how she must have hurt him. "I knew we didn't want to share our relationship with them and I thought it would be impossible for us to live together without being intimate. I hurt you when I panicked and let them sucker me into their little plot. Maybe it was the alcohol in my system or my worry that they could hurt you with that stand-in nonsense, but I felt like I didn't have a choice. I love being with you, Nairn. I want to be with you and if what we do naturally as a couple ends up on film, I'll cope with that. I know you would never disrespect me."

"Like Boys Night? That was hot, baby."

"I wanted you," she said. "And I liked taking control." Loosening, she gave him control of her weight. "And there was no pressure, it was just us, you know, enjoying each other. I like having fun with you, Trick. But I don't like being conned."

"So, we do what comes naturally… and if we feel uncomfortable."

"Blueberries."

"Right," he said and bowed to kiss her. "Blueberries."

After another kiss, she took his hand to take him back inside. Trick closed the door and she carried on into the living room. Except as soon as she approached the back of the couch where the twins were sitting with their mother and hers, they all turned to look at her. Drea and Josie were on the loveseat and they looked just as pitying as her family.

"What is it?" she asked.

Avril pressed the mute button on the television and the volume came back up. Lyla hadn't even looked at the screen until she heard the reporter speak. "…Ms. Levine has refused to confirm or deny the identity of the child's father. But our station has been told by sources that it is without doubt Nairn Strickland. Given the recent footage of their getaway, we would say that's a safe bet." Pictures of Kira and Trick were shown on screen as well as images from Opposites Marry. "Also given that Ms. Levine is pursuing a civil case against the Prem channel, it seems certain that Trick, as he's known to his friends and colleagues, is the perpetrator. While details of the suit are just coming to light, it's understood that Kira asserts contraceptive protection provided by the show may have been tampered with, deliberately damaged to ensure failure. The accusation is serious and—"

Spinning around, Lyla gasped as she fixed on her stunned husband. "Oh, God, Trick," she said.

"Trick," Drea exclaimed. "Son, is it true? Is Kira pregnant with your child?"

"That's not why Lyla's upset," he said, searching his wife's face with concern. Lyla struggled to breathe in. "Baby, it'll be okay."

Linking her fingers, Lyla pressed her hands to her abdomen as he came to her and scooped his hand around the side of her head. "Nairn," she whispered.

"We'll deal with it, okay?" he said, fixating on her eyes and smiling. "We'll deal with it. I love you. It'll just be a little ahead of schedule, that's all."

"I don't get it," Josie said. "She's not upset that you slept around?"

"He didn't sleep with Kira," Lyla whispered, calming as she focused on her husband. When she could breathe normally again, she spun around to look at her sister-in-law. "We used their condoms."

***

"HONEY, WHERE'S YOUR wallet?" Lyla asked.

Lying on her stomach on Trick's bed, she had his laptop open in front of her. She'd just peed on the stick and was trying to distract herself as they waited for the results to develop. Trick was clearing space in his closet that he said hadn't been cleaned out since he moved in.

It had taken her a while to get to sleep last night, but Trick had been great at calming her down. The mood in her mother's house when she left was somber. Cece would miss having her there, but the sooner they all returned to their lives, the sooner they could start to process how life would be now that her dad was gone.

Lyla knew it would take time to grieve for her father, but she also knew he wouldn't want them all sliding into a pit of depression and stopping their lives. At every low moment she'd had since her first breakdown, Trick had been there for whatever she needed and he was still here now as they prepared his apartment for her officially moving in. Permanently.

It would just take a couple of minutes to find out if they were going to have a third, tiny, roommate moving in too.

Trick came out of the closet and pulled his wallet from his back pocket to toss it to the bed. Picking it up, Lyla sat to cross her legs and began to look through it. When she found the condom he'd put in there on the night of his party, she looked at it for a second and then tossed it to the trash can beside the door.

When it went in, she raised both hands up.

Trick laughed. "Nice shot, baby."

It was a fluke, but she wasn't about to tell him that. So, she just went back to peeking at his cards. "Which credit card can I use?"

"The black one in front," he responded. Staying in the bedroom, he frowned at the inside of his closet. "What are we buying?"

Pulling the card out, she tossed his wallet aside and began to type in the numbers. "Porn," she said.

"Hmm, cool," he said, doing a double-take. "Wait, what?"

Lyla was only halfway through the number when he came over to sit on the bed beside her. Instead of looking at the screen, he pushed her hair aside and leaned in to kiss the side of her neck.

When he snaked his hand under her skirt, she laughed and pulled it out before he could touch her. "Don't distract me."

"You need some loving, you don't need to pay for it," he murmured and put an absent hand on the top of the laptop screen, but she caught it before he could close it and opened it again. "Your man's right here, baby."

Taking her hand, he guided it from the computer to his lap and began to rub it against his groin.

"I want to see this," she said, sliding her hand out of his to put another couple of numbers into the screen.

"See what?" he asked, flipping onto his front. "What the hell can be so interesting that—"

"Us," she said. "We're live right now."

"We are?" he asked, glancing around the room.

There were still cameras there, but they wouldn't be linked to this low budget website. "Yep, we're live having crazy, wild sex apparently," she said. "I want to see us having sex."

"We'll make a sex tape," he said.

Lowering, she rubbed her mouth in his hair. "We don't have to, because this website says we're having sex right now."

"Then I've been doing it wrong for a long time," he said.

Lyla laughed as she put in another number. "I want to see this… especially since some of these tags are things I've never heard of… what is bukkake?"

"Okay, we don't want to watch that," he said and this time succeeded in closing the laptop.

"Trick," she whined.

He rolled to his back and began to stroke her thigh. "It's a con, Malloy," he said. "You put in your card details and they take all your money to show you some grainy video of crappy porn actors wearing bad wigs and reciting lines from the show."

Laughing, she bowed and kissed him. "Is that the voice of experience?"

"Watching porn? Sure, I've watched porn," he said and grinned. "Got an offer to star in one once."

"Really?" she asked, climbing on top of him. "Did you consider it?"

"My life was a porno back then," he said. "I probably would've done it if someone had dared me."

"You'll do anything on a dare," she said, pushing up his tee-shirt to expose his torso. The sight of his form made her whimper. Man, he was hot. "You know if I get fat we're not having sex."

"Fat?" he asked. "I don't care if you put on weight… and I'm confident in my ability to get into your panties. But why would you get fat?" Turning to look toward the bathroom, Lyla figured that the stick would probably be ready by now. "You don't mean fat, you mean pregnant."

Pressing his hands to her belly, Trick drew her attention back to him. "I'm nervous," she whispered.

"If you're pregnant, we'll deal with it. It's not a disaster. We talked about having kids."

"Yeah, in the future," she said. "Not today."

"Nine months is in the future," he said. "We only used their condoms those first three times, after that they were all ours."

"I say we throw out every condom anyway, just in case," she said.

"We don't need them now," he said. Wearing that mischievous glint in his eye, he picked up her skirt. "Slide that pussy on up here, baby, and we'll go live right here."

He flicked his tongue at her, but she bent over him to press a hand over his mouth. "We have to be in the studio in an hour. What are we going to do if they got us pregnant? I guess… we don't know where Kira got her information from… And you said she was on an IUD, how can she be pregnant? They can be removed… and I guess no contraception is a hundred percent effective. Oh, God, Trick," she sighed out his name and collapsed on top of him, tucking her head under his chin.

When his arms closed around her, she started to feel better. "If they got us pregnant, we sue them," he said.

But Lyla shook her head. "How would our baby feel if we did that? It would be like we didn't want him."

"Then we'll settle for an undisclosed sum," he said. "Whatever you want, babe. I'll do whatever you want."

"Anything?"

"Anything," he said. "Especially if it involves punching Bunny in the face."

Smiling, she thought about how nice it would be to see Bunyan taken down. But that was a dream, not a reality. "Then he'll sue us." Sitting up, she planted her hands on his chest. "You'll do anything?" He nodded and caught the ends of her hair between his splayed fingers. "Will you check the stick?"

His playfulness lessened as he got serious. Driving his fingers into her hair, Trick pulled her down for a long kiss. Turning her onto her back, he stroked her face, and kissed her again before rolling away to climb off the bed to head for the bathroom.

Risk jumped up on the bed and she reached for him, he bunted her hand and came over to rub his face on hers. "I love you too," she murmured, picking up the cat as she sat up to look at the bathroom door. The stick wasn't difficult to read. It said pregnant or not pregnant. But Trick hadn't come back. "Nairn?"

He came into the bathroom doorway and lifted the stick. "Not," he said, "we're good."

Flopping onto her back, she gave Risk a kiss before letting him go. The cat wandered off and she put both hands over her heart. Trick came to the bed and sat beside her. Throwing the test across the room, he got it in the trash can and then rested a hand on her belly.

Grabbing his hand, she squashed it against her lips. "I'm disappointed," she said, uncertain as she sought his eyes, but when she did, his were smiling.

"Me too."

"Gosh, it's so weird."

Curling around him, Lyla put her face in his lap and brought her knees up at his back. "It's okay," he said, stroking her hair. "The next one will be positive and we'll be ready." Nodding, she pressed her mouth to his thigh. "Babe, if you're really upset, we'll get you pregnant."

Tipping her face, she looked up at him. "We have a meeting."

"Malloy," he said, catching her wrist as she rose.

Looking back at him, she smiled. "I'm okay," she said. "Next time."

It was nuts that she was this disappointed. They weren't trying for a child, they hadn't failed at anything. Now wasn't the time to have a baby. The show was still going on. The studio was on them every minute. They needed breathing room to get to know each other.

Lyla had to focus on being the best wife she could be. On her parents' porch, she and Trick had agreed to be themselves, to do what came natural and to have fun, and that was what she was going to do.

TWENTY-NINE

INSTEAD OF WATCHING Opposites on their nine-week anniversary, they were going to a nightclub. Trick had tried to say no when Tate and Green had suggested they go clubbing to celebrate. But Lyla was feeling buzzed after her surprise appearance on a live Boys Night show earlier that week, making it twice that she'd been on now. So she'd railroaded her husband into saying yes.

Lyla was super excited, until the cab reached their destination block and then she started to get nervous. But it was a kind of excited anxiety that made her stomach flip-flop.

Turning her smile on Trick, she didn't expect to see him looking so concerned. "What's wrong?" she asked.

He hadn't let go of her hand since he took it to lead her out of their apartment. Twisting toward him, she laid her opposite hand on his chest.

"Nothing, baby. I'm good," he said and picked up their joined hands to kiss the back of hers.

"I promise to do my best not to embarrass you," she said. "I've never done shots, but I can—"

"No," he said, his attention flying to hers. "Just… pace yourself, okay? I'm gonna look after you." His grip tightened as his gaze drifted to the side window. "I'm gonna look after you."

Was that what was worrying him? He felt responsible for her at the best of times, now they were going into an uncertain and volatile situation where people were going to expect him to lose control.

"It's okay for you to get drunk, you know," she said. "And to flirt."

"I'm not going to get drunk," he said, letting go of her hand to put his arm around her. "And I plan to flirt, constantly." Swallowing, Lyla hoped she'd be able to handle that without retreating into herself. Trick pushed his mouth into her hair. "With you."

"With me?" she asked.

Before she could tip her head back to tell him she'd never been hit on in a nightclub, the car stopped and Trick was leaning forward to pay the driver then ushering her out into the street.

Those in the roped-off line called out when they saw Trick and as he tossed a casual arm around her shoulders, he waved at the group and walked straight toward the door across a red carpet. The security guard stepped aside, letting them head to the entrance without hindrance.

Trick exchanged a fancy handshake with the guy who was just inside the door and they laughed at whatever was said. Lyla focused on the double doors at the end of the lit space behind them. There were security guys here and a few clubbers. But no one else stopped them after Trick was done talking, though he did slap a few hands.

Lyla could feel the music before they even got to the door. It was so loud and the bass seemed to slam into her chest. She couldn't tell where the thumping came from, whether it was her heart on the inside or the external music.

Infused with adrenaline, she kept herself close to Trick when he moved her body in front of his and reached for the door over her shoulder. "Ready?" he said into her hair and she nodded.

Lyla couldn't wait. A brand-new experience was waiting for her right on the other side of that door. She didn't even have to be nervous because she had the most experienced guide she could hope for.

Trick pushed the door open; she gasped at the intensity of the noise. She struggled to hear her own thoughts. Quelling an impulse to put her fingers in her ears, she figured if everyone else was okay with it, then the volume couldn't be doing any serious damage to her hearing.

The vast space was dark, but regular colored lights flashed and there were recessed blue lights around a central bar area. Right at the back of the room was a huge space that was almost completely black. Even the colored lights didn't really help her pick out details, all she knew was that there was a mass of bodies, maybe hundreds of them all moving up and down, dancing to the music.

After giving her a few seconds to absorb the scene, Trick wrapped an arm around her shoulders from behind and guided her down the half-dozen stairs into an area filled with booths. But they didn't sit at any of these. He pointed over her shoulder to an area on the right-hand wall and guided her through the clubbers, many of whom stopped to exchange high-fives with him or fist bumps.

At least the volume meant it was virtually impossible to have a conversation, so they didn't need to stop. The crush got worse, but Trick tightened his arm around her shoulder, pinning her back to his body as he curled himself around her and kept moving forward.

When they got to another set of stairs, they went up and a security guard opened a roped-off area to let them inside. Exhaling shock and excitement, Lyla looked up to see a booth in front of them. Large and circular with white leather seats, Tate and Green were there already with Samantha, and Sadie, and a few other people she recognized from the network.

Trick guided her toward the booth and urged her to sit down first before he leaned over the table to exchange handshakes and kisses with everyone who was here. When all the hellos were done, he slid in beside her and wrapped an arm around her neck to pull her close to him.

"You okay?" he shouted into her ear and she nodded, grinning as she turned around to make eye contact.

She'd meant just to assure him that she was actually okay, but her excitement overtook her and she pushed forward to kiss him. The table cheered, but Trick tightened his arm around her neck, pulling her closer still and deepening the kiss.

If they kept this up, they were going to have a short night. Patting his chest, she eased him back and puffed out some of her adrenaline as he swept her hair away from her neck and bowed to kiss behind her ear.

"Usually takes a couple of hours in a club before I get a kiss like that," he said into her ear.

The feeling of his breath tickling her neck made her shiver, but she turned herself against him into the cocoon of his body, keeping her back pressed to his ribs beneath his arm. Being here was a new experience and she'd expected to learn something about the thrill of clubbing, Lyla hadn't expected to learn something new about her relationship with Trick, but she had.

Belonging to him, in this room full of people, was a powerful sensation. Lyla felt a need to keep herself against him, to get as close as she could, to maintain contact as the rhythm of the music overtook her.

A tray of drinks was brought and the tray was circled with shot glasses that were duly handed out. One was put in front of her and she glanced at Trick who narrowed his eyes and shook his head once before he leaned in again.

It was so loud that any time he wanted to talk to her he had to scream in her ear. "You don't have to."

Stroking her hand over his thigh, she gave him a reassuring body nudge and lifted her glass in time with everyone else. Tossing back the shot, Lyla inhaled as soon as the liquor hit her throat and coughed once. Trick turned her face to him and immediately closed his mouth on hers, giving her cover for the response to the drink that had hit her harder than she'd thought it would.

Lyla had drunk alcohol, did on a regular basis, but she'd never been one for binge drinking, so shots had never featured.

"Want to dance?" he asked, rubbing his cheek on hers as he found her ear after their kiss.

She hadn't really done any dancing in public. But they were at a nightclub, so she pushed aside her initial urge to say no and took his hand. If they were going to do this, she was going to do everything.

***

TIME DIDN'T EVEN have a meaning in this building.

Without any windows and only artificial light they could've been here for an hour or a week and she'd have no way to know. They'd danced, they'd drank; she'd even done another couple of shots. Everyone was laughing and flirting or hooking up as they all sank into drunkenness.

Under Trick's arm, seated at the booth, Lyla was bouncing along to the music and sipping from her straw. It was amazing to see how all these normally civilized people suddenly became party animals as soon as a little music and some alcohol was introduced. She'd never got it. Never understood the thrill. Until tonight.

Trick's lips touched the side of her neck, then rose to the back of her ear, but he didn't speak to her, just blew gently and kissed his way back down. He had a high tolerance for alcohol, but she hadn't really been keeping track of what he'd been drinking. Lyla didn't know where his inhibition level was, not that he usually suffered from having high inhibitions like she did.

Grabbing his wrist, she put down her drink and twisted toward him, pulling his arm tight around her so she was pressed into him.

Pushing up, she sought his ear and he ducked to offer it. "Can we make out?" she asked.

Leaning back, his eyes stayed heavy though his brows rose. Lowering, he pressed his lips to hers, in a quick but sensual peck. Was he teasing her? He tipped his head the other way and did the same thing again. Yes, this was a tease, but it was a nice one. The adrenaline fused with her endorphins, the alcohol surged through her and she felt her body loosen.

Kissing Trick made her feel alive while it deadened her ability to control her own body, or even hold herself upright. Scooping a hand through her hair, he cupped the back of her head and pulled her mouth up to meet his.

Yes.

This was what she wanted. His tongue, exploring her mouth, hot, wet, wild. Here they were, in public, surrounded by their friends and colleagues, enjoying each other and she wasn't even thinking about the camera crew that was somewhere loitering around. She wasn't thinking about the future, or the past, she was thinking about now.

This minute.

This man.

Man, he was hot and he was hers. Undoing a couple of his shirt buttons, she slid her hand inside without even thinking about whether it was appropriate. Lyla wanted to feel good and Trick was taking her to ecstasy.

Letting go of her hair, he moved onto her neck when her head fell back. But he crouched a little and hooked an arm under her legs to pull them up over his. If she was allowed to stroke his chest like this then he was allowed to caress her legs.

Lyla didn't even realize she'd parted them until his finger pushed into her. Opening her mouth in a gasp that may have been silent, or a thousand decibels, it was impossible to tell since it was drowned out by the music, she broke their kiss, but stayed close enough that they could share oxygen.

With her wide eyes on his, she curled her fingers into the edge of his shirt as he withdrew his finger and then pumped it back into her. This had to be breaking some kind of rule, but when his other finger began to massage her clit, Lyla didn't care about rules anymore.

Releasing a breath of bliss, her head fell back again. But Trick's supporting arm curled to catch her head and he tucked it in against his neck, concealing the look on her face against his skin as he kissed her face then her mouth as he manipulated her position.

His hand kept working between her thighs as his mouth teased hers. Lyla wasn't even sure she was breathing, he might have been doing that for her too because he was certainly the guy in control here.

It was only as she whimpered and tensed that his tongue stopped teasing her mouth. Keeping their lips together, he took her to orgasm, covering the curse word that slipped from her mouth with another kiss.

When she was gasping and shaking from the force of what he'd just done to her, he slid his hand from her panties and reached for her drink to put it in her hands. Usually they were having sex not long after he did that to her.

But as she regained her equilibrium, or at least tried to, Lyla figured that couldn't happen here in this public place. Those around the table were carrying on their conversations, or engaged in their own make-out sessions, and she wondered what else might be going on beneath the table.

Taking a long drink, she let her eyes wander to Trick. He was peering at her, and damn he looked proud of himself. She wanted to ask him if they could leave because she desperately wanted to feel him inside her.

But… this was her first clubbing experience and could be her last for all she knew. The last thing she wanted to do was be the party pooper who cut the night short.

Shoving her glass to the table, she boosted up to sit in his lap. But as she tipped her chin up toward him, she heard his groan of satisfaction like he liked this position and from the lump in his jeans under her ass, she'd guess he was having thoughts of his own.

Except he wasn't asking to go home to be with her, so she'd just have to accept this desire as part of the night, and it would lead to an explosive union… if they could have one. With the cameras in the bedroom, they'd been avoiding having sex in there. Their usual kissing and cuddling wouldn't be enough to satisfy her tonight if she didn't calm herself down and they might be too drunk to do it in the shower.

Curling an arm around to the back of his head, she pulled him, and felt his hands close around her breasts at the same time. Given what he'd just done for her, Lyla wasn't going to object to his hands going anywhere. Apparently, this place had the same rules as Boys Night: anything goes!

But instead of kissing him, she sought his ear. "I'm going to the restroom."

There were bathrooms on this private level, and she'd gone with Sadie already, but her friend was currently on the other side of the booth wrapped around some guy she'd met at the bar.

Trick nodded and put his lips to her ear. "Want me to come with you?"

She didn't need an escort; the restrooms were just in the back corner, accessed from a square hall that was down a couple of stairs. She couldn't get lost and because they were in the roped-off VIP area, their particular bathrooms were quiet, so no one would be able to hurt her.

Pushing his hips up, Trick gave her a hint of what was in his mind.

But, wait, he wasn't suggesting… Was that allowed?

Twisting further, she made eye contact and from the mischief in his eyes, she'd guess that maybe… really? Was he thinking what she was thinking?

No. No way. Surely, they couldn't…

But Trick took her hand as he slid to the end of the booth and because she was on his lap, when he stood up, she was forced to. He didn't let her body part from his, but he probably didn't want the whole club to see the erection in his jeans and it was still there as he led her away from the booth and down the stairs to the bathroom.

There were people outside, but no one said anything when Trick pushed into the ladies room. Oh God, they could get into serious trouble for this. Except when they went inside, there was no one in the main part of the bathroom. Some of the stall doors were closed, but no one actually witnessed Trick leading her to the end stall and guiding her inside.

Pushing her to the wall as soon as the door was locked, he stole her mouth. "Can we do this here?" she whispered, but he was already opening his jeans and hiking up her skirt. "Oh my God, Trick."

But it was a laugh that accompanied her words, not any kind of horror.

Picking her up, he hooked her legs over his hips and kissed her as he slid himself into her. "Oh, God, Trick," she said again, but this time it was a long moan of pleasure that flavored her words.

"This isn't romantic," he said, kissing her neck.

"It's hot," she said, moving in time with his increasing pace. "Oh, Trick!"

"Shh," he said, laughing as he captured her mouth.

Yes, okay, they were doing this, but it probably was against the official rules. To keep herself quiet, Lyla did her best to kiss him as hard as she could. But as he groaned and slammed into her, Lyla couldn't concentrate on kissing anymore.

God, he hadn't even taken her panties off, he'd just slid them aside. Lyla had never had sex like this, never been so bad. But it felt amazing.

Now she didn't have to worry about them not being intimate when they got back to the apartment. Squeezing around him, she struggled to control her panting. Sealing her lips, Lyla tried to trap her moan, but it ended up just sounding pained and high-pitched.

Arching forward, her mouth burst open as she hit climax and slammed her hand against the stall door beside them. "Trick, fuck!"

Hissing through his teeth, he pushed hard, slamming her hips against the wall again as he came inside her. Slumping on him, Lyla couldn't lift her head from his shoulder, couldn't even bend her own arms.

"Oh, baby," he grumbled and the mist of his breath moistened her hair.

"You're... you're... I don't even know what you are, Trick," she whispered only now becoming aware of what she'd done at climax. Shock made her head dart up. "Oh, I..."

"Screamed my name? Yes, you did, baby," he said, rubbing his nose on hers to tempt another kiss. "I love you."

Redundant as it was now, she whispered. "You said to be quiet."

He shrugged and kissed her again. "As long as we both finished, it doesn't matter. Getting thrown out during, that's a bitch, after, I'm okay with."

A smile helped her to relax and she kissed him again. But as they sank into the pleasure of their make-out session, Lyla began to wriggle and Trick lifted his head.

"I'm sorry it had to be fast and dirty, baby," he said, putting her on her feet.

Pushing down her skirt, Lyla watched him tuck himself away as she rested on the wall. This wasn't like at home when they could kiss and enjoy each other for as long as they wanted to afterward.

"I loved it," she said, rising to kiss him again. "I love you... Thank you for tonight. I've had so much fun... all because of you."

Bowing, he put his head to hers and murmured. "It's not over yet, gorgeous... Let's get back out there."

Stroking his face, she smiled. "Give me a minute, I'll follow you."

"You're not going to hide in here all night, are you? Trust me, everyone's been impressed with you tonight. No one's going to—"

"No, I just need to..." Rolling her eyes downward, she shrugged. "Clean up."

"Okay," he said, grinning and stealing another kiss. "I'll get you another drink."

"I love you," she mouthed.

He opened the lock and curved himself around the door to slip out. He winked at her before he ducked out and pulled the door closed. "Ladies," Lyla heard him say on the other side of the door and as those in the bathroom giggled, she smiled and rolled her eyes. That was her man and she'd never been so proud of him.

***

WHEN SHE CAME OUT of the bathroom, Lyla was already missing her husband and in need of another drink. The last person she expected to find standing outside the restroom was her friend, Curtis.

"Curtis," she said and he turned toward her.

"Lyla," he said and the two of them embraced. "What are you doing here?"

"Trick brought me," she said because the last place he'd probably ever expected to find her was in a club like this. But when he made a face, she returned it. "Yes, my husband, and don't even start."

"I'm sorry," he said, driving a hand through his hair.

Concern made her look at him closer. "Curt… are you okay?"

"Yeah, I…"

A group came down the stairs into the small hallway, crowding them. He took her hand, and looked around before pulling her toward a door at the edge of the space.

Lyla didn't really register the handle on the door, but when he pulled her through it, she was shocked to be hit by cold air. The door closed with a click behind them and he pulled her across the alley into a shadow.

"Curt?" she asked.

Her friend wasn't usually frazzled like this and he didn't look drunk, just frantic as he put one hand to his hip and rubbed the back of his neck with the other. "I… I think I screwed up."

"How?" she asked, moving nearer to him.

"I… I had a big fight with Bunyan."

"At the studio?" she asked, having not expected that because she didn't even know the men knew each other. "Why? What happened?"

"I laid into him, told him how it wasn't right how they'd portrayed you in this show. I was so pissed. I saw him and I… I just took the chance to say my piece, you know? But he's not the most understanding guy and…" Curt took her arms to pull her closer. "I think he might fire me… I can't lose my job, Lyla. What will I do if he fires me?"

"Okay," she said, putting her hands to his shoulders to reassure him. "It's okay."

Part of her was pissed off; she didn't need Curtis defending her. Yeah, the show had painted her in a kind of negative light, but she and Trick had decided weeks ago to let the show do whatever the show was going to do. They weren't going to get themselves upset about it. Unfortunately, Curtis hadn't been included in that decision and might have just risked his career to stand up for her.

"No," he said, holding her face. "It's not okay. If I lose this job… Bunyan knows everyone in this industry… I'll never get hired again. I'll lose my apartment, my life! Lyla, what the hell was I thinking?"

"It's okay," she said again and smiled as she pulled him into a hug.

What the hell was she going to do? She couldn't leave him out here like this. But they were outside, would she be allowed back into the club without Trick? The alcohol in her system wasn't reacting well to the cool night air and her head began to spin.

"Are you okay?" Curtis asked, probably feeling her waver on her feet.

"Yes," she said, trying her best to smile, but keeping her arm around him as he supported her and they walked to the end of the alley. "Let me get Trick and we'll go home and talk about this."

Curtis slowed and scowled at her. "He hates me. He doesn't give a damn if I lose my job. He'll probably tell Bunyan to fire me just 'cause they're buddies and he can."

Boy, was that a misconception. It was easier to smile after hearing that assertion. "They're not buddies," she said, pulling him forward to keep moving. "And Trick will care; he'll appreciate you sticking up for me."

Even if he didn't, she would hope that her husband wouldn't tell her to turn her back on her friend. They carried on around to the front of the club, but she was shocked to see the doors were all closed up. "They don't let people in this late," he said. "I think security let people out the back when they want to leave."

Okay, well he could've told her that before they walked around to the front. But she'd only taken a single step when Paul came around the corner of the building.

As soon as he saw her, he lifted his arms. "Where the hell did you go?" Paul asked.

She'd think that was pretty obvious given that she was standing right here. "We need to get Trick," she said. "He's inside—"

"I'll get him," Paul said. "What's the problem?"

"Nothing," she said because she knew Paul did have a relationship with Bunyan, so it would probably be best that he didn't know about Curtis' fight with the man, at least before he had to.

"I asked Lyla back to mine," Curtis said. "I'm only a few blocks over."

"You did?" she asked. Curtis made a face at her that suggested she should go with it. "Okay, but I need to get Trick and—"

"Okay," Paul said and put an arm around him. "They won't let us back in this late. I'll radio our sound guy; he'll get Trick and meet you over there."

"Meet me over there?" she asked because she hadn't noticed that Curtis had gone ahead to stop a cab.

"Sure, we won't all fit in one car anyway," Paul said, smiling as he urged her forward. "We'll be five minutes behind you."

Yeah, because he'd want to make sure that everything was filmed. That could cause problems for Curtis. Anything the show got on film could be seen by Bunyan and that wouldn't be good for her friend if he said anything negative.

"Okay," she said, ducking into the cab after Curtis. "Tell Trick to meet me there."

"Yep," Paul said, urging her into the car.

Something felt off. She couldn't tell what it was, but she was thinking about it as the cab pulled away from the curb. When Curtis picked up her hand in his, she looked at his profile. Why was he holding her hand? For comfort? Did he need the physical connection to make him feel better?

Curtis was her friend, he'd been her only friend for a

long time, she trusted him… didn't she?

THIRTY

TRICK NEVER SHOWED UP.

Lyla would have been pissed off except when she woke up on Curtis' couch, she panicked. What if something had happened to her husband and she hadn't been there for him?

After talking to Curtis for a while last night, she'd been ready to go home. But she hadn't taken a purse to the club. Trick had assured her that she wouldn't need anything because she'd be with him all night. Except that meant she didn't have her cell phone to call him and had no money for a cab.

Curtis let her use his phone, but Trick's just kept ringing out over and over again. If he was still in the club, he'd never hear it over the music. She couldn't get in a cab if she didn't know Trick was at the other end with his wallet, and she didn't feel confident walking the streets that late by herself.

Trick would probably be mad for endangering herself like that anyway. He didn't like her out and about at night alone. At Curtis' she was safe, and so when he offered her a blanket and a pillow, she conceded. Trick would show up when everyone was done at the club and he noticed she hadn't come back from the bathroom. When he did, she'd be on the couch, ready to shout at him for not answering his phone.

But she fell asleep and no one ever knocked on the door.

Curtis offered her breakfast, but she wasn't going to hang around at his place. They were both due at work anyway, so she persuaded him to take her straight into the office. She went to reception and requested to use the phone. The receptionist said she had to dial the number out and when Lyla said she was calling Trick's cell, she was told that Trick was already here… in a meeting with Bunyan.

Good.

Thank God.

At least he wasn't in danger or dead.

Curtis was there at her shoulder when she turned around. "Do you think I should go to Bunyan and apologize?"

"Couldn't hurt," she said, racing toward the elevator.

Trick was never at work this early unless he'd been called in for something. But what could he have been called in for? What did Bunyan want with him?

"Will you come in with me?" Curtis asked.

To Bunyan's office? "I'm going there anyway," she said and it made no difference to her if Curtis buddied her up the stairs.

The elevator seemed to take an age to ascend. Eventually it got to the executive floor and she dashed to Bunyan's office. If Trick was in there, she didn't need to knock, so she strode straight in.

Trick was standing at the desk opposite Bunyan. Sadie was on her feet at the end of the desk. Everyone turned when she came to a rushed halt. "Trick," she said, but his eyes were cold as they scanned her figure up and down.

He exhaled a tut and then his lips sloped. "Guess I do have it in me to corrupt even the purest," he muttered. "Haven't been home yet, sweetheart?"

Damn.

Looking at herself, Lyla saw that she was still in last night's outfit. It hadn't even occurred to her that she'd be a mess, but she hadn't combed her hair or brushed her teeth, all she'd thought about was getting to Trick.

"I didn't have money for a cab," she said.

Trick looked over her head. "You're a real gent."

"There, you have your answer," Bunyan said, dropping into his seat. "She was screwing this guy."

Her jaw swung loose and she gasped. "No! No, I wasn't… doing that." Bunyan was evil, through and through, but she didn't think that Trick would believe him, at least not until she looked into her husband's stony eyes. "Trick," she said and took a step to him, but he took a reflexive step back and cast his attention to Curtis.

It was fine, Curtis would tell him the truth, and then she could be pissed at Trick for believing the worst of her. "I'm sorry, Strickland," Curtis said.

Spinning around, Lyla couldn't even recognize the man she'd once thought of as her friend. His look of contrition. His shifty posture. What the hell was he doing? "What the…? Curtis!"

But Curtis was still looking at Trick. "We've had feelings for each other for a long time… But I guess you knew that. That's why you went off at me, right? You saw how we felt about each other."

"How we…?" The shock of this was making her numb, but she couldn't shut down, not now. Pivoting to set her sights on Trick, Lyla sought for some sign that he was messing around. "Nairn, you don't believe any of this."

"That I never deserved you. That I always knew you were going to find something better? Someone… better suited to you. I told you if you did that you should go for it without hesitating, didn't I?" he said, his words almost callous. "Congratulations, Malloy… Be happy."

When he headed for the door, she tried to reach for him, but he twisted his whole body away from her and kept on going. The door slammed so hard that she was sure the room shook and for a minute she just stood gaping.

But it was when Sadie began to move that she snapped out of her daze. "Sadie," she said. The woman stopped, wearing a look of such hurt and disappointment on her face that Lyla sank into a pit of shame. "I promise you… I wouldn't—"

"Guess it wasn't him we should've worried about playing away," Sadie said. "I'll have your stuff packed up and sent back to your apartment. Don't call him. Don't come near him. Stay the hell away… from all of us."

Her apartment was on the market, due to be sold; she'd already had an offer on the place. Lyla was supposed to be living with Trick, dedicating her life to him as he did the same for her.

One night out and everything had fallen apart.

Sadie carried on out of the room, leaving Lyla alone with Bunyan and Curtis. When her eyes crept up to Bunyan, she was disgusted to see the satisfaction pasted across his face.

"When an asset is no longer valuable, we sell it," he said, reciting what he'd said before. "I think this news will be getting to Ms. Levine later today… She'll console Trick for you and I'd expect her to be a regular feature in his life from now on if I were you… They do make a very beautiful couple, don't they? And now that she's expecting his child…"

"That child is not his," Lyla spat out. "Is she even pregnant? Was this some kind of game all along?"

"It's all a game," Bunyan said, opening his arms to the ceiling. "It's entertainment."

Heartbroken and infuriated, Lyla couldn't stay calm. "These are our lives," she said. "That petition was right. The lawsuit… it's everything you deserve. You do enjoy playing with people's lives… with their happiness… and their sanity. Why would Kira want to be anywhere near this station after the—"

"The footage of you and Trick waiting for the results of your pregnancy test was golden, some of the most interesting we've had. And let's face it, Miss Malloy… you're not exactly interesting to watch… unless you're taking your clothes off on Boys Night."

Was it spite? Was this guy really that pissed at her for having fun on Boys Night and not playing by his rules? Or was it less contrived than that? Was he so shallow that he'd do anything to produce what he thought was great television?

"Trick is smarter than you, he'll figure it out," she said. "And when he does, you're going to lose your biggest star."

"Trick is in contract for another three years, he's not going anywhere… You on the other hand…"

Oh, she was happy to jump, she didn't need to be pushed. "You can consider this my notice."

"Accepted," he said. "Though you're required to fulfill your Opposites Marry contract."

"Whatever," she said. If Trick was going to hook up with Kira, they wouldn't be filming much of her and there was less than three weeks left on that contract.

"Consider your credentials revoked. If you have to come back to this building, you'll be escorted by security."

"Fine," she said, turning around to head for the door. She didn't even look at Curtis, couldn't bring herself to. The bastard had sold her out and whatever he'd been paid was blood money that ruined any chance of her finding happiness.

"Lyla," Curtis said.

The apology in his voice meant nothing to her. "Go to hell," she said, and marched out of the room, sick, heartbroken, and pissed as hell.

THIRTY-ONE

SHE DESERVED EVERYTHING she got.

It didn't take Lyla long to realize that Curtis had to have been in on the con from the start. When she got the call from Paul to say she'd be required to go to the Prem Halloween party, she hadn't been surprised. The Wild West theme was an excuse for the guys to carry guns, because she'd eat her braids if a single one of them weren't thrilled to have an excuse to carry fake weapons… at least she hoped they were fake.

The Native American costume that had been couriered to her was short and low-cut, but as she entered the studio that had been cleared for the in-house party, she saw that she was in good company.

"The restrooms are in the east corner," the guy at her side, Ivan, said. "You can use those, but you are not permitted to leave this room for anything else."

"Sure," she said.

The tall guy was built like a quarterback. When he'd come to her apartment door, she'd almost swallowed her tongue. Despite reminding herself not to be intimidated, it was difficult when he got into the cab beside her not to be because he took up more than three quarters of the backseat, just with his shoulders.

But, as Bunyan had reminded her by email, she was technically no longer a Prem employee. She was merely a participant in a show, so she had to be escorted on and off the premises. Fine by her. All she wanted to do was show up, play the damn games and leave again. The sooner the better.

They'd lost a week of filming when her father died, Bunyan had decided to write that off, but it did mean that Opposites was airing only a week behind. Watching their clubbing night had been difficult. She and Trick looked so happy and then there was the alleyway footage.

Now she understood exactly how they'd cut the footage to look like Trick and Kira had done more than they had in the woods, because they'd cut the footage of her and Curtis in the same way. It did look incriminating, but she didn't care.

The world knew she and Trick had split up. The tabloids had been outside her apartment. But it didn't matter. She had nowhere to be. Paul came to the apartment to do her interviews; she wasn't even invited into the studio for those.

The cameras in her apartment seemed to be on constantly. Lyla knew they couldn't use all the footage, but she was so tired of seeing the red lights beaming from her walls.

Her aunt had come to visit her and it was infuriating. Lyla couldn't ask her if she wanted to go anywhere because the paparazzi were outside. But the studio was inside. It didn't help that all her aunt wanted to talk about was Trick. Lyla tried to remind her about the cameras, but Ann just didn't understand that everything they said was being recorded.

Ivan, her security guard and escort, pointed at the barrel of miniatures that flanked the stairs, but she shook her head. "I don't want a drink."

"It's pot luck," he said. "It's fun. Some are liquor, some are fruit juice."

He'd been so stern that she was sure he'd been instructed to be mean to her. But when he offered his arm, she smiled.

"I like your costume," Lyla said, if she was stuck with him, then she might as well be polite.

"Thank you," he said.

Descending the stairs, she hoped they'd just find a table in the corner and keep to themselves. Somehow, Lyla knew it wouldn't be that easy.

***

"SHE BROUGHT THE goddamn Hulk," Tate said.

Trick saw Green and Tate's shock and Sadie slanted to the side to get a better look. Turning around, Trick saw Lyla at the top of the stairs with a guy four times the size of her. But she was smiling at him as she took his arm, and he saw her lips move in speech as the couple descended the stairs.

"Good for her," Trick said, turning his back on the room again.

All he wanted to do was get blitzed, Sadie had told him to keep his wits. The cameras were in the room and they'd be looking for any kind of drama because there was less than two weeks left of filming. Less than two weeks and they'd be able to divorce.

Damn.

Divorce.

Grabbing his drink, Trick swallowed down the rest of it and snapped at the bartender for a refill.

"Yeah, you're handling this well," Green said.

Trick was so sick of his friends looking at him with that damn pity in their eyes. Yeah, he'd been treated like a chump, but it was his own fault. He had known that Lyla would figure out she was worth more than he could offer her, he should never have fallen for her. He should've stuck with his original plan and just been a dick the whole time.

Damn Josie and her bright ideas about honesty.

"I wonder why she didn't bring the other guy," Tate said.

Green snorted. "He's probably scared that Trick would beat the crap outta him, that's what I would've done to any guy who thought about touching Sam."

Sadie put her hand on his arm, and he tried to pull away, but she persisted. "You could forgive her," Sadie said. "If she's not with him tonight, maybe they're not together... If it was just a one-night thing..."

Trick had thought about that, actually thought about asking her to stay with him. He had even considered giving her permission to mess around if she had to. He'd had years of indiscretion. Years of being crazy and sewing wild oats. Lyla was just starting out.

Yeah, twenty-eight was a late start, but she had time to screw around and make her mistakes before settling down. He'd just been the first in what could be a long line of guys and relationships for her. Shame, he'd wanted her to be his last, and he'd been her first. Their timing was shot and he was paying the price.

But he shook his head and took the drink from the bartender, God bless open bars. Though it was probably only provided so the studio could write off the liquor and if it was free, they probably didn't need a license, what did he know? What did he care?

"He can't forgive her," Green said. "That kind of thing messes with a guy's head. And after Kira..."

He was just a piñata for women, and Trick couldn't even argue or feel hard done by. This was karma. Green had been stupid when he was young, but he'd found Samantha. They'd stayed the course. Stayed together. Got stronger every day.

Trick figured that love obviously wasn't on the cards for him. It was impossible for him to picture himself with anyone other than Malloy. Lyla had come into his life and he'd wanted that to be it. He wanted her to be it.

Kira had shown up on his doorstep last weekend; just a couple of days after he'd walked out of Bunyan's office. He'd laughed in her face. It was hilarious that the woman thought he might be stupid enough to take her to bed.

But she'd tried. Boy, had she tried.

Paul appeared between Green and Sadie. Trick groaned and sank his mouth into his glass again. Just the sight of the director made him sick and angry. "Damn, what do you want?" he asked. "Film, do whatever the hell you want, just stay the hell away from me."

"The games are about to start," Paul said.

"So?" Trick asked.

He wouldn't be playing any damn games. He was staying right here, propping up the bar, with his best friend… liquor.

"Ladies and gentlemen!" the host on the dais called for the attention of everyone in the room. "Welcome! It's time for the first in a series of games, our scavenger hunt! Everyone will be given a list and a basket. Every couple must bring every item on their list back to the stage in their basket."

"Tate," Trick said, slugging from his glass. "Wanna forfeit with me? I'll race you to the bottom of the bottle."

Picking his partner quickly was vital. Sadie would give him earache and Green was competitive, Tate cared only about having fun.

"Everyone's name is on the screen above me!" the host shouted and a list of names flickered up on the huge screen over his head. "You're listed next to your partner, seek them out, then come up here and grab a list!"

"Trick," Sadie murmured.

He didn't even have to look at his friend or at the list to know whose name was next to his. "Let me guess, I'm spending some time with my lovely wife this evening."

Sadie touched his arm again. "If you can read maps with Kira, you can scavenge with Lyla."

Growling, he quickly downed his drink. Yep, he wasn't going to make a big deal about this and damn him, but he wasn't going to embarrass Lyla by refusing to participate with her.

"Grab me a list," he said and turned around to stalk through the crowd.

This was the band-aid moment; he had to just do it. Rip it off fast and breathe through the pain.

Swiping a couple of handfuls of miniatures from the barrel he passed, he opened one and downed it fast. He expected it would take him a while to find her because she'd be moving around looking for him too. Instead, the crowd cleared and he saw her there about twenty feet away, her head tipped all the way back and her arms folded.

Angled away from him, she didn't see him and he slowed. This was kind of like the day in the canteen; she was at the same angle then when he'd walked up and grabbed her ass.

Hell. Why not?

Striding over, Trick increased his swagger before he slapped his hand on her tight butt and squeezed her hard. Funny thing was, she didn't even react, didn't look at him, didn't squawk or chastise him, she kept her eyes on the Hulk who didn't seem to be going anywhere fast.

"Hi, honey," he said and ducked to kiss her cheek.

Still nothing.

What the hell?

"Well can you check for me?" Lyla asked the Hulk, her focus on him was complete.

Trick couldn't figure her mood, she wasn't looking at this Hulk guy like she adored him, but she wasn't pissed off either, she was just, there.

"Ly—"

"One way or the other, I have to know, Ivan," she said.

"I can't leave you alone," Ivan said, and eyed him.

Good, at least he was getting a reaction from someone. Trick grinned. "I'd tell you that there's nothing to worry about, but I guess she does have a history of screwing around," he said. "But my dick stays in my pants, I swear it. God knows where her pussy has been in the last nine days… No offense, I'm sure you're clean as a whistle, man… Not so sure about the last guy, so… check yourself, you know?"

It felt so wrong, so revolting, to even suggest that Lyla might be unclean. This Ivan guy didn't look too impressed. He glared for a minute then bowed and whispered something into Lyla's ear that Trick didn't hear.

Her slow smile made Trick itch. She put a hand to Ivan's chest and patted him gently as he eased back. "I promise," she said to him and the pair made eye contact before Ivan turned around and walked away.

"Sadie's going to bring a list over to—"

Turning, Lyla pinned icy eyes on him. "Touch me again and I'll have you arrested."

What?

What the hell?

She was pissed at him? How the hell had that happened? "Wow, is your boyfriend the possessive type?" Letting his attention float in the direction Ivan had gone, he gave her a casual shrug. "Funny, I'd actually be scared if a bastard that size threatened to hit me. Thank God he leaves the threatening to you."

"It's not a threat, Nairn. It's me telling you that you do not have my permission to put your hands on me."

Who the hell was this woman? If he told himself to stick to his character, he stuck to it. He'd never been pulled from it against his will. When he'd been himself with her on camera, it had been a choice, just as it was to play with her character.

But he couldn't see her character now. She wasn't doing what was necessary. As she folded her arms and looked away with that disdain all over her face, he snapped.

Grabbing her arm, he yanked her toward him, she was right there anyway, but he wanted her attention on him. "Do it," he snarled, dragging her into his arms. "Go on, sweetheart." Running his hands down her back, he ignored her wriggling and her hands pushing his chest, and grabbed her ass in both hands. "Mm, baby, your man's missed his honey."

"Nairn!" she objected. Pushing with all her strength didn't make any difference to how close he held her. "Let me go! Stop it!"

Grabbing the fabric of her costume, he clenched his fists to pull it up over her ass as he spun around and pushed her to the wall beside them. "Not a chance," he said.

"Trick!"

Didn't matter to him what name she used, he ducked to pick her up from the floor. He didn't even see her hand coming, but he felt the harsh slap she planted on his cheek and the shock of it made him stop.

What the hell was he doing?

She was panting and red-faced. This was Lyla, why was he treating her like this?

"Trick?"

Sadie's voice beside him sounded just as shocked as Lyla looked. Dropping her to her feet, he backed away and rubbed a hand over his jaw. "What the hell," he breathed.

"Yeah," Sadie said, smacking his chest. He looked down to see a stupid basket with a piece of paper in it. He only just caught it before it fell and Sadie moved between him and Lyla. "Are you okay, Lyla?"

"He should be in a zoo, not on television!" Lyla said.

Damn.

"He's had a couple of drinks, and—"

"I don't give a damn," Lyla argued with Sadie. "The studio will never show that, but I can subpoena the footage. I could get him into a lot of trouble! He needs to be thinking! And what the hell would Kira say?"

Kira?

That cleared some of his confusion and he frowned at her. But she was straightening her clothes, doing her best not to look at him or Sadie.

"You've got some nerve," Sadie snapped. "You mess around on him then come here threatening to get him into trouble? What the hell gives you the right—"

"Wait," he said, reaching past Sadie to touch Lyla's arm. As soon as he did, they all looked at the point of contact, so he opened his hand and eased it away. "Sorry… But… Why did you mention Kira?"

"You're together," Lyla said, shrugging a few times, probably trying to shake off his assault and that's what it was. There was no other word for it. Man, he was an idiot. "I bet she was thrilled when my name popped up on that screen next to yours. It's some weird kind of karma, I guess. Though she *wanted* sex when we were together, I don't. Kira has nothing to worry about. I'd just as soon never be in the same room with you ever again."

What? Lyla. Was this really Lyla? She wouldn't look at him. She seemed far more interested in watching the crowd.

Maybe she knew the camera was out there, or didn't want it to look like they were talking. But she wouldn't look at Sadie either. It was like she was waiting for something, but what?

"I heard you left the network," Sadie said.

Lyla nodded and folded her arms. "Twelve days and then I leave for good."

"The network?" Sadie asked.

Lyla shook her head. "The city."

Where the hell was she going? Why was she leaving? She loved her job, she'd been in it for five years, it gave her everything she wanted… or it had, until him. And why the hell hadn't Sadie told him that she wasn't at the network anymore?

"When did you leave the station?" he asked her.

"About thirty seconds after you walked out of Bunyan's office," Lyla said and perked up. A hopeful smile spread on her face and he glanced around to see Ivan approaching. "Well?"

Ivan reached them. "Answer's no."

"Oh," Lyla said, losing the smile though it twisted to one side of her face first. Plucking the sheet of paper from the basket, she scanned the list. "There are twenty things on here, I'd say eight of them will be in this room for sure… the other twelve… well…" She dropped the list back into the basket. "They're your responsibility, Trick, sorry."

Lyla began to move away, and he lunged forward to catch her arm. Again, everyone looked at his grip and he slid his hand away. "Sorry," he said again, feeling like a prize prick.

"Want me to get you one of those minis now, Lyla?" Ivan asked.

Lyla smiled at him. Why did he get a smile? Anger made Trick surge forward. It didn't even matter that the Hulk was bigger than him meaning he'd get his ass kicked for sure, Trick couldn't ignore his rage. "You know she's married," Trick heard himself saying as he put himself between Lyla and this Ivan guy.

"You're not serious," Ivan said, looking him up and down like he was a gnat. "You want to take me on?"

"Yeah, I do," Trick said.

"What the hell is wrong with you?" Sadie asked, swatting his shoulder. "First you attack Lyla, now you're going after this guy. Are you having a nervous breakdown, Trick?"

Maybe. That might be the only explanation. "No way he's smarter than me," Trick said, returning the guy's glare. "She was supposed to get with a smart guy. A better guy. No way this guy is better than me."

Ivan exhaled a laugh that made Trick's blood simmer to a boil. "You idiot."

"He's not my date," Lyla said, in a fed-up tone. "He's my chaperone. A Prem employee… He's Bunyan's monkey… Sorry, Ivan, honey."

"Hey, I've been called worse," Ivan said.

Okay, maybe he was an idiot. Trick's bluster left. A chaperone. She wasn't with the company. She quit the last day they'd seen each other. Bunyan had to be pissed at her if he was keeping eyes on her at all times. They'd told her that he was with Kira…

Spinning around, Trick locked eyes with Lyla. "You didn't screw him."

Her smile was tight. "Only took you nine days to figure it out."

"Wait," Sadie said. "But, Trick, you were sure, you knew that—"

"There was footage," he said and exhaled disbelief as he ran his hand into his hair. "Damn, they set you up… and I fell for it like an idiot because I… believed I wasn't good enough… They set you up." Lyla rolled her eyes away from him and squeezed her lips together even tighter. His hand drifted toward her face, but as soon as the back of his fingers touched her jaw, she flinched away and he clenched his fist. Damn. Had he really scared her or was she that disgusted by him? "Baby, I'm so sorry."

"Cliff was fired too," Lyla said, but she was talking to Sadie, not to him. "He came to me at the start of this week, told me he heard about the setup after, said he would tell you guys the truth and show you the footage they weren't using that showed what really happened."

Sadie was as shocked he was… Well, almost as shocked, it would be hard for anyone's surprise to match his. "Why didn't you let him—"

Lyla sneered. "I don't give a damn what the public think. We agreed the show didn't matter. Whatever they chose to show, it didn't matter."

"As long as we knew the truth," he murmured. "Damn, baby, I let you down."

"Yeah," she said and her anger was tinged with hate. "You did… I told Bunyan you'd figure it out… I didn't know that you'd figure it out too late."

"Too late?" he asked, but he didn't let himself panic, instead, he smiled. "Babe, I'm not with Kira, I didn't touch her."

"I really don't care whether you did or not," Lyla sighed and it twisted his guts that she sounded like she meant it. "I thought it was a stretch that you'd screw around with a pregnant woman who was carrying another man's child. But…" She shrugged. "Then I found out she wasn't even pregnant, so, I guess you knew that."

"Knew that?" he asked. "I didn't know that… Didn't know until right now. She's not pregnant?" He couldn't even blame Lyla for refusing to look at him. "Malloy, I'm sorry—"

"It doesn't matter," she said. "Ivan, you could help me look in here since I can't leave the room. Trick, you'll have to find the other things. I heard someone say there's a prop room downstairs. You'll probably find everything you need in there if you're quick."

"Quick?" he asked. This time when he caught her arm, he didn't even care that she glared at his hand, he wasn't letting go. "I don't give a damn about the game. Love, we have to talk."

"About what?" she asked and he hated how calm she became.

"About this, about us, about…"

"All you had to do was trust me, Trick," she said. "Like I trusted you."

And that was why she was hurt.

Even when people told her he was messing around, she didn't believe it. She hadn't cared that Opposites showed him and Kira in the woods like there was something going on. Hadn't cared when the world acted like he was nothing more than a horn dog. Didn't care when she was portrayed as frigid, when in truth she was one of the most sexual people he'd ever known... even if she didn't know it herself.

"I'll fix this," he said, seized with determination. "I'm going to fix this."

"No," she said, shaking her head. "It's too hard. I... I can't."

"Yes, you can," he said. His hopes rose when he brushed his fingers along her jaw and she didn't pull away this time. "We fixed it before, remember?"

"No," she said. "They don't want us together. It was never supposed to work out. The premise of the show was never to make us fall in love. We were supposed to aggravate and upset each other. It was never supposed to work out."

"I don't care about supposed to. I don't care about the show... I made you promises, on your parents' porch, remember?"

"I remember," she said. "I also remember telling you that losing you so soon before losing my dad was more than I could handle, yet I had to do it again. I lost you twice... was it fun for you? Did you pick me up just so you could drop me again?"

"You and Curtis were... you were a thing before we got together," he said. "I figured your feelings—"

"I never hid my feelings," she said. "Curtis was the guy who asked me out last year, the date I never went on. I told you about that. If I'd wanted to be with him, I would've gone on that date. I never wanted to be with him. The only man I ever wanted to be with, to have forever with, was you."

"And you have me—"

"No," she said, backing away from his hand. "It's too hard... You were supposed to trust me... you didn't... I can't get over that. I can't do it." Moving away from him, she lifted her concentration to Ivan. "We have scavenging to do."

As she walked away, Ivan went with her, and neither of them looked back. Sadie closed in beside him. "Damn, Trick," Sadie murmured. "You screwed up."

That much was clear. "I'm gonna fix it."

"How?"

He didn't have a clue.

But he would.

He'd let her down.

That wouldn't happen again.

THIRTY-TWO

TRICK CAME BACK with all the items on the list in record time. Lyla added her items and they presented the basket to the dais. There were already baskets up there, so they weren't first, but it didn't matter. Prizes weren't awarded until the end of the night and she had no intentions of still being here when the night came to a close.

The host dismissed them and took the basket away. Lyla heard Trick inhale as he turned to her, but she wasn't waiting to hear him. Instead, she went to the bar.

Ivan had been a good help during the scavenger hunt. For one thing, he was taller than her, and he was good for getting other people out of the way when she was reaching for the same thing they were.

Lifting herself onto a stool at the bar, she waited for the bartender to come over. "Just a lemonade, please," she said.

"Sure thing, Mrs. Strickland," the bartender said and she exhaled.

That name was going to take a long time to go away. The sad thing was, she'd never actually changed her name anywhere officially. It had never been brought up that she should, which she guessed worked out well on reflection.

"So, I think you should wear a toga."

Rolling her eyes, the sound of Trick's voice was enough to set her on edge. "Excuse me?"

"At the wedding," he said. "I figure instead of having our honeymoon in Greece, we should do the full shebang and have a wedding too." He leaned in so close that she tensed and raised her shoulder, trying to keep him away. "And you'd rock a toga, baby… I'd just have to deal with having a hard-on all day in front of our guests."

"Mm hmm," she said.

The one thing she'd promised herself that she wouldn't do tonight was engage him. Trick wanted her to react. But Lyla had shut down her emotions now. He wasn't getting in. No way. She'd needed him and he'd screwed her over. That was it, his one chance.

Done.

"They might do weddings at that Acropolis place; I'll look into it… I'll get the guys to come over, make them dress as gladiators or something."

"Gladiators are roman," she muttered as the bartender brought her drink. "Togas too, for that matter."

"Huh," he said. "So, we move the wedding to Italy or go naked?"

Closing her lips around her straw, Lyla drank and reminded herself not to loosen. "They wore clothes in Ancient Greece, similar to togas, they just weren't called that."

"I was thinking about the Olympic thing," he said. "You said the dudes were naked."

"Are you planning to take part in an event?" she asked.

"If you want me to," he said. "We could host our own naked Olympics… We could sell tickets… that would pay for the wedding, and a vacation for everyone… Though they'd have to entertain themselves, 'cause you know, we'd be at a hotel *far* away from everyone we know… preferably far away from everyone else on the planet… Do they have a desert out there or something? Somewhere we could camp?"

Turning her eyes to his, she wasn't impressed. "You think you could survive camping in the desert? Without a cellphone? Without running water?"

He shrugged. "We can take water. As long as I'm alone with you, I don't need to talk to anyone else and you know more than the internet anyway, so we're set."

She couldn't look at him anymore, so she returned to her drink. "How would you find out the score of the game?" Of whatever game or sport was on at the time, not that she'd have a clue about it.

"Are you kidding?" he asked, leaning closer. "If we've just hosted the latest naked Olympics, that's the only sporting event anyone will be talking about for weeks." Her lips twitched, she wanted to smile, but picked up her straw with her tongue instead. He got so near to her that she felt his breath on her ear. "I saw that."

Damn him.

His finger slid onto her knee, but she quickly pulled her legs away. "Don't," she murmured.

"I love you, Malloy," he whispered and leaned in to touch his lips to the side of her neck.

Oh no. Why did he have to kiss her there? His lips were so slow in their caress, so tender and delicate as they tasted their way to her shoulder and around to her collarbone.

His hand slid across her stomach and he eased her body toward his. "Nairn," she whispered.

"I got you, baby. Oh, sweetheart, I got you," he murmured and touched his lips to her earlobe.

"You hurt me," she said, telling herself to pull away but finding herself incapable of moving. "Again. I needed you. You told me you would always be there and I… I needed you."

"Uh, Trick?"

Sadie's voice was close by. As soon as she heard it, Lyla pushed at Trick, remembering that she was supposed to be keeping her distance.

He loosened, but didn't go far. "Say, not now," Trick said, growling the words through his teeth.

"But… something's happening, look."

She was right. The music died and there was a hubbub. When she spun her stool around, Lyla was surprised to see the crowd spreading wide around something… around someone… And cops, why were there cops?

"Damn, is that… Bunny?" Trick asked.

The cops closed in around the sweating man on the dancefloor. He was grabbed and turned around. As cuffs were slapped on his wrists, one of the cops began reciting Miranda.

Another cop turned to the group. "Go back to your party, folks, nothing to see here," the cop said.

Nothing to see? That was Prem's network director being slapped into cuffs, and led away. "Oh, God, I wonder what he did," someone nearby said.

"What didn't he do?" Sadie said.

"I heard he's been sleeping with his assistants."

That wasn't an arrestable offence as far as Lyla knew. As she turned her stool back to the bar, she saw the Opposites cameraman turning his lens onto the director. Ha, now he knew what it was like. Turning off her microphone from the pack on her back, Lyla unclipped it and tossed it onto the bar.

"I think that's enough from me," she said and took a mouthful of her lemonade before she hopped off her stool. "Ivan, can I walk out alone or do you need to escort me home?"

"I can take you home," Trick said behind her.

In a move that was usually his, she released a single burst of laughter and turned around to pat his cheek once. Oh, he was persistent, and gorgeous, and an idiot… in the best possible way and she loved him.

Losing her father had taught her one valuable lesson: life was short.

"You can call me," she said. "In twelve days."

"What's twelve days?" he asked her and glanced at a smiling Sadie.

"The end of your Opposites contracts," Sadie said.

"So, once we're done…" he asked, and it was sort of sweet how the light of hope met his eyes.

Even though there were no cameras around, Lyla cupped her hands around her mouth and skirted her stool to lean in and touch her lips to his.

Trick grabbed her hips and pulled her into the vee of his thighs. She didn't mind him holding her, but wasn't going to share the tenderness of this kiss with anyone.

As soon as his tongue tried to find hers, she stepped back out of his arms and reached over the bar to grab her purse. "By the way," Lyla said, taking a half-step backwards. "Todd and Stacy are going steady… he's very grateful… you should call him."

Trick grinned and it made her return the expression as she tiptoed backwards. "I will," he said.

Half turning away, she kept herself loose as she spun back and this time she paused, though she was six feet away from him now. "Oh, and one more thing…"

"Yeah, baby?"

"The test was wrong," she said and tried her best not to smile when he lost some of his delight to confusion.

"The test?"

"We're pregnant," she said and his jaw sank.

Lyla winked at him before spinning away from his stunned expression.

Yep, shocking him was still fun.

Thank you for reading this tale!
If you can, please take the time to review.

~

Ask your local library for more Scarlett Finn
novels!

~

For all things Scarlett Finn
check out:

www.scarlettfinn.com

CHECK OUT

SCARLETT FINN

OUT NOW!

www.ingramcontent.com/pod-product-compliance
Lightning Source LLC
Chambersburg PA
CBHW060746190726
48285CB00002B/321